TO POISON A KING

S.G. PRINCE

SUMMERHOLD PUBLISHING
CALIFORNIA

TO POISON A KING Copyright © 2023 by Summerhold Publishing

All rights reserved. Printed in the United States of America. No part of this book may be used or reproduced in any manner without written permission except in the case of brief quotations embodied in critical articles or reviews.

This book is a work of fiction. Names, characters, businesses, organizations, places, events and incidents either are the product of the author's imagination or are used fictitiously. Any resemblance to actual persons, living or dead, events, or locales is entirely coincidental.

ISBN: 979-8-37-259781-5

First Edition

For Dad, with love.

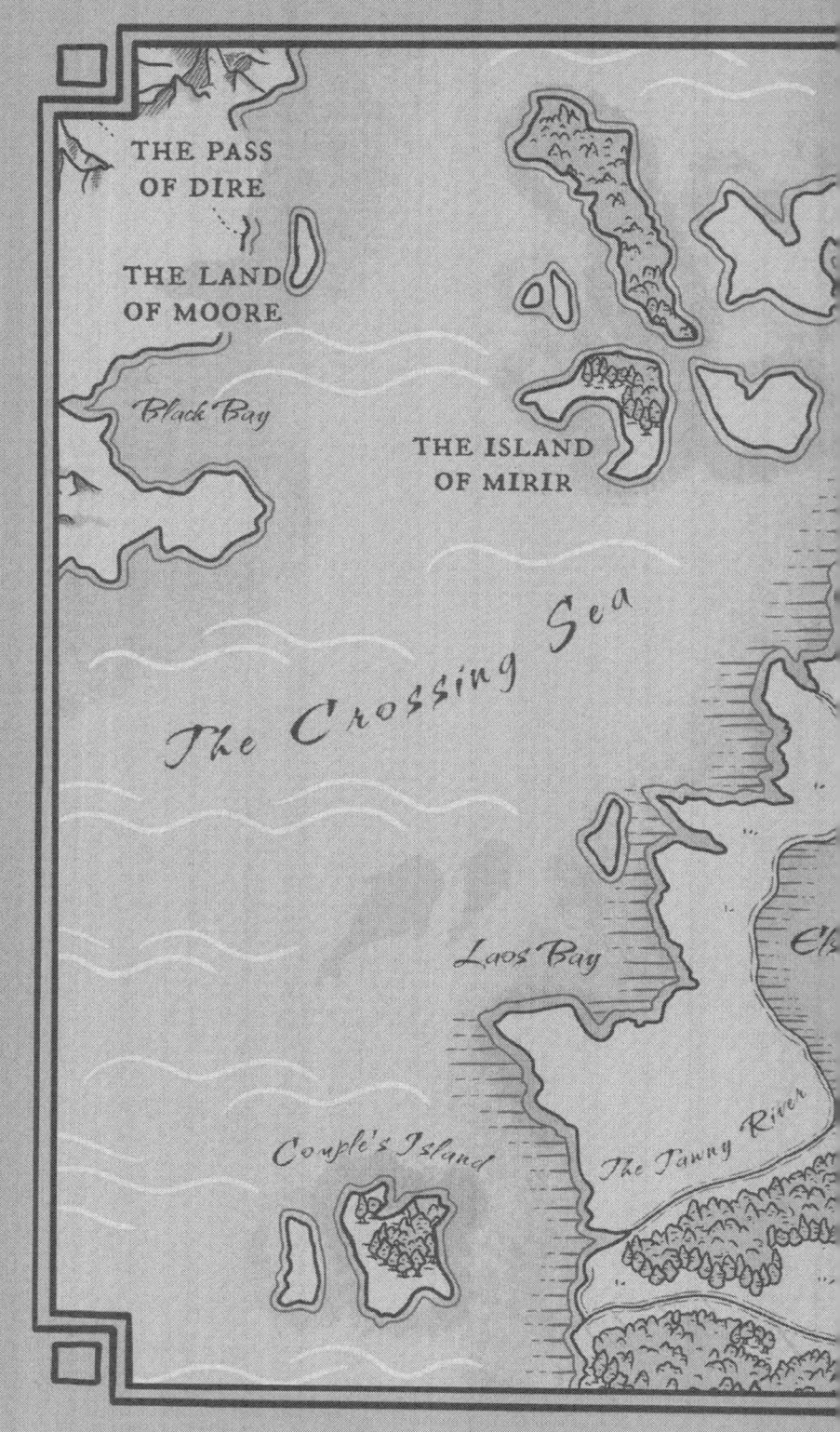

Author's Note

Every time I write a book, I go in with a different vision for how I want it to feel. The characters are one thing, and the setting, and the plot, but there's this whole other element that's kind of like a story's aura. It's the atmosphere of a book—an intangible sensation that falls into place before there's ever a plot, before the characters even have names. I carry that feeling with me all the way through the writing, and use it to guide me if I get lost.

To Poison a King is, in my mind, a dark fairytale. It's written for readers who want to know a character from the inside out, who are in it for the build, who like to watch a transformation take place over time, because that's how you really feel it. I wrote this book from the heart, as true as I could make it. I think it changed me to write it. I hope it changes you, too. - S.G.

Content Warning

This book contains reference to attempted suicide, attempted sexual assault, violence, gore, death of an infant, and sex.

ONE

My hands did not shake on the day I killed the king.

I was confident, though perhaps it could be said my confidence was that of a child climbing a high tree. I had never suffered true pain in all my life, and my sheltered upbringing made me naive. Fearlessness and bravery are not the same, for in order to be brave you must first understand the danger, but you can be fearless and also a fool.

I was a fool.

My childhood was an easy one. I lived in the king's palace under the care of my father, who was a carpenter, and my mother, who served as the royal physician, as had her mother before her, and her mother before that. Though I was only fourteen, I had taken to the family craft like a fish to the sea. I had a particular affinity for herbwork, yet since I had been hip-high I could do it all: stitch wounds, check fevers, set bones, birth babies. I was often called upon to administer whipstarch and bellwarth, remedies of my own invention to clear a cough or stop a sniffle. Sometimes I worked beside my mother, studying her art and honing my own, though more often I worked alone. The instinct for medicine ran in my blood, a gift passed down through generations, and I did not need supervision.

It is strange to look back on those days. I thought myself clever. I did not care that the other palace children whispered about me behind their hands. I did not care that the ladies of the court fretted over my strange interests or my nighttime jaunts in the woods. *A blessing*, they called me when they needed me. *A witch*, they called me when they did not. It is not hard to imagine where they got the notion. I was a scrawny thing, my hair often frizzy from leaning over cauldrons, my hands burned and scarred from one too many experiments. I did not care to dress in the latest fashion or wear my hair in braids, and I found friendship frivolous. I had a reputation among the court, even then. And that was before.

. . .

As the royal family's personal physician, certain honors were bestowed upon my mother. She sat at the king's table at mealtimes and was given her pick of the finest robes, the fastest horses, the most handsome escorts. Though she did not wear jewelry, she seemed to sparkle in the halls, burnished gold and white. Like a falling star she drew all eyes, but she was charming enough that her beauty could be forgiven, particularly by the women. The court adored her.

"Persaphe, you are not eating," said a lady in waiting, one of the queen's women who had somehow found her way to my mother's side instead. There was always someone fawning over my mother, someone to ask after her health and happiness. The court flocked to her like bees to flowers. "Are you quite well?"

"She is glowing," said another, a tittering handmaiden. "She is with child."

We were in the great hall for the midday feast, my mother in her place of preeminence at the king's table and I at her feet, scraping the bark off a young willow branch to reach the flesh underneath. I looked up.

"No," my mother replied with a lazy smile. "Freestone women bear only one child, and only daughters. You know this."

Their eyes met across the table. But then, why wouldn't the handmaiden suspect my mother to be with child? She was said to have slept with half the court, men and women alike, anyone who caught her fancy. She took lovers like she took her tea: at her pleasure. The rumor was that my father was sometimes even allowed to join, and what an honor that must have been for him.

I went back to my scraping. It had always been just the three of us in my family, my mother, my father and me. I was never one of those children who yearned for a sibling, and indeed, I did not like the idea of a brother or sister sharing my parents' attention. But then, it was as my mother had said. Our women produced only one child, and only daughters. Persaphe would bear no more children, no matter how many courtiers sought her bed.

I do not think I imagined the handmaiden's disappointment as her eyes dropped to me.

I returned to our chambers that afternoon, my hands sticky with willow sap, my nailbeds caked with bark. My family lived in our own quarters of the palace, a sprawling set of rooms that opened into the gardens and beyond that, the orchards and grazelands. I had my own bedroom and even my own workroom where I was allowed to do whatever I pleased.

I had planned to use the willow to make a poultice, but as soon as I pushed through the workroom door, I discovered I had no energy for the task. I set the willow on my worktable and looked around, feeling strange.

Fresh air, I told myself. That is what you need.

I walked the palace gardens. They glowed in spring's finest glory: the geraniums a carpet of scarlet, the roses nodding on their stems, the spider plants and salvias and weeping figs. I ran my finger across the fat head of a coneflower, its petals soft as a baby's cheek. The thought made me recoil my hand.

My mother found me there later that evening, lying among the rhododendrons. "Selene, it is late. Won't you come inside?"

It was unusual for her to call me home. Persaphe knew I often liked to sleep out in the gardens, or in the nearby forest. I had grown up on those grounds and was as comfortable there as I was anywhere. But she must have seen the thought in the handmaiden's eyes, as I had. *What a shame, Persaphe, that you will not make a better one than this.*

I did not bother to shake the dirt from my hair as I stood and looked at my mother. Those proud cheeks, the wide mouth. Her eyes were silver while mine were gray. Her hair was golden while mine was mouse-brown. She said, "You have a perfectly good bed inside. There is no need to sleep with the worms." She smiled to soften her words, though, and I felt myself softening, too.

"Of course, Mother. I am coming."

I often wonder how differently my life would have gone had I but a fraction of my mother's allure. She was a burning flame and I, the shadow she cast. But then, we had always been different in that way. Even our medicines were different. Persaphe relied on charms: little feints of the wrist, a smile offered at just the moment, words spoken softly in time. Her art was in convincing patients they truly were better, and their belief made it real. I, on the contrary, worked best with my hands. Berries ground to a paste, roots picked under the half moon, potions brewed over an open flame, balms and creams and sharp little tonics. My mother's gift seemed to spring from her like a river while mine had to be worked and molded and drawn, drop by drop, from the stone. I learned slowly through much of my own experimenting, but I did learn. Charmed or not, I was a Freestone, a gifted daughter in a long line of gifted daughters.

That was our art. A little science, a little magic, a little luck. It is unclear where our abilities came from, but there was no denying the truth. We were the best.

. . .

It cannot be said that I did not attempt to learn my mother's ways, at least for a time. As a young girl, I often tried to emulate her, asking her to teach me her trick of lifting the eyes to make a woman blush or a man pull out her chair, the thousand little flirtations I saw her use every day. My curiosity into such matters never failed to perplex her. Persaphe could not imagine what it was like to struggle socially. "You are a Freestone," she would say. "Your gift is medicine."

My father understood better. He was a cheery man, but also plain and rather quiet. He was happy to let my mother make the rules while he focused on his woodwork. Before they were wed, my father had begun the building of a temple, what would have been the largest in the world. Persaphe, however, had other plans.

"Temples are dull, Aegeis," she told my father. "We have a thousand already. What need is there for one more? You will make something new."

My father was a pious man, which is to say, he needed somewhere to aim his devotion. Before, it had been toward the Goddess. After, it was toward my mother. He did as she ordered and spent the following years inventing instruments to help Persaphe's patients: a crafty device to peer into someone's ear, a double-cane to be tucked under the arms, and my favorite, a wheeled chair with carved spokes.

"What is the chair for?" I asked one afternoon, watching him sand the wood. He was sitting outside in an area that had been cleared for this work. Around us, servants bustled between the kitchen and gardens; the sky was bright as a pearl.

"The sheepherder's son broke his leg. This will help him move around until he is healed."

I studied the designs my father had carved into the chair's backrest, leaping fish and rolling waves. It made me think of the temple he would have built, if not for my mother. "What do the carvings do?"

"Nothing." Aegeis had smiled. "Not all of us are magic."

My father did not understand Persaphe's prescriptions, which seemed to come from thin air, but with me it was different. He would wander into my workshop, tap a finger against my long worktable, which he had built for me himself. He would ask questions about this ingredient or that, nodding as I explained. Aegeis might not understand his wife's work, but here was something he could appreciate. He knew what it was to work with his hands.

One afternoon when I was eight years old, my father invited me to walk the palace gallery. It was an unseasonably sunny day, springtime, and a new painting of the royal family had recently been commissioned. He wished to take me to see it. I did not care much for paintings, but I went to please him. Even as we wandered, I was thinking about the brew sitting over my fire, one of my earliest attempts at a tonic to ease a headache, which I would later name *myrtaceaeas* for the plant from which it came. I was reciting the steps in my head, and I must have been murmuring aloud as well, because two palace children caught sight of me and sniggered.

I ignored them. I was used to ignoring other children by then. We seemed to have so little in common. There was once a time when they might have asked me to play, but their games perplexed me as surely as my mother's allure did. I simply did not understand.

"How do you know who wins?" I once asked the cook's son after he explained the rules of tag.

"If you tag someone, you win."

"No. If you tag someone, that person is it, and the game continues. Winning means the game is over."

The boy rubbed his neck. "Then no one wins, I guess."

"Why would you play a game no one can win?"

"Because it's fun."

"It does not sound very fun to me."

That day in the gallery, my father saw the children giggling and frowned. I could hear his heart pick up pace, the subtle thrum that meant he was angry. The ability to hear heartbeats was an unusual skill, though not unheard of in our line. Still, I was different enough as it was, and I preferred to keep that particular power a secret. My parents were the only ones who knew of it.

"You should turn them into toads," said my father.

I did not like that he had seen them laughing. When I was alone, it was easy to be indifferent. I told myself I wanted nothing to do with those children anyway. I had work to do, important work, and there was no time for games. I learned how to avoid eye contact; how not to let my curiosity get the better of me when I was working in my shop and could hear others playing in the field outside my window; how to keep my chin high, even as whispers followed me down the halls. I knew I was not like others, not in mind or spirit, and trying to fit in would only be to fight my true nature. *Your gift is medicine.*

But it was different with my father there beside me. I could not help but see myself as he did, as if through his eyes. Suddenly, I was not the person I had conjured in my head, the competent potion maker. I was a scraggly girl who muttered to herself. I glanced at my father, all my insecurities crowding up my throat. Was I as odd as they said? Did he think it too? He saw my expression and draped an arm over my shoulder. I felt the weight of his protection and wore it like armor.

...

It was autumntime when King Alder fell ill with his cold. The first chill of the season had just touched the air, my favorite days. Isla was a kingdom known for its glorious summers and pristine, snowy winters, but it was those in-between times—the gloomy autumns, the half-frozen springs—that I loved most.

A footman arrived to our family's quarters to request a remedy for the king. I remember my mother's hand on the door, her stitched brow. A cold? How unfortunate. I will have the medicine delivered at once. When we were alone again, she pulled me aside and whispered the words I had been waiting to hear for nearly a year, the ones I dreamed of and clenched my teeth over, anxious and fraught with waiting.

It is time.

The poison was my mother's creation, a concoction she named *nightlight* for the way it emitted a faint purple glow. Untraceable, she told me, dangling the bottle before my face. The poison was odorless, tasteless and—when diluted—colorless. A few drops into the king's medicine was all it would take.

I arrived at the king's chambers as promised, doctored medicine in hand. Though I had lived in the palace all my life, I could count the number of times I had seen the king up close. My mother was the formal physician, and while I was allowed to tend other members of the royal family, I was rarely sent to tend the king. Still, this was the natural progression of my role; as I aged, I would be given small tasks such as these, working up to more involved treatment alongside Persaphe and, eventually, on my own.

I was escorted into King Alder's study by his mother, the dowager queen. She was tall and straight-backed and fierce. I was small and imagined myself sly. The rabbit who slides right under the fox's nose.

I did not understand the details of the scheme. Later, I would marvel at how I never thought to question why my mother wanted the king dead. But then, I was not in the habit of questioning my parents. I was still at that age where I believed them infallible and would have done anything they asked.

I approached the king. He was hunched over a writing desk, his sleeves pushed up to the elbows, his corded forearms exposed. A feather quill danced in his hand. His forehead pinched as he scribbled.

I do not know what I expected. A sickbed, maybe. A withered old man with wrinkled lips for spooning broth. But the king looked healthy, besides the stuffy nose. He was young, scarcely past his twentieth year, with tawny hair and a striking, marble-cut face. It was often said that King Alder had all his father's looks and none of his heart, but I could not remember the late king—dead after a hunting accident when I was only six—so I could not compare.

I did not look too closely at King Alder, nor did I let him look closely at me. I was just another face among the hundreds, another eager servant waiting to help. I handed over his medicine, muttered well wishes, and was gone.

For a time, the poison simply sat in his veins. This was the nature of the drug. It must be slow working so as not to be tied back to my family. The king appeared to recover from his cold, but his recovery would not last. In nine days, my mother explained, he would begin to show symptoms. They would be subtle at first—a throbbing behind the eyes, a bit of lightheadedness—but things would deteriorate quickly from there. The king would soon lose his ability to walk, his eyesight, his consciousness, and by the following morning, he would be dead.

As I have said, the poison was not of my invention. If it had been, it would have worked.

At first, things seemed to happen as my mother foretold. I watched from across the breakfast hall as the king rubbed his temples. Later that day, he had trouble traversing the stairs, and by nightfall, he had lost not only the use of his legs, but his hands and arms as well.

His eyes grew dim, then blank.

Death, I whispered to myself, was next.

Except, the king's eyesight began to return. He regained his ability to speak. By morning, it was clear that something had gone terribly wrong. The poison did not work, and the king did not die. Rather, he came back to life, and while a lesser court might have called the incident accidental, an undiagnosed health condition, a message from the Goddess, the people of Isla were more clever than that. They suspected this was no mere illness. Rumors began to spread, and by the second day everyone agreed—the king had been poisoned, and his attacker was on the loose.

Let me tell you this. I was young and naive, yes, but not blameless. I understood I was killing a man, even if I did not know the reason. So, in the end, perhaps I deserved what came.

. . .

My family name, Freestone, means *a stone fruit with a pit that can be easily separated from the flesh.* They say names have power, and sometimes even the power of prophecy. My mother had no patience for talk of the divine, but my father was a firm believer, and so they disagreed. Now I know my father was right. I was the pit.

It was the evening the king had woken from his stupor. I do not remember exactly what my parents said to me then. There were bags packed in the night. Sharp words spoken under breaths. I began to pack my own belongings, the fear coming to me like a storm over the ocean. There would be an inquisition. The poison would be traced back to my family. It would be traced to me. I would be hung for my crimes, or worse. My mind conjured a hundred gruesome images, each more disturbing than the last. They would tie rocks to my feet and drop me in the ocean. They would string me up by my hair and whip me scarlet. They would release earbores into my ears to eat my brain.

My mother stopped me with a gesture. "No, Selene. You must stay."

Her words did not register. I continued my packing.

"I am sorry, my sweet." She pulled the bag from my hands. She did not look sorry. "You tried to kill the king. It was your hand that dealt him the poison."

My hand, yes, but only under her instruction. I was fourteen years old. I did not even know why we wanted him dead.

"Please." My voice scraped from me. "Please, do not leave me."

"They will show you mercy," my mother said. "You are only a child."

I remember my father glancing at his wife. The briefest hesitation. Yet when Persaphe turned her eyes on him, he only nodded his agreement and muttered, "A child will have mercy."

My breath had gone tight, everything taking a strange gray sheen. My mother's face was cold when she commanded, "Do not follow us." I felt the power of her voice lock my legs into place.

They pushed through the back door and were gone.

TWO

The king's mother came for me. *Queen Althea*, she had been called during her husband's reign, now *Queen Mother Althea*, or simply *my lady*. Such she would have been to me that day, had I been able to speak.

She appeared with a knock later that same night, filling the doorway to my family's chamber with her regal severity, her shoulders draped in white, the crest of the Goddess hanging heavy around her neck. I had known she would come and was waiting silently by the door, yet still I quaked. I would have thrown myself at her feet and begged forgiveness, but I was too afraid to move. It was that fear, I know now, that saved me.

"Where is your mother?" Althea scanned the entryway as if she might find Persaphe hiding behind the coatrack. My mouth worked uselessly. I could not breathe.

The queen's irritation deepened. "Well?"

"Her sister is with child," I managed. "My mother went to Esmond to help deliver the baby."

It was a clumsy lie. An obvious one. The queen should have seen right through it. This was known—Freestone women bore only a single daughter. My mother had no sister. She was an only child, as I was. But Althea merely said, "Persaphe is needed here."

It struck me then. Althea did not suspect my mother. She did not suspect me. And why would she? My family had served the crown for generations. Our success was tied to theirs, some even saying our two families had *gilili*, twined blood. It was that link that allowed Freestones to heal Alders with such innate efficiency. My mother had no reason to wish the king dead. To call for his death would practically be to call for her own, since King Elias Alder had no wife or children and therefore no heir to absorb the crown. If he died, the kingdom would be thrown into mayhem, the balance disrupted as men vied for the throne. A new king would rise to power, and along with him, a new royal physician, since Freestones only served Alders, and our magics were tied to that bloodline. Without the king, my family was nothing.

"I will send a letter," said the queen. "Your mother must be summoned back at once." I nodded quickly, dipping my head, *of course, of course*. "In the meantime, you will attend my son."

Her words dropped like stones. "I...what?"

"His Majesty's condition is unstable. He needs a healer, someone who knows our ancestry. And you are your mother's daughter, trained by her hand, born to one day take her place. You will attend King Alder until Persaphe returns."

I do not know whether Althea truly believed I was far enough along in my training to attend the king, or if she merely assumed any order she gave would be obeyed, because she was a queen, and queens got their way. I stared into her icy face and made myself reply. "As you command, my lady."

· · ·

Althea did not want to wait. She took me to the king straightaway.

The king's suite felt somehow different than it had on the day I delivered his medicine, though at first I could not place the change. The furniture was as it had been, the tables set at exact right angles, the pillows fluffed and arranged. Golden busts sat on their pedestals, the candelabras in their corners. Overhead, a crystal chandelier hung like a star.

As we moved through the rooms, I began to notice more. A feather quill, abandoned, the nib crusted with dry ink. Dust on the bookcases, the tabletops, clinging to the curtain folds. There were shadows in the corners and wax caked to the candleholders, and a sourness in the air that made me yearn for a flung-open window.

Althea guided me deeper still, through the king's study and into his most private rooms, his bathing room and bedchamber. Here, the disarray was worse. Clothing lay in heaps across the floor. A half-drunk wine bottle was discarded on its side. Broken glass crunched underfoot and food, untouched, sat cold on the tables. And there at the center of it all lay the king.

He was propped up in bed, his eyes open but cloudy, face unshaven. We came closer, and I saw more. His hands were frozen to claws. His legs were twisted under the sheets. The room smelled not of death, as I had imagined, but urine and bile.

I stopped looking. I dropped my gaze to the floor and did my best not to think the words, certain they would show on my face. Yet at that moment I spotted a bucket brimming with vomit and my mind slipped, the thought coming as plain as the moon to the sky. *I did this.*

"I have brought your physician," Althea said.

Apart from his milky eyes, King Alder's face appeared untouched by the poison. He had an angular jaw, a perfect bow mouth. He still wore his day clothes, the ones he'd been wearing when the paralysis hit: a high-neck tunic, long sleeves, trousers with a sash. He tipped his chin down, tracking our movement across the room with his limited vision. Then his lips twisted downward, and his expression seemed as marred as the rest of him. "Finally."

Althea turned to me. "You are not to speak of what you see here. If anyone asks, you will tell them the king is doing well, that we expect a full recovery. When you come to this room, you will come alone. Aside from our immediate family, no one is allowed to enter."

"No," the king drawled, "not even the maids."

Althea shot him a look. "No one should see you like this."

"Are you worried I'll frighten them away?"

"Elias."

"Or is it that you fear word will reach Princess Mora?"

"It is not about that," Althea said, in a tone that made it clear it was about that exactly. "We cannot have people talking," she continued doggedly. "This sort of thing can spell disaster for a nation. If our citizens discover the extent of your condition, there will be panic. Unrest, loss of faith in the crown. And that is to say nothing of our enemies, who are always looking for an opportunity to strike. You nearly died—"

"As one is wont to do, when poisoned."

"—but kings are not supposed to die. You are not supposed to be susceptible to ailments or disease or afflictions of any sort. These things are signs of weakness, and weakness cannot be tolerated in a ruler. To the outside world, you must appear a god."

"That is ironic," King Alder said, "coming from a king's widow."

Althea's shock was open-mouthed. She breathed into the empty air. "How—" Her teeth snapped together. "How dare—your father was—"

"The greatest ruler Isla has ever known. Yes, you've told me."

"In the name of the Goddess, you will not speak ill of the dead."

"Well." He turned his cloudy eyes to the ceiling. "If it's in the name of the Goddess."

Althea looked like a kettle set to boil. For a moment, she merely stood there, rigid, seething. I felt like a fawn caught between two lions. Deliberately, and with great effort, the Queen Mother turned away from her son and focused on me. "Let us move," she said stiffly, "to the subject of your duties."

Althea began explaining what they knew of the poison and its effects. The king could not walk. He had regained the use of his arms but not his hands. He could see light and shadows but not details. "Your tasks will extend beyond medicine," Althea said. "You will bring my son his meals three times a day, do the washing and cleaning." As she began speaking of his recent medical conditions, the king cut her off. "Mother, quit flapping. Persaphe knows my history."

His vision must have been even worse than thought, to think I was my mother.

Althea pursed her lips. "This is not Persaphe. It is her daughter, Selene."

Not once during Althea's tirade had King Alder shown signs of surprise. Not when she announced the necessity of his seclusion, or called him weak, or spoke of his poisoning as if a shameful secret. But this—the realization that my mother was missing—had the king gaping. "What do you mean? Where is Persaphe?"

"Absent. She will be returning shortly. Until then, the child will see to your needs."

"A child? Mother, you cannot be serious."

They continued to bicker. I concentrated on taking slow, deep breaths. The world had begun to turn, everything dizzy and warping. I was going to faint, I thought. I was going to faint on that very spot. I refocused, locking my eyes on the opposite wall to steady myself. There was a painting above the king's head. It showed a man with a lion's face and a woman beneath him, one breast exposed, her neck offered up for a bite.

I do not think it hit me until that moment that my parents were truly gone. The truth trickled cold over my skin. I had been drawn into a scheme I did not understand, tasked with poisoning the most powerful man in Isla, only to be abandoned by the two people I loved and trusted most. There was no one who would come for me, no one to pull me to safety. No one to say, it's alright, Selene, it will all be alright. I had somehow become the royal physician, responsible for overseeing the king's needs until my mother returned, but my mother wasn't returning. She wasn't returning, and everything was going to fall apart.

"Enough," King Alder snapped in his monarch's voice, the one that allowed no room for argument. "Both of you. Get out."

· · ·

Back in my family's chamber, I stared at the empty rooms. Stone and wood, the cold hearth. There was an east-facing window by which we ate our breakfast. I had spent nearly every morning of my life watching the sun lift from behind its leaden glass. The window was dark now. A part of me believed it would never show the sun again.

I would pack, I thought. I would pack my things and run. But where would I go? This—these palace halls, my bedchamber and workroom—was all I had ever known. I had no money of my own, no one to call upon for help. I had my herbs and my pots and the forest. I had the palace cat with her fluffy bobbed tail, the spiders and mice who, like me, wished mostly to be left alone.

I picked up a golden pen from the table, engraved with the faces of animals. I could sell it, but how would it look, a young girl wandering the streets selling the king's items? Who, even, would I sell these things to? And then a worse thought: if I did run, my absence would be quickly discovered. Once Althea realized all my family had fled, she would be forced to confront what she had thus overlooked—we must have reason to run.

That was when the trembling began.

I shook and shook, unable to control myself. A new fear was lifting within me. All my life, I had been living inside a ring of firelight. I knew nothing of the blackness beyond, knew nothing about anything, but now I had been thrust into that dark world without so much as a match. I could brew potions, but that was nothing. Worse than nothing. There in the palace people knew me and appreciated my remedies, but who outside those walls would trust such a young physician?

The trembling deepened. My parents were gone. But—gone? How could this be? How could they just…leave, as if it were easy? As if I did not matter? My mind churned, searching for purchase. I stood there with that pen clutched in my fist for a long time.

I remembered a letter. Althea had said she would send a letter to Esmond to call back my mother. But what would happen when the messenger discovered Persaphe was not there, or worse, that there was no sister and no baby?

I focused on that thought. It calmed me a little to focus. I saw that letter like an ingredient in one of my tonics, a single step in the larger process. Add an ingredient too soon and the tonic would go sour. Add it too late, and you might create something else entirely. But you shouldn't think of every step at once. One thing at a time.

Outside the window, the moon was lifting. I looked at the stars, their tiny smiling faces.

I pulled on my cloak and went out the door.

THREE

I found the messenger in the stables readying to ride. I was fortunate. Usually these stalls were teeming with people, stablehands tending the broad beasts, lords readying for a hunt, servants sweeping straw. It would have been impossible to pick the messenger out of the crowd, especially since I did not even know which messenger I sought. Althea, however, had placed the palace under a state of arrest. Everyone must be interrogated, every member of the imperial household subject to scrutiny. The question was on everyone's lips: who had poisoned the king? No one was allowed to leave unless they had the queen's seal and special permission. That night in the stables there was only one other, a young man dressed in messenger-yellow.

"I come by order of Queen Mother Althea," I said. "I am to retrieve her letter."

The messenger peered at me over his horse's back, his eyes raking my grubby trousers, my mess of hair. He knew who I was, of course he did. I saw the word in his smirk. *Witch*.

"I am also under orders," said the messenger. "I am meant to have this letter delivered."

"Your orders have changed."

"For what purpose?"

"The queen needs to make an amendment."

"What kind of amendment?"

"That is none of your concern." I held out my hand. "Give it to me."

How must I have looked? I imagine myself as I was then, standing like a warhorse, my feet planted, my mouth set. While my mother might have wooed and charmed, batting her eyelashes and tossing her hair, I was blunt as a block of coal.

The man barked a laugh. "I don't take orders from *spinikkas*."

I gaped; my face burned. *Spinikka*—it was a dirty word to describe someone who was uncomely. I knew what the court said of me, but insults of this nature were usually whispered or implied. Never did anyone speak so bluntly, and certainly not to my face. "That was—" My voice was small. "That was uncalled for."

His grin widened. "Are you saying it's untrue?"

"No—yes. Yes. It's untrue."

"Ugly *and* stupid."

My throat was clogging. The king was poisoned, my parents were gone, and now this man was being cruel for no reason at all. The task, I told myself. Focus on the task. "Regardless, I...I will have that letter."

"Didn't you hear me? I'm not taking orders from the likes of you."

"Is that what you wish me to tell the queen when I return empty-handed? Perhaps you will give me your name as well, so she might know who has caused her such trouble."

My voice trembled. These were more words than I had spoken to anyone but my parents in months, more than I had ever said in all my life. I expected more of the man's disdain and was surprised when instead he looked uncertain. "Now," he hedged, "it doesn't have to be like that."

"I agree." My hand was still outstretched. My open palm felt like a promise. "And it will not, once I have what I have come for."

"You'll be sorry," he snapped, but the words were empty, and only half-sensical. It was, I would come to learn, the kind of knee-jerk response an opponent gives when they have lost.

I can still recall the moment the messenger set the letter in my hand. Never before had I bent another's will with words alone. Was this how my mother felt when she spoke the world into her vision? I turned to hide my face before the man could sense my lie, exiting the way I had come.

⋯

I have mentioned my family's quarters opened right onto the palace grounds. I cannot tell you how lucky I was for it, or for the fact that the queen—though she stationed a palace guard at every other entrance—had not thought to place a guard there. If not for that oversight, I would have been stopped on my way back into the palace, searched and questioned. The letter in my pocket would have been uncovered. And what would have happened to me then?

Back in my workroom, I burned the letter in my cauldron fire. I wiped a poker through the ashes to be sure there was nothing left. Then I merely stood and twisted my hands.

I would like to say I began to think. That one plan turned into two, into three and four. I would like to say, yes, of course, the solution was obvious, I knew it all along. I was young and naive and all the things I have said, but I did possess a bit of wit, and was not entirely a fool.

And yet, the truth is I did not see the answer, not that night, nor the following morning when another knock came at my door, this time a footman sent on Althea's behalf. *It is the king. You are needed.* It was not until later, much later, when the king was still not dead and I was deeply entrenched in my new life that the thought finally occurred to me, like a sprout pushing through loose earth: I made this mess. Perhaps I may also unmake it.

· · ·

I did not sleep that night. I tossed and turned until the dawn crept blue through my window. Then the knock, and the footman, and my summoning.

It did not occur to me to fix my appearance until we were halfway to the king's chambers. I caught sight of myself in the gleaming belly of a vase and was momentarily dismayed. My eyes were dark holes in my face. My shoulders showed their knobs. My head looked too big and my neck too skinny, like a flower bulging on its stem. *Ugly* and *stupid*. I had a memory of my mother preparing to attend the king, pushing her breasts together, dabbing perfume over her wrists. The monarch of Isla would surely expect a certain amount of pomp in his presence, but there was no chance to turn back, and nothing much to be done for my appearance anyway. I reminded myself that the poison had afflicted King Alder's sight. To him, I would seem little more than a blurry blotch. It was some comfort.

The guards stationed in the hallway outside the imperial wing knew who I was and allowed me to pass with little more than a glance and a nod. I should have nodded back and continued on with whatever small authority I could summon, but instead I hesitated. The doors to the king's chamber had been crafted by my father. We had never discussed it, but I recognized the mark of his work: the perfect seams, those delicate details. I wanted to touch my hand to the patterns, press the design into my palm. I sought…comfort, maybe. Solace in the thought that my father had made these doors, and they would hold me, as he once had.

I might have stood there forever, staring at the wood until the sky went dark, if not for the fact that the guards had begun to peer at me. I shook myself; I was being ridiculous. My father left me for dead, he could give me no comfort, and now I looked like a simpleton who had forgotten how to work a door.

With an inhale, I pushed inside and moved past a series of rooms: the cloakroom, the observatory, the dining room, the drawing room. At each turn I expected to meet someone. A courtier, perhaps, or one of the many handservants. Althea had ordered no one besides family enter her son's chambers, but the king was a king. He had every right to overrule his mother and send for company. Yet the rooms were all dark.

King Alder, at least, was in bed where I expected him. I stepped through his open bedchamber door and began to offer a greeting, stopping short when I realized he was fast asleep. It took me a moment to recover from the shock of it. Childishly, I had not really thought the king slept. I expected to find him awake, his angry mouth ready to deliver another lashing. For a long minute I simply stood there, afraid to go forward, afraid to move back. I felt as if I was witnessing something I should not, something private.

Strangely, it was this same thought that finally drew me closer.

In sleep, the king looked terribly young. Three and twenty, he would have been—a man by all rights, yet with a hint of boyishness still hidden underneath. I could see the slow rise and fall of his chest, the scattering of fine hairs along his arms. His breath rasped a little. His eyes danced behind their lids.

I stood at his bedside for another half an age. What did I expect? For the king to spring from the covers? For him to pin me as his assassin? *You did this to me*, I imagined him saying. *I knew it all along. You are a traitor, and now you will be hung!* Yet the king's face remained loose with sleep. His head dented the pillow; his mouth was slightly parted. I could hear his heart in his chest, a low, steady rhythm.

I considered my situation. Queen Mother Althea had instructed that I tend the king until my mother returned, or truthfully, until I could think of a better plan. Last night, the idea of caring for King Alder had filled me with dread, but there with him asleep before me, it no longer seemed so impossible.

I began by tidying the room, clearing away the worst evidence of his sickness, cracking the curtains to let in a bit of light. I kept one eye on the sleeping king, hoping he might wake and tell me what he needed. When he did not, I fetched a cloth, a bowl of water and a stepping stool. The king was high in his bed, and I had always been small, but the stool gave me reach.

Up close, I saw more details. There was a small scar over his browbone. Thin white sunlines fanned his eyes. His hair curled a little around his ears.

I lifted the cloth to his forehead.

The king's eyes snapped open; he flung an arm between us. I jerked away with a startled cry, the items flying from my hands.

"You do not," he breathed, "have permission to touch me."

His chest was rising and falling, his cloudy pupils dilated. I could hear his heart pounding like mine pounded, matching pace. "I beg pardon,

Your Majesty. Queen Mother Althea said—"

"I do not care what my mother said."

His heart continued its furious pounding. This was not like it was with others, that faint thrum. I could feel the king's pulse beating in my chest as if it had become my own. The sensation upended me. Was this another part of our twined blood, that I might not only hear his heartbeat but feel it too? Yet if that was true, why had I never experienced it before?

I struggled to keep my voice measured. "A damp cloth is good for fever."

"I do not have a fever."

But he did. His brow was shiny, the color high in his cheeks. I could practically feel the heat rising off him, and I could smell it too, that sickly scent. "I apologize," I said, scrambling to recover the situation. "I should have woken you first. If you would allow me—"

"I want you nowhere near me."

I shrank at his tone. I wondered if the king would tell Althea how I had startled him, and what she might do. It was a thought that spoke my age; I expected every son or daughter to answer to their parents, as I answered to mine. It took only a moment to remember the king needed no permission. He could punish me himself.

The idea turned my stomach. I had been a fool to believe this would be like caring for anyone else. King Alder was not anyone else. *The most powerful man in Isla*, my mother used to say, *and suited to it. He stays closed off from others, and rightly so, if he is to effectively rule such a vast and prosperous empire. It takes a certain mind to hold such power. A certain…density of character. This you must remember, Selene.*

Elias Alder had been groomed to rule, just as I had been groomed to serve. I felt us each firmly in our roles, as mortar sets between brick.

And then there was my secret, hovering in the air between us like a static charge. It shivered across my skin. I was terrified he could feel it, too.

Not knowing what else to do, I clasped my hands behind my back. "I...understand my error, Your Majesty. Please forgive me. I will not touch you again." A pause as I hunted for the right words. Something my mother would have said. "Is there...anything you would require of me?"

"Yes," he replied. "Your departure."

FOUR

News of the king's poisoning spread quickly over the coming days, and theories began to pour in. Some suspected a foreign enemy, the warlords to the north or the Mad Horsemen to the south. Others speculated the poisoning was of a more personal nature, one of the king's distraught relations, perhaps, or a bastard child come to pay his due. King Elias Alder did not have any bastard children—my family would have been aware of it due to our twined blood—though he did have a bastard brother, who lived among the court. His name was Hobore.

No one seemed to suspect Hobore, despite his obvious claim to the throne. Perhaps this was because Hobore was timid and willowy, a weed in the current. He was four years younger than the king, though he appeared younger even than that, a boy who had not yet reached manhood. Anyone who met Hobore could see he was not the conniving, murdering type, and besides, he had always worshiped his older half-brother. No, the court agreed. Hobore was not behind King Alder's poisoning.

As the days went on, I began listening. I paid attention to all the gossip, eavesdropping at doors, or sometimes climbing high into the eaves to peer down on council meetings. I was not alone. The palace staff could often be seen lingering near the imperial wing, whispering at each other's necks. What was known about the poison? Who could have delivered it? It was the cook, I am certain, he had access to the king's food. No, the steward, he always did seem wily. Or no, it was the king's own mother, that uptight bitch.

I waited for their eyes to turn to me, yet they never did. If the court thought of me, it was only to wonder what it must be like tending the king in Persaphe's absence. Some tried to ask, but I always gave the same meatless answers. The king is doing well. A full recovery is expected. Yes, Persaphe will be returning soon, very soon. Eventually, they grew bored of me and sought their gossip elsewhere.

Several days after I had burned the letter, I arrived to the king's chamber with a breakfast tray in hand. We had scarcely spoken since the incident with the cloth, yet I did my best to carry out my new duties as if nothing was amiss. This, I had decided, was the safest route—I must continue on as normal for as long as possible. Three times a day I would collect a prepared tray of food from the kitchen, nod to the guards stationed outside the king's doors, enter his bedchamber, leave the food on the first flat surface I could find, and exit again without a word. Usually, King Alder was asleep in bed and I was able to leave his meals without incident. That day, however, the king was gone.

My heart spluttered in alarm. I rushed from room to room, my mind conjuring a rash of images, each more wild than the next. The king had been poisoned again. He had been kidnapped. He was hiding behind the curtains and planned to spring for me after all.

I found the king in his study, leaning heavily on a sideboard as he pulled himself toward the window. My first thought was a startled, *he's walking*. This was not exactly true. He was upright and moving, but his legs were sluggish, his feet leaden. His hands twisted where they clutched the sideboard, his shoulders set at hard angles. He had not changed his clothing, that stuffy, done-up outfit that looked as comfortable as a box of pins, and the stiff fabric only seemed to heighten his struggle. He used the furniture to maneuver himself forward before dropping heavily into a velvet chair.

He raised his eyes to mine. I realized I had been gawking and felt a rush of shame. Was I no better than those gossiping servants? Would I take what I had seen and ridicule him for my own amusement? I knew what that was like. I did not want to do it to him. I dropped my gaze to the tray in my hands.

"No," he said. "You have seen me. There is no need to pretend otherwise."

I hovered in the doorway. When he did not beckon me forward, I gathered my courage and moved into the room, setting his breakfast on the low table before him.

As in all the other rooms, the curtains of the study were drawn, the dim glow of the wall sconces casting shadows. The king's features were muted by the low light, but even still, he looked sickly. His skin was pale; there were bruises under his eyes. A line of sweat had formed along his brow, and he was breathing heavily, as if he had just walked a flight of stairs.

"I may be half-blind," he said, "but I can see you staring." A pause, as he waited for me to speak. I did not. "Well?" he prompted. "Is my mother right? Do I deserve to be hidden away? Am I a monster?"

Was he? The thought sat on my chest like a weight: Persaphe wanted you dead. There must be a reason, even if I did not know what it was. But the king did not look like a monster to me then. He looked young, and terribly alone. I remembered he too had lost a parent. He had been thrust onto the throne after the unexpected death of his father, King Adonis Alder. That was eight years ago, meaning Elias would have been fifteen at the time—scarcely older than me.

He squinted. "Will you not speak?"

I dipped a small curtsy, fumbling for my voice. "You are no monster, Your Majesty."

"How reassuring."

I marshaled a bit more courage. "You have been poisoned. Forgive me, but I fail to see how that speaks to your character."

"The failure is yours."

My cheeks heated, though the insult should not have surprised me. I knew what was said about our king. He had a reputation for callousness, if not actual cruelty. *Frigid*, people called him. *His heart is made of stone. It's made of ice. That is why he has delayed taking a wife—because he doesn't know how to feel.*

The king asked, "How well has your mother trained you?"

"I…suppose she has trained me quite thoroughly, Your Majesty."

"And what," he continued, "has she told you about me?"

It was not the question I was expecting. I could not fathom its meaning.

The king must have seen my face, or else read my silence, because he continued. "Persaphe has been my physician since I was a boy. Seeing as you are her daughter, and the next royal physician, I would assume she has been preparing you. Sharing…information that might be relevant."

In truth, Persaphe did not often talk about the king. I had seen them together at mealtimes and during daily outings, but I did not know how they behaved behind closed doors, whether my mother was her usual slippery self, whether the king was cordial or irritable or abusive. That last thought gave me pause. Could this be the reason my mother wanted him dead? Had the king abused her in some way? Yet try as I might, I could not picture it. My mother was a glowing idol for whom the seas parted. She had never been a victim.

"Persaphe considers your relationship a private matter," I said. "She does not often speak of your history, but…I assure you it is no hindrance to my abilities. I can see that you have a fever. Likely, your body is still fighting the aftereffects of the poison. If you would like, I could—"

"I told you already," he snapped. "You are not to touch me."

His heart sped at the words. As before, I could feel my own heart quicken in reply, the strange overlay of a second pulse. It was the oddest sensation, as if his fear had become mine. Last time, I thought his fear was due to me startling him awake, but there was more to it than that. The idea of me touching him frightened him in a way I did not yet understand.

"I do not need to touch you to cure a fever," I said. "I could have a remedy prepared this afternoon. You could take it yourself."

"I have no interest in any remedies."

"It is a simple thing." I did not know why I felt the need to push. What did I care if he suffered a fever? I was his poisoner. Supposedly, I had wanted him dead. Even without those simmering truths, I had overstepped my place already and was not eager to repeat the mistake. Yet I found myself saying, "It's a combination of yarrow and *thistlevein*. Quite subtle. You can take it with your tea. You will barely even taste it."

"I am sure."

Was this an agreement? The king's tone was dark, his face closed. Before I could say any more, he spoke again. "I tire of this. Go now. And don't bother leaving the tray. You might as well take it with you."

This, too, had become part of our routine. For all the food I left him, he hardly touched any of it, and each day I would return to the kitchen with full platters. The poison, in addition to peripheral paralysis and loss of vision, had affected the king's appetite. Or so I thought…until I reached for the breakfast between us. I looked at the spread. An orange and a mango, steaming tea, porridge with a little silver spoon. Of course he was not eating. How had I not thought of this? I could see the king's hands, twisted and stiff. How was he expected to hold a spoon, or peel an orange?

I glanced up at him. For the second time that day, I had the sense that the king was reading my thoughts. His jaw was tight. His eyes dared me to speak.

I held my tongue, but after that, I began bringing meals he could actually consume: peeled fruit, chunks of soft bread, porridge that was runny enough to drink from the bowl. He made no mention of the change, but from that day forward when I returned the platters to the kitchen, they were empty.

I left him the promised fever remedy in a cup that was easy for him to grasp. This, he did not touch.

• • •

Let me tell you what King Alder was not. He was not patient or particularly forgiving. He was not the kind of man who allowed for weakness or deficiency. Above all, he hated for others to see these things in him. Althea might have been the one to order his solitude, but I believe the king would have chosen it for himself just the same.

I learned King Alder might tolerate my presence if I did not linger. I crept about like a mouse, doing the things I thought needed doing: airing rooms, washing linens, sweeping the floor, tending the fire. My mother would have choked to see me performing such servant work, but the king did not truly expect me to act as his physician. It was part pride, part mistrust. King Alder was not one to submit easily to another, not even for his own benefit, and it would grate against the very essence of himself to take orders from a one such as me. He wanted me nowhere near him.

Althea, for her part, did not care to check in on our day to day. She had begun splitting her time between the palace temple, where she spent long hours in prayer, and the stateroom, where her interrogations continued in earnest. A reward had been offered to anyone who could provide information about the poisoning, anyone who had even a sliver of insight to help uncover the king's assailant. People began flocking to the palace to share what they knew, and I watched them as I walked the halls. That man dressed in an embroidered cloak, was he not an old friend of my mother's? That woman wearing the red robes of the House of Healers, had I not seen her in my father's company? Who were these people and how much did they know? Who else was in on the scheme…and what would they say about me?

It was one of those times that I came upon two women whispering excitedly near the imperial wing. They could not have been much older than me—sixteen, seventeen at most—yet they seemed otherworldly, clad in pinks and blues, their necks weighted with pearls. I saw their shining eyes and felt immediately on edge. Had they learned something new about the king's poisoner? What gossip was passing among the court now? Without thinking, I approached. "Has there been news?"

The ladies looked down at me with furrowed brows. I wondered if they had not heard me.

"Well?" I prompted.

"News?" said one. "About what?"

"About the king."

They exchanged a glance. "We were not discussing the king," the other offered, motioning to her companion. "We were discussing Hermapate's complexion. She is looking rosy in the cheeks, wouldn't you say?"

I hesitated. This did not seem like the kind of topic worth whispering about excitedly. Had I misread the situation? Or were they lying?

I wanted to smack my forehead. Of course they would lie. I had been indelicate, and they had no reason to share their gossip. I thought again of my mother, what she would have done to gain the trust of these women, to have them begging to spill their secrets. I plastered on a compliant smile. "Your complexion is indeed lovely," I told Hermapate. "And your hair, it practically shimmers." She seemed pleased by the praise, and I was encouraged. "Are you expecting?"

Her pleasure dried to dust. "I am not married."

"And so?"

"I have no husband. How could I be expecting?"

"One does not need marriage to conceive a child."

"Of course you think so," said the other. "Your mother is the palace whore."

I froze. "She is not."

The women were gleeful. "She's slept with half the castle. That's how her power works." They flapped their fingers. "Didn't you know? If you want her to heal you, you have to pleasure her first."

My face burned. "That's not true."

But the women had collapsed into a fit of giggles. I realized too late what this was—another heartless joke at my expense. I stormed back to my workshop, my ears on fire. Since I could not slam out their words, I slammed the door instead.

I kept a better distance from the courtiers after that, yet continued my listening. I was aware my time was limited. Althea was expecting Persaphe to reappear any day. In the meantime, every new face in the palace meant a new witness who could potentially expose me. I had already decided fleeing was not an option, but what else could I do? The anxiety was beginning to wear on me. I was not sleeping well, not eating. I had fallen in the habit of looking over my shoulder as if the guards might lunge for me at any moment. I thought, if only I could cure the king, perhaps they would stop hunting his poisoner. Perhaps these people would go away, and the entire ordeal would be forgotten. I would be free again. I would be safe.

They were foolish thoughts, but I clung to them with all my strength. I began thinking of solutions to the king's paralysis—a formidable task in itself, even without the brooding man to contend with. I had no experience counteracting the workings of poison. Indeed, it would have been easier if I had created the poison myself. At least then I would have known what was in it.

But I had seen it, I reasoned. I knew the liquid was a deep purple, so dark as to be almost black. I knew it was odorless, its shape and consistency, how it stuck to the sides of the vial like honey. And if I knew these things, perhaps I could decipher more: how it was made, and what it would take to unmake it.

A regular remedy would not be enough. The king's paralysis would require a *gaigi*, a true potion of undoing. I had never created a *gaigi* before, though my great-grandmother was the first to invent such a brew. I thought, if she could do it, surely I could too, for I was of her blood.

Over the next few days, I began to study the king for more clues. I noted the color of his skin, the deepness of his breaths. I brought him his meals, soups and stews mostly, breads and soft cheeses, whatever I thought he could manage. I sometimes had to help set the items into his ruined hands—a task we both loathed, and bore in utter silence—but it provided an opportunity to see him up close, and I paid attention to this as well: which foods seemed to energize him, which drained him, which left him annoyed or thoughtful or hungrier than before. I did all of this as secretly as I could, always afraid of the moment when he would grow weary of me and send me away.

Inevitably, he would send me away anyway, and then I would go to the forest. There I could breathe again. I knew those trees better than I knew my own name, had grown up wending between their thick limbs, drawing out their secrets as the charmer draws out the snake. I had spent much of my childhood exploring the palace grounds, climbing rocks, dipping into ponds, building rafts, hunting for beehives. I knew where to find elderberries and wild plum, how to start a fire without kindling, how to snare and skin a rabbit for stew. I could make a torch using tree limbs and sap, and navigate home by the stars.

One crisp autumn morning, I ventured to a favorite grove of mine in search of *istilla*, a small, white flower that blooms at the base of trees. I had named the flower myself, for I had never encountered the species before, not in paintings or botany books or anywhere. I believed it grew only in those woods and, truth be told, only for me.

I found a cluster of the flowers and plucked them by hand, setting them in my basket and covering their broken stems with a damp cloth. An idea had been brewing in my mind for some days, a potential remedy to counteract the king's paralysis. I rushed home, my thoughts spilling, but as soon as I entered my workshop I felt doubt, as I had never doubted myself before. My wooden worktable with its hatches and burn marks. My knives smiling their silver smiles. And I, a child with her kitchen tricks.

Stop it, I told myself. You might fail at everything else, but you will not fail at this.

Yet all I created were failures. Tonics that burned the tongue, infusions that melted to nothing, ointments too dry to be useful. I tested each concoction on myself, thinking I might know when I landed on the *gaigi*, but how could I have known? I was not the one who had been poisoned, and besides, this was not as simple as healing a minor cough or cold. The workings of the king's affliction were deeply complicated, and so too must be the remedy. Yet I kept on as only the desperate do, grinding and mixing and boiling and baking, adding this ingredient, then that, in this order, then that one.

I counted the days with tallies on parchment. Althea remained preoccupied, wrapped in her interrogations and prayers and the running of the kingdom in her son's absence, but she would not stay distracted forever. Already, she had begun to wonder why my mother was so delayed. I heard her ask after the whereabouts of the messenger, and her letter to Esmond, but that messenger had since been sent on another far-flung journey and was not around to answer questions. I thought, another letter will be dispatched, one I could not prevent. Or the original messenger will return and point his finger at me. Even without those looming threats, I knew I must find a cure quickly, I must, or else the queen would reexamine my story, and all my lies would unravel.

Well, can you guess? They began to unravel anyway.

FIVE

It was early one afternoon. I was in the king's study to deliver his midday meal. The days were growing shorter as autumn drifted toward winter, the room chilly despite the high-stacked fireplace. I had already poured the king his tea and set the cup in his grip. I was arranging bread on a plate when he spoke. "What is in this tea?"

My hands stilled. The king rarely acknowledged me, nor did he ever show any interest in what he was fed. I risked a glance up. "It is chamomile, Your Majesty."

"No. There is something else."

I had added a tincture to the tea, a mix of primblossom and *istilla*. It was not the cure I had been hoping for, nor did it have any of the usual properties of a *gaigi*, but as the days wore on, I was running out of options. I knew the king was gripped by moods. I knew, too, that stress was bad for the body. I had the idea that if I could ease some of the king's anger, his body might begin to heal itself. The tincture was a delicate thing, and I had only mixed the smallest of doses. I had not thought he would taste it.

He watched me over the rim of the cup. "You've added something."

"Only a bit of blossom," I replied, fussing with the bread. "To keep up your spirits."

"My spirits."

I nodded.

"You thought to fix me." His voice was dangerously even. "Is my attitude not to your liking?"

My heart began to race. "No."

"Need I remind you that I was recently poisoned? Do you think I enjoy people meddling with my meals?"

"No."

He sneered. "I do not care if you are a healer. I do not care if you are the bloody physician of the ages. You have tried to drug me without my consent. I should have you whipped."

The careless mention of punishment, the knowledge that he could easily see it made true. My fingers dug into the bread. "I'm sorry. I never meant—"

"I do not care what you *meant*." His anger flashed like a weapon. "You are a child, and an idiot one at that. You are a placeholder until your mother returns. Have you forgotten that? My spirits." He spat the word. "We'll see about my spirits. Fetch me a knife."

"For—for what purpose?"

"We are going to make you like me."

I spluttered. "What?"

"We'll cut off your hands and see what it does to *your* mood."

I fled the room. I rushed through the halls, past hanging tapestries and arched windows, all the way to the kitchen. There I stood in the center of the afternoon bustle, gulping air.

Knives lined the tables, hung from the walls; a great pot bubbled on an iron trivet. Nearby, the cook was preparing a pig on the counter. He brought his cleaver down with a wet *smack*.

I did not return to the king's chamber that night. Instead, I went to the forest. I crouched to the earth, pressed my fingers into the soil. I wished for my parents then, as I had not allowed myself to wish for them. I yearned for my father's sideways smile, my mother's quick laugh, no matter that they had abandoned me. I tried to imagine where they might have gone. Had they fled the country? Or were they in the King's City just across the valley? The thought was so painful as to make me ache. It was possible, wasn't it, that they were still somewhere nearby? Surely they were realizing their mistake, were missing me as much as I missed them. They would reappear any moment, I thought. They would sweep me back to safety. But it would not be.

The next morning, the king said nothing about the tea or the knife. I was cautious, uncertain of his mood, but as the morning drew on and he remained silent, I became guardedly hopeful. Perhaps he regretted his harsh words. Perhaps he realized I was only trying to help.

I was wrong. Rather than forge a new understanding between us, the king became even more brooding, even more difficult. He began thwarting my attempts to aid him. I would open the blinds and he would order them shut. I would offer fresh clothing and he would insist on his dirty ones. He was self-sabotaging for no other purpose than to spite me, and if ever I tried to push or coax, he would resort to insults. You tried to trick me once, why should I trust anything you suggest? Look at you, with your cracked nails and muddy boots. Is it true what they say? Is that why your hands are so scarred? Maybe you really are a witch.

I do not know if the king had a knack for sniffing out insecurities, or if it was only chance that allowed him to cut right to the heart of me.

It was no less than anyone else said or thought of me, but hearing that word come from him, *witch*, was painful, the implication being that my methods were dangerous and uncivilized. To be a healer was to be an upstanding member of the medical society; to be a witch meant something else. A barbarian. Crude. Wild.

With each of the king's insults, I would turn away, tears threatening my vision, only to return to my workroom for another sleepless night of boiling and mixing and picking and mashing. I tried to remind myself that the king was suffering. I reminded myself I had made it so. In the weeks since his poisoning, King Alder had seen little improvement. His mother was busy with her interrogations, still insisting her son take no visitors. The kingdom hung in some unsteady place, everyone waiting for the king's promised reemergence, but no reemergence was coming. I knew it. The king must have known it, too.

I continued adding the tincture to his tea in secret, masking the taste with an extra squeeze of lemon. There was a risk in it, oh, I knew that. I was practically asking the king to make the connection between his poisoned medicine and me. And yet, I had become desperate to reverse his paralysis for a new reason—to save myself from his ire.

My eyes often strayed toward the King's City in those days. Sometimes it tempted. Sometimes I thought, let the world have me, it cannot be worse than this. More than once, I went to the forest and stood at its edge, staring out across the valley into the metropolis beyond. The King's City was the closest city to the palace and provided the crown with foodstuffs and supplies, entertainment, labor. The buildings glowed reddish in the distance. The sun moved along its track. I would think, just start walking, no one will stop you. But always I would turn back. In the end, I was more afraid of life outside the palace than the hardships awaiting within. I would return to my workshop and continue my experiments, one failure stacking on top of the next like children's blocks ready to topple.

The problem, as you might guess, was that I was attempting to find a cure for a poison I did not understand. I had hoped my gift for herblore would guide me to the answer as it had always guided me before, but I was a fisherman without the hook, my line dangling uselessly in the sea. In order to undo the workings of the poison, I would need to understand what had truly happened to the king, down to the level of blood and bone and muscle. I would need the thing that ruined his body.

I would need to first recreate the poison.

I sat with that thought for a long time. I knew nothing of poisons. I was a healer, not a murderess. Which was a foolish thing to think, as I had of course been both. Still, the thought of creating something to kill gave me pause. What if my experiments went wrong? What if I hurt myself in the process? And what if anyone learned what I was attempting?

Across my worktable lay the carnage of my failed trials, scattered petals and mushed berries, flax lily and liregrass, fuzzy yellow pollen and of course, *istilla*, which was the base of all my creations.

I tossed it all out and began again.

SIX

I had been putting it off for as long as I could, but the queen's questions about the messenger and my missing parents were becoming more pointed, and I knew I could delay no longer. An afternoon came when the king and his mother were together in the king's study. I took my chance. "There has been word," I said. "My parents are dead."

Their eyes snapped to me. I was not interrupting—they had not been speaking—yet I felt already as if I had misstepped. Althea did not often visit her son's chambers. I cannot say what their relationship was like before the poisoning, but the tension between them after was thick enough to taste. Usually, I would have left during the queen's visit, found somewhere else to be while they glared at each other, but I could not afford to miss the opportunity to speak to them both at once.

"It was—it was a fire," I continued, pulling the forged letter from my pocket. "In Esmond. It happened shortly after they arrived. An accident. Word has just come…"

Althea blinked once, her only sign of dismay. Then her expression smoothed into something like sympathy. "You poor thing."

I had thought there would be questions, how and where and why. I had thought there would be suspicion. Was it not suspicious that two of the crown's most valuable subjects disappeared on the eve of the king's would-be assassination to tend a sister who could not possibly exist, only to die before they could return? The lie felt paper thin to me. It would blow away in a breeze. I had prepared the whole story, how a lantern was overturned, how they became trapped in the blazing building. Additionally, I had taken a dose of *risphini*—a drug used to reduce one's heartrate—in order to curb the more obvious signs of my deception: reddened cheeks, shaky voice. But Althea's expression remained pitying.

"I have been uneasy about your parents' journey," she said. "To depart in such swift fashion…it is permitted, certainly, yet I have sensed something amiss. I wonder now if the Goddess has been whispering to me in warning." She touched the crest at her neck; her expression became intense. "My mother was gifted with such premonitions. She was favored by the Goddess, as was my grandmother. I have never seemed touched by that same foresight, no matter my devotion, but perhaps…" She trailed off, then seemed to come back to herself. "Death is the will of the Goddess, child. Your parents have been embraced. We will conduct a ceremony in their honor—discreetly, I think, will be best. We have had enough turmoil of late, and our allies need no more reason to doubt us."

The ceremony was held right then and there. It was only the three of us, the king, his mother and me. Althea and I lit tapers, speaking the customary words while King Alder watched in his iron-plated silence. I knelt on the floor as I might have knelt before a casket, holding my flame over my head, conducting the ritual according to tradition. As I recited the verses, I stared at the rug beneath my knees. I felt the king's gaze on me, but I did not falter. I had thought I might struggle to feign grief over the people who had abandoned me, but my hurts were real enough. If only they hadn't left—or maybe, if they had taken me with them…why hadn't they taken me with them? I swallowed and cleared my throat, and it was no show. As far as I was concerned, my parents truly were dead.

After, Althea extracted a small, jeweled brooch from her gown and pinned it to my lapel. "It is not the symbol of the healer, but it will do for now." It took me a moment to realize what she meant. She was dubbing me the new royal physician.

I stared dumbly down at the brooch. It showed a dove with a pear in its beak, crafted from glittering citrine and sunstone. I should have expected this. I had always been next in line for the role of physician, meant to take my mother's place when she could no longer carry on herself. But this, the lack of formality, the ease in which my mother had been supplanted, neatly replaced with a few small words…it shook me. I gazed up at Althea, who appeared satisfied, her mind already moving to other matters. *There*, her face seemed to say. *All better now*.

After Althea departed, I began gathering the candles, doing my best to hide my red face. The king watched from his velvet chair by the window. He had at last changed his clothing, switching into a loose nightgown that did nothing to soften his appearance. As he tracked my movements, I braced for it: his insults, his mocking voice. Look at you, he might say, crying like an infant. I lost my father too, you know, I did not make such a scene. But the king remained silent, as he had been all throughout the ceremony. There was something in his face. Not cruelty, I thought. Not anything I recognized.

. . .

I returned to my workroom. My parents' funeral had unearthed something within me. I no longer felt like crying. I felt like smashing something.

The feeling began to build. I looked around. What would make the loudest sound? The mirror? A porcelain plate? I snatched up a glass decanter and held it over my head.

The moment passed, all my anger draining. I remembered entering the king's chambers that first day, how I had stepped around broken glass. I set the cup carefully back in its place and rubbed fists into my tired eyes. I did not want to be like him. I could use my anger another way.

I went to the window. On the sill was a vial, fat around as my fist, the stopper sealed tight. It had taken many attempts to create the concoction inside, dozens of iterations of brews and strains and brines and mixes until at last, a poison that looked like Persaphe's *nightlight*. Dark purple. The way it stuck to the bottle. I had finished it two evenings ago but had not yet summoned the courage to test it.

I tipped a measured amount of the poison onto a spoon. It looked elegant in my hand. It was the elegance of a lioness before she tears out your throat.

I suppose you might be picturing me in my stuffy workroom in the middle of the night, the candles burned low, the shadows deep. That is not how it went. I had never been afraid of the dark, but nor did I want to tempt bad omens. The first time I poisoned myself, it was midafternoon. My workshop was clean, swept and tidied. The view through the window showed a perfect late-autumn sky.

I lifted the spoon to my lips, watching my own distorted reflection in the poison's liquid surface. This time, my hands did shake. I was afraid, of course I was. It was not death I feared, exactly. I had the *gaigi* ready and waiting on my worktable, three times the dose I thought I would need. Even if the antidote failed, I had been precise in my measurements—this spoonful was not enough to kill me.

But this was not what I thought. I thought of my parents, who had vanished. I thought of the king and his artless malevolence; the messenger and his cruel words; those two ladies-in-waiting with their glittering eyes, their shrieking laughter. If I died here in this room, would anyone care? Althea had not truly seemed bothered by my mother's death. Rather, she replaced Persaphe as you might replace a candle, one for the next. Perhaps these sorts of dealings were easy for the dowager queen, who had learned to rule a kingdom in the wake of her husband's death, and was ruling it again during her son's recovery. Perhaps it was easier still, since she had me to replace my mother, an understudy waiting in the wings. But there was no one to replace me. There would be other physicians of course, though none quite as skilled. If I were to die, would they mourn my passing, or merely the end of the Freestone line?

I lifted the poison to my tongue.

I was unprepared. *Nightlight* was supposed to work over the course of days, not moments, yet the instant the poison touched my lips, I seized. I tried to catch the table and missed, tumbling to the floor where I began to writhe, the pain burning me up inside. It felt as if my blood was boiling, as if I was being cooked alive. Overhead, the antidote sat in its silent glass, high on the table out of reach.

I clawed my nails across the stone floor, arching my back and trying to scream. My mind was scrambling, everything a scattered mess of pain and pumping adrenaline. I thought, I must have miscalculated, I have given myself the wrong dose. I am going to die after all.

With a gasp, I forced myself to my knees and reached for the antidote. My fingers wormed along the table; my forehead pressed into a wooden leg. After an eternity, my fist closed around cool glass. I swallowed the inky serum in a single mouthful.

Unlike the poison, the antidote I had prepared was no guess. Recreating *nightlight* meant I knew exactly what was in it, and therefore I knew how to counteract its ingredients. Purified witchwood to bind to the hellbane. Distilled liverwing to deactivate the fool's mushroom. And my dear *istilla*, which gave the whole thing life.

I do not know how long I lay there on the floor. It might have been hours. It felt like days. Eventually, the feeling returned to my limbs, and I could stand.

I went to the mirror. My eyes were bloodshot, my nails jagged from their scraping. Ugly bruises had formed under my skin, spreading pools of green and purple. I looked like a rotten fruit. But worse was the sinking feeling in my stomach—this was all wrong. The king's poison had not bruised him. It had not affected his blood, merely paralyzed his muscles. The poison I had created was not *nightlight*, and therefore its sister *gaigi*, its reversal cure, was useless.

I should not have expected to get it right on the first try. I was going by memory alone, attempting to recreate a poison on sight, a feat even the most accomplished potion makers could hardly hope to achieve. Yet the weight of my failure clouded me. I stared at myself, the mottled skin, the bloodied fingers.

I do not like to recount the thoughts that came to me then. That I deserved my misery. That the poison showed a person's true nature. This is what you are, Selene, it's like they have always said. You are a *spinikka* and a disappointment. Is it any wonder your parents left you?

I turned away from the mirror, hugging my arms to myself. Everything hurt. Even the smallest movement made the bruises scream. Step by careful step, I limped to my bedchamber. I crawled into bed, buried my head in my hands, and for the first time since it all began, I let myself cry.

• • •

I did not sleep. I considered giving myself a draft, something to elicit sweet dreams, but the king's suppertime was approaching, and I could not hide forever. I did my best to cover the bruises. I smeared ointment over my skin to help with the swelling, dressed in long sleeves, wrapped a scarf around my neck. There was nothing to be done about the discoloration on my face, but I tried to reassure myself. The king's vision was still poor. His rooms were dark. I would leave his meal quickly and depart before he noticed a thing.

Yet the king did notice. He was there waiting for me in his velvet chair, his tawny hair hanging around his cheeks, a book in hand. He frowned as soon as he caught sight of me. "What is wrong with your face?"

I could not meet his eye. I hesitated in the doorway as I had that first day, wishing for once that I was a proper witch. Maybe then I could have waved my hand and magicked the bruises away. Maybe I could have magicked myself away, too.

He said, "You look like you've been playing with a hammer."

I did not want to tell him the truth. There was a reason I said nothing of my experiments; it would be dangerous to admit I was trying to recreate the poison that had nearly killed him. No one was supposed to know what poison had been used on the king. If I admitted I believed I could recreate it, I would also be admitting I knew more about the poison than I ought, what it looked like and how it worked. Once that truth was revealed, the rest of my secrets would quickly follow. I kept my eyes on the platter in my hands.

The king's tone was cutting. "I am speaking to you."

"The bruises were an accident."

"They're hideous."

But what I heard was, *you're hideous*. It might have been said that after weeks of such jibes, I had grown used to him, but I had not. If anything, the longer it went on, the farther each insult seemed to reach, like a tunnel made deeper with each pass of the shovel. My skin grew hot with humiliation, which I am sure only made the bruises stand out more. "I would leave," I croaked, "if it pleases you."

"It does not. Come closer. I want to look at you."

My stomach turned. I wondered what would happen if I simply fled. Would he send the guards after me? The dogs? Slowly, I forced my feet forward.

"Look at me."

I did. When I met his gaze, my pulse leaped.

His eyes had cleared. The cloudiness was much less than it had been, the hazel of his irises shining through. I realized he had noticed my bruises from a distance. And this, the book in his hands. He had been reading, he must be able to see the words. Was it the tincture I had been adding to his tea? Had it been working to counteract the *nightlight's* effects? Through my humiliation, I felt a bump of something that could have been excitement…quickly extinguished by the way the king was peering at me. He asked, "Why are you looking at me like that?"

"You can see," I blurted, then pressed my lips together, worried it was the wrong thing to say, since everything seemed to be the wrong thing with him.

His smile was a cruel twist of his mouth. "The view was better when I was blind."

SEVEN

Winter came early that year, and with it, my fifteenth birthday. I tried not to pay the calendar much mind, but like a messenger hawk, my thoughts kept banking home. Five more days. Then three. Then two. If my parents had been there, my father would have baked my favorite rhubarb tart, my mother gifting me something from the city market: a new mortar and pestle, a rare herb from Hillshire, a glass beaker that could withstand my fire's heat. We would have all sat around the table, my father holding my present to his ear and giving it a shake. "What could this be, I wonder?"

The morning of my birthday, I stood in my empty kitchen. Everything was just as I left it, the herbs in the window, the cutlery in their cabinets, pots and bowls and knives and the rest. It was not the items that were lacking. If I wanted something for my workshop, I need only send a request to the queen. But a gift is not the same when it must be asked for. I wished I had at least learned the recipe for the tart.

When I arrived to the great hall for the morning meal, the feast was in full effect. During the dinner hour, men and women sat grouped by order of class, the king's mother and uncle and cousins at the king's table, advisers and council members at the next, nobles and knights, sages, ladies in waiting, all the way down to the palace staff. For breakfast, however, these practices were relaxed, and people intermingled as they wished. I had my new chair at the king's table, which had been my mother's, and remained empty. It felt wrong to sit in her place, and anyway, I did not like to eat in the grand hall, exposed to the tides of the court. I would much rather gather a plate and return to my chambers in peace.

The feast that day was fit for a king, whether or not ours was present. The tables overflowed with offerings that showed the changing season, squashes rather than corn, bitter greens rather than berries, apples and potatoes and turnips and pomegranate. Maybe the servants still expected King Alder's reappearance, though by that time people understood their monarch's ailments were worse than originally described. The rumors around his seclusion were endless, and more farfetched than could possibly be believed. The king had grown a second head. He had shape-shifted into a fox. He required a vat of blood a day to sate the demon who had taken residence in his body. I wondered if Queen Mother Althea knew how the king's disappearance spurred such hideous fictions, and whether those stories ventured to Skylin or Acaca or Hillshire, to Princess Mora, as Althea feared.

I moved through the great hall, my ears open as always for new gossip. I reached for an empty plate, careful to keep my sleeves down to cover my wrists.

Over the past weeks, I had continued my attempts to recreate *nightlight*, and alongside it, the reversal cure. I tested each of the poisons on myself, the tiniest of doses dropped on paper and swallowed whole, followed quickly by their antidotes. Never again did I make the mistake of starting at the table; instead, I sat on the floor. I measured the quantities exactly, timed my poisons with the remedies, all prepared beforehand. I knew even the slightest miscalculation could lead to my death. Sometimes, the poisons were terrible enough to make me wish for it. Many nights I was so violently ill I had to take a needle and shoot the antidote into my own veins, only to wake the following morning—sweating, nauseous—to attend the king as if nothing was wrong.

Most of my attempts were for nothing. The poisons were not the same, they were not right. One temporarily took away my hearing so that I had to lipread the king's orders. One gave me a bloody nose that did not let up for days. One left a ringing in my ears, and another made me forget how to breathe, so that I had to mechanically force my lungs in and out until I could tweak my antidote to make it stop. None took away my ability to walk. None stole my vision. They left their marks, surely, but in other ways: rashes on my arms, boils on my skin, blackened nails and red eyes and clumps of falling hair. I did my best to hide the damage, donning long sleeves and keeping my patchy hair tucked under a scarf. I had a reputation for always looking bedraggled, and for once I could be glad of it. Still, I wondered what would happen when someone finally took a closer look. My scars were one thing, those could be explained away, but boils? Rashes? This was a bit much, even for me.

That day in the great hall, I made myself a plate, adding an extra helping of sugared rhubarb. Nearby, a group of girls burst into laughter. I glanced up, feeling that familiar drop in my stomach, but they were not looking at me. Their laughter seemed aimed at one of their fellows who was trying to balance a spoon on her nose.

My hands lingered over the rhubarb. The girls were not clothed in dresses but in black work trousers and boots, their hair done simply, faces bare. The brooch on their lapels showed the symbol of an apron, which marked them as kitchen servants. Likely, their parents worked in the palace and apprenticed the girls as well.

I hesitated. There was an empty seat at their table. I found myself wondering what would happen if I slid into it. I would not tell them it was my birthday, that seemed too much. Maybe instead I could start with a compliment. Something better than the one I had used on Hermapate, something honest. That would work, would it not?

I added a third helping of rhubarb, my plate teetering. The girls would thank me for the compliment, that was the polite thing, but what would we talk about after? I would need to find some common ground. Would they care that the winterberry bushes had begun to bloom? I could explain how the bright red berries were used to make dyes, and they would say…but my mind could conjure no further. Those girls were kitchen workers, not seamstresses. They would not care about berries or dyes. More likely they would want to discuss their duties, or people: the women they worked with, the boys they liked, their teachers and friends. It was the topic I found most difficult, since I had nothing to contribute. I worked alone. I had no teachers or family to speak of. The only person I could remark on was the king, and that was not allowed.

By that point, my plate was nearly overflowing. I came back to myself with a start. How ridiculous I must look, standing in a daze, piling rhubarb. And what was I thinking, anyway? I must be touched, some aftereffect of a recent poisoning. If anything, I had more reason than ever to keep to myself, what with my experiments and my secrets and Althea's ongoing interrogations. The queen had recently doubled the reward for information regarding her son's poisoner, which spurred a fresh wave of people into our halls, some traveling from as far as the Crossing Sea to share what they knew…which was little. Most of these visitors were only enticed by the gold and had come to toss false accusations in hopes something might stick and win them the prize. Still, it seemed only a matter of time before one of those accusations, founded or not, was tossed at me.

I checked again that the rashes on my wrists were covered, my headscarf firmly in place. I set back the serving spoon and gathered up my plate.

On my way out of the hall, I passed the king's half-brother Hobore. He caught my eye; his expression pinched slightly.

I did not know Hobore well, though I might have. As the son of the late King Adonis Alder and an unknown woman, he was of the Alder family and therefore tied to our Freestone bloodline. It was unusual for a bastard to reside within a royal residence—scandalous, even—and surely Hobore would never have done so, if not for my mother.

I'd heard the tale told many times. Persaphe was in the city market when an impoverished woman approached and pressed a baby into her hands. Please, the woman said, this is a son of the king, you must take him. My mother could sense his bloodline was true and whisked the baby away. She used her charm to convince Queen Althea to give the bastard a place among our halls, and she even had a hand in raising him. Persaphe felt responsible, I think, since she was the one who had brought the child to the palace. Or maybe she was just curious. Here was an unwanted son when she was destined to bear only a daughter.

Hobore was five years old when I was born. I cannot say if he resented me. I think I would have, had our roles been reversed. I was my mother's true child, while he was merely a pastime. Yet if there was any ill will there, he never showed signs of it. Or, he almost never did. That day in the great hall, Hobore passed me with a look that was almost a frown.

I wanted to panic. I wanted to launch myself out of the room and hide in the nearest cupboard. Had he noticed my bruises? Could he guess the reason behind them? No, I told myself, no, be calm. Hobore knows nothing. How could he?

I tried to carry on the morning as usual. I finished my meal in the safe security of my workshop, the one place besides the forest where I felt I could truly breathe. After, I brought the king his breakfast.

King Alder was in a quiet mood that day, his limbs folded, his face turned toward the fire. He seemed to take up less space than usual, his attentions focused inward. Twice, I almost asked what he was thinking. Both times I stopped myself. What was wrong with me? Maybe I really was afflicted by one of my recent experiments, like a truth serum that had you babbling without control. I was not usually keen on conversation, particularly not with the one person who liked me least.

I should have been eager to leave. I did not trust myself, not while I was in this strangely sociable mood. And yet, as with the girls at breakfast, I found myself hesitating, hovering, drawing out the day's tasks. I dusted shelves that did not need dusting; I polished flatware that did not need polishing. I entered the king's reading room, his parlor, his observatory, wondering what else might benefit from my touch. The sideboard. I should clean out the sideboard.

The drawer stuck, and it took a good bit of jiggling to slide it open. Inside was a hodgepodge of items. An hourglass, an old book, a set of dice…and a nameday candle.

My breath seemed to slow. Nameday candles were rare. They could only be produced by a nameday craftsman, and there were few enough of those. On the day of the baby's birth the candle was poured, seventeen little notches etched into the wax. Each year on the child's birthday, the candle was burned down to the next notch, meant to signify another year passing. It was said that if you wished upon a nameday candle, your wish would come true.

Tentatively, I reached to pull it free. The candle was wide as my wrist, creamy and matte, the wick blackened. It stuck a little under my fingers, warming from my touch as I counted the notches. The king was behind on his wishes. The candle hadn't been burned since his fourteenth mark.

Already, my hands were digging through the drawer for a match. I felt oddly shivery. Today was my fifteenth birthday. I was in sync with his candle. I did not know if the power of nameday candles could be transferred to another, but if they could, if I could make one wish…

My pulse was rising. I glanced around to be sure I was alone, then lit the wick. I thought of Althea's interrogations. I thought of Hobore's frown, the king's ceaseless insults. This could be my chance to change my fate, to protect myself, an opportunity as pure as it was brittle. I tried to think of how to phrase my wish. I must get it perfect. I must speak the words clearly, and I had better—

"What are you doing?"

I spun, clutching the burning taper to my chest. The king had pulled himself into the doorway. I had not heard him approach.

He frowned. "Is that my nameday candle?"

My face heated. "What?"

He shifted his weight. "It's singeing your shirt."

Startled, I blew out the candle. The wick smoked thickly, curling upwards. "I'm sorry. I didn't—I didn't mean…" My words tumbled over themselves. "I just saw that you hadn't…that is to say, the candle, I shouldn't have…"

He wasn't listening. He was watching my face, my splotchy red cheeks. He would accuse me of stealing, and what then? The law on theft in Isla was clear. They would cut off my hands. Or maybe since they still needed me to work, they would settle for just one hand. A few fingers.

His frown deepened. "Is today your birthday?"

"No. I mean—yes, but that doesn't excuse…there's no excuse…" I made myself stop. Nameday candles were not meant to be shared, and the king was not a generous man. He was still watching me. Thinking of my punishment, no doubt. Trying to imagine how many fingers he could sever before I could no longer do my job.

He asked, "Do you have any family in the palace?"

I did not understand the question. Would he call my family to bear witness to my be-handing? Would he make one of my relatives wield the blade? "No, Your Majesty."

"What about in the city?"

"No."

"Friends? Visitors?"

I realized then what he was asking, and it was almost worse than punishment over his stolen candle. Burning, I swallowed. I could not even answer.

He seemed to regret his question. Suddenly awkward, he looked away. "You are dismissed," he said. "Take the rest of the day for yourself."

He thought he was doing me a favor. That I might want to spend my birthday—what? Swimming in the pond with the frogs? Weaving spells under the stars? It was what everyone else said of me. But I could not admit the truth, either: that I had nowhere to go, nothing to do. That I had chosen to linger there in his unpleasant company rather than be alone.

I set the candle carefully back into the drawer, dipped a curtsy, and escaped the room.

EIGHT

Later that evening, a knock came at my door. I flinched, my knife going sideways on the rosemary stem I'd been working, making a ragged chop. I never received visitors, and certainly not at so late an hour. Had the king decided to punish me after all? Or was it the guards, come for me at last?

I darted a glance around my workroom. Though I had lit no tapers, my cauldron fire burned brightly, illuminating the evidence of my latest experiments. There were poisonous mushrooms and deathberries, hemlock and hogweed, snake venom and even the snake herself, a gorgeous diamondback contained inside a large jar. The knock came again, louder this time, and my pulse began to rise. What would happen if someone saw this place? I did not know how obvious these ingredients were to the untrained eye. Could the average person recognize which plants were for healing and which were for killing? I could not risk it. It must all be destroyed.

It had taken weeks to collect those ingredients. Each had to be sought and found, picked at the right time and carefully transported, cut a certain way or distilled or milked to draw out the plant's full power. It had been an arduous process, but it was even more painful to see how quickly everything disappeared into my fire—everything but the snake, who was carefully released through the window. In a bare minute, my shop was clean.

I scurried through the kitchen into the entryway, brushing my hands down my front and doing my best to school my features. I paused before the door, listening hard. Just one heartbeat on the other side. Whoever it is, I told myself, you must show nothing.

I believe I did show something, though, when I saw who was waiting behind the door. It was not the king, or a guard, but one of the girls I had seen in the great hall earlier that day, the kitchen worker who had been balancing a spoon on her nose.

"Hello," she said brightly. She was taller than me by a full hand, with a freckled face and bright blue eyes. She wore a dress of simple cloth, and her hair was unbound for bed, flowing around her shoulders in pretty waves. I realized with a jolt I had forgotten to don my headscarf. My hair was at its thinnest from my poisonings, the scalp showing through in places. I battled a wave of discomfort.

"I hope I am not troubling you," she continued, rocking onto her toes, "but my little brother has fallen ill. A head cold, it seems. I was told you might have something to help?"

As the royal physician, I was not supposed to tend anyone but the king and his immediate family. If a palace servant took ill, they were instructed to make the quarter-day journey to the King's City to seek a healer there. It was a clear rule. Everyone knew it.

"I am not allowed," I said, forming the words slowly. "The crown forbids it."

"Oh, I know." She was smiling, as if the concepts of law and punishment were foreign to her. "But it is a rather outdated rule, isn't it? Anyway, I would not be asking, except that it's late, and I am so tired—too tired to walk to the city—and I do not imagine it would be much trouble?" She said this last as if it was a question, clutching her hands together hopefully.

I felt as if I had been nailed to the spot. My skin prickled. Did she know what she was asking? No, of course not. She worked in the kitchens, probably doing something simple and carefree. Baking bread. She looked like the kind of girl who baked bread all day, laughing and balancing spoons, then going home to her little brother, and probably a mother and father too. Maybe they played games together. They probably all loved each other. Meanwhile, I had not slept a full night in ages, and when I did sleep, it was fitful and worried and broken. My body ached constantly from my poisonings, the experiments an endless torment. I was exhausted to my bones, and I had just destroyed weeks of work for her intrusion. I thought, you are tired? You know nothing of tiredness.

"I am sorry." My nails dug into my palms. "I cannot break the rules."

"Oh, but—"

"Goodbye."

I tried to close the door, but she stuck out her foot to jam it. I inhaled, practically frothing, only to stop short when I realized there were tears in her eyes. "Please," she said. "I lied. I cannot go to the city because we have no money for a healer."

My anger lost its rabidity. "Oh."

"Please. My brother is very sick."

I wavered. It would not take long to create the needed draught. But what if the king learned of it? By all rights, I should have been punished for the candle debacle. It seemed utterly insane to press my luck with a second disobedience on the same day. I was no heroine. I did not know this girl's brother; I had no reason to care whether he was sick. Why should I risk myself? What would such a thing gain me? Yet I found myself saying, "Give me a moment."

I left the girl to wait outside the door while I returned to my workshop. Luckily, I had all the necessary ingredients for a cold remedy on hand: elderberry, ginger, sap from my *istilla*. There had been a time when I kept these items fully stocked, but I had not made this draught in ages, not since that last and fateful night. That time, the remedy was for the king, with one unforgettable difference—his had been mixed with poison.

My fire crackled. A breeze whined against the window. In the distance, my hands went about their preparations, reaching for the mortar high on the shelf, unstopping the vial of milky *istilla*. My mind, however, was tugging on that memory. I saw my mother dangle the bottle of *nightlight* before my eyes. I saw her tip the contents into the king's medicine. She gave it a little shake to be sure it was dissolved.

My hands were cold on the pestle, my gaze a thousand leagues away. I felt as if a great chasm had opened beneath me, and I was falling, falling. How had I not thought of this? *Nightlight* was a brew just like any other. If you combined it with different ingredients, its properties changed. Of course it had not killed the king. My mother—clever with her words, but hardly a master of potions—had mixed the drug with another, a draft for a cold, and so changed its composition. This was her oversight, her grand mistake. And it explained, too, why I had been unable to recreate *nightlight*, why all of my experiments were failures. I had been administering it to myself in the wrong way.

My mind spurred, galloping forward. This was a missing piece of the puzzle, a crucial link I had not considered. It was the answer I had been looking for. It changed everything.

Already my gaze was darting around my workshop, cataloging what ingredients I had in store, which must be recollected. I would tell that kitchen girl something had come up, she must return another night, and meanwhile...

I rubbed my temples. No. If not for that girl, I would never have made these connections. I owed her in some way, didn't I? Besides, another hour would make little difference. With careful deliberateness, I finished the draught for her brother. I donned my headscarf and my long sleeves, checking that the worst of the damage was covered. When I stepped out into the corridor with the medicine in hand, the girl beamed.

We walked together toward the servants' chambers. The king's palace was built like a system of locks so you must pass through each room to get to the next. There was the library, the great hall, the throne room, the gallery. Tapestries hung at even intervals, with guards and butlers alternating between them. Overhead, intricate murals splayed the ceiling, mighty lions and coltish lambs, grinning lords and fawning maidens, all painted by the great artists of our age.

I saw none of it. My mind was ensnared, looping over itself again and again. Every noise, every whisper, the tiled floor beneath my feet, the night pressing in on the windows, was all of it lost to me. The air itself seemed to have vanished, and I felt weightless, drifting like a planet through space.

The girl's voice came from far away. "I am Ophelia," she said. "I cannot tell you how thankful I am. My mother will be too, once she sees."

I nodded distantly.

"If not for your help, I do not know what we would have done."

My voice was scarcely there. "Yes."

"It must be wonderful to possess such a knowledge of medicine." I could feel her eyes on me. "What talent you have!"

At this, I looked at her. It took me a moment to process what I was seeing: her hopeful eyes, her mouth quivering with more to say. She was making a valiant effort, and I was in the clouds.

I tried to pull my attention back to the present. What had she been professing? That I was talented? My instinct was to rebuke this. *You are not really in a position to think so, you have not yet seen my work.* The other part of me, however, sensed that pointing out her fallacy was the wrong thing. I dug for a better answer. "I am grateful for my gift."

"It is not just a gift," Ophelia insisted. "Everyone knows how hard you work."

Did they? It seemed most people did not know anything about me, besides the fact that I was a caretaker to the king. But again, I tried for diplomacy. "I suppose it must be both."

Ophelia nodded, her entire body bobbing with the movement. "Your private garden, too. It flourishes even in winter when the kitchen gardens are dead. I've often heard the cook wondering how you manage it. But of course, as a Freestone, you have an instinct for these things. You can root out power at its source."

I peered at Ophelia. Surely the cook had never spoken so favorably of my abilities. "There is no need to invent stories to flatter me. I have already agreed to help you."

Ophelia's expression shifted. "They are not stories."

"I know what people say of me." My cheeks were hot. "I am not a fool."

"You don't believe me?"

"Of course not." I glanced away, battling a surge of resentment. "Just look at me."

Ophelia did look. Her expression softened, and I bristled. I feared she would say something falsely conciliatory, or worse, pitying, but all she said was, "We are here."

The servants' quarters were located on the east end of the palace. Built for practicality, the rooms were devoid of fanciful flourishes, but this only lent them a homey, lived-in feel. Ophelia led us through a common room and into a final chamber, which belonged to her family.

I realized I had been wrong. Ophelia did not just have one brother. She had a dozen.

"Everyone," Ophelia chirped. "This is Selene."

It was overwhelming, all those eyes on me. Ophelia was the oldest by a handful of years and clearly in charge, but I could not make much sense of it beyond that. So many children. So many siblings to battle for attention, and noise to speak over and fights to break, and bodies to bathe and clothe and feed. Each servant's chamber was built to comfortably house a family of three or four, but not...how many were there? Eight? Ten?

The boys did their best to smile politely as Ophelia hurried us through, but it was impossible not to see how they eyed me, their gazes scraping my headscarf, my mottled skin. My face burned. *Just look at me.*

"Through here," Ophelia said, hurrying us to a room in the back separated by a curtain. "Icharu and Mother are waiting."

"So many," I said vaguely.

"Brothers?" Ophelia nodded. "Only Icharu is my sibling by blood. August and Desius are my cousins—their parents died in that stable fire a few years back, do you remember it? And then there's Ulphan, whose mother was a close family friend, but passed away during childbirth, may the Goddess give her peace, and Perseus, who heard we take in lost boys and just showed up one day, and—Mother, look who I've brought."

Ophelia swept back the curtain to reveal a little boy in bed, their mother perched on the mattress beside him. At the sight of us, she pressed a hand to her heart. "Thank the Goddess," she said. "Miss Freestone, I am so glad to see you."

I went about my work, administering the boy his medicine, handing the remaining draught to the mother—she was Daphne—and explaining how and when to administer the next dose. Ophelia came closer to take note, and side by side, it was easy to see how similar mother was to daughter. They had the same nose, the same eyes, the same scattering of freckles. As they listened, they tilted their heads, nodding with their bodies. "We are so thankful," Daphne said. "If not for your help, I do not know what we would have done."

I cleared my throat. "Just be sure he eats something with that next dose."

"You are a blessing, child. Truly a gift from the Goddess. Just wait until the others hear!"

"Oh, please don't—" I toyed with the hem of my shirt. "Please don't tell anyone I was here."

Daphne blinked. "You don't want others knowing?"

"It is my duty to help the royal family." I could not tell by her face whether she understood, so I added, "Only them."

"Well yes, but...that is a very old rule, isn't it?" Daphne peered at me. "You aren't in any trouble dear, are you?"

The way she looked at me. It was as it had been all those years ago when I walked arm in arm with my father through the gallery, and I could suddenly witness myself through another's perspective. I had grown thinner these past weeks. There were dark bags under my eyes, a tremor in my hands. I was never hungry, never at ease, exhausted by both my work and my thoughts, which chased themselves like a dog chases its tail. I knew I was not the picture of happiness or good health, scarcely even the picture of modest adjustment. Rather, I was a winter wolf run ragged. So what if I had just uncovered a new revelation in my quest to heal the king? It was only further proof of my hopelessness, for if I was truly competent, I would have thought of it ages ago.

Yes, I wanted to burst. I wanted to throw myself into her arms and weep. *Yes, I am in trouble, help me, please help me*. But I only shook my head. "No." I forced a smile. "Of course not."

NINE

Word came that a soldier was to be punished. He had given King Alder a new title—the Cripple King—and had been overheard singing a bawdy song by the same name. Such insolence could not be tolerated, especially among the king's own men. The soldier must be brought to justice.

The court gathered in the palace's back courtyard, a motley group of vassals and advisers, cupbearers and pages, ladies and lords and their many red-nosed children. They came all at once, their robes spilling, eyes full of glee and fear. Who knew how many of them had called the king cripple themselves, how many had a hand in crafting that soldier's song? They had come to show their loyalty to the crown, lest they be next.

The day was clear and cold, the sky a pale stretch of canvas. I stood deep within the press of bodies, unable to see the offending soldier. A maiden bumped my elbow. When she turned to apologize, she caught sight of me and gave a start.

I moved to the outskirts of the courtyard where an old elm grew. It was a simple thing to scale the tree for a better view, and at once I could see the crowd's puppet faces, the soldier with his quivering lips, and the captain of the guard, holding a war hammer.

The soldier was younger than I expected. He had a patchy beard, a thin neck. His eyes were white all the way around, darting here and there. He had been chained to the cobblestones by the wrists and ankles, his hands up by his head, legs spread wide through hoops staked into the ground for this purpose. Pinioned on his back, he looked like an animal for dissecting.

The captain of the guard stepped forward. I knew him—he'd once had a place at the king's table beside my mother. He was a hulking man, his head bald and shining, his neck like an overstuffed sausage. His hammer was a thing of stories, beautifully forged, heavier than most could lift. A weapon meant for smashing skulls.

He hefted the hammer. His expression was grim. The captain demanded perfect discipline from his soldiers, and this was his chosen punishment. The young soldier had called the king a cripple and would be crippled in turn.

I drew back, bracing. I was no stranger to blood, but wounds were usually brought to me after the wounding had already been done. The closest I had ever come to witnessing real pain was childbirth, but this would not be the same. I glanced around for King Alder, but of course he was not there.

The hammer came down. The soldier's knee shattered. He let out a terrible cry and the crowd surged forward, everyone vying for a better view. I squinted my eyes to slits so as not to see too clearly, my fingers digging into the branches. I hoped the soldier would pass out for his own sake, but he remained awake, eyes rolling in pain and terror as the hammer was brought down on his other knee. The bone bent at an awful angle. This time I could hear it. *Crack.*

I made myself stay for the whole of it, as the captain methodically broke both of the soldier's knees and one of his wrists, to mimic the damage that had been done to the king. I was still squinting, my head turned partway. Though I peered through fuzzy lashes, I could not block out the soldier's crying or the methodic crunch of the hammer.

My thoughts began to feel strange; my ears buzzed. It occurred to me that I myself might pass out. I should get down from the tree. I saw myself in the soldier's position, my knees broken one by one, my bones reduced to a mangled heap. The soldier's punishment had been wellannounced, a public event meant to remind people that the king was still their king, regardless of his absence, and should not be crossed. But I had already crossed the king, and my offense was worse than some silly song.

The captain lifted the hammer a final time. He was meant to break the soldier's last wrist, but brought the weapon down on the boy's skull instead. Later, the captain would say he misaimed, that his hand slipped. It was the sort of lie that could be forgiven. The soldier was the captain's own man. The captain had trained him from boyhood and was pledged to teach and guide him. If the captain had been the one to decide the soldier's punishment, he had done it for duty, but if he ended the soldier's life, he had done it for mercy. There was no future for a soldier who could not fight.

I clung to the elm, breathing deeply through my nose as the crowd dispersed and the soldier's body was wiped away. It had been a full turn of the season since the poisoning. The queen's interrogations had yielded little, but that was nothing. She had a lifetime to put the pieces together, and meanwhile, I could only wait and hold my breath.

I could not stop thinking of the captain and his soldier. If the king discovered what I had done, would he show me that kind of mercy? If he did, would I deserve it? But those are questions you ask when you already know the answer, and hope for a different one.

...

I did not immediately return to the imperial wing after the punishment. I was not ready to face the king, not with visions of gore still playing in my head. I went instead to the forest, that place of quiet introspection. It had given me answers before, but now all was winter-silent. I tried to dig up roots, something to do with my hands, but my trembling fingers made a mess of the task. Eventually I gave up and simply walked between trees, trying to remember the trick of breathing.

When I entered the king's study later that afternoon, he was there in his velvet chair. The window stretched tall behind him; the sun illuminated hazy rainwater stains. On the mantle was a stout clock, and on the wall beside it was another. The two clocks were not in sync, and their ticking eclipsed each other. The king's heartbeat made three, a deeper rhythm that I felt more than heard.

He waited for me to come forward. Over the past weeks, the king's eyes had come fully clear, reflecting light like a tiger's, sometimes green, sometimes gold. That day they were an in-between color, the hue of autumn leaves glimmering in his shadow face. "You saw the punished soldier?"

I nodded.

"And what did you think?"

I instantly suspected a trick. The king never asked for my thoughts.

When I did not immediately reply, he leaned forward and set his elbows to his knees. "Do you think the soldier got what he deserved?"

A trick indeed. This felt dangerous, as if the king had read my earlier thoughts and wanted to lure them out of me. I chose my words. "It is not up to me to say what he deserves."

"You must have some opinion."

"Apologies, Your Majesty, but no."

"Then invent one. Do you think it was a fair punishment? Did the captain sentence him fairly?" I had never seen the king like this. There was an energy about him, a glint in his eye that seemed almost…earnest. It was a look I would come to know, that spark of mind, the way his words could become like an ocean, ropes of purple current to draw me in. At the time, though, I was only aware of his intensity, and a surprising desire in myself to meet it.

"It was a harsh punishment for a small crime," I said, "but if the aim was to prevent future indiscretions, I think the captain achieved it."

"And what of that final blow? The captain ended the soldier's life."

This answer, at least, was easy to give. "I would not have wanted him to end my life."

The king thumped back in his chair. His tone was flat. "So you would choose the life of an invalid."

"I would choose *life*," I said simply.

"Naive as ever." But the words held no bite. "Have you considered what that kind of life would mean for you? Imagine. What would you do if you could not care for yourself? If at every moment you were at the mercy of another?"

I held his gaze. "I do have some sense of what it is to be at one's mercy, Your Majesty."

He blinked, but did not concede the point. Rather, my boldness only seemed to spur him. "Then what if you could not engage the things you enjoy? If you were deprived of your spellwork?"

"It is not spellwork," I said automatically.

"Do not change the subject."

So I considered it. What would I do if I could no longer practice my medicines? If I could not wander the woods, stopping here and there to pick wildflowers or mushrooms, or spend long hours shut away in my workshop, so absorbed that days might pass without my notice? I had not chosen my gifts, but that only meant they were more a part of me, less like a locket to be worn around the neck and more like a limb that could be severed.

I looked at the scars on my wrists and palms, old burns crawling pink around my fingers. I could not even blame the poisonings for their ugliness; these hands were all mine. They mapped my existence, and yet...life was not merely about what my hands could make. If I was immobilized, I would still have my mind, and wasn't that more important?

I returned my gaze to the king. He had not taken a single visitor since his poisoning. No family visits, no council meetings, no hearings or strategy sessions or meals with friends. He met with his mother to discuss the more pressing issues of the kingdom, leaving the rest to her judgment. I had thought stubbornness was what kept the king in isolation, or misplaced pride, but of course it was not so simple. *The most powerful man in Isla.* What must it be like to watch yourself reduced, stripped before the eyes of a people who expect you to be unfailing? We all face the judgment of others, that is something even the lowest among us must endure, but the king faced the judgment of millions, tens of millions, and that had been when he was strong. What now that he was bedridden, lost to himself, with graveyards in his eyes? I had seen the shadows in his face. I had seen how he still spent many days in bed.

He did not keep the curtains closed because he liked the dark.

"Things would be different," I said slowly, "but I would make adjustments. I would allow myself to lean on others."

That only made him defiant. "They would grow to resent you."

"Those who love you cannot truly resent you."

He huffed a laugh. "My mother must not love me then. Oh, do not look so shocked. Althea is competent enough. And she has a mind for ruling, there's no doubting that. But she does not want the responsibility. She is a devout woman, insistent on tradition, and my reign has been anything but traditional. When she looks at me, all I see is shame."

He was no longer watching me. His eyes were distant, gazing into some memory I could not see. Before, I had thought he was self-pitying, but it struck me that the king truly believed he deserved this misery. Almost as if the poisoning was something he had done to himself, rather than something that had been done to him.

I wanted to say something. To offer him comfort, maybe. A kind word. When was the last time anyone had spoken to him kindly? I do understand the irony of that, but I couldn't help it, not when he was sitting there before me, broken and dark and hating himself.

I thought of the woman who had pulled away from me in the courtyard. Ophelia's brothers eyeing me, the king himself mocking my scars. I thought of all the hours I spent poring over my potions, the burns and marks I tried to cover. When I spoke next, I spoke with conviction. "I would always choose life, Your Majesty. It might not look the same as it once did, but a changed life is better than none." I waited until he met my eye; I wanted him to know I meant this with all my heart: "We are more than our bodies."

Did he soften a little? I'd like to think so. Yet whatever effect my words had on him did not stick, because three days later the king would attempt to take his own life, and it would become clear he did not agree with me after all.

TEN

I smelled the blood first.

I had arrived to the king's chambers early that morning. I was restless. I wanted to get a start on the day's work. Truly, it was for no good reason at all. I was fortunate, yet not so fortunate as to stumble upon him at the moment of injury. I went about the morning as usual, taking my time. I folded fresh linens and set them in their cabinet; I refilled a useless water pitcher normally meant for guests; I drew open the curtains to give light to the houseplants. I might have continued that way all morning, stalling until it was time at last to bring King Alder his breakfast, until it hit me. That metallic scent.

I darted into the king's bedchamber. He was there in bed, eyes open but dim, hair a tawny halo around the pillow. One of his wrists was a mess of red. Atop the sheets beside his thigh was the knife.

I launched myself into his bed, tearing away the covers. He winced but did not protest, which frightened me more. He was weak, quickly growing weaker. My heart pounded; everything took on a keen, sharp edge. His wrist bore a deep gash. The blood was dark red and oozing—

some small fortune, he had missed the artery at least. But how long ago had he cut himself? How much blood had he lost?

I thought our *gilili*—the power that bound my family's healing abilities to him—might have alerted me to some change in him, that my senses would have taken over, guiding my hands as I drew him back to life. My mother had always seemed touched by that kind of unseen magic, her powers pouring into her like water into a glass, but that was never how it had been for me, and it was not that way then. I felt no special power, no shimmer of enchantment, nothing but jittery terror at the sight of him like that, broken and bleeding beneath me.

"Please," he croaked, and that frightened me most of all. I had never heard him beg. "Don't."

But I did. I snatched the knife from where it lay among the bedsheets, using the same blade that had done this to him to tear a section of the cloth, which I wrapped around his upper arm in a tourniquet. With my free hand I pinched the vein down by his wrist to stop the immediate blood loss, ignoring the sticky warmth and trying to think.

I needed to stitch the wound, but I did not have needle and thread on hand. I wavered. How long would it take to fetch the supplies? What might happen if I left him alone? A part of me warned against it. There was no telling what the king might attempt in those few spare minutes. "Don't," he murmured again. "Selene."

It was the first time he had ever used my name. That seemed to decide things.

I bolted to my workshop as quickly as I could to fetch what I needed, pausing long enough to snap a command at the four members of the King's Guard who stood sentry outside the door. "The king is hurt. You," I pointed to the largest of the group, "go to him, make sure he does himself no further harm. You," to the bald one, "bring water and clean cloth, quickly. And you two, stay here, let no one else enter. Not even the queen."

The men were alarmed; their hands dropped automatically to their swords. For one wild moment, I envisioned my orders backfiring. They would draw their weapons on me instead, demand to know what had happened to their king, what I had done to him, why my fingers were dripping with his blood. These four men had been hand-chosen for both their skill and dedication, sworn to protect King Alder at all costs, while I was only a young physician, yet untested in my new role. They should have questions at least, demand a better explanation. But in the end, the men only nodded and obeyed.

I returned from my chambers to find the king exactly as he had been, his guardsman hovering anxiously beside the bed. The king's eyes were hooded, his face frighteningly pale. His breath was coming short and fast—his body's response to being starved of oxygen. I climbed back into his bed and straddled his chest.

"What are you doing?" the guardsman asked.

"In case he tries to fight me."

The supplies were in my hands. I did not bother with a numbing serum. I cleaned the site, administered a topical balm for infection, then stitched the wound with the most perfect sutures my mother taught me to make.

Once it was done, I accepted the water pitcher from the second guardsman so I could make the king drink. He refused, turning his head like an insolent child. I could have forced it down. There was a part of me that wanted to. Now that the immediate work was over, my nerves were setting in. I wanted to shake him. I wanted to rage at him for his idiocy. *How could you do this?* I wanted to get close to his face and scream. *How could you care so little for your own life?*

Gently, I lifted the cup to his lips and coaxed him to swallow.

After, he was exhausted and immediately fell asleep. I scrubbed my hands in the nearby washbasin. The guardsmen were watching me with new eyes.

I said, "Someone needs to tell the queen what happened."

"The queen knows," replied the larger of the men.

"Is she…is she coming, then? Or here already, waiting outside?"

The man's face showed no emotion. "She is in the temple. Praying."

They left to retake their guardsmen positions outside the door. Alone once more, I cleaned my tools, gathered the ruined sheets. My limbs felt distant; my own fatigue tumbled over me. Though it was only midmorning, the craving for my bed pierced me like a lance. I pulled a chair up beside the king instead, curled into it like a cat, and set my chin in my hands to keep watch.

. . .

The king woke later that afternoon. I could feel his heartbeat rise and was there at once, offering more water. This time, he drank and drank. I watched the column of his throat move as he swallowed.

He wiped his mouth with his unbandaged wrist and tried to give back the cup. I gripped his hand, turning the palm over, ignoring his weak complaint. My eyes traced the tendons, the muscles, the thick blue veins. He coughed. "What are you doing?"

After his poisoning, the king's hands had been frozen stiff, but now they were easy, the skin supple, fingers loose. When I released him, he drew the limb back and clenched his fist as anyone might. They looked like normal hands.

I wanted to rage at him all over again. You begin to regain your mobility, and this is how you choose to use your newfound power? To grip the hilt of a knife and carve into yourself?

He saw my thoughts and gave a wan smile. "Never fear," he rasped. "It seems I have failed even at this."

. . .

He was asleep again. Outside the window, a storm was moving in. The steel sky threatened rain.

I had not left my chair except during those few brief minutes to fetch him water. I kept watch, silent and gray, a gargoyle in her portico. Under the green eye of the storm, I memorized new details. His unbound hair. The lock brushing his forehead, curled like a shell. His nose, surprisingly delicate, and his ears, surprisingly small. His mouth that had shaped my name. *Selene*.

If you had asked me last summer whether I wished for the king's death, I would have said yes. It was what my mother wanted, and I was her sheep, roped to her will. Later, in the months after the poison failed, when the king was at his cruelest and my life was shrunk to the size of pebbles, my answer would have gained nuance. I would say I no longer knew what I wanted. That it was not so simple.

And if you asked me after? After I had witnessed the king's life bleeding away, and fought to bring it back? After I glimpsed the pain he must be suffering, pain he had been masking with anger and malice? What then? Did I still want his death?

No, I realized, never, I could never really want that.

I shifted in the chair, tucking my legs more tightly up under me. Through the window, the wind twisted the trees. The glass windowpanes rattled in their sockets. It was late in the season for a thunderstorm, but the weather felt fitting. Perhaps this was the Goddess' way of showing her grief over the king's actions. Perhaps the king was a god himself after all, and the grief was his.

I thought of my mother. It was in our blood to serve the Alder family. The instinct was woven right into our bones. So why had Persaphe conspired to end the king's life? Was she acting under another's command, as I had acted under hers? I imagined a nameless face pulling strings from the shadows. It was possible, I supposed, though like my earlier theories, I could not truly picture it. *Power*, my mother used to say, *is that asset which should never be compromised. Without power, we are all just prisoners.*

Persaphe hated to think of herself as an unwilling servant; rather, she called herself a steward of the throne. This was not mere pride. Her mother, my grandmother, had been captured by a band of Mad Horsemen while on a foraging expedition in the Forbidden Lands. Persaphe had witnessed the abduction firsthand. She had been young then, and I believe the fear of imprisonment followed her into adulthood. It was part of the reason Persaphe was so careful to retain her own autonomy. My grandmother was never found.

It was not until much later, after the fireplace burned itself out and the gray clouds sunk to dusk that the sky finally opened to wash the earth. Hunger gnawed at me, and I yearned for a bath, but I was afraid to leave. What if the king woke and I was not there? What if his condition worsened and he never woke again? The thought filled me with inexplicable dread. Yet there were rules to the craft, which my mother had often lectured. The first was this: you cannot care for others if you do not care for yourself.

When I exited the king's chambers, I was surprised to find Hobore there, sitting against the wall across the hallway. At the sight of me, he stood. The king's half-brother was lanky; it seemed to take a long time for him to straighten. "The guards wouldn't let me pass," he explained, glancing at the four men stationed beside the door. "They said you ordered it."

I glanced at the King's Guard, but they kept their eyes resolutely forward. "Actually," I said, "Queen Mother Althea ordered it. No one is allowed to enter."

No one but family, Hobore might have countered. It would put me in an awkward position. I did not think Althea meant to include her late husband's by-blow in that count, but nor would I offend Hobore by saying so. If he made that point, I would have no choice but to concede. Yet if Hobore saw this obvious loophole, he did not take it. Maybe he was too gentlemanly for that. Or maybe his mind simply did not work that way. Not everyone was made of teeth and claws, and Hobore did have a reputation for being simple.

"You were spotted running through the halls with blood on your hands," he said. "I think, under the circumstances, the queen would understand."

"We will have to ask her to know for certain."

"We could ask the king."

"He is sleeping."

"Well." Hobore stood a bit straighter, his eyes skittering over my face. I was reminded of the way he had looked at me in the great hall and felt a fresh wave of unease. "Will you at least tell me what happened?"

I did not want to lie to Hobore, but nor did I want word of the incident spreading until I had spoken with Althea. This was the royal palace, and that kind of information would trade hands like currency. I replied as best I could. "There was an…accident."

"What kind of accident?"

"His Majesty cut himself."

"Cut himself?" I could hear Hobore's pulse jump. "How? How could you allow this to happen?"

I was startled by his vehemence. "I did not allow anything."

"He was hurt under your care."

"If you have an issue with my methods, you can take them up with the queen."

I did not mean it as an insult, yet I saw the words land. Bastards of the court were not usually allowed a place in our halls. It was the single favor the queen would ever grant Hobore. He would not be asking for more.

A shadow moved through his eyes. Hobore took a step forward—to force his way past? To spit his reply into my face? I do not know, because at that moment one of the guards gripped the sword at his belt. A warning.

Hobore blinked. "Forgive me." He took a step back. "I only worry for him." He was all civility again, a snail retreating back into its shell. "The poisoning…has been difficult. I have wanted to visit before now. I should have tried. I know the Queen Mother's order, but I think Elias would allow me. He is my brother, and I…" A swallow. "May I return when he wakes?"

"His Majesty is weak. His condition is still unstable. I think it would be best to give him time."

Hobore did not seem intent on arguing. He glanced once more at the guards before nodding. "I will return again in time, then."

I waited until he was out of sight before dropping my shoulders. I needed that meal and bath more than ever.

I turned to face the King's Guard. My next words were difficult for being so unpracticed, but I forced them out. "I would know each of your names."

They gave them. Yorvis, who was tall and lean. Kurton, who had the look of a great bear. Arch, whose smile was like his axe. And Freesier, the one who had dropped his hand to his sword. These men guarded this hallway day and night, yet we had never spoken before today. I repeated each of their names back to them. "I owe you a debt," I said, "and my thanks."

"No, *rahvika*," said Kurton, using the ancient word for what I was. It meant *healer*, but also *comrade*. "We know what you have done for our king. It is us who owes you."

Unsure of how to reply, I gave an awkward curtsy. Yet beneath the awkwardness was an undeniable pleasure. I departed for my rooms, feeling different than before. As if I had dipped my hands into my pockets and discovered something I had forgotten, yet had been there all along.

ELEVEN

We took the next few days the only way we could: one at a time. The king recovered and regained his strength, and I suppose it could be said I did as well. At first, the horror of his accident was all I could think about. I replayed it again and again. That initial whiff of blood. Lunging into his bed, pulling back the covers. And the king, with his fading eyes and his ghostly skin and the way he had said my name.

As the days passed and those images began to fade, however, my old thoughts of fear and punishment did not retake their place. Rather, something new was rooting within me. For so long, I had been the rabbit in the lion's den, forever afraid of the moment the beast would wake and take his dinner. But I had seen the lion grin, and he had no teeth.

I went about my duties with renewed purpose. I sent a footman with a message for the queen. I delegated the delivery of meals to a kitchen servant. I carried what supplies I could to the king's suite, setting my cauldron over one of the fires, organizing my vials and jars and pouches around his bedchamber. My knife clicked on a marble table as

I chopped. Newly picked herbs hung to dry in the window. The room smelled pleasantly of my oils and washes, the afternoon light suffusing us in a warm glow.

"Close the curtains," the king said.

"No," I replied.

I made a draught to help ease the king's pain and another to ward against infection. I ordered him to take both, then turned back to my work, watching from the corner of my eye. He scrutinized the bottles, rolling them in his hands before finally bringing them to his lips to drink.

Had you asked me even a week ago if this was where we would find ourselves, I would have laughed. Yet I had given the king a command and he had obeyed. I felt an unfamiliar prick of satisfaction.

Day by day, the color returned to his cheeks. He began sitting up in bed to watch me work. His heartbeat regained its old rhythm, and that too gave me strength. There was something comforting about the feel of it sitting beside my own pulse, similar but different, like a stamp in relief. Or maybe the comfort lay in the fact that its sound was proof of his life, and my efforts.

When there were no more draughts to prepare and no more chores to be done, I began brewing elixirs. I did not work on my poisons with him watching—I was not daft—but rather resumed my old experiments, the ones I had scarcely had time for these past two seasons. I lined my beakers along the mantle and hauled up as many botany books as my arms could carry, leaving them open to the relevant pages.

"You are turning my bedchamber into an apothecary," the king remarked.

"Apothecaries are for selling medicine," I replied. "Nothing here is for sale."

He did not say thank you. He did not say, I might have underestimated you. Where did you learn to make a tourniquet, Selene? Where did you learn to stitch a wound or craft an antibiotic? I did not expect him to ask these things; I knew him better than that. Yet he began to look at me differently. No longer did his face hold such malice, always primed to fight. Rather, he deferred to me, allowing me to assess his wrist as often as I liked, to bandage and rebandage, to relay instructions, *you must not, you must be sure to, every day it is important*, and nod his agreement.

Althea had not yet answered my summons. I sent another.

The king still hated physical contact. Each time I redressed his wound, he would hold himself perfectly still, his eyes set on the opposite wall as if he could stare it into oblivion. On the fourth day, I was halfway through assessing his stitches when I realized he was holding his breath.

I paused. It was difficult not to feel a twinge of those old familiar hurts. I knew I had a reputation, and my scars might have been unsightly, but this was unwarranted. "I am not going to hex you, if that is what you worry."

His eyes shot to mine. "What?"

"I am not," I repeated slowly, "going to hex you."

The sound he made was like a laugh, if you sucked out the joy. His next words seemed to come from somewhere deep within. "I...do not like to be touched."

I think it took something out of him to admit that. I gave a small nod, though inside my blood was running clear with relief. So he was not just that way with me, then. "I promise to make it quick." I went back to my task. Rather than return his attention to the wall, however, the king regarded me.

That joyless laugh was still in his voice when he said, "Tell me why you saved my life."

"Tell me why you wanted to die," I shot back, then widened my eyes. I had not meant to speak so freely.

His lips twitched. "I think it should be obvious." He pulled his gaze to the ceiling. "I no longer wished to bear witness to my own demise."

And ending your life was the solution? I might have rejoined. But I knew that was not what he meant. He meant, the demise of who he had been. The slow demise of his power, his position, his kingdom. I thought of the king's face the day he asked if he was a monster. At the time it seemed a test, but I realized that was not all it was. He truly wanted reassurance. He wanted to know he was not ruined, not changed beyond recognition, that he could still be well-regarded, as his father had been, the king with a heart. I wondered if he actually believed what people said of him—that he had none.

"I saved your life," I replied, "because what you did with that knife was a mistake. You have…value. Not just as a king. As a person. A human. I know your spirit has been…wounded." He eyed me, but I continued. "It is no reason to give up. I do not wish to see you dead."

"Do your wishes matter more than mine?"

"In this case, yes."

"That is insolent."

"I will not apologize for it."

"Unless I order you to."

I pulled back a little. This was another test, I thought. The king was flexing his fingers, seeing just how deeply things had changed between us, how far his power still reached with me. I had the sense that my entire future hung on my answer. "No," I said. "Not even then."

He actually smiled at that, if you can believe it.

Eight days after the king's attempt on his life, I coaxed him out of bed into his study. Once he was settled in his chair, I gathered up one of my botany books and came to sit on the rug before him. The late morning sun shone hazily through winter clouds; the room was stuffy but not uncomfortable. The king wore a set of day clothes, a shirt with a drawstring front, trousers that hugged his long legs, a set of simple deerskin loafers. It was an improvement over the nightgown, to be sure.

He tapped a finger against the chair's curved arm. "Tell me what you are reading."

It was one of my favorites, an encyclopedia of all the plants that grew not just in Isla, but the neighboring regions as well, Hillshire and Skylin and the Island of Mirir. That last most interested me, for it was the place my mother had once traveled to hunt for the rare seeds of a near-extinct wildfruit. This had been before my birth, during King Adonis Alder's reign, and he had given her special permission. The story was famous among the court, favored for its novelty. Never before had a royal physician left the king's side for more than a month at a time, and my mother was gone for six. Likely, she had charmed the king into agreeing, as she charmed everyone. I often wondered what that trip was like for her, the ships she would have sailed upon, the mountains she would have seen, the color of the dirt beneath her sandals. Was it brown like ours, or red, or gray? Did it excite her to walk upon it, or frighten her, so different as it must have been from home?

As far as the story goes, my mother never found the seeds.

"I am researching roots," I told the king. "This book lists their properties."

"Roots?" He dropped his chin into his hand, arching a brow as if to say, *really?*

"I would have you know roots are quite interesting."

"To be sure."

I pursed my lips. "This knowledge doesn't just fall into my head. It must be learned." I almost said, *I am not my mother*, but stopped myself, saying instead, "You should be grateful I care to know my craft."

"I am grateful."

I cut my eyes to his, expecting more sarcasm, but he was sincere. "Oh." Now the room *was* too stuffy. "Well."

He said, "Tell me what you do with the roots."

So I did. I explained how roots could be mashed to make a poultice or boiled into a brew, how fibrous roots had one purpose and taproots another, how I might spend hours searching for root hairs that were just the right shape and size. When I finished explaining about roots, our conversation turned to algae, then fungi. My words came haltingly at first, and I stumbled more than once, unsure of what was worth explaining and what better left out. I was not used to such an audience, and the king was not the easiest of listeners. He could become intense, probing into my methods, his sleek mind sniffing out inconsistencies as the fox sniffs out the mole. Rarely did he ask a direct question, instead saying *tell me*, as if giving an order. *Tell me why you cut them this way. Tell me why they must be picked under the full moon. Tell me what happens if you add two to your brew instead of three.* That was part of being a king, I suppose. Or maybe it was just part of being Elias Alder. In time, my words evened out, my voice finding its cadence. I discovered I did not mind the king's intensity. After so long with only myself for company, I enjoyed the challenge of his attention.

By the eleventh day, king had made large strides in his physical recovery. Althea still had not come. I did not send a third letter.

He said, "Tell me about the mixture you have been adding to my tea."

We were in our usual places in his study. I had been focused on an entry in my encyclopedia regarding mosses, my mind exploring a new path for a potential *nightlight* recipe when his words yanked me from my thoughts. "Mixture?"

"You have been including lemon to mask the flavor. Did you think I wouldn't notice?"

Last time, he threatened to cut off my hands. A part of me believed those days were behind us, but how could I be certain? Maybe the king's temper would be like the sun, rising and setting and rising again. Maybe the peace we had found was an idyll, a watery reflection to be broken at the smallest of splashes. "It is a mixture of primblossom and *istilla*," I replied uneasily, searching his face for clues. "It is meant to help you relax." I explained the rest about stress and recovery. Then, venturing, "It seems to be working."

He held his hands before him, opening and closing his fists. "Yes."

I let out a silent breath. He was not angry. He was not going to threaten me, or worse, accuse me of poisoning him. The king must place more belief in my Freestone oaths than I had thought, to continue drinking his altered tea. It gave me the courage to say more. "I have been experimenting a little. There are other remedies I would like to try, ones like the tincture that I believe could help your recovery. If you will allow it."

His eyes came up swiftly. "Experimenting."

"The remedies are safe," I hastened to add. "I always test them on myself first, so you needn't worry about ill effects."

The king had frozen; his mouth hung open. He was looking at me as he never had. "You test them on yourself?"

"Yes."

"Tell me—" he started, but stopped. Whatever he intended to say, he did not want it to be a command. "Will you tell me…is that how you got your bruises?"

Oh, I wish he had not asked that. Without thinking, I tugged my sleeves more firmly over my wrists, my cheeks heating. His gaze followed the movement, his confusion morphing into thinly-veiled horror. "That's the reason you cover your arms," he said. "Your hair."

I do not know where my voice had gone. I could only nod.

His eyes were dark. "Show me."

If he ridiculed me now, I thought, I will not crumble. I am done with that. Yet I was not so brave as to hold his gaze as I fumbled with the knot at my chin, undoing my headscarf, then pulling up my sleeves.

The marks of my most recent poisonings were all over. Around my shoulders, my thinning hair hung like tumbleweed. My forearms were splotchy with rashes, my wrists covered in hives. The itching wasn't so bad thanks to a poultice I brewed for the purpose, but I had not yet figured out how to quell the redness, or speed its healing. Even if I could, it would hardly matter, because I would only poison myself again, and there would be new rashes and new bruises and the cycle would start again.

I kept my eyes down. I did not think I could bear to see the king's face just then. I listened for his heartbeat instead, but it was difficult to separate it from the pounding of my own. He was quiet for so long I thought he would not speak. Then, finally: "I do not understand."

I glanced up, and I was right—I could not bear it. His face had drained of color, his lips a pale slash. His eyes were stark, almost angry. I dropped my gaze again. "Sometimes, combinations of ingredients cause unwanted reactions. My experiments—"

"That is not what I meant. I mean, you have been trying to find a cure for my paralysis."

I gave a cautious nod.

"You have been suffering, and hiding it, because of me."

Again, I nodded.

"When I have been nothing but—" He broke off. If my face was pink before, now it was blazing. I wanted to melt into the floor, make him forget he had ever seen my marks. What had I been thinking, bringing up the remedies? What a foolish thing to do.

"Look at me," he said. Reluctantly, I obeyed. He was doing his best to keep his voice even, but I could feel his heart swelling, the pressure reverberating in my chest. "You are no longer to test these remedies on yourself."

My mouth popped open. "But I must."

"No. We will find someone else for your experiments."

"I won't subject others to this."

His nails dug into the armrests. "Yet you subject yourself?"

I could not explain the whole truth—that in order to find *nightlight's* cure, I must first recreate the *nightlight* itself, and these marks were not from remedies gone wrong, but poisons. I could not explain that his paralysis was my fault, that I had allowed my mother to use me, had fallen into her mysterious plot. I had been a fool of the worst kind, one who is blind even though her eyes are wide open. It almost did not matter why Persaphe wanted to kill the king. How could I possibly defend her when I myself did not know the reason?

"I must test the medicines on myself," I said, trying instead to appeal to his sense of reason. "It is the only way for me to understand them. If I gave my remedies to another, how would I know their exact effects?"

"The participants will describe them to you."

"They might miss something."

"We will increase the number of test subjects."

"I cannot conscionably experiment on more people."

"You can if I say you can."

"Your Majesty, please. These are human lives we are discussing."

"Yes," he said. "I know."

I thought of the king's reputation for ruthlessness. His singlemindedness, his ability to make hard decisions for the greater good. There was never any doubt that King Alder cared for Isla, but his methods were known to be severe. Once, in order to build a quicker route from Esmond to the King's City, he had ordered the construction of a road, straight and wide. When the Master of Labor asked what would happen to the farmers whose land would be destroyed by the new road, the king had waved a hand and said, "They can plant around it."

I did not know if this was another example of the king's merciless governance, or if it was impulse, or simple selfishness. I spoke frankly. "This is my duty."

He was unconvinced. I could see it in the set of his neck, the narrowing of his eyes. I expected him to switch to his monarch's voice, to command me to do as he bid, but the king did not command me. Rather, he turned his face to the window. The sunlight struck his profile; the light limned his nose. "You asked whether I would be willing to try new remedies," he said at last. "My answer is yes. If it helps you, I will take what you give me."

This statement was so unexpected that I could only stare. I had been plunging through my tasks because they were necessary, meeting the king head to head at every turn. Never did it occur that I might win his trust. That I might want to win it. "Thank you, Your Majesty."

"It's Elias." He pinched the bridge of his nose. "Just Elias."

Not even my mother referred to the king by his first name. It was too much, and I nearly said so, but at that moment he dropped the hand and looked at me. His eyes were more green than gold that day, and bottomless as oceans.

I could not help it. I smiled. "Elias."

When the impressionists paint us, they paint us like that, he in the velvet chair and I on the rug before him, book in hand, grinning. The smile means something different to the artists, I am sure. They did not know the way things were between us then. But the gist is the same.

TWELVE

The next morning, I went to find the queen.

A doorman confirmed she was in her chambers and asked for my calling card so he might pass it along. I told him I did not have such a card, and I would appreciate if he simply told Althea of my arrival. This seemed to offend the man, and he began to explain the reasons for palace protocols and the value of the queen's time, none of which I absorbed. What did it matter if I had the card or not? I was there, Althea was there. I needed to speak with her, so let me in.

Eventually, the doorman relented, leaving me to wait. When he returned, he looked down his nose. "She is displeased."

That makes three of us, I thought. "I can escort myself."

Althea did not immediately acknowledge me upon arrival. She was seated at a small writing desk in her receiving room, a prayer book in hand, sunlight cutting hard across her cheek. Her reading glasses hung so low on her nose I thought they must be held there by magic. At the edge of my awareness, I could hear her heartbeat, that soft tick.

At last, she looked up. "Well?"

She did not ask, how is my son? She did not say, I have been meaning to come. Two letters I had sent, both of which she ignored. There was a kindling in my chest—started by the doorman, fueled by Althea's shortness—that had me speaking bluntly. "Your son tried to kill himself."

"Yes," she replied, "so you said in your letters."

"Do you not wonder how he fares?"

Now it came. "I have been meaning to visit."

"It has been twelve days."

This was bold of me. A month ago, I would never have dared.

Althea closed her book with a muffled *snap*. "I have been busy with the investigation." When I merely looked at her, she relented. "He does not want to see me."

"I think he might."

"We have nothing to say to each other."

"You could start with an apology."

"An apology? For what? I hear he is recovered."

"He is doing better, yes. But he nearly died."

"And you saved him. Are you seeking a reward?"

I felt my anger rising. Was this Althea's expectation, that I would use her son's health as bargaining tool? Was that what my mother would have done, or my grandmother?

"If you cannot give your son your time," I replied in a voice quite unlike my own, "you might at least end his seclusion."

Althea turned her chin. "Elias is free to reemerge if he wishes."

"You have counseled him against it, and he heeds your advice. You could change your counsel."

"I cannot."

"Why?"

Althea tossed her glasses to the table. "You are a sharp child, Miss

Freestone. Surely you can see the difficulty."

I did not. Elias was suffering in more ways than one. He had survived his poisoning only to step into a haunted prison. If he never left his rooms, if he never took back his old life, how could he truly recover? This was obvious to me: he was alone, and in need of help. Support. Not from me, a girl he barely knew. From his mother. His family.

Althea gave a long sigh. "Elias is betrothed to Princess Mora of Hillshire. You know this, do you not? It has taken years of doing, mostly due to my son's impertinence. He wants nothing to do with any woman, or any man either, as far as I can tell. Yet he is the ruler of our kingdom, and a kingdom needs heirs. He has agreed to marry Princess Mora once she comes of age."

I knew of the betrothal. When it was first announced, it had been the subject of much excitement among the court. Though I had never met the princess, there was talk of her. *Hair like the smoothest silk*, people said. *A smile like the brightest star, a nose like the smallest button.* They were ridiculous parallels that did nothing to describe what the princess was actually like. Besides her engagement to our king, my knowledge of her was slim.

I said, "I do not see what the princess has to do with it."

"Don't you? The Queen of Hillshire would have rather married her daughter to someone from Skylin or Acaca. Those are alliances worth making. Hillshire and Isla are already allies, with many marriages between us. Queen Rendimire has no reason to wed her daughter to our king, except for the fact that Princess Mora took a liking to Elias. She finds him handsome, I think, and convinced her mother to consider the match. But what will Mora think when she learns of my son's condition? She does not love him—she barely knows him—and attraction is a fragile thing. She will change her mind. The marriage will be broken, and once again the future of Isla will be thrown into question. So no, Miss Freestone. I will not encourage Elias to return to the public eye, not until he is recovered."

It was hardly a convincing speech. I wanted to say, he is your son. He is a king and a man in his own right. Does everyone truly believe his physical impediment matters to such a degree? He is the same person, for Goddess' sake—steely, quick witted. Humorous at the most unlikely of times. Thoughtful, underneath all the anger. And what of his happiness? But Althea had already returned to her book, and I found myself unceremoniously dismissed.

To this day I do not know if it was my imagination, but I do believe Althea's heart beat just a little faster than was natural, which, you understand, means it was smaller.

. . .

I sulked through the palace and out to my gardens. I stomped around, making a thousand promises to the sky. I would show Elias it did not matter if he never walked again. I would prove he deserved better than a princess who desired him for his looks alone, or a mother whose priorities were so distorted as to put politics over her son's wellbeing. My parents had abandoned me, and I thought that unbearable. But what of Elias, whose mother had abandoned him as well, yet stuck around so the wound could again and again be reopened? Every cold remark, every uncaring order, he was forced to bear. No wonder he was so callous.

I did not mention the meeting to Elias. As far as I was concerned, it would have been better if Althea and I had never spoken, so I acted like we had not.

Over the course of that winter, Elias began taking the medicines I prescribed. He liked to take his time, examining the vials, asking what each would do. Mostly, they were iterations on the primblossom mixture, supplements that would improve his stamina or aid his sleep, if not actually reverse his paralysis. Elias knew these remedies were mere placeholders, that my true goal was to create a *gaigi* to counteract his debility for good, but he did not often ask about it. When it came to the subject of his immobility, he was uncharacteristically shy. Only once did he ever ask outright what I thought his chances were. "Tell me," he said, "will I ever walk again?" His face was so vulnerable in that moment, so full of cautious hope, I could not help but give the answer he most wanted. *Yes.*

The king could still be blunt. He had his moods, same as ever. His reputation for being frigid was not overblown; he was a beautiful painting, every detail perfect and untouchable. I used to think coldness was his true nature, but it was in moments like that, when he asked questions that revealed his desires, I caught a glimpse of a deeper Elias, like a statue hidden inside granite. There was more to him than anger and moodiness, just like there was more to me than silence and servitude. Irritability was a mask he wore, and I began to wonder at the true shape of his face beneath.

I do not like to be touched.

It was curious. Though we never spoke of it, I was always aware of Elias' aversion to physical contact. Even after all the time we spent together, his neck would still tense when I came too close, his pupils dilating. He reacted to physical touch as you might react to a boar in the woods.

I was careful. I kept my hands to myself unless absolutely necessary.

It occurred to me that if Elias was forced to marry, he was wise to have chosen someone from Hillshire. Those lands were set to the far north, too far for easy travel. Due to heavy seasonal snowfall and unpredictable storms, the roads were only passable in warm months. Elias could court Princess Mora from afar, if he courted her at all.

I wondered about the princess. Queen Mother Althea said the wedding would take place once she came of age. In Isla, that meant turning seventeen, but Hillshire women did not come of age until they were twenty. How old was Princess Mora now? And what was she like, actually? I considered again how little anyone seemed to know of her, besides her glowing smile and perfect skin. I looked at my own skin, my blackened nails, my hands with their marks. I tucked my fingers away self-consciously.

Foolish. If I was self-conscious, it was my own fault for making comparisons where no comparisons should be made. Princesses were meant to be beautiful. I was meant to be useful.

And yet, I caught Elias staring sometimes, too. Every so often his eyes would catch on a fresh burn, an old scar. His brow would crease, his expression growing troubled. I could feel our unfinished conversation hanging over us, and I twisted with discomfort, forever anticipating the moment he would reopen the subject. *You are no longer to test these remedies on yourself.*

But I did. Despite my initial fumbles, I was making progress. By mixing my poisons with a draught for a cold, I was able to narrow my search, coming closer and closer to recreating *nightlight*. There was still pain. I still subjected myself to it. But I no longer despaired as I once had.

Why did I no longer mind? I have mentioned I feared for my life. I believed if I could find a cure for the king's paralysis, I would in turn protect myself, either by erasing the crime or—should I be discovered—through absolution. I have also said I'd begun to feel the full scope of my guilt, and was finally confronting my culpability. *Am I a monster?* the king once asked. I thought, if he was a monster, then I was too, for I was the one who made him.

Yet looking back, it is clear there was a third reason. All my life, I had been living in the shadows. I kept to myself, kept away from others, spoke little, smiled less. Some might have said I was devoted to my craft, and that was true, but it was only half the truth. I surrounded myself with the familiar, dipped deep into the safety of my herblore. My world was as narrow as my smallest finger, and I preferred to keep it that way, lest I stretch too far and the finger snapped. I had always been sheltered, but now I'd gotten a glimpse of how it felt to walk among the world. I had saved a man's life. I had confronted a queen. I thanked men who deserved thanking and helped a boy in need. I was changing, reaching, exploring what I could withstand. The pain of my self-inflicted poisonings was terrible, but I found myself wondering, could I bear more? How much more?

I tried to imagine my mother doing what I was and could not. I reminded myself she was not the golden angel everyone believed. She tried to kill the king, but brews were never her specialty, and she had failed. It made me realize something. My mother's charms had their limits. She was sly and beautiful and full of wiles, but she was not strong. And I was more than just her shadow.

THIRTEEN

The birds returned, the trees thick with flowers. There were morning showers, patches of blue sky in the afternoons. Most days were still chilly, but sometimes the sun would shine through my kitchen window and I would shed my headscarf, lifting my face to its warmth. I was eager for spring, which is to say, I was eager for a fresh beginning.

I arrived to the king's chambers one afternoon when Kurton stopped me with a look. "You should know the king has a visitor."

My heart leaped. A visitor? Elias had allowed a visitor? But my excitement quickly faded at the look on the guard's face. "It's Hobore, isn't it? The queen allowed him entrance?"

"The king allowed it," Kurton said.

The chamber doors were silent on their hinges, my footsteps silent on the tile. I moved through the imperial suite, breathing the scent of fresh blooms through the windows, the faded tang of cleaning lye and lemon-scented wood oil. I do not think I meant to eavesdrop, merely to enter without interruption, but as soon as I came near I heard Hobore's soft tone: "—not what you think she is."

"Why?" came the king's dry reply. "Because people call her a witch?"

I froze. The two men were in Elias' study out of my line of sight, but the thin double doors leading into the room were cracked slightly, as if they had been shut but not fully latched. Hobore's voice came again. "Most rumors do not simply spring from thin air."

"Interesting," Elias said. "Does that mean the rumors about you are true as well?"

"There are no rumors about me."

"Not so. For instance, they say you've been entertaining a secret love affair with a maid from the city. You sneak over to meet her in the night."

"That is—" I could hear Hobore's huff. "That is not the same."

"So it *is* true."

"You are trying to change the subject. I'm only saying the girl is secretive."

"Private."

"She is strange."

"A breath of fresh air."

"The scars on her—"

"Do not speak to me about appearances." Elias' tone dropped its good humor. "You will understand I have no patience for it."

My heart was pounding, my thoughts darting like silver fish. Was this Hobore's revenge for the way things had gone outside the king's chambers? Or were his suspicions born of substance? I had not been paying close attention to the gossip among the court, not since Elias' incident. It was possible, wasn't it, that some new rumor had surfaced, something that threatened to reveal me?

"Brother." I heard Hobore sigh. "I have always respected your judgment. You see things as others do not. But something has changed in the palace since the poisoning, something we all feel, and it cannot be ignored. That girl—"

"That girl saved my life."

"And we are indebted to her for it. But you have been closed away in these rooms for too long. How can you make a fair assessment if you are not there to see what we see? Perhaps, if you were to emerge..."

"And how am I to do that?" Elias snapped. "I can barely pull myself out of this chair, let alone walk down the stairs. Would you like to carry me, Hobore? Or shall I crawl, like a toddler?"

Hobore was silent a long moment. "We could figure something."

"And in doing so, give my kingdom one more reason to ridicule me."

"No one will ridicule you. People love you."

"People loved our father," the king rebuked.

Hobore's voice dropped too low for me to hear what he said next. Then, abruptly, their conversation seemed to end. I had no time to react before the door swung open and Hobore appeared, his eyes widening at the sight of me. "Have you been spying on us?"

My face went blank with surprise. "Of course not."

"Eavesdropping on the royal family is a punishable offense."

"It is a good thing, then, that I was not eavesdropping."

Hobore's expression was like logs in a fire, stacked upon itself. He threw a glance back at the king, who remained out of my line of vision. "Your physician has not seen fit to announce herself, so I will do it for her."

"Selene does not need to be announced," came Elias' reply.

I do not know what silent look passed between the brothers, only that it made Hobore darken. With a final glance in my direction, he strode away.

"Selene." Elias.

The king was not in his usual velvet chair that day, but seated behind the study's desk. He looked troubled, his hair pushed back, his sleeves rolled to the elbows. His pulse was slightly elevated, linking up with mine as I drew near. "You overheard our conversation?"

I considered lying again, but I did not want there to be any more dishonesty between Elias and me. I nodded. "Some of it." A pause. "I am glad you agreed to see him. More than glad. It has been too long since you've had company."

"It was easier," Elias admitted, "than I expected."

I nodded. "And yet, Hobore seemed…tense."

"My brother worries…" He let the thought trail. It could have meant anything. *My brother worries a lot about nothing. My brother worries about the most ridiculous rumors. My brother worries you had a hand in my poisoning.*

"He cares for you," I hedged.

"He wants me to give you a truth serum."

My pulse stuttered. So Hobore did suspect me. "There is no such thing as a truth serum."

"That's what I told him." Elias leaned back, tracing circles around his index finger with his thumb. A contemplative motion. "Apparently, Hobore knows a potion maker in the city who spent the last year working on such a serum. The man invented something that seemed to do the trick. A few drops onto the tongue and you'll be spilling all your secrets."

"But?" I squeaked.

"But," he continued, "the serum kills you as soon as it's done."

Relief, like ice on a burn. There was no truth serum. I would not be forced to take it. Potion makers had been attempting to create truth serums for centuries, but those kind of brews—ones that dealt with the mind—were complicated, and little understood. Only a true master might ever have hope of success, but most master potion makers were sponsored by noblemen with other pursuits in mind, like gold or women or the expansion of their estates. Exploring the limits of human physiology did not often make the list, nor garner the funding.

I asked, "Will the potion maker try to tweak his recipe?"

"He cannot. That is the problem. He tested the serum on himself. He babbled on and on before dropping dead." Elias pinned me with a look. "I am sensing a theme here."

"It is an unspoken rule of the craft. We do not test our experiments on others."

"That is sentimental nonsense."

"It's the right thing."

"Is it?" Elias leaned forward, propping his forearms on the desk. There was that look again, the one like a beacon to draw me in. "What if there is a potion maker who is the greatest mind of her age? What if she is destined to find the cure for, say, a plague that will kill millions, but dies before she is able because she insists on testing her remedies on herself? Is that still the right thing?"

"You are not giving her enough credit," I countered. "Maybe she knows her limit. Maybe her breadth of knowledge allows her to experiment safely."

"Or maybe she is overconfident, and thinks too highly of her own abilities, and makes a mistake that ends her."

"That would be a big mistake."

"I think the truth serum maker would agree."

I was silent.

Elias said, "I worry about you."

I knew he worried. That in itself was stunning. Since when had we reached a place where Elias worried about me and I knew it? But I saw the way he watched me. I saw how his gaze often lingered on my arms, my headscarf, searching for new injuries. The way he darkened when he found them.

"I am trying to heed your wishes," Elias said. "You asked that I not interfere with your experiments, and I have not. But I have an entire kingdom at my disposal, thousands of willing subjects who would gladly trade their lives for mine, or yours, if I asked it."

"You cannot ask it."

Elias merely looked at me.

"It would be an abuse of power," I said.

"Is it any different than when my soldiers go to war for me? When my King's Guard swears an oath to protect me at any cost?" Elias sighed. "I am requesting only that you reconsider your methods."

I did not reconsider. Instead, I began to take seriously the danger of Elias' concern. He could end my experiments with a word, and I believed he would, unless changes were made.

From that day forward, I began placing new emphasis on healing the visible damage from my poisonings. It set me back, taking time away from the greater task, but I deemed the delay necessary. I created ointments to reduce scarring, pigmented pastes to hide redness. Eventually, this led me to the invention of *formacia*, which reduces inflammation, and *moxikin*, which relieves congestion. Over the course of that spring, my skin began to heal; my hair regrew. I gave up my headscarf, and when the weather was warm enough, I switched to short sleeves.

The king noticed, as I hoped. "Your skin…" he began one afternoon, trailing off uncertainly.

"Oh, yes," I replied with a smile. "My experiments are going much better."

Elias was not the only one who noticed. The courtiers began throwing me funny looks, their frowns deepening as if I was a puzzle they could not solve. When I passed them in the halls they would turn away, shrugging their shoulders like birds their feathers. The King's Guard, too, seemed intrigued by the change, though theirs held none of that underlying malice. "*Rhavika*," Kurton said to me in the great hall one day. My hair was down, my shoulders bare. There was still some scarring—there always would be—but the marks were faded, no more noticeable than the moon in a noonday sky. "You are looking well."

His cheeks immediately pinkened, and mine did, too. But I gave a shy smile. "Thank you, Kurton. That is a kind thing to say."

My body was changing in other ways, which I was slow to acknowledge. When I looked in the mirror, I did not see myself as a normal fifteen year old girl might, but with a clinical eye, assessing my features the way I would assess a patient. My breasts had grown, my hips widening. I touched my face, ran my hands through my hair. I was still too skinny. I should do my best to eat more. I prescribed myself food as I would prescribe medicine, three full meals a day, with snacks in between. It is for your own good, I told my reflection. Do not argue with me. If you are strong enough to consume poison, aren't you strong enough to consume three square meals?

I grew taller, as should be expected with age and proper nutrition. My cheeks filled out and took on color, my knees and elbows no longer so knobby. I was further encouraged when I discovered this new growth came with new stamina, which allowed me to spend longer hours foraging for ingredients, later nights spent in study. My mind, too, felt clearer than it ever had. It was as if before I had been seeing the world through a film, and someone had come to rinse the film away. I remembered altering the king's meals—that felt like ages ago—and how small tweaks seemed to produce drastic improvements in his energy and outlook. I marveled at how I had never thought to do the same for myself. Food was medicine, and I promised to neglect it no longer.

It was around that time Hobore began visiting his brother with more regularity. We would cross paths in the imperial wing, each doing our best to ignore the other, and I would listen to his pulse, though it gleaned me little. I did not find the chance to eavesdrop again, though really, there was no need. I knew Hobore continued to whisper his doubts about me, just as I knew Elias refused to heed them.

Undeterrable, Hobore began aiming his misgivings at members of the court. I would find him sulking around the temple or the outbuildings, speaking in low tones to minor noblemen, butlers, clergywomen, heralds. More than once, I caught Hermapate at his arm, that glittering lady-in-waiting who had once laughed at my expense. Their heads would bow together, their faces intent. Their gazes slid to me as they spoke, and I would hold their eyes and think, *Say what you like. I am not afraid.*

But I was.

FOURTEEN

An idea had been sitting in my mind for some time. I was not sure the king would like it, but it nagged at me like a splinter that needed to be yanked. Queen Mother Althea might have her reasons for ordering her son's isolation, and Elias his reasons for agreeing, but imprisonment had many faces, and there were freedoms still to be had.

I had seen only one of these contraptions in my life, which was crafted by my father. I remembered him sitting under the sun, his hands methodic, working the wood with a kind of reverence. Aegeis once said not all of us are magic. And yet, is magic not merely the act of creating something from nothing? I had seen my father's work. I had seen him take the unbending wood of an ash or oak and transform it into marvels.

The wheelchair had been built for the sheepherder's son. He was young then, but had grown significantly, and seemed surprised to find me at his door. He lived in a tidy cottage on the west end of the palace grounds, one of a dozen identical homes built to house the fieldworkers. The breeze was swift that day, the sky bright. Overhead, dragonflies dipped and wove.

"I am wondering about your wheelchair," I said.

The young man scratched his beard. "What for?"

"It was gifted to you by my father. I would have it back."

"For the king?"

There was no coyness or mockery in him, just curiosity. I decided to answer honestly. "Yes."

He nodded. "This way."

We walked around back to a storage barn. The structure was run-down, its boards in need of patching. The door was crooked, and its edge dug an arc into the earth as the sheepherder's son heaved it open. I stepped into the dark space, and there was the wheelchair.

It looked just as I remembered. The chair was crafted entirely from wood, with two large wheels on either side and one smaller behind, plus a little ledge to set your feet. It was sturdy, and heavier than it looked—I had some trouble pushing it across the gravel path back to the palace. I passed the outlying houses of the fieldworkers, the gardens and grazing herds. My breath puffed, my feet digging ruts into the ground. I had not even made it halfway when the young man reappeared. "You look like you could use some help."

I had not realized he was watching. "I am fine."

He gave an easy smile. "I insist."

Though the lad was not particularly tall, he was well-muscled from his days in the field and maneuvered the wheelchair without trouble. Once the wheels met the courtyard's stone cobbles, they turned easily, as if newly oiled. That was the mark of my father's work. His designs were built to last.

At that point, I assumed the young man would give the chair back and be on his way, but instead he continued onward through a pavilion into the entrance hall. I hurried after him. "I thank you for your help," I said, "but I can take it from here."

That smile again. "How will you make it up the stairs?"

And so we worked together, me pulling and him pushing, up four flights of stairs to the imperial wing. By the time we reached the top we were both puffing, but I found myself smiling, too. "I am indebted to you. I never would have managed on my own."

"Anyone would have helped, if only you asked."

My mouth opened. Was I merely surprised, or did I plan on arguing the point? I do not know, nor did I have the chance to find out, because then he was saluting me playfully and saying, "Good day, Miss Freestone."

It was not unusual that he might know my name. Most palace workers did. Yet shouldn't I ask for his name as well? I had done that with the King's Guard and the sky had not fallen. As the young man turned to leave, I gripped the wheelchair's handles and thought furiously, just ask him. Just ask. But the moment passed, and he was gone.

· · ·

Elias took one look at the chair and drew back like I had brought him a three headed snake. "I am not sitting in that."

He was in his usual spot in his study, the windows cracked to let in the day. Nearby, the palace cat lazed in a square of sunlight. I tried to hide my smile. "My father built it."

"I don't care if the bloody Goddess built it."

"There is no reason for such stubbornness. Look, you can even wheel it yourself."

"I will be ridiculed."

"You will be mobile." He continued to eye the chair with mistrust. I gave it a friendly pat, as if it was an old friend. "I will let you think about it."

It took three days for Elias to ask, "How does it work?"

I took my time explaining the simple mechanics, how he could rotate the wheels to move himself along. When he was still unconvinced, I sat in the chair and gave a demonstration. I knew I had made my point when he said, "Let me try."

I held the wheelchair steady while he maneuvered himself into place. It was an awkward business, and I had to contain my urge to help, to reach out a hand as he struggled to navigate over the footrest while simultaneously twisting into position. I bit the inside of my cheek instead, waiting until he was seated and reasonably secure before moving to stand before him, feeling more than a little pleased. "Well? Where to?"

He ran his fingers along the wheel as a blind person might come to know an object. "I would see my library."

The king's private library was one of the rooms I had decided was better left closed off. I knew it would smell of dust and disuse, but I only nodded cheerfully. "To the library, then."

It was a short distance, just up the hall on the other side of the imperial suite. I walked alongside the chair, watching Elias from the corner of my eye as he pushed himself forward. Was he pleased? Unimpressed? He kept his expression deliberately blank, as if he knew what I sought and aimed to thwart me. Still, I had the sense he was not wholly unaffected as he put on a bit of speed, then more, so by the time we reached the library door it had become a race, him flying and me sprinting to keep up.

He glanced back at me and flashed a smile. "I win."

I set my hands to my hips, feigning annoyance. But oh, that smile. It was pure as summer sun, a true smile, the first of his I had ever seen.

The library was small, stocked only with the king's favorites. The walls were paneled in dark wood, the furniture thick and cushioned. The windows were fitted with diamond panes, and there was a liquor cabinet at the back, stacked high with bottles and books. I wondered if Elias had a hand in designing this room. It suited him in a way the rest of his chambers did not.

"There is a book I desire," he said. "*The River of Reversal.* I believe it is up on that shelf."

An old tale. Though I had never read the book myself, it was one of the most popular stories among the court. At the annual wintertime festival, women liked to dress up as the story's heroine, while men donned the cape and horns of the demon she falls in love with. It was all a good deal of fun, so I had been told, men and women pretending to be someone else for the day. I understood the appeal, I supposed. What I did not understand was why everyone wanted to dress as the same two characters. It was a bit redundant, wasn't it? Not to mention, an excellent opportunity to compare yourself to others. But then, that was exactly the kind of thing the court would enjoy: a contest to see who'd done it better.

I found the book and tried to hand it over.

"No," Elias said. "It's for you."

"For me?" I frowned. "What for?"

His mouth twitched. "Reading."

It took great effort not to roll my eyes. "I mean, why this book?"

"I only ever see you with your botany books." A pause. "Have you ever read *The River of Reversal?*"

I drummed my fingers along the cover. My father had once told me an abbreviated version of the story. I had never explored the tale myself. "No."

"I thought not."

That *did* make me roll my eyes. "You don't have to look so smug."

"I'm not smug. I'm appalled. This is one of the most famous legends in Isla. In all the continent, even. How have you never read it?"

"I suspect you have some guesses," I quipped, "seeing as you already knew I hadn't."

"My guess is you work too much."

I drew up a brow. "I work for you."

"And now you will read for me."

Always an order with him. Part of me wanted to resist. Leisurely reading seemed a grotesque waste of time, especially when there was still so much work to be done. But I caught that look in Elias' eye and knew I would not be winning this argument. I swallowed a sigh. "Do you force literature on all your subjects?"

"Only the ones I spend all my time with."

"So just me."

"You'll like it," he insisted.

He was right. I began reading *The River of Reversal* that afternoon and finished the same night. The story was unlike any I had come upon, the cursed prince doomed to remain a demon without a soul, the brave maiden risking everything to bring him to the River, which was said to draw you back in time and make you who you had once been. The maiden saved the prince's life, undoing his curse, but when she pulled him out of the River, his memories were undone as well. He could not recall who she was. It was a curse all its own, and a sacrifice, for love.

When I admitted how much I liked the story, Elias only smirked. *I told you.*

I read *The River of Reversal* three times in as many days. I was about to begin it a fourth when Elias wheeled over and pulled the book from my hands. I made a noise of protest. "That's mine."

"Actually, it's mine."

"You gave it to me. Why not let me enjoy it?"

"There are other books."

"I like *this* book."

He gave a longsuffering sigh. "I think you're missing the point."

We returned to the library where Elias suggested a second novel, and a third. It became a game of sorts. He would pick a story, and I would read it and love it and ask for another. Elias would pretend to think, dangling his next suggestion like a carrot over my head. "I have one in mind, but I am not sure you're ready…"

"I'm ready," I would insist.

"It's a bit old for you."

"I am fifteen."

"I know," he would say. "Exactly."

I swallowed those stories like a fish swallows flies: in great, sucking mouthfuls. When Elias ran out of suggestions, I began venturing downstairs to the palace's larger communal library to hunt for my own. I would return with my arms full, tipping the volumes right onto his lap. Have you read this one? What about this one? You read that, and I will read this, and then we will switch.

Elias just smiled through it all.

"Don't take too much credit," I told him one day. The weather had turned balmy, the skies pristine. On the mantle, incense burned, juniper and lavender and palmberry. "I would have discovered these stories eventually."

Elias shot me a look. "I very much doubt that."

I did not fall behind on my work. I was too devoted for that. I will admit, however, that over the course of that summer my experiments lost their fervor, my old fears like distant mountains. I could see them if I looked. They stood there with their gray faces, same as ever. And yet, after nearly three seasons, Althea's interrogations had yielded nothing. Hobore's malice had progressed no further, and Elias' condition was stable. Things were going well, as well as I could have hoped. Wasn't there a bit of spare time for stories, too?

I made time, of course I did. Once again, I was discovering a new dimension to the world, one that took me outside myself and my work. It was mesmerizing, almost addicting—not merely the tales, but the discussions that followed. For the first time since his poisoning, Elias and I had common interests to discuss, characters and plots and places and what-ifs. I loved to sit before him on the rug as the room blued to dusk, watching the light soften his sharp features. I loved to set my opinion down like a cup, to see what he might pour into it. I especially loved when I suggested something that perplexed him, because then I would get to watch his thoughts grow deep, like an oak putting down roots. These were the pleasures of true conversation, which were new to me. I would complain about one ending, and he would ask how I would have preferred it. Why did an author choose to write their story this way? What might we write, if ever we took the chance?

"You would write a romance," I told him. I do not know what made me say it, but I can still see the look on his face, the swift surprise.

"And you would write a tragedy," was his reply.

It is strange to think it now, but I remember how I smiled at that.

FIFTEEN

On my sixteenth birthday, Elias left his suite for the first time in five seasons. There was no preamble, no warning. He simply wheeled himself out, pointed at the first servant he could find and said, "Every set of stairs will be replaced with a ramp."

Later that day, dozens of horses could be seen hauling up supplies from the city. The sounds of labor filled the palace, hammers and saws and hollering men. The corridors smelled of cedar and crushed stone, and dust coated everything, sticking to my teeth. After three days, the work was done.

The news seemed to clang through the palace like bells: the king was come. As Elias moved through the winter halls using the new-built ramps, men and women clambered forth, lining the corridors like streets at a parade. I followed at a slight distance alongside the King's Guard, my eyes on every face, every twitch, every muttered word. I was expectant, tensed for a blow to fall. Elias had been locked behind closed doors for over a year. It was longer than a monarch had ever been absent from the public eye. What would happen once he returned to the light?

The congregation played their part perfectly. There were blushing maidens and grinning lords, nodding councilmen and guards at attention. Courtiers and visiting city folk came forward, eager to compliment the king, to remark on his good health, to marvel at his chair. The king's return was a sign from the Goddess, they said, and just in time for the new year. It was a mark of good things to come.

Queen Mother Althea appeared at the opposite end of the hall. She gazed upon her son for a long moment before turning her eyes to me. I saw in them, for the first time, a cautious hopefulness.

Satisfied we were not about to witness some kind of revolt, I turned my attention to Elias. I had never seen him interact with his subjects, not since I was old enough to notice or care. He was formal, returning the well-wishes with a nod, or sometimes a word. His black tunic was straight and neat, his face freshly shaved, a gold sigil ring glinting on one hand. It was strange to look at Elias through my own eyes and also through theirs. I could see what people saw when they looked at him, the way he held himself, the quiet authority. I could see how he commanded the room, for he was their king. But I saw, too, how he tried not to flinch as the crowd closed in on him. How every so often his eyes would search for me. The subtle relief when his gaze met mine.

A woman fluttered over. I recognized her, though not by name—she was one of Althea's ladies who had often lusted after my mother. The woman was gushing over Elias, her lips drawn back in a wide smile. She set a hand to his shoulder, leaning in as she spoke.

The change was instant. All the color drained from Elias' face, and I could feel his heartbeat lurch, the twin pulse pushing between my ribs. Oblivious, the woman prattled on, her skirts brushing his knees, her breasts in his face. Elias looked like he wanted to snap at her to remove the hand, but he could not do that without ruining the celebratory mood of his reemergence. He tried to physically extract himself instead, but the woman was overexcited, and the movement only made her cling tighter. His panicked eyes met mine.

I started toward them. I did not know what I planned. My own pulse was climbing, my palms turning clammy at the thought of inserting myself where I was not invited. Before I knew it, I was standing before them, a strained smile plastered to my face. "Benadine! What a pleasant surprise. Have you returned from Hillshire?"

The woman looked at me with a mixture of confusion and surprise, but it worked—she withdrew her hand. "I…what?"

"Oh, my apologies." It was not difficult to feign embarrassment. We were the center of attention, and my cheeks were red enough. "I mistook you. Benadine is an old family friend. I do miss her, it has been years." I babbled on. "You look so alike! She moved to Hillshire some time ago to pursue her work. She…keeps goats."

The woman flinched as if struck. "You mistook me for a goatherd?"

Elias, recovering himself, gave a nod. "I am acquainted with Benadine. You two bear quite the resemblance."

The women appeared dazed. "I…well, I don't think…"

"Perhaps there is some relation?" I offered. "Do you have relatives in the country?"

Shock gave way to offense. "I am of House Donmore. We are not laborers."

"Are you certain?" the king pressed. "You have an air about you."

"Quite certain," she replied. Then, clearly eager to escape this conversation and all the damage it was doing to her reputation: "I have taken enough of your time, Your Majesty. Goddess be with you."

After she was gone, Elias caught my eye, his face full of mirth. "Goats?"

"It was the first thing I could think," I muttered.

"It was brilliant."

I know I should have been beyond such things, but his praise seemed to reach inside me and bloom. "Oh," I said. "Well."

I did not have to scare away any more women after that. Most people seemed to know their boundaries and kept their hands to themselves. Still, I stayed closer to Elias, catching his eye every now and then, a secret smile lingering between us.

A face appeared in my vision. It was the sheepherder's son, heading my way. He grinned when he caught my eye, jerking his chin toward the edge of the crowd to indicate he wished me to meet him. "Excuse me a moment," I told Elias.

As we approached one another, the sheepherder's son pushed his hands into his pockets, tipping his chin down to look at me through thick lashes. "You know," he said, "I guess I can say I'm glad I broke my leg all those years ago."

I knew what he meant, but asked the question anyway. "Why would you be glad of such a thing?"

"If not for that, your father would have never built the wheelchair." He gave a little shrug, his gaze skating across my face. I noticed his eyes were very blue. "You can tell the king I don't require much in the way of payment. A palace of my own should suffice."

It took me only half a beat to realize he was joking, and I laughed, a tinkling bell-sound that was a surprise even to me. On the edge of my vision, I was aware of Elias' head turning.

"I believe that can be arranged," I quipped. "But only if you ask very nicely."

His smile turned mischievous. "I can be nice."

I felt myself warming and scrambled for safer ground. "How did you break your leg?"

"Ah." He rubbed the back of his neck. "It was stupid, really. Fell from a tree. Snapped the shin right in two."

I grimaced, more for show than out of real disgust. I had mended too many broken bones over the years for such visions to affect me. "That must have hurt."

"Not so badly."

"Only because you are very brave."

I meant to say it in a playful manner, to joke with him as he had joked with me, but the words came out sincere. I blushed, and he shrugged again, though he looked pleased. We fidgeted for a moment. He took a breath, his expression suddenly earnest. "I was wondering—"

"Selene." Elias' voice made us both swing our heads. He was in discussion with the Master of Labor, an elderly man with eyes like a bloodhound. "Argorn wants to know how the wheelchair was built. Come explain it to him." Though Elias' expression was measured, there was something in his voice.

I turned back to the herder's son. "I—"

"You should go." He mustered a smile.

Not sure what else to say, I dipped a small curtsy. As he began to turn away, I burst, "What is your name?"

He turned back. "Gellert."

"Gellert." I smiled. "I am glad you broke it, too."

• • •

The feast that night was a jubilant affair. The kitchen staff outdid themselves, bringing forth mead and ale, platters of spiced meats, pickled vegetables and warm bread. There was music, and dancing, and lots of stomping feet. Toast after toast was given to the king's good heath, the king's speedy recovery, the king's long life.

I was dazed by it all, the noise and color, the high tune of the piper, the great belly laughter rippling between stone walls. When a bell chimed to signal it was time to take our seats for the main course, I felt a wash of relief, if for no other reason than it meant we were one step closer to reaching the end. Do not be mistaken; I was glad of the celebration, glad the palace welcomed their king with such high spirits. But I was used to the quiet of my workroom, or Elias' study, just him and me. The raucousness was taking its toll on my nerves. As I started to move through the great hall to take my chair, however, Elias held out a hand. "No. You will sit by me."

I darted a glance down the table. The chair to Elias' left was empty, but that was only because it was meant to one day host his future wife, Princess Mora. I tried to protest—I was happy to sit in my spot farther down the table, or better, no spot at all—but there was something in Elias' face. His voice was quiet when he said, "I need you here."

The Queen Mother was seated to Elias' right, her brother—a soft-spoken man named Toromond—beside her, with more cousins and council members and family beyond that. Hobore was there as well, chatting amiably with the Master of Coin. It was impossible not to feel their eyes on me as I pulled out the chair meant for Elias' bride and took my seat.

"Elias." Queen Mother Althea's voice was a low warning; her eyes flitted between us. "Have you lost your sense of propriety? Have her move at once, before people notice. This is not—"

"Of any concern to you," he finished curtly.

"There are expectations," she insisted, voice dropping lower. "That chair is meant to remain empty for your bride, Princess Mora."

"Am I to sit alone until I am wed?" Elias asked. "Selene is my friend. I welcome her company." And with that, he turned away.

More food was served, bone-in pork leg arranged on ceramic plates, mounds of roasted potato, tangy cheese made from goat's milk. Elias kept up conversation with his uncle, discussing the status of some distant country estate, pausing now and then to glance at me. He had relaxed since his initial appearance and was leaning to one side, an arm thrown across the back of his chair. In the candlelight, his hair shone like autumn wheat; his eyes were two bright stars. When he spoke, heads turned to listen, and again I had the thought: it was strange. I had grown used to Elias as he was in his velvet chair, set against the backdrop of those high, black-paned windows. A lone presence.

Now, he was anything but alone. I watched people vie for his regard, tempting him with questions and half-finished entreaties, waiting to see who he would next bequeath his attention. The court was enraptured; this was better than a play. I could practically hear them keeping score, could sense the changing counters of rank and status. *This is whom King Alder finds worthy of notice, and this is whom he does not.*

I wondered what would happen if I spoke to him then. Would he turn toward me, and lean in close, and hear nothing but what I said? Or would he listen with only one ear, as he did with his big-toothed cousin Prisiponan, or his mother? I should have known the answer, of course I should have, but it had already been a long night, and I felt out of place in that chair by his side. Exposed. I could not help but notice people throwing me strange looks, some even making signs to ward off evil when they thought I could not see. I did not know it then, but the rumors about me were changing, shifting from a wood-witch with black magic in her blood to something I understood far less. I pushed my food listlessly around my plate, trying not to meet anyone's eye.

"Selene." Hobore's voice made me lift my gaze. "You have been awfully quiet this night. And you have hardly touched your food. Do I sense you are…unhappy?"

"Leave her alone," Elias said.

"The question bears answering. Today is a day of celebration, and she is looking like she would rather be anywhere else."

Elias' voice went dark. "Do not make me say it again."

There was a tense bubble of silence. Courtiers could sniff out conflict as a shark scents blood, and this was as good as chum in the water. I shrank as heads turned, everyone watching to see what would happen next. I did not want the brothers fighting again, not so publicly, and certainly not about me. After a moment, Hobore gave a shrug and turned back to his meal.

That was twice Hobore had aimed barbs directly at me, three times if I counted the incident outside the king's chambers, and that was to say nothing of the mistrust he was fanning behind my back. His veiled hostility was troublesome, more so because it went against his character… or at least, what I knew of it. Had he indeed learned something about my role in his brother's poisoning? Or could there be another explanation? Determined to give him no more reason to suspect me, I dove into my meal with vigor. I would drink and feast all night if that was what it took. I was prepared to down every last bite.

No sooner did the spoon touch my lips that I knew—my plate had been poisoned.

I gagged and tried to spit, but it was too late. My throat was on fire, my lungs seizing. I toppled from my chair and hit the floor, too stunned to scream, to move, to do anything but gasp for breath. There was a commotion around me, the scrape of chairs. Several soldiers appeared, the King's Guard among them, Arch with his axe, Kurton with his sword, Yorvis and Freesier close behind. They cast about wildly for an enemy to fight, something to sink their steel into, not yet realizing the enemy was already inside me. The fire spread down my throat into my chest, my belly. Murderous. I felt as if my flesh was paring away from my bones, as if someone had taken a hot iron to my heart. Every moment I thought, surely the pain can get no worse. And then it did.

I remember once standing in my workshop, wondering what limit of torment I could withstand. That night, I do believe I found it.

Somewhere behind me, I heard Althea ask a high pitched question, and over her, Elias' swift command. "She has been poisoned. A healer, fetch a city healer *now*."

But it was too late for that, didn't he see it was too late? And oh, the irony. I knew what poison had been used on me because it was one I had tested on myself. *Lily of the Night*, it is called. The poison comes from a delicate pink flower that grows in abundance in Isla. This is a flower every child knows to avoid. Even so much as touching the spores can bring hallucinations. And to ingest more than the smallest of drops? Well.

I wanted to explain this to Elias. As the room erupted in a flurry of motion, I wanted to reach for him, take his hand in mine. *Please*, I would have said. *Please, stay with me, just for these few final moments.*

Someone scooped me off the ground—Kurton, I think. I felt my body rock with his long strides. My vision was fading, my thoughts like distant stars. I could hear Elias close behind, speaking in that same, urgent tone. "Selene, listen to me, damn you. Don't close your eyes. Do you hear me? Don't you dare."

But I did close my eyes. It hit me like a wave: I was so tired.

"Selene." His voice cracked. "*Don't.*"

In a twisted way, I had prepared for this moment. Had I not poisoned myself a hundred times? Had I not imagined what would happen if I miscalculated, if my antidotes failed? I used to picture it, how the toxins would seep into me. I would fight at first, kicking and thrashing, until at last my energy was spent. I would fall still there on my workshop floor, my limbs rigid, my hair sprawled around me. My breath would cease, and I would die alone, surrounded by the silence of my herbs and my tools.

Well, I was right on one count—it was poison that would kill me. But even as I had the thought, I could feel Kurton's thick arms holding me. I could sense the other three men of the King's Guard with their weapons uselessly in hand, hearts thundering. Over it all, I could hear Elias' voice turn to pleas as he begged me to live.

I would die by poison, I thought. But I would not die alone. That was something.

I tipped back my head and surrendered to the blackness.

SIXTEEN

Years later, I would hear a tale told of that dinner. The storyteller was wizened, white with age. Her voice rose and dipped like a ship on the wave. *The girl lived. It was a miracle. A marvel. A gift from the Goddess.* It made for a good story, even if she was mistaken. Had the storyteller known the truth, she would have used a different word.

Mithridatism. It is the practice of protecting oneself against poison by slowly administering nonlethal doses in order to build up a tolerance. I had ingested enough Lily of the Night to fell a bull, yet whoever wished me dead had not accounted for the fact that over the last year, I had been steadily consuming a wide range of poisons. Through my experiments, I had unwittingly built up an immunity, and so I lived.

I recall that night only in pieces. There was a dash to bring me to the servants' quarters—the first location within easy reach, with access to an empty bed—and a swift message sent to the city. A woman from the House of Healers appeared to administer an antidote, but I was too weak to explain that she had used the wrong proportions, that a proper counter for Lily of the Night was two parts hoghemp and three parts *carisa*, and she had arrived too late for it to help me anyway. Her concoction would do nothing but give me something to retch, yet the woman was determined to force it down, plying me first with bribes, then with threats until eventually I relented. The mixture was bitter and pasty. It sat in my gut like a rock. I willed myself to keep it down, lest we have to do the whole thing over again.

After—perhaps regretting the violent measures she had been forced to take with me—the healer was pliant as new weeds. She did her best to make me comfortable, applying a cool compress to my forehead to battle fever, coaxing me to take sips of water. Sometimes I could lift my head on my own. Sometimes she had to do it for me. It was a relief when she was finally gone.

At some point, I was moved out of the servants' quarters into Elias' private guest room. I did not question the change. It did not matter where I was kept, so long as there was someplace relatively quiet for me to sleep. By that time, it was clear I would survive the poisoning, though the worst was not yet behind me. My head felt full of cotton. My eyelids scraped like claws on stone. The ticking of the clock, the tumble of logs in the fire, the sickly smell of my own skin, all of it wore on my over-heightened senses. It was as if the very fibers of my being had been strung tight and would snap at the barest of touches. I took a draught for the pain, but it did nothing—my only true respite was in dreams. I surrendered to them eagerly, and when the pain became too great and kept me from sleep, I took another draught to induce it. The poison needed time to work through my system, but I did not intend to be awake for it.

Still, there were waking moments. I could never quite tell what time it was, for the curtains remained drawn, but I could sense whether it was day or night based on who was by my side. During the day, the King's Guard stood watch, sometimes one man, sometimes two or three. We did not speak—I was in no state for it—but I began to learn their heartbeats by ear. Kurton, whose pulse was the loudest. Freesier, the fastest. Arch, the quietest. And Yorvis, the most irregular. I do not know whether the king commanded his men to guard me, or if they took the task upon themselves, but during the daylight hours I could count on them to be there.

At night, there was only the king.

Elias' presence was gravitational, ever pulling at my awareness. He wheeled his chair to my side where he would sit for hours, sometimes in stillness, sometimes restless with angst. Mostly he was silent, but occasionally, he would read to me.

"What is love, if not surrender?" His voice floated from somewhere far away. "What is surrender, if not a sacrifice?"

It was the story of *The River of Reversal*, which had quickly become my favorite, but never more so than when told in his voice.

"Those who seek the River must be truly desperate, for the way is a curse all its own. The journey starts by entering the Crossing Sea and sailing toward the Evening Star, which can only be located with use of a special compass crafted from the River itself. The path is treacherous. There are leviathans, and krakens, and sea dragons with two dozen heads. There are whirlpools and storms and the simple issue of dehydration, which has killed more travelers than any monster…"

During those times when my fever was at its worst and my body was rejecting everything in it, Elias held my hand. A part of me that apparently cared wondered how he could stand to touch me while I retched. Another part of me, however, marveled at what it took for him to do this, to initiate skin to skin contact and sustain it. Elias' hands were warm and dry. Strong, with fine hairs along the back, too fair to see. I tried to memorize these details. I was afraid when my fever finally broke and I emerged from this ordeal, I would forget how his hand felt in mine, or worse, I would forget he'd held my hand at all. That was not uncommon in poisonings, and Lily of the Night did have a reputation for inducing hallucinations.

This is not a dream, I told myself as I doubled over. He brushed the damp hair from my forehead. I screwed my eyes shut, shaking and shaking. *This is real.*

Later though, when the worst of the poisoning was past and I could think clearly again, I was not sure it had been.

. . .

I woke to the smell of spices. Nutmeg, I thought, and something earthy. Slowly, squinting, I pushed myself upright.

I was in a bed in a room I knew, because I knew all the king's rooms. This was the guest chamber situated across the hall from his, the one with doilies on the tables and a flowerbox outside the window. The walls had been done in sky blue, the ceiling painted with elegant white swans. The nightstand bore the evidence of my illness, rags and a wash bucket, various vials and draughts. Standing beside the door keeping watch was the guardsman, Arch.

He smiled to see me awake, tipping his mug in my direction. That explained the smell. It was *kriva*, a brew soldiers used to stay alert. "Alright there, *rahvika?*"

I dragged a hand through my tangled hair. For the first time in days, the motion did not give me vertigo. "How—" I cleared my throat and tried again. "How long have I been here?"

"Four nights. Six if you count the two you spent in the servants' quarters." Arch was still smiling. Of the four members of the King's Guard, he was the most menacing, with his shaved head and small, ice-blue eyes—until he smiled. Then he was all kindness. "You've been through it, haven't you? Gave us a right scare. His Majesty will be pleased you're awake. Never seen him so worked up."

I pressed my fingers against a building headache. "Is he here?"

"Just in the other room. I'll tell him you've woken."

I wanted to stop Arch, to ask for a moment to collect myself, but before I could find the words the guardsman was gone. A moment later, Elias wheeled into the doorway. "Selene."

He did not come any closer. He was dressed in his day clothes, hair washed and combed, black jacket, black waistcoat, a cravat about his neck. He looked surprisingly composed for someone who had spent the last six nights tending a sick girl. When he spoke, his tone was formal. "How are you feeling?"

I dropped my eyes to my hands, smoothing my fingers over the sheets. "I am fine."

"Your color is looking better."

My color. He might as well have been noting the weather. I had almost died, had vomited into a bucket while he held back my hair, yet he spoke as if we were strangers. "That is good."

"Arch has not wanted to leave this room." The hint of a smile. "None of the men have, actually. It seems you have cast a spell on them."

I noticed he did not include himself in that count. The disappointment was worse now, clawing at my throat. I gave another bland answer. "They are good men."

Silence. I continued to study my fingers, trying to rein myself in. What had I expected? For Elias to rush over and take my hand again?

For him to look into my eyes and say, Selene, you scared me half to death? I should have known better than that. I did know.

The silence expanded. It became obvious one of us must work to fill it. It was not going to be me.

"I owe you an apology," Elias said at last. "Once again, you have suffered on my behalf."

I was suffering alright, but I do not think he meant it the same way. "I don't see your meaning."

"That poison was intended for me. It appears whoever tried to murder me the first time came back to try again, but there must have been a mistake with the plates. You were nearly killed, and for what? A miscalculation." He looked away. "As it is, I do not know how you survived."

"People will say it's a miracle."

"I do not believe in miracles."

"Fate, then."

"I do not believe in fate, either."

My tone was bitter. "You and my mother are in agreement."

Elias' mask slipped for the briefest moment, his expression hardening. Before I could understand it, the mask was back. "I have been advised to hire a food taster," he said. "Someone to test my plates for poison. And yet, to be thorough, wouldn't such a person need to try every bite? It seems a poor solution."

I shrugged.

"Do you not agree?"

I did not agree or disagree. I just wanted him to leave. I was confused by myself, by my desire to hear him proclaim his care for me. What did it matter if Elias acted like nothing had changed between us? Maybe nothing had. Maybe near death experiences were expected from those who served him. I remembered him once saying as much.

He still had not budged from his place in the doorway. I could hear my own voice, as if from far away. "Well, if that is all."

A line appeared between his brows. "Are you...dismissing me?"

"I am very tired, Your Majesty."

He looked as if I had aimed a tomato at his face. "Your Majesty."

"That is your name."

"I told you—"

"I know what you told me."

A pause.

He said, "You are angry with me." His hands came to the wheels of his chair, yet still he did not push himself closer. When I made no reply, he said, "Tell me why you are angry."

I had poisoned myself, and had been poisoned by another. I had cut my hands and burned my wrists and suffered a thousand scrapes and bruises and strains. Yet these wounds were nothing compared to the fear that had rooted inside me ever since my parents abandoned me: that all of it was for nothing.

I recalled how Althea had reacted to news of my mother's death. The ceremony she cobbled together. How there were no mourners or flowers, and my mother had been loved. What, then, of me? I had spent my life hunting the woods and looming over cauldrons. I had no real friends, no family or allies. I feared if I was harmed, no one would care. If I died, no one would mourn. I wanted someone to prove me wrong, to prove my parents had been mistaken to leave me, that I held value beyond that of my work.

I wanted it to be Elias.

It was a painful thought. An impossible one. Elias was the King of Isla. He was a man whose position required him to view his subjects for their usefulness. If he spent more time with me than usual, it was only due to our circumstances, the unfortunate twist of fate. Whatever affections he might have for me were no more lasting than a rose in winter, a fluke, a mistake a plant makes when it is confused. Elias would be confused to care for me. I was confused, to think I deserved his care. How could I ever deserve it? I was his poisoner.

"Selene?"

"I am not angry with you," I replied weakly. "Only with myself."

Once, I thought if I was good and obedient and hardworking, no harm would ever come to me. *My strong girl*, my father used to call me. When I was very little, I wanted to be strong, to prove I was worthy of his praise. I wanted to be what he thought. But I had not really been strong, only fearful, which can sometimes look the same. And then my father had left me.

"Tell me why you are angry with yourself, then."

I drew my arms around my knees. "Because I am a fool."

I do not know what Elias saw in me that day. I cannot say if he sensed my desolation, or if he simply understood on a deeper level, because self-blame and hidden wounds were things we shared. He scrubbed a palm down his face, sighed, and wheeled to my side. I thought—hoped, a hope bursting bright as a shooting star—he might take my hand again, but he only motioned for me to unwind myself, then pulled the covers up to my chin. The movement was gentle but uncertain, underlaid with awkwardness. I clung to the gesture anyway, as a drowning woman clings to the raft. It was enough, I told myself. It could be enough.

SEVENTEEN

The King's Guard asked to see me. No, Elias said, she is resting, come back later. Twice more they tried, all four of them crowding the door like eager puppies. "It's alright," I told Elias. "Let them in."

They circled my bed, each speaking over the other to offer their sympathies. Yorvis, with his lean frame. Freesier, with his thick beard. Arch, whose smile was gone. And Kurton, towering above them all. They had been so afraid, they said. This attack on me was an assault on the king, an insult to the very pillars of their oaths. They swore upon their honor that they would find the poisoner and have his head.

"Justice will be served," Kurton promised gravely.

I tried not to fidget. "You will do your best, I am sure."

"No." The man seemed to swell, his deep voice like an iron band. "We have been asleep at the helm, allowing ourselves to be distracted by other matters. That ends here. The poisoner must pay for his deeds. We will hunt this coward where he sleeps, and cut out his soul, and water the earth with his blood."

There was a silence. If I looked a bit paler, I hoped they would attribute it to my weakened condition.

"Well," Arch said brightly, clapping Kurton's shoulder. "I think we have imposed long enough."

"Indeed," Freesier agreed, lifting a brow. "Promise us to stay away from poisons for a while, will you, *rahvika*?"

That had me smiling. "I promise."

I did not stay bedridden long after that. Elias was skeptical, demanding I not push myself, but I assured him a bit of activity would do me good. "I cannot stay in this room forever," I insisted, realizing too late what I was saying.

He held my gaze. "As you say."

During my recovery, I had taken no news from the outside world. I was therefore surprised to discover that in response to my poisoning, the palace had again been placed on lockdown. As before, servants and courtiers were called for questioning, visiting citizens subjected to interrogations. It felt as if we had gone back in time, back to those gray months when my life was turned on its head and talk of poison was on everyone's lips. The court seemed to believe, as Elias did, that the Lily of the Night was meant for him and not me. That the king's poisoner, having failed once, had taken their first opportunity to try again.

But I was the one who had poisoned the king the first time. Clearly I had not done it again. As the days ticked by, I fell back into the habit of looking over my shoulder, my mind looping through possibilities. Could there be some truth to the court's suspicions? Had my mother returned to finish what she'd started? That was a startling thought, but worse still was the idea that she had not returned, that the poison was not meant for the king at all, but for me. If that was true, it begged a different question…who wanted me dead?

Three days after moving out of Elias' guestroom, a footman found me in the library. I had been browsing the stacks, more for light exercise than any real desire to read. I was still weak from the poisoning, still easily tired. My throat felt scratchy, my skin sensitive to chill, which was difficult to avoid—it was the middle of winter. The movement was good for me though, and helped clear my head, and so it was in this setting that the footman approached and said, "Queen Mother Althea requires you."

I did not believe Althea was summoning me to ask after my health. More likely, she wished to question me about the poisoning, whether I had noticed anything suspicious at the feast, if the incident might provide clues to uncover her son's assailant. I thanked the footman and started toward the breakfast room where the queen waited. On the way, I passed a group of courtiers, one of whom I recognized—Hermapate, that young woman who could often be seen conspiring with Hobore. She was shorter than I remembered, dressed prettily in light green, a girlish gown that seemed to highlight her hauteur rather than diminish it. She ran her eyes over my body as you would a stray dog. "Miss Freestone, my dear, are you on your way to a royal audience? If so, you must do something about that pallor."

I halted. "Pallor?"

"You look positively ghostly. I understand you were poisoned, but that is really no excuse. Have you no cosmetics to brighten your features?" She clicked her tongue, her companions clucking at her sides. "And your hair. Must you always wear it loose?"

I stiffened. "My hair has never been a problem before."

"Because you are young and are therefore given license. But that will not last." Another perusal of my figure. "Not long at all."

I searched the woman's face. This was why I avoided courtiers. They never spoke straight. "I do not understand."

A sigh. "You will be of age—when? This year? You must learn how to properly comport yourself." She startled me by gripping my shoulders and pushing me onto a nearby bench. "Ladies?" She snapped her fingers at the others. "What do you have on hand?"

"My rouge," said one of her companions, rifling through a small reticule. "Charcoal, eye drops."

"A tube of balm," said another, pulling the item from between her breasts.

"And powder!"

The women crowded me, dabbing my face and neck with powder, painting my cheeks and lips and eyes. I tried to protest, and once even attempted to stand, but I was dizzy and weak, and their bodies blocked me in. It all happened so quickly. In a matter of minutes, they were stepping back to admire their handiwork. I lifted a hand to touch my face, but Hermapate smacked it away. "The cosmetics will smear."

"What…?" I blinked from woman to woman. "What did you do?"

"We fixed you," Hermapate said. "No one will think you look sickly now. Oh, but we have not made you late, have we?"

Her words jolted me. How long had I delayed? The queen was waiting; I could waste no more time. I stepped away, barely pausing to utter my goodbyes. I rushed through the halls, passing courtiers and their companions, ministers, a traveling troupe, the servants. People saw me and frowned. Some suppressed giggles. A feeling was niggling at my belly, the voice in my head urging me to stop and find a mirror. I should not waste more time but…what had Hermapate done?

I took a detour down a hall where a golden mirror hung. I wish now that I had instead chosen to peer into a window or vase, something that would have shown my reflection less perfectly. Then maybe the shock of it wouldn't have cut so deep.

They had done me up like a clown. My lips were overlarge; my face was caked with white paste. My eyebrows were drawn high and bushy, as if perpetually surprised. Behind me, curious onlookers toed closer. They smiled in open amusement.

I felt rooted to the spot. I stared at myself as the smiles turned to laughter. I needed a washroom, somewhere to quickly towel off my face. But I could not move my feet.

A figure emerged from the gathered crowd, snapping at the spectators. *Are you really just going to stand there? You should be ashamed.* The group—properly scolded—tucked their chins and fled. Ophelia appeared in the mirror at my side. "Come," she said. "There is a washroom up the hall."

Ophelia did not speak as she helped wipe my face in the washroom's bronze water bowl, and I was too rattled to fill the silence. Hermapate's prank was low, though it was not difficult to guess the source of her newfound animosity. Hobore—unable to convince the king of my untrustworthiness—had been working for months to pit the court against me. . Yet…to what end? Did he wish me gone? Dead? Was Hobore the one who had poisoned my plate? But why would he do that when he had the power to accuse me directly?

"There," Ophelia said, toweling off the last of the cosmetics. "Good as new. I have to get back to work, but—"

"Thank you," I blurted. Ophelia blinked. I had not meant to interrupt, but what she had done, scattering the crowd, guiding me here, helping remove the damage…who else would have come to my aid in such a way? "Thank you for helping me."

Ophelia gave a smile. "Oh, Selene. You are welcome."

...

Queen Mother Althea's breakfast room was quaint, done in pinks and golds with pretty woodwork details my father would have admired. There was a balcony, which was closed off for winter, and a shrine to the Goddess, placed in the corner opposite the dining table. It was there I expected to find the queen, but instead she stood by the high window, gazing out across the lawns.

It was Althea's habit not to acknowledge a person when they first entered a room. I believe she liked to use this as a judge of character. Did silence make you uncomfortable, and if so, would you try to fill it? Well, I was uncomfortable, mostly because I was late. Yet I was good at silence too, and so I stood upon the threshold until the quiet had gone on long enough that it was my making as well as hers.

At last she said, "Can you create a truth serum?"

I blinked. Of all the questions I had expected. "My lady?"

"Twice now, someone has aimed to take my son's life with poison. I have personally interrogated countless suspects, yet my questions have yielded little. A truth serum would greatly aid my efforts."

"I wonder," I said carefully, "why you are asking me?"

"Is it not obvious?" Althea turned to face me. She wore a gown not unlike mine that day, solid in color and simple in design. Like Hermapate, it looked wrong on her. Althea was a woman best suited for armor. "You have invented potions before. You created whipstarch. It cured my brother's cough."

I was surprised she remembered. The queen's brother Toromond had once contracted an acute case of *aspithia*, the Hacking Cough, which was known to cause lung damage in its victims, and sometimes even death. I had invented a cure, but that was years ago, and anyway, my mother had been the one to deliver the remedy. As far as I knew, Persaphe had taken credit.

"That is true," I replied slowly, "but this is different. Whipstarch is a type of bodily medicine, which is within my domain of study. A truth serum is…something else."

"What do you mean, something else?"

"It would require an alteration of the mind. I am not sure a physiological alteration is enough, though. There would be an element of psychology, too, and I think—"

"So you cannot do it?"

If ever there was any decorum between us, it was gone. Yet what I said was true. I was a healer, trained in medicine. Even if such a serum could be invented, I had neither the knowledge nor the skill for the task. My gifts were specialized to the body and its fluxes. Altering the mind was another science entirely.

But the mind is part of the body, a small part of me whispered.

But you improved your own mind by changing your diet.

How can you be sure you are not capable?

Foolish. What did it matter if I was? I would never be the one to invent a truth serum. That would be as good as contriving my own downfall. I had my own secrets to keep, after all.

I held the queen's gaze. "Apologies, my lady, but I cannot."

EIGHTEEN

"I have something for you," Elias said.

We were sitting in his study the following night, he in his wheelchair and I perched on the edge of the chaise, reading. I looked up from the page.

"It was meant to be a birthday gift." He was dressed casually in a shirt and trousers, the neck unbuttoned to reveal a triangle of skin, his hair damp from a recent bath. Nearby, the fire emitted warm light. "I'd planned to give it to you after the feast, but…" He gave a helpless shrug, then seemed to catch the look on my face. "Have I surprised you?"

"You got me a gift," I said dumbly.

"Yes."

"For my birthday."

His mouth quirked. "Yes."

"But how did you remember my birthday?"

"It would be hard to forget."

After last year's candle debacle, he meant. I conceded the point. But still. "You did not have to get me anything."

There was that smile again, the one I wanted to cup in my hands and carry. "Humor me."

It was a compass, beautifully crafted. The face was obsidian, the casing done in polished gold. Curiously, there was not one needle but two, the first pointing north and the second west, tipped with a little etched star. The symbol was familiar, though I could not quite…

I blinked, my thoughts scattering like marbles across hardwood. "Is that—?"

"The Evening Star, yes."

"But that means—this is—" My jaw continued to work. "This is the compass from *The River of Reversal*. The one the maiden uses to navigate the Crossing Sea…" I recognized the details better, the lens said to be blown from the River's sand, the bezel hand-carved by its stewards. The particulars of that story were etched into my mind, worn smooth with love and repetition. "But where did you find such a perfect replica?"

"Replica?" Elias had wheeled himself up beside me, close enough that our shoulders could have touched. "Who says this is not the original?"

My smile was so wide it hurt. "But it's just a story."

"A legend. There's a difference."

"What are you suggesting? Do you believe the River exists?"

"No. Maybe." Another shrug. "Either way, this compass is not only for finding fabled rivers. It works normally, too, and I hope"—this he said with some gravity—"it may one day be of use to you."

A feeling bloomed in my chest, warm as melted butter. I thought of how my mother had once departed to sail the world. Never before had it occurred to me to do the same. I had never left Isla, had scarcely even left the palace. Would I have the courage? Could I ever do as Persaphe had done and venture into the lands beyond the sea?

As I was working through this, I realized Elias was watching me. His mouth was pulled in slightly; his eyes searched my face. He was the picture of anticipation, that moment when the gifter is held in suspense, waiting to see how his present will be received. His heart, too, gave him away, thumping slightly offbeat. It struck me then. Was Elias…nervous?

Novel. Elias' nervousness was novel, and unlike him, and so wonderfully endearing. Unthinkingly, I set my hand over his. "It's perfect."

He went utterly still. I snapped my eyes to our joined hands, stunned by my mistake, but before I could yank away, his other hand came down on top of mine. "No," he managed weakly. "Wait."

I waited. Though Elias and I had touched before, the contact was always clinical, swift. I watched as he warred with himself, his gaze fixed on our hands, his expression set with effort. This was no affectionate embrace. Rather, it was a testing of his limit. His teeth ground together; my heart pounded as hard as his. I was never more aware of Elias' fear of physical contact as I was in that moment.

An eternity seemed to pass. After a time, Elias' shoulders settled. His racing heart slowed. With a small inhale, he withdrew his hands.

I had a thousand questions. "When—?" My voice had gone hoarse from the strain of those long moments. "When was the last time you held someone's hand?"

His eyes were hidden behind thick lashes. "I cannot remember." A pause. "I am not sure I ever have."

"And now. Was this…?"

"Not terrible, if that is what you wonder."

"But not pleasant, either."

A sigh. "No."

"Could it be?" Slowly, with more courage than I knew I possessed, I reached out again to brush his wrist. We never discussed Elias' fear of touch, yet the door to conversation had been inadvertently cracked, and I pushed it wider. "Could this ever...could it feel good for you?"

He watched my thumb trace his skin. A shudder moved through him. "I don't know."

"Elias." I faltered. I had always wondered what made him this way. How could he be so repulsed by something so fundamentally human? "Why—?"

"Please." His breath was ragged. "I would rather not speak of it."

I nodded. There were wounds in him, depths I could scarcely fathom. I would not push. He would come to me when he was ready, if he ever was. Still, this was a step forward, and I was glad he had chosen to take it. Which is to say, I was glad he had taken it with me.

• • •

I carried that compass with me often in the months that followed. It was heavy in my pocket, but I did not mind. I liked the feel of its solid face pressing against my leg. I liked that I could take it out and consult it, the needles wobbling gently, the metal warming at my touch.

I was remembering the streets of the King's City, which I had visited on rare occasion with my father. I could envision the tangled network of roads, the merchants and vendors calling out their wares, wide strips of cloth strung between buildings to keep off the sun. I held Aegeis' hand to prevent myself from becoming lost, wondering how anyone ever found their way in such a place. I wished for a compass as we passed the sights: the market, the city hall, the wandering rose gardens. My father walked us by the House of Healers, that sanctuary where women renounced their past lives to devote themselves to the craft. The people we met on the streets were not like the polished courtiers of the palace, but stiffer, more serious. Or, so they were until nightfall. Then they transformed, shedding their business wool for satin and organza, their frowns for smirks and winks. The drinks began to flow around dusk, and by dark the city was changed, like a painting that becomes another when you turn it upside down.

"Look," said my father.

He pointed to an ancient temple. It sat at the end of the main thoroughfare, composed of white stone and huge, needlepoint towers. The construction alone had taken decades, to say nothing of the cost. *The Flame atop the Match*, my father named it. The largest in the world, the temple was an architectural marvel as well as a place of worship. Only one other equaled it, a black hall called the Shadow Temple in the Land of Moore, which was built deep into the ground—and also, interestingly, the place where the River of Reversal was fabled to flow. It was said that if the two temples were joined, they would appear symmetrical opposites, like a reflection in water.

We stared at the Flame's brilliant, sculpted face, its endless spires and thousand windows. The structure was made of the earth's oldest sandstone, and was as old as the earth, or nearly so, itself. My father's eyes held their tears. "Imagine the men who built this."

• • •

The compass was a treasure, not merely for what it symbolized, but because it was proof that there was someone who cared enough to remember my birthday, and gift me a present. The timing was apt as well, as I began to see less of Elias in those days. Now that he was reemerged, councilors and dignitaries sought him out, their calling cards piling on his desk. They wanted him to attend their meetings, their dinners, their evening libations. A part of me expected Elias to turn them away, if only to prove he was not one to be summoned, but he seemed pleased by the requests. He did not ease back into his kingly duties, but swallowed them as you might swallow a pill: all at once.

I should have been glad to see him resume his work. For too long Elias had been aimless, wasting his days with no one but me for company. I wanted him to take back his life and rediscover his purpose, yet I would be lying if I said there was not some heartache there, too. It was selfish of me, I know it, but I had grown used to our days in his study, he in his chair with that look in his eye and I on the floor by the fire, a pillow tucked under my belly, book in hand. I did not realize how much I had come to enjoy his companionship, or how dearly I would miss it once it was gone.

I filled my time as I only knew how—by diving into my experiments. Nearly two years had passed since my parents' departure, two years since I'd begun hunting for the king's cure. That number stuck like a briar in my thumb. I wanted to see Elias walk again. I wanted to undo the devastation I had wrought upon his life. Sometimes I berated myself for not having come farther in my experiments, but other times I tried to be gentle. Who was to say how long it should take? Who was to say it was possible at all?

I began spending more hours out of doors, in the gardens and pavilions, wandering the distant fields. There were always people about, despite the cold. Servants trimmed hedges, herded sheep, hefted sacks of grain. Some nodded to me, but most kept their eyes lowered as I passed. They were aware of me, I could hear it in their beating hearts, but they were hesitant to acknowledge me. They waited for my shadow to pass.

The courtiers never ignored me. Even when they pretended not to notice my presence, they did it in a way that made it obvious they were pretending. Their murmurs chased me down the corridors, their glances full of puzzling resentment. I thought Hobore must be whispering to them like he'd done with Hermapate, though even so...would that explain their bitterness?

I cannot say why it took me so long to put it together, except I had never been good at reading social cues, or anticipating the petty jealousies of others. I was not a part of the court, really, but separate: a girl looking through the glass.

But let me not jump ahead.

• • •

The spring rains came, but in between there were bits of sun, and that is when I went to the forest. I tied my hair with a strip of leather, donned an old apron, dug out my favorite knife and spade. I still loved to walk those trees, seeking out the hidden shoots and ferns, collecting wildflowers for my potions. Sometimes I brought a basket, though more often I simply put what I found in my pockets, to sit beside the compass.

Despite carrying that compass wherever I went, I never actually used it. I might have. The forest was expansive, stretching so far north it eventually met the mountains. There were leagues of uncharted lands between there and here, great stretches of trees waiting to be explored. Sometimes I felt them call to me, like a whisper against the back of my neck. What secrets did the deep forest hold? Would I be brave enough to venture onward, where the trees grew wide as houses, the canopies so thick no light could enter? This was my forest, I had always thought—if anyone was to explore it, it should be me. But rather than pull out my compass and set my course, I always turned back, keeping within sight of landmarks that could easily guide me home.

It was during one of these forest wanderings that I stumbled upon a species of toadstool I did not recognize. It was an unusual color, that shade between purple and blue. I knelt for a better look, my knees sinking into the damp detritus. Overhead, the trees shifted and sighed. I harvested the specimen with my knife. Not wishing to let it be crushed in my pocket, I carried it home in my hands.

A strange feeling was moving within me, like a memory, or a recognition. Back in my workshop, I set the toadstool on the table. It seemed to hum with energy, its gills soft and gray, the cap as perfect as a painting.

I began slowly. I had spent years wandering that forest and had never before encountered this species. Did it only sprout one day a year? Or perhaps it only grew under exact conditions, when there was a steady northern wind, and the trees shaded precisely one quarter of its surface, and three worms tunneled beneath its cap. I did not know. What I knew was whatever this mushroom was, it was rare and therefore deserved prudence. I could not count on finding another.

I started with the stem, paring a small sliver, testing its sponginess between my fingers. Next I moved to the ring, the gills. Each of these parts I handled carefully, peeling off small pieces, sniffing, examining, mulling over what to try. As I worked, my mind emptied. I let my instincts guide me, choosing at last to focus on the cap, which bore a scattering of white spots. These I made sure not to touch with my bare hands, for I sensed their power straining to be released. I used my knife to take what I wanted, then worried my lip, considering. I could brew them over my fire, or mince, or bake...but none of that seemed best. Instead, I procured a mortar and pestle and got to work grinding the pieces of cap to a paste. The resulting mixture was thin, watery. That was not right. My mother's *nightlight* had stuck to the sides of the vial. Like honey, I thought at the time.

Now, I had another thought.

I found a clean knife and turned it on myself. The skin of my palm parted easily beneath the blade. I allowed my blood to drip into a bowl, giving it another few turns with the pestle for good measure.

The potion thickened. Eventually, the metallic smell faded, leaving the blend curiously odorless. But this was not what excited me most. In the dim light of my workshop, the concoction gave off the faintest purple glow.

NINETEEN

We were in Elias' study, he in his chair and I standing before him. I held the vial to the light, squinting as if to examine its contents for the first time, though really I could have drawn their perfect likeness from memory.

"What will it feel like?" Elias asked.

"Like drinking too much wine."

"How are you to say? You've never tasted wine."

I had, actually. I had tried sips from my father's cup at dinner, and was once given my own glass during a toast. I did not know why so many people worshiped the stuff. I found the taste vile. "Then it will feel like falling asleep."

"Those two are not the same."

"Why not try it yourself and tell me what you think it's like?"

Elias took the vial from my hands. He was dressed well that day in an outfit befitting his position, a silken tunic, polished boots, waistcoat shining with gold buttons. He looked more a king than ever. All that was missing was the crown.

He unstoppered the cap to sniff the vial's contents but did not drink. I tapped my foot, but Elias could not be rushed. "Tell me about the sheepherder's son."

I stilled. "What about him?"

"You were seen together in your gardens. I wonder what he wanted with you."

Gellert had indeed found me in my spring garden the previous day. He wanted to know what I was growing. It surprised me. No one besides Elias ever took any interest in my work. I had named the sprouts for him, what they would grow to be, how I cared and cultivated each in their way. Gellert had listened with attentiveness, and after, he asked if he might return to see how the plants were coming along.

I tucked an errant strand of hair behind my ear. "He wanted to say hello."

"That's all? He just came to say hello?"

"He wishes to be my friend."

A half-bitten laugh. "I doubt that."

It was as if I had been slapped. I flinched, my mouth opening and closing like a fish out of water. Elias had not spoken to me like that in ages. "Excuse me?"

"I doubt he wants to be your friend."

I did not know what made me more furious, the words themselves or the carelessness of their delivery. I stood in stiff outrage, my eyes darting over Elias' neatly combed hair, his gleaming belt, the perfect cuffs.

His kingly appearance seemed to gain new meaning. Maybe now that he'd reclaimed his position, Elias had once again decided I was beneath him. This decision was surely helped along by Hobore, whispering venom into his ear, and the court as well, imparting their own misgivings. I still did not understand the palace's renewed animosity toward me, nor did I know the rumors that had begun to circulate, but even I could sense I was a target among the circles.

"Is it really so hard to believe?" Bitterness turned my tone to rinds. "Not everyone thinks so poorly of my company."

It was his turn to look surprised. "What?"

"I might not always be the easiest…the easiest to talk to, but Gellert is nice."

"That's not—"

"The perfect gentleman."

"I didn't mean—"

"And it is not for you to say whether he might wish to be my friend. In fact—"

"Stop."

I stopped.

"Selene." Elias' eyes had gone round. "You misunderstand. I only meant that boy wants to be more than friends."

"He what?" I squeaked.

"He fancies you." Elias spoke carefully, every word like tiles laid. "If he is after your attention, he is not thinking of friendship. That's all I meant."

I could not help it. I laughed.

Elias frowned. "Don't laugh."

That only made me laugh harder.

"You don't believe me?"

No, of course I did not believe him. Gellert, interested in me? It was absurd. Young men did not look at me that way. No one did. "Well done," I said. "You aimed to distract me, and you succeeded. But enough of this. Take your medicine, Elias."

He was still frowning, looking at me in that way he sometimes did.

I thought he would argue, insist I was wrong, that I did not see things clearly, but in the end Elias did not argue. He only tipped the vial to his tongue and drank.

· · ·

Imagine, then, that you have suffered an accident. Your knife slipped when you were chopping carrots. A horse who had always been gentle stomped your foot. You are brought to me, and I hand you a bottle of pale liquid. When you drink, you are surprised to discover not only has your most recent injury vanished, but all your injuries. You feel as if you are floating, as if you never had a care. You are delightfully relieved of pain.

That is what my serum did. After successfully recreating *nightlight*, it did not take long to finish the sister cure. As always, I tested the poison-antidote combination on myself to judge its effects, and finally, two years from the start, I had met success.

I named the remedy *eithier* after the Goddess' famed lover *Eithieros*. It was a *gaigi* of a sort, a potion of undoing, but it was unique in that it did not discriminate. Rather than merely reverse the paralyzing effects of the *nightlight*, *eithier* cured all the body's ailments. Once the remedy set in, aches and pains would subside, old wounds diminishing. You could remember the concept of pain but could not truly fathom it.

There were two problems. The first was that the reversal only lasted as long as the antidote remained in the body. As with all edible medicines, the subject's metabolism would slowly begin breaking down the *eithier* and flushing it from the system. After, wounds would revert to their former stages, ailments returning. For all my efforts, I had not yet figured out how to make the change permanent.

The second issue was that the *gaigi*, like the *nightlight* itself, required the use of my blood—and my blood only—as an ingredient. This surely had something to do with the inherent Freestone-Alder *gilili* blood ties, but it made me uneasy. If my veins held the key to Elias' recovery, it meant our fates were well and truly entangled. If something happened to me, his cure could be lost forever.

Nearly an hour passed before Elias started to feel the remedy's effects. After a time, his muscles began to relax. His face became pleasant. Some say my *eithier* does not affect the mind, merely the body, but the mind and body are so intertwined I do not see how that could be true. There is a peace that comes over you in the absence of pain, a sort of bliss. Elias looked up from the vial and asked, "What have you done?" But he was smiling.

"Come," I said. "Let's get you standing."

I spoke with careful nonchalance, as if this had already been discussed. When I went to pull Elias out of his chair, he gripped my forearms with none of his usual hesitation.

I let go. For a moment, I thought he would fall back into his seat. But a minute passed, then another. He looked down at himself. He was standing on his own without the use of crutch or hold. "Selene." His voice, like the purest honey.

I examined the king. His spine was straight, his stance easy. The *nightlight* had twisted him up, but this remedy allowed his muscles to loosen enough to hold his weight.

"This antidote only masks the poison's effects," I explained. "It is not permanent."

"Do you think you can make it permanent?"

He did not really care to hear the answer. I could see it in his face. For now, it was enough just to feel like his old self again.

"I am working on it," I said. "Try to take a step."

He did, but this seemed to be his limit. After two years of immobility, Elias' atrophied muscles were not strong enough to balance this shift in weight. He began to fall forward, and I rushed to catch him. His hands came down on my shoulders; his face was suddenly close to mine. We locked eyes, and I heard my breath catch.

Slowly, I helped lower him back into his chair. His eyes were still on mine, serious again.

I wanted to say something, I do not know what. Some lighthearted comment to pull us back to the present, to celebrate this accomplishment, but I found myself oddly strangled. The moment congealed. He cleared his throat. "I think that is enough for today."

He wanted to be alone. I could understand that. The *eithier* had a way of making you feel both more and less yourself, and while I did not like the idea of leaving him unsupervised, I also appreciated the desire to experience the effects in peace.

I said something then, I do not remember what. A bid goodnight, a promise to return in the morning. I walked back to my workshop in a kind of daze. The evening sky was shot through with pink. The days were growing long again, another turn of the season. Soon, summer would come.

I felt myself deflating. I had thought…what? The king would stand, and we would rejoice. He would call for a celebration, and I would get to see him glow with happiness. He would thank me in a way that proved his gratitude, and the court would come to respect me as they had respected my mother.

Is that all, Selene? Will they also write songs in your name and make you queen?

I distracted myself. I spent the evening doing as I pleased, walking the gardens, visiting the horses, luring the palace cat to me with treats, then running my hand down her silky back. I ventured to the kitchens and nicked a ball of leavened dough from the table, pulled it apart to eat piece by piece. I hummed a made-up tune, caught a butterfly for its wings, then changed my mind and let her go, watching her dart into the sky, farther and farther until she was nothing.

Night came, yet I continued my whims. I did whatever I wanted, whatever came to mind. I deserved the break, I thought. I deserved some time to myself. Yet the more I wandered, the worse I felt. *Why? My work is done, my evening free. What else could I possibly desire?*

As if in answer, a vision of the grand hall shimmered in my memory. The long tables, the smooth stone floor. The sound of laughter overhead, my mother's slender legs crossed at the ankles. I was kneeling below her with my herbs and my knife, crouched like a suppliant. I kept my eyes on my work, but my ear was always turned to her, listening for her voice, awaiting the moment she might shift her focus to me.

The black night stretched to its edges. Overhead, the stars danced. And far below, I stood knee-high in shrubbery in the center of a dark garden, watching from afar.

I think now you must begin to see, it was not time to myself I wanted. Really, it never had been.

TWENTY

I sat bolt upright in my bed the next morning, sleep retreating from me as a wave retreats the shore. Something was wrong.

I looked around my small bedroom, the bare floors and slender bedframe, wooden chest and wooden door. I listened hard, my thoughts going where they had not gone in months: guards in my chambers, guards come to take me. But I could hear no heartbeats beyond the door. I could sense no stomp of boots or drawing of swords. Quickly, I slipped from my bed into a pair of house shoes, breathing, straining to hear. At last I realized what had alarmed me. Not a sound, or a sight, but a smell. A strange scent hung in the air, wafting into my bedroom. If I had to name it, I would say it smelled of freshly shaved woodchips.

I knew, I cannot say how. A whisper from the Goddess, maybe. Another fear, an older one, reawakened.

I pushed through my chambers and there it was. My workroom, which I had spent a lifetime cultivating, and relied upon to conduct my experiments, had been massacred. Every pot was overturned, every glass vial broken. Someone had taken a hatchet to my worktable, the one my father had built me. And there, gouged with a knife into its broken surface was a single word. *Whore.*

The world seemed to drain of color. I stumbled forward, my breath juddering out of me. My dried lavender pots, my *istilla* and winter-picked yuleberries. My cauldron, my tools and my books. On went the destruction, and on and on. They had even smashed the windows, all the glass panes fractured. But who had done it? Why? And how, oh how had I not woken from the noise? My bedchamber was located on the opposite side of these quarters. Its thick door was made for privacy, but I still should have heard the clamor. I would have, surely, had I not stayed up so late into the night, or later been pulled under by exhaustion.

I looked again at that word. *Whore*. So ugly, so plain. It would have been better if they'd stuck to the old narrative of *witch*. At least then it might have made some sense to me.

It was a final tribute to my innocence that I was so blindsided. I had seen the way the courtiers looked at me, not with their old superstitions, but with bitterness. When had it started? Was it when Elias asked me to sit in the chair meant for his bride? Or had it begun before that? People must have noticed how much time the king and I spent together. They must have seen how Elias reacted when I was poisoned, how he moved my recovery to his private suite. Though I was only sixteen—nine years his junior—I would be of age that winter and eligible for marriage. Maybe the court believed I was wooing their king, asking him to make me promises. Maybe they believed I wanted him to choose me over Princess Mora, or worse, that I wanted him to choose me in spite of her.

I didn't. It wasn't like that. Elias was a...*friend* seemed too light a word. A kindred soul, maybe. A heart ship, sailing with me by the bonds of our *gilili* and that strange connection of our pulses. But still my king.

Regardless, I should have realized something like this would happen. Like a compound whose properties were known, this was the natural order of things. If you give a plant sunlight, it will grow. If you throw water on a cat, she will flee. And if you offend the court, they will retaliate.

I had offended the court—endangered their class hierarchy and threatened to come between their king and future queen—and here was their retaliation. They did not even know Princess Mora, but they adored her for her beauty and her sweetness, and they would defend her with all their teeth.

I sank to my knees, too numb even to cry. I knew I should rummage through the debris to see if anything could be salvaged, the rare *mintis* leaves I had gathered three summers ago, or the remains of that poisonous mushroom that allowed me to recreate *nightlight*. But all I could see was the pointlessness; there was nothing left. I thought of the endless hours I'd spent collecting those ingredients, how many times I had pulled myself from bed at the crack of dawn or stayed up late under the moonlight searching, wandering, harvesting. Years. It had taken years to amass this collection, to fill every cupboard and vial and jar. And now it was gone.

I continued to stare. My knees were starting to bruise, my eyes like arid rocks. I thought, I should do something. Cover up that word. But I could not move. I felt sucked dry, like the kernel of a nut left in the sun. I do not know how long I would have gone on kneeling there if not for the arrival of two figures at the broken window. I recognized their heartbeats at once.

"What in the Goddess' name happened here?"

Kurton and Arch leaned through the shattered windowpanes. They were not dressed in their usual uniforms but in city clothes, scanning the destruction with abject horror. It was the look on their faces, I think, that finally shook me loose. My throat went tight. I buried my face in my hands and choked on a sob.

No words were exchanged between the men. Rather, in the way of two comrades who had worked together long enough to share silent understandings, they quickly disappeared and then reappeared through the back door. Kurton strode over to put a comforting arm around my shoulders while Arch tipped the table to hide that word. "There now, Selene," Kurton soothed. "There's no need to cry." Which, of course, only made me cry harder. I wept for my table, which I had cherished. I cried for my parents, who were not there, and for Elias, who did not know. Finally, I cried for myself. For the pain of being young, the bitter sting of unfairness. I cried because I had been attacked by strangers, and it hurt as deeply as they intended.

"We need to tell His Majesty," Arch said.

"No." I lifted my stricken face. "Please don't."

"This was no mere prank. Whoever did this must answer for their crimes."

"Please," I begged. "It will only make things worse."

"I am sorry, Selene." Arch did indeed look sorry. "This is our duty."

Kurton helped me to my feet while Arch marched off to find the king. "Come on," Kurton said. "No need to stay here looking at it. I think I know something that will cheer you up."

We left out the back door. I did not pay much attention to where we were going. My eyes were swollen, my heart sore. I felt bone tired; I could have fallen asleep on the spot. It was only when we entered the stables that I had the sense to look around. The space was mostly empty, save for a few workers and, of course, the horses.

"What are we doing here?"

"You'll see," Kurton answered gently.

He led me to one of the empty stalls. Inside, a mother hound whelped her pups. They were tiny, squeaking creatures, each no larger than a hand. They could not have been more than a few days old.

"The Master of Hounds says it's a litter from the Goddess," Kurton explained. "Don't know about all that, but they're sure cute." He pulled one of the puppies from the straw and set her in my palms. I sniffled, cupping her loose body to my chest. A litter from the Goddess meant all the puppies were female. The dogs were thought to be lucky.

"I can't imagine why anyone would want to ruin your workroom like that," Kurton said, "but we'll help you rebuild it, *rahvika*. We know how important it is to you. To the king, too."

I could only nod. Whatever help the guardsmen could offer would not undo the damage. It would not protect me from future attacks. And yet...it did ease the pain, a little. There was solace in the moment, in the knowledge that if I had to suffer, there was someone there who would try to make it better, fumbling a way as this might be. A wounded heart that ends with a puppy in your hands, and an offer to help rebuild.

...

Elias found me in the palace's communal library later that day. The *eithier* from the night before had fully worn off, and he was back in his wheelchair, looking grim. "We need to talk."

It was midafternoon, that hour shortly after lunch when most of the palace was still gathered in the great hall. I had specifically chosen to come to the library at this time to avoid running into anyone. I did not want to see how people looked at me, the vindication or the pity. I did not want to know how the court would split. Would anyone take my side, or did the entire palace believe I had gotten what I deserved?

As it was, there were a few others in the library that morning, a pair of women lounging in tufted chairs, a trio of men chatting quietly. Until then, we had all been happy to ignore each other, but at a glance from the king they up and left the room.

Elias asked, "Do you know who did it?"

I had an idea, maybe. But naming names would help nothing. "It doesn't matter."

"It matters to me."

"My tools can be replaced. The table and windows, too. The herbs—" I swallowed. "They will take longer to recollect, but it can be done. I do not want more trouble."

"Is that why you were not going to tell me? Because you do not want more trouble?"

I shrugged.

He drew his eyes upwards. "Will you ever not suffer because of me?"

The question lodged in my throat. I felt as if I would start crying all over again. "It's not your fault."

"Of course it is."

This was typical of Elias, this reflex of self-blame. But the incident was not his doing. If anyone should be sorry, it was me. "I must have offended someone without meaning to," I said. "The court can be harsh that way. I just need to be more careful."

"You are not listening. I do not care who you offended. I do not care if you put a knife through one of their hearts. Someone broke into your private chambers and destroyed your workshop because they knew it would hurt you, and seeing you hurt hurts *me*." He gave a harsh exhale. "You are more than just my physician, Selene. You are an extension of myself, which makes any attack on you an attack on us both. I will have the perpetrator brought to justice. Do you understand?"

I had a vision of a soldier with his legs broken. I imagined it was Hermapate chained to those courtyard stones, that it was her blood spilling across the cobbles. The image gave me no pleasure. "I understand, and still I ask that you not seek justice."

"You would let them get away with it?"

"If you react in any way, you will only prove their theory."

"And what theory is that?"

But I could not say it. I could not look the king in his eye and admit the court believed us more than just servant and master. Elias' father had a reputation for infidelity—Hobore was proof of that—and my mother a reputation for promiscuity. Who was to say their children were any different? I swiftly dodged the question. "My father once told me aggressors lose their power if you do not cower. If they see they cannot affect you, their game loses its fun."

"This is not a game."

"It is always a game."

"But they have affected you."

"They do not need to know that."

Elias' face was carved in deep lines. I saw my words push regret across his features, slat by slat, like the unfolding of a fan. I cut him off before he could speak. "I can handle this, Elias. I do not need a savior."

That was unfair of me; Elias did not deserve my scorn. Before I could draw the words back, however, he gave a short nod. "If that is what you wish."

I had thought that would be the end of it, but Elias was Elias, and could not be so easily deterred. From then on, as if to prove a point, he began inviting me back to his private library to read and discuss books as we once had. When the first invitation came—folded, unsealed, scribbled in his hand—requesting my company after dinner, I felt a pain so deep as to be physically exhausting. I clutched that letter to my chest, even as I knew I could not accept.

Thank you, I wrote back, but I must decline.

The King's Guard helped me repair my workshop, as promised. It lifted my spirits to watch those battle-trained men sweep the floor and bend over mop buckets and handle cracked pots, delicately gluing. They joked with me as they worked, telling stories about the enemies they'd fought and critiquing each other's handiwork. It was not until the third day that the topic of my table was raised. Would I prefer to replace it entirely? Or recraft using the same wood? They knew it was a gift from my father.

I hesitated, touching the splintered chunks.

Once, my mother brought me to the Master of Horses. He had stepped on a nail and gouged his heel, but the man stubbornly refused treatment, and without proper tending the wound had festered. I remembered standing in his small bedroom. His skinny legs were pale against dark sheets; the gash had sealed over with yellow pus. My mother ran a knife through the fire, then handed it to me.

I was nine years old. The man was elderly, balding, his face scattered with liver spots. He nodded as if to reassure me, when really I should have been the one reassuring him. I set the tip of the knife to the abscess. The metal sank in; thick fluid oozed.

Some things are like that. If allowed to remain, they will fester. As I stood in my shop touching one of my last remaining links to my former life, I thought of my aggressors, and what weakness they must have seen in me to believe they could destroy this room without consequence. I thought of the young girl I had been and the woman I was becoming, and I recalled my mother's words clearly. "There is only one solution," she had told the Master and me, "when an abscess grows too large."

You must cut it out.

• • •

New trees were felled. Lumber was sawed and sanded and nailed. Soon, my new table began to take shape. We burned the old one in the field out back.

Even after my workshop was repaired, I began to notice the King's Guard was never far away. Arch would grin at me in the great hall, tweaking my hair as an older brother might. Freesier developed an interest in the apple tree near my forest, while Yorvis often came to read on the little bench outside my window. Kurton especially was always near, greeting me kindly and calling me *rahvika*. It seemed that while Elias may have agreed not to pursue those who had destroyed my shop, here was something he would not concede. I was still to be looked after by the men he most trusted.

Once, I might have loathed such supervision. I would have turned away and shut those men out. But now I looked for them, smiling whenever our paths crossed. When I saw Yorvis on the garden bench, I invited him in for tea. When I spotted Freesier under the apple tree on my way to the forest, I asked if he wished to walk with me. Their company was not like Elias', underlaid with things unspoken, but bright and clear, playful as a spring creek. They were friends. My very first.

Meanwhile, the king's letters kept arriving. *I have a new book for you*, Elias wrote. *I think you will like it. Come read with me?* The more requests he sent, the more confused I became. I wanted to accept his appeals, of course I did, but was it worth risking the court's ire to spend time with him? I wished I had someone to ask, yet I could think only of the King's Guard, and though I might have turned to them for any number of matters, I could not turn to them for this.

Days passed. I stewed over the issue. Maybe I should confide in the King's Guard after all. There was no one else.

Except, actually, there was.

TWENTY-ONE

My knock was quiet on Ophelia's door, the sound like a little pulse. When one of her many brothers answered, I tried for a smile. "I am here for Ophelia."

"She is out in the kitchen gardens."

I found her there among the herbs, looking more grown up than the last time I had seen her. She wore a simple gown and apron, her hair coiled neatly at the nape of her neck, her cheeks bright with color. The picture of a young lady.

"Selene." Ophelia smiled, which is to say, her smile grew wider. She never seemed to stop, really. "I am glad to see you looking well."

She had a right to her sarcasm. I had come straight from my chambers, determined to seek her out before I could change my mind, which meant I had not delayed to comb my hair or switch out of my stained work clothes. Strangely, though, her comment did not seem barbed. Ophelia spoke like it was a joke we shared.

"Beauty rest," I said.

"We should all be so lucky."

I searched for a way to broach the topic of the king's letters and found myself wavering. I motioned toward her garden tools. "Do you need help?"

"If you have time to spare."

Which is how I found myself shoulder to shoulder with Ophelia on a warm midspring day, harvesting basil. The plant was fragrant but flimsy, overgrown from lack of good pruning. Ophelia employed a pair of kitchen scissors, but I worked with my hands, as had always been my preference. "You should trim these stalks more often," I said, moving along the row. "If you want a better harvest, basil should never be allowed to flower."

"Is that how you get the basil in your garden to grow so well?"

"That is part of it."

"And the other part?"

I shrugged. The private garden behind my chamber had always flourished without much help.

"I saw you speaking to Kurton in the great hall the other day," Ophelia remarked. "I wonder, has he yet made mention of the apple tree?"

It took me a moment to catch her meaning. There was an apple tree that grew near the forest. The tree was odd in that it had stood there for ages, alone, uncultivated. Odder, however, was that the tree put out apples in the winter: green, shiny, and juicy as you can imagine. When a man liked a women, he might mention he would enjoy taking her to the apple tree.

"If not," Ophelia continued, "you should expect it. He fancies you."

This again. I wished people would stop with their presumptions. "You are wrong," I said, "but I do believe you fancy *him*."

She blinked at me. "What?"

"Do you deny it?"

"I...do not deny it." A little laugh. "How can you tell?"

Because I could hear her heartbeat speed at the mention of his name. "Because I can see it in your face."

"I hope I am not so obvious to everyone."

"Why not? Maybe he feels the same."

"We have never spoken," Ophelia admitted.

"Never?"

She brought a dramatic hand to her forehead. "It is love from afar."

"I consider Kurton a friend," I said. "I could introduce you."

I do not know where that offer came from. I was hardly one to play matchmaker. Yet I enjoyed it, the way Ophelia's eyes turned hopefully luminous. She lowered her scissors. "You would do that?"

"Yes. If you wish it."

She reached for my hand. I nearly flinched away but managed to smother the reaction—I was not the king, I did not have his aversions. Ophelia's skin was soft and warm. She gave my fingers a squeeze, and I felt the contact in a deeply human way. "Oh, Selene." Her smile was different now, full of mischief. "When Kurton and I are wed, we will name our firstborn after you."

I smiled back. "How about instead, you give me some advice?"

"Ah." Her eyes twinkled. "There *is* someone."

"No." My face flamed. "Not like that. It's...about the king."

Ophelia waited, the basil forgotten, as I told her everything. I had planned on leaving out certain parts, particularly those that might reach the wrong ears, but once I started speaking I found the whole story about my destroyed workshop and the king's reaction pouring from me, every name and detail included.

"It is foolish," I finished miserably, "isn't it? To accept his invitations. Spending more time with Elias will only bring trouble."

Ophelia's gaze was as steady as I had ever seen it. "You call him Elias."

My blush deepened. "He asked me to."

"Yes," she said. "I know." A breeze tugged at her braid. Behind us, the garden fence fluttered with wild creepers. "I was born in the palace. Did you know that? I have lived here all my life and have known King Alder since before he was king. He has always been a serious man, made even more so by his father's death. Yet now, the court sees him change."

"The poisoning—"

"I do not speak of his poisoning. I mean, he has softened. In a council meeting last week, the Master of Labor asked to extend the working hours of the cook—and by extension, the kitchen staff—in order that midnight meals might be made possible for those within his rank. The king declined. He said the cook worked hard enough, and if the Master wanted a workhorse, he might find one in the barn."

"I am glad of it," I said impatiently, "but what has that to do with me?"

"You are the reason for the king's change."

"What?"

"Oh, come now. Surely you've seen it? Everyone knows Elias Alder's reputation. *The king with a stone for a heart.* He was always so closed off, so unforgiving of mistakes. Ours, yes, but also his own. Then he spends a year locked away with you, and suddenly he can be heard arguing on his servants' behalf. He listens to us. He *smiles*. I nearly dropped my teacup the first time I saw it. The king has always been easy on the eyes, everyone knows it, but that smile? I tell you, it sent us kitchen girls into a frenzy. Do not try to say that was the poison's doing. No, Selene. It is because of you."

My eyes fell to the basil. "If that is true," I mumbled, "I think you are making my point."

"Not at all. You are good for him, and it seems," she touched a knuckle to my chin, bringing my gaze back to hers, "he is good for you. Accept his requests, if you wish it. Spend time with him. Why not? Because you fear more retaliation?"

"Yes, actually."

"Tell me something. How do you get your garden to grow?"

"You already asked me that."

"And you gave half an answer. I'm asking for the other half."

I tried to come up with a reply that did not sound boastful or mad. In the end, I settled on the truth. "It just grows for me."

"Without care," Ophelia pressed.

"Yes."

"As if summoned by magic."

I had never thought of it that way. "I don't know. Yes. Perhaps."

She pinned me with a look. "Are you, or are you not, a witch?"

All the years spent hiding from that word. All the years ashamed of it. Now, it sparked something new within me. "I...maybe."

"Could you take your vengeance, if you desired it?"

The feeling continued to grow, like horns on a ram. "I could."

"Then what have you to fear? The courtiers are spineless snakes. You, dear Selene, are the hawk that will devour them."

TWENTY-TWO

The next time Elias sent a letter requesting my presence in his library, I scrawled my answer right there beneath his signature and sent it back at once. *Yes.*

I was returning from the forest later that afternoon when Elias intercepted me. "I received your reply."

He was in his wheelchair, though he looked taller somehow, his eyes green and meadow-bright. Behind him, the sun dipped toward the horizon, crowning his hair like one of the princes from our stories. I felt my cheeks redden. "And you came to tell me this in person?"

"I am pleased." He searched my face. "I wanted you to know it." His eyes dropped to the basket I carried. "Are you coming from the forest?"

"Yes."

I expected him to ask about the *eithier*. Since the day my shop was destroyed, my first priority had been to regather the ingredients needed to create it. Having done that, it was decided Elias would not take the *eithier* on a daily basis, since it required time to brew and—more significantly—the use of my blood. I could not drain myself just to give him a few daily hours of mobility. Rather, we would save Elias' ability to stand for public occasions, and in the meantime I would continue to work on making the transformation permanent.

If Elias wondered how my foraging went, however, he did not ask. Instead he said, "You remind me of a story."

I fell into step alongside him. We were in a well-used courtyard on the east end of the palace, the same place the young soldier had once been punished. The rings in the ground were gone, the stains long since scrubbed. Out of the corner of my eye, I could see Arch's bald head as he trailed us, keeping watch. "Which story?"

"The one about the girl who loved the woods."

"I remember that tale." It was one of the first novels he had given me after *The River of Reversal*. "She adored the woods so much, she begged the Goddess to grant her the freedom to live there forever. The Goddess obliged and turned her into a tree."

He was amused. "You do not like the story."

"I detest it."

"Oh?"

"The girl was a fool. She should have known better than to bargain with the Goddess. She should have been wise enough to spot the trick." I did not admit the story also reminded me of myself. I did not say, what if I was tricked, too? What if I made a mistake I cannot undo, and what if you cannot ever forgive me, and also, must we walk here on the grave of a man your captain ordered beaten?

I said, "I wish I did not remind you of her."

"Then I take it back," he replied. "It does not."

I made a face. "You cannot change your mind so quickly."

"I am a king. I may do whatever I please."

"Stubborn."

"One of my more endearing qualities."

"And self-satisfied, too."

"You like that I'm self-satisfied."

I met his gaze. A moment, like warm breath on cold hands.

I said, "I would like it better if you were silent."

"Selene." The way his mouth cradled the syllables. His face, rich with mirth. "That sounds like a complaint against your king."

"One of many, I assure you."

"One of *many*. This I must hear."

"Shall I make you a list?"

He laughed, a full-bellied sound that winged through me like a bird on a breeze. "If you are so certain—"

His chair gave a thump. We looked down. One of the wheels had caught in the crevice between two cobblestones.

A moment passed. We were not the only ones in the courtyard that day, and I was painfully aware of the turning heads, and of Elias' pulse, which seemed to lift through my skin. His cheeks were stained with color, his mouth gone tight. After a short deliberation, he set his hands to the wheels and gave a great, determined heave, but it was no use. He was stuck.

His eyes shifted to mine. All humor was gone from him, leaving only resentment and defeat. Here was a man who did not like to ask for help, who had found himself suddenly and very publicly in need of it. Without speaking, I moved around to the back of the chair and used my full strength to free it from the crevice. The chair lurched forward, the spokes spinning. The wheels clattered noisily as they came back down.

"I thank you," he said stiffly, avoiding my gaze.

"Elias." I hated to see him like this. I knew he did not want sympathy, and surely not pity, either, but he had no reason to feel ashamed. "It's me."

He did not seem convinced.

"It doesn't matter," I insisted. "Or—it does matter, because it upsets you. But this—your wheelchair, the way you sometimes need help—there is no shame in it, and it does not…" I realized my volume had grown rather loud. "It does not define you." I was blushing furiously. "It does not change the way I see you."

He was staring at me. "I…well, that's…" I was surprised to see his cheeks were as red as mine. "I am glad of it. That it does not…change your view of me. Be that as it may…" He grimaced. It was rare to witness Elias struggle for words. I fought the impulse to throw my arms around him. "What I am trying to say," he continued more firmly, "is thank you."

I smiled. "You're welcome."

He shook his head. "Shall we continue?"

We meandered the path, passing several smaller courtyards until we finally came upon the Garden of Statues. Here, all the prior kings of Isla were erected in stone, set in granite for eternity. We passed Elias' great-grandfather, and his grandfather, and finally, his father. The statue was twice the size of a normal man, carved in white and gray, the details so fine as to make me wish for a magnifying glass. Elias' hands skipped over his wheels as we passed. The slightest hesitation.

"Tell me about him," I said.

His eyes slid sideways. "There is not much to tell."

"He was your father."

"He was a king."

"Are you saying all kings are the same?"

His tone was stubborn again. "Clearly not all kings are the same."

"Because you are not like him?"

"Selene."

"You can tell me." I spoke in the same way I had said, *it's me*. I wanted to know his thoughts. I wanted him to give them to me.

We had stopped again. Elias was looking past me, squinting into the sun. When he began speaking, it was haltingly, with the air of someone doing so against their will. "My father's flaws were exactly the kind you would hope for in a king. He cared too much. He was often too kind. The Master of Coin joked he had to reel Adonis in, lest he donate the entire royal treasury to the needy. Growing up, I wanted to be like him. I wanted to be the sort of king people could love, and I thought I would be, in my time. But then there was my father's accident." Elias gave a weak laugh. "So senseless. Have you ever heard the full story of how he died?"

I shook my head. It was a hunting mishap, like everyone said. The details were not discussed.

"He fell off his horse." Elias' voice was like a sword hidden within its scabbard. "He and his hunting party were chasing a bear. His horse's reins came loose from the bridle. A faulty ring. He tumbled down and broke his neck."

I felt the words soak through me. I had never known.

"In the months after," Elias continued, "I was angry. At him, for dying. At my mother, for diving so deeply into her faith she might as well have died, too. And at myself, for how helpless I felt, how unprepared. I was grieving, and newly to the throne. I was trying to rule a nation before I was ready. I could feel the attention on me. The pressure. I thought back to my father's reputation, how he was good and kind and patient, and that made me angry as well, because it seemed absurd. How could anyone be patient when they were in charge of the lives of millions? How could anyone be logical or kind?"

"It sounds like a lot for anyone to handle."

"It was too much," Elias said curtly. "I snapped at a Master one day and that was it. People had been waiting to see what kind of king I would be, and there was their answer. From then on everyone decided I was an angry king, and that *made* me angry, and so they were right." He glanced at his father's statue. "Things might have been different had my mother taken my side, but all she could talk about in those days was the Goddess' will. She blames me for Adonis' death."

I blinked. "How can that be?"

"It was my duty to ready my father's horse. It is said to bring luck to a hunt for a prince to prepare the horse of a king. An old tradition. But I arrived late. The task was given to Hobore instead. My mother thinks… well, she thinks Hobore brought the Goddess' ire. That his hands cursed the saddle. She said to me, *If you had been on time, your father might have lived.*"

"That is ridiculous."

A shrug.

"She cannot blame you for the bridle." I felt my indignation rising. "Is she really so superstitious?"

"Althea has always been ruled by custom. She was heartbroken. She used her faith to make sense of the accident and convinced herself Adonis' death was meditated by divine hand. But the Goddess does nothing without reason. My mother needed someone to condemn, and that person was me."

I knew, by how he said the words, that this was not a secret he ever shared. It was one of the most vulnerable admissions he could have given me, and it made me ache for him, more so because it made so little sense. How could Althea choose to blame her only living son? Why set herself against him at a time when they needed each other's strength more than ever?

"Your mother is a fool," I said.

Elias did not deny it.

"If anyone, she should blame Hobore."

He gave a dry laugh. "Oh, she does. After the accident, she nearly had his head. It was your mother who intervened."

My mother. The mention of her was like a splash of cold water. "Persaphe spoke on Hobore's behalf?"

"She always had a soft spot for Hobore." Elias' face was clouding again. I noticed it often did this when discussing my mother, and I felt the first hint of something, like spider silk along my spine. But I did not want to talk about Persaphe.

"You know," I said in an attempt to move the conversation onward, "you do not have to be who you once were."

He cocked a brow. "Oh?"

"I have been hearing rumors. The palace staff has noticed you acting…differently. They say you've taken their side in recent matters, and spoken for their wellbeing when you would not have before."

He harumphed. "They exaggerate."

"I don't think so. I think this could be the start of something new. You could prove people wrong. Show them your kindness."

"I am not kind."

"You are kind to me."

"I wasn't always."

"You changed. You can always choose to change."

"Like you have?"

I thought of the strength I was discovering within myself. My mother's charms, and my poisons, and Ophelia's praise.

Are you, or are you not, a witch?

"Yes," I agreed. "Like me."

TWENTY-THREE

The leaves shifted from green to gold, the blue skies giving way to clouds. In the mornings, glittering blankets of frost covered the fields, melting as the sun rose. Later came the sleet, icy downpours that turned the roads to mud. Autumn passed into winter, and back to spring. I was seventeen.

We were in Elias' library after dinner. I had chosen the tufted divan and was curled up with a pillow between my knees, a book of Elias' suggestion in hand. The story told of a girl who fell in love with the sun. She would sing her longing to him, and he would take the shape of a man, coming to her at night when the moon could stand in his place. One day, the sun did not return to the sky in time for the dawn, and the world fell to darkness.

Elias was reading as well, but after a time he began to grow restless. There was a bowl of peanuts on the table beside him. He flicked one at me. "How is the book?"

I did not look up. "It would be better without the interruption."

The plot was getting good. I had just reached the scene where the girl and the sun were about to kiss. Elias spoke again. "Which part are you on?"

"Are we talking, or are we reading?"

"We are talking." That smile. "I know what chapter you've reached."

"You cannot know that."

"Halfway through. The kiss. That's why you're blushing."

Was I? I touched a hand to my cheek. Carefully, I put my bookmark in its place and set the book aside.

He said, "There is no need to be embarrassed."

"I'm not embarrassed."

"It is a good story. The kiss is the best part."

"Don't condescend to me."

He clicked his tongue. "Touchy."

My eyes fell to the king's hands, his forearms corded with muscle. I thought of how he held back my hair when I was ill. I thought of his hand trapping mine, later, when he gifted me the compass. That sure, solid warmth. "It is merely a kiss," I said. "I have encountered those before."

"In books."

I am sure now he did not mean it as an insult. I can remember how Elias looked that day, his mind somewhat engaged, his body aloof. He hadn't the slightest idea how his presumption would scrape into me like a nail into glass, yet I hated, deeply, his nonchalance, and how he spoke as if I was a curious child rather than a young woman. The truth, of course, was somewhere between, but that fact only made my pride rear higher.

It lit in me a wicked fire.

"I was wondering," I said abruptly, "if I could request a favor."

The king must have heard my change in tone. He eyed me warily.

"What kind of favor?"

"Do you remember Gellert, the sheepherder's son? Or," I gave a little laugh, "I suppose he is a man now. A sheepherder himself."

I watched my words play across Elias and oh, I liked that. His eyes had gone storm-dark. I could feel his heart squeeze. "I remember."

"He is the benefactor of your chair."

Elias took his book back in hand, a poor imitation of disinterest. "I thought your father was my benefactor."

"My father crafted that chair for Gellert, and Gellert gave it to you."

"I see."

"Gellert has become a dear companion of mine," I continued wistfully. "We spend a good deal of time together." This was untrue. Gellert did sometimes seek me out, but his work prevented him from coming more often. Still, he'd opened an invitation to meet any time, and I had returned the offer. "Gellert's shed needs repair. It is practically falling apart. I thought it might be kind if you—"

"Had it fixed?" The king clutched his book. "My servants are not slaves. They receive a wage. If his shed is in disrepair, he can pay to fix it himself."

"Yes, but a shed is quite an expense…"

"That is none of my concern."

"I thought you were resolving to be nicer."

"When have I ever cared for being nice?" He tossed the book down again. "When have you ever cared for it?"

My mirth, which had been growing, slipped. "I can be nice."

"Don't bother. I do not value you for your likability, Selene, merely for your mind."

"Well, I used my mind to think this through, and I have decided helping Gellert would benefit you as well, since his work directly—"

"My answer is no."

I pouted.

"Don't pout."

"You are being difficult."

"I am in good company."

We frowned at each other, neither willing to look away first. As our eyes held, something…caught.

Elias sliced a look at my novel, breaking the moment. "Your two lovers both die at the end, by the way."

I dropped my jaw. "They do not."

"Oh yes. It's tragic. The sun is so lovestruck he cannot return to the sky, and the world freezes."

"I do not believe you. You would never give away a story's ending."

"Why not?" He stretched back in his seat, easy again, cradling his hands behind his head. His shirt lifted, revealing a sliver of skin. "I can do anything, whatever brings me pleasure."

"Not without consequence."

His smile was indulgent. "Is that a threat?"

"A promise."

"Ah, Selene, you need not start making me promises."

I rolled my eyes and went back to my book, yet my blood was biting at my neck. He could never know what he did to me, simply by looking smug and saying the word *pleasure*. He could never know how it was to feel his unexpected jealousy rising up in his heart as if it rose up in mine.

When I look back at our story, there is no single place where it began. Our tale is not like the horizon over the sea, a single line that might be traced, but a constellation, a scattering of silver points through which our history is woven. Still, when I think of how it all started, I think of two nights. The first is the night I poisoned Elias.

The second is this.

• • •

Our jabs continued, traded back and forth like playing cards. I would mention Gellert and feel Elias' heart swell. He would refer to my inexperience and watch me redden. We were like two dancers circling each other before that initial meeting of hands, the music lifting, our brows beginning to sweat. Like our exchange of books, our banter was becoming a game of sorts, a meeting of wills, though I chose to ignore the underlying tension, or consider why it felt so much like anticipation.

During the day, I began saddling one of Elias' horses to roam the land. I was hunting for something, I was not sure exactly what. A new ingredient. A root or thorn or leaf. Elias and I had tested the *eithier* twice more, but I had come as far as seemed possible and was still unable to make the change permanent. My frustration continued to rise. What poison had no cure? Surely my mother had not created greater harm than I could fix. I felt pitted against her, my power versus hers. Who was the stronger witch between us? Who would win, in the end?

My eyes strayed across the field to the forest. Not for the first time, I imagined venturing straight into its heart, farther than I had ever dared. Did my answer lay somewhere in the forest's depths? Or were those trees simply luring me like an anglerfish lures the eel? I could sense the power of the woods straining against their invisible bonds, and though I was tempted to uncover their mysteries once and for all, better sense warned me away. I did not want to be like the truth serum maker, too foolish to recognize my limit.

At night, I returned from my field wanderings, my hands full of speckled clover, my pockets stuffed with berries. I'd hurry though the door and sweep an anxious look around my workshop, checking that the windows were still intact, the bottles in their rows. Though I kept my chamber doors locked, that had hardly stopped my aggressors the last time. If they wanted to punish me again for the time I was spending with Elias, they would find a way. Really, it seemed inevitable.

I frowned at my sages and petals, the briars clinging to my skirts. I let out a slow breath, like a dragon waking.

I returned to my original poisons, the ones I had written off as failures. I recreated those concoctions, lining them up in beakers along my new worktable. There was soap to disorient, gel to halt motor function, cream to cause blindness. There were mild toxins with small effects and stronger brews with larger ones, and under a loose floorboard below the wash bin were my true poisons, foxseed and liverhex and anthiem, the ones to bring death. I gathered those vials as a squirrel gathers nuts, though I knew I would not put them to use. Not then. I did not wish death on anyone, then.

I outfitted my shop with a few well-placed traps at the windows and doors. If an intruder attempted to enter, they would inhale a face full of my newly-created anthem powder, which caused the recipient to fall into an instant coma. Though the effects were generally harmless and would wear off within the day, the powder made one look as though the victim had dropped dead. All the signs were there, the rigor mortis, the bloating, the releasing of one's bowels. It was a frightening thing to experience, even more frightening to witness. Which was, of course, the point.

I walked the palace halls with my chin lifted. Though I told no one of my brews or traps, the evidence of their power was written over me, and courtiers are nothing if not attuned to power. They gave me a wide berth, their ears dragging with baubles, hair piled so high as to bend their necks. Had I ever truly feared them? I remembered my mother, how she had sat in the great hall like a queen, surrounded by men and women falling to their knees at her feet. *Freestones are not servants*, my mother had once lectured me, *but keepers of an old and forceful craft. The only position higher than ours is the royal family itself. As such, there are many who envy our status and wish to undermine us. What have I always told you about power? Without it, we are prisoners. Yet the only way to have power is to take it; the only way to keep power is to fight.*

Days passed. My confidence grew. I wondered, if I reached my chamber and found my aggressor's body comatose at the door, would I leave them where they had fallen? Or would I call upon a footman to have them removed? Leave them, I thought. Word will spread better that way.

It took twelve nights.

I was returning from my usual reading with Elias, my nose deep in a book. I reached the antechamber that led to my rooms when my shoe hit something soft. There was a wheeze. I looked down. The book went loose in my hands.

I hardly recognized her. Hermapate's skin looked like overworked dough; her hair frayed from its confection. My healer brain instantly sprang to action, cataloging causes and possible remedies, until I remembered it was I who had set the trap, and my sleeping powder that made her so. I paused, forcing my feet to stay. The air smelled of urine and sour skin. The door to my chamber was thrown open, though this time it had not been forced—I had not wanted them to smash another lock, so I left up the bolt. I was like a spider drawing in her prey, but there was no shame in me. Only grim vindication.

I stepped over Hermapate's body as if she was a doormat.

The following morning, Hermapate was gone, my shop untouched. When I arrived to the great hall for breakfast, Ophelia caught my eye. "Selene. You are looking well."

This time, there was no sarcasm in her.

She continued, "I have heard the strangest tale. One of the queen's ladies dropped dead last night, only to rise again by morning. They say she has been cursed, like the prince from *The River of Reversal*. She has fled the palace for shame."

"Really." I poured myself a cup of tea. "How terrible."

Ophelia arched a knowing brow. "It was said to have happened outside your chamber door."

"Is that so?"

"It seems she might have been trying to break into your rooms." Ophelia's amusement rose. "Do you truly know nothing of this?"

I sipped my tea. "I cannot be responsible for every odd thing that happens within my vicinity."

A laugh. "You *are* well."

"That reminds me," I said. "There is someone I would like you to meet."

Kurton was shy at first, his movements at odds with his towering figure. He spoke in a lowered voice, as if worried his regular boom might offend Ophelia. And yet, she was so enthusiastic that he soon felt comfortable speaking at his normal volume, his laughter eclipsed only by hers. It filled me with a strange sense of rightness to see them there together. That rightness was followed by another feeling, one that had me thinking of a library, and a low-glowing fire, and tiger eyes illuminated in the dark.

I retired early that night, undressing before my mirror. My hands lingered over my hair, my simple clothes, the healer's brooch at my breast. Queen Althea had eventually replaced the sunstone dove with a red ruby encircled by a crown, which was the traditional symbol for a healer. The token was meant to mark my position as the royal physician, a person dedicated to healing.

I wandered my chambers, checking my powder traps, listening for hidden heartbeats. I wondered if word of what I had done to Hermapate would reach Elias, as it had reached Ophelia. The thought filled me with belated worry. I had poisoned a courtier. Would the incident reveal my true capabilities? Would it raise new suspicions about my role in the king's poisoning? I imagined Elias calling me to his rooms, the way his face would shift as he took in this new side of me. *Tell me why you did it.*

I was tired of being helpless, I would reply. *I was tired of letting others decide.*

But as the next day came, and the next, and I woke and dressed and carried on my duties, no one confronted me. Perhaps the palace had liked Hermapate's flair for viciousness and assumed if I bested her, I must be the better villain. Or maybe they truly believed I had nothing to do with it.

The spring days lengthened; the air smelled of rain and weeds. I dressed each day in boots and trousers, a simple braid for my hair. I left the healer's brooch where it rested on my nightstand. I never wore it again.

TWENTY-FOUR

Later that spring, Elias oversaw a hearing called the grim-moon. Twice a year, at midspring and midautumn, the crown hosted the event to settle matters that could not be resolved in the lower courts. The grim-moon was a public affair, well attended, and though Elias would remain seated for its majority, we discussed whether he should take a dose of *eithier* so he could stand to greet each new attendee. In the end, Elias decided against it.

"That potion has a way of meddling with my thoughts," he said. "The lack of pain...it is almost too liberating. Like I lose control of my inhibitions. That is all good and well on a normal day, but for this, I need a clear head."

Unlike most royal undertakings, the grim-moon was hosted not in the stateroom but in the great hall, where guests could first avail themselves of the kitchen's best offerings. This was meant to ease some of the formalities and stymie the tension, which was said to help settle arguments more easily. Though the day was still early, the hall was already crowded and smelled strongly of bodies and fires, soot and yeast. Servants brought trays of hot pastries and steaming cups of *kriva*, and the guests partook with enthusiasm, many drawing from personal flasks dangling at their belts. Elias sat in his chair at the head of the center table, his mother in her usual place to his right. The king's uncle Toromond was in attendance, and Hobore too, looking slim and subdued. When Elias offered me the seat to his left, I caught the look in Althea's face. She was frowning, her gaze darting between us. I knew Elias was trying to prove a point, but I had stirred up enough trouble lately with my traps and Hermapate, and I thought it best not to push my luck. I told Elias I preferred to stand.

The grim-moon proceedings were surprisingly civil, even for the most heinous accusations: theft, adultery, armed assault. Elias was a fair arbitrator, logical and efficient. Only once did the trials grow heated, one family accusing another of meddling in their daughter's courtship. This had apparently come to a head when a lowborn son asked the lady for the first dance at a midspring ball. Elias handled the dispute using the same calming tones he sometimes used with me. The matter was settled, the sons pulled into line, and both families walked away with their honor intact.

"I do not understand," I said in the interim between cases, coming to stand beside Elias' chair. "Why does it matter who dances with whom?"

Elias shot me a sideways glance. Behind him, his mother and uncle were in discussion, Hobore staring moodily at nothing. "Have you ever been to a ball?"

I tried to shrug as if the answer was of no consequence. "No."

"Dancing is a kind of language. A ritual. But there are rules. If a man asks an unwed woman for the first dance, it means he is romantically interested in her. It is a public statement of courtship. Yet what if this woman has already been promised to someone else? What if she accepts the dance anyway? Now there is a feud."

"So it is her fault," I said. "Such a woman should be more discerning."

"It is not so simple. Perhaps the woman has her own desires, which are different from her family's. Maybe she is unable to express them outright, and so accepting a dance from her true love interest is her way of stating her own intentions, or of rebuffing another courtship."

I looked across the hall, trying to wrap my mind around this convoluted explanation. I wondered how well I would fare if ever I was invited to a ball. I would probably make a fool of myself, or give the wrong impression. Not that I need worry about that; my social schedule was as empty as ever.

"How do you know so much about this?" I asked Elias. "I have never seen you dance."

"A king who uses a wheelchair and is averse to human touch." He turned his green-gold eyes to the cup of *kriva* on the table before him. "No, I suppose you haven't."

I flushed scarlet. "Elias. You know I didn't—"

"It's fine," he cut in, then turned to greet the next citizen, ending the discussion.

A man came forward. He was middle-aged, assured in his movements. His clothes were fit for a prince, his boots made of supple leather, sleeves and collar ornately embroidered. He wore a dagger at his waist, and his hair was cut short, close enough to see the scalp. "I come bearing a request of a different nature."

The great hall, which had been filled with the din of voices and clattering silverware, hushed.

"I am a merchant," said the man. "I make my living selling the world's marvels to those who understand their worth. I have traveled through each of our great continents, and many seas besides, and have witnessed miracles fit for dreams. Only recently, after twenty years away, I returned to my childhood home. I met with old friends, and we laughed and toasted, yet there was one friend missing."

The crowd leaned forward. This was not the way grim-moons usually went, yet the merchant was an expert storyteller and had his audience captured.

"Ularis was my missing friend's name," the merchant said. "As a boy, he was my dearest companion. I asked after him, but oddly, no one wished to disclose his whereabouts. Only after much insistence was I directed to a cottage on a hill some distance from town. I set off that very night, yet the moment I saw Ularis, I could not believe my eyes. In twenty years, he had not aged a day."

Murmurs, then. I saw people lean into one another, knocking elbows and grinning. This was a tale, clearly fabricated, and though storytelling had no official place among the grim-moon, the morning had been long and, at points, dull. The court was eager for a break, and they loved nothing if not a good tale. Elias was motionless in his seat. I glanced at his face and was startled by its intensity.

"At first," said the merchant, "Ularis did not seem to recognize me. Then he said, *Qyre, is that you? But you have grown so quickly!* I was confused. I had aged as normal; it was he who remained unchanged. We sat and talked, and eventually I came to understand that Ularis had not failed to age. Rather, he had gone back in time, though he did not remember the event. I learned, too, how this time-turnaround occurred. The River of Reversal."

There was a rush of excited chatter. *The River of Reversal* was a long-standing favorite among the people of Isla. It had inspired many offshoot tales, some nearly as popular as the original. This story, however, was new.

"I have seen almost every corner of the world, Your Majesty," Qyre continued, spreading his palms. "Though legends differ from country to country, there is one we all share." He took a step forward, and the depth of his expression seemed to emerge, like sunlight touching a jewel. "Like you, I grew up hearing tales of the River. They say if you step into its waters, you can reverse the very fabric of your life. Many believe it is a mere story, but if you travel as I have, you begin to see patterns: old men reverted to children, knights with wounds undone, troubled lovers rediscovering happiness. All my life I have wondered, what if the River is not just a tale? What if it exists? After seeing my friend Ularis, I am convinced. I believe the River is real, and I wish to find it. To map its path and bathe in its waters and, of course, share the knowledge I uncover with you, Your Majesty. I have the ship to make the journey, but not the funds. I will need a strong crew, and warriors to fight the monsters that lay in my path. I come here today to ask these things from you."

The gatherers were no longer grinning. *Can he be serious?* someone whispered. *No, surely not.* The audience had thought this was only a story, an entertaining reprieve from the tedium of the grim-moon, but now the merchant was asking for resources?

Elias spoke into the silence. "The River does not exist."

"I believe it does," Qyre continued valiantly, "and I am willing to risk my life to prove it. I only need a benefactor. The goodwill of the crown, and perhaps a blessing from the Goddess, to see me through."

"My son," said Althea. It was the first time she had spoken directly to Elias since the start of the hearings. "I counsel you to give this man no credit. The River is just a tale. We cannot be wasting our resources on such a mission."

For once, the queen and I were in agreement. It would be absurd to grant Qyre's request. Elias did not know this merchant—he could be a madman, or an enemy sent to bleed our assets. Even if Qyre was honest in his purpose, it was as Althea said. The River of Reversal did not exist. Yet Elias hesitated.

"Brother," said Hobore. He was entirely out of line to speak, yet no one did anything to stop him. "You cannot be considering this."

"I am hearing his case, as I have heard everyone's."

"This man speaks of our warriors as if they are steeds to be loaned. And the gold he demands? If he had brought his proposal to the Master of Coin, he would have been laughed out of the room. He is using the grim-moon to bypass the usual means of inquiry."

Qyre stood serenely, waiting. The gatherers shuffled and murmured. Elias turned to me.

Like Hobore, I was not there to give council; it was wrong for the king to seek my opinion so openly. The moment our gazes met, I could feel the room shift again, like an agitated snake curling in on itself. Althea stiffened. Toromond frowned.

I gave the smallest shake of my head.

"I must heed the council of my mother and brother," Elias said in diplomatic tones, turning back to Qyre. "My answer is no."

TWENTY-FIVE

After the grim-moon, there was a rush of new gossip, everyone speculating over the merchant's claims and the tense exchange between Althea and her son and Hobore and, of course, the way the entire episode had ended with my single headshake. The stories became more eccentric with each retelling, until people were swearing Qyre came bearing trinkets from the River, that he had been there himself and could prove its existence, but I had used my witchcraft to thwart the man in order to prevent Elias from ever journeying to the River himself. Althea finally managed to put an end to these stories, reinstating order among her court. She did not do it to protect me—I was under no illusions. When she caught my eye in the great hall, hers were troubled, but nothing more was said.

Things settled down after that. The palace was turning toward the summer harvest, our busiest season, and soon there was no room for talk of the lavish merchant or his far-flung requests. Yet neither Qyre nor his story were forgotten. Not entirely.

．．．

We were in the king's library one late-spring evening, Elias in his wheelchair and I on a nearby pile of floor pillows. The fires had died to embers, the clocks ticking. I was taking notes from my encyclopedia, though I had lost my place on the page some time ago and was making no effort to get it back. The evening had dimmed to shadows; my eyes were heavy. The black font warped on the page.

Elias was watching me. He had been observing me for some time. I roused myself. "Elias?"

He did not immediately speak. He traced a finger along the arm of the chair. "Princess Mora arrives tomorrow."

I sat up, the book tumbling. "What? Tomorrow? Why was I not told of this?"

"Should it matter?"

A laugh caught in my throat. Should it matter? "You are not yet recovered. I thought the queen wanted to wait until…" I had to recover my breath. "Until you could walk again."

"I can stand with the help of your *eithier*. It might be as far as I'll ever come." His expression was unreadable when he added, "My mother believes the princess' visit is overdue. She wants to reunite us, and to bring our people together in feast. Our engagement will endure for some years yet, but that does not mean we must ignore each other until the wedding day."

My heart plummeted at his words. *The wedding day.*

I had known this was coming. I had always known. Yet somehow, hearing it then was like waking from a dream. Elias was engaged to another. A princess, someone whose status was equal to his. They would be married, and go on to live their lives together, and my place in Elias' life would shrink down to nothing. I swallowed my dismay. "You should have told me before."

Those tiger eyes. "I am telling you now."

Princess Mora arrived the following morning. She came in a white carriage woven with flowers, her entourage fanning behind her like the train of a gown. I watched from a high window as men and women crowded the courtyard, the princess's personal assembly of vassals and couriers and lords and maidens. Their bodies were hunched and travel-weary, but their faces appeared eager as they took in our lush lawns, the spring rosebushes. They exchanged glances, flashing their teeth.

I welled with protectiveness. Our home was not a clothing shop where you might run your fingers along the fabric. It was not for sale. I wished to shut those newcomers out, send them back from where they had come. I clenched my jaw and shut the curtains instead.

A feast would be held that night to welcome our guests. I spent the preceding hours in my chambers, unable to focus on any one task. I wanted to go to Elias, but I knew he would be with the princess. The thought dug into some soft, vulnerable place.

It was a relief when a knock sounded at my door. A servant had been sent for a dose of *eithier*, which Elias would take before the gathering; unlike the grim-moon, this event would require him to stand, mind-altering side effects or no. I had the vial ready, but when I collected it from its place in my bedroom dresser and made to exit my chambers, the servant held out a hand. "I will take it."

I clutched the vial as if he might snatch it from my grip. "I am the royal physician. It is my duty to deliver the king his medicine."

"His Majesty's orders were clear." The servant was old enough to be my grandfather. He gave a weak smile. "He wishes not to see you."

My voice was sharp. "He said that?"

"Not in so many words. But his meaning was understood."

I felt choked. I was aware of the man's probing gaze and I wondered if he, too, believed me romantically involved with the king. Was he tallying my reactions to report back to his fellows? Would he try to bring me justice, as Hermapate had?

I held out the vial in loose fingers. He plucked it from my palm and was gone.

. . .

I considered seriously the idea of missing dinner. I could fake an illness. I could take a draught to make the illness real. I thought of my hidden collection of poisons, their hideous aftereffects, hives and warts and rashes. I could make my skin so pale as to be translucent, my teeth so brittle as to split and crack. I fingered my bottles, my mind running through the possibilities. Yet when the hour struck, I arrived to the great hall on time, exactly as I was.

My stomach churned with trepidation and reluctant curiosity. Elias and the princess had not yet arrived, and meanwhile, the guests mingled. Up close, I could see the people of Hillshire were not unlike us. I had imagined outsiders with strange clothes and unusual habits, but the princess's people fit well in Isla. In fact, once they disseminated into our halls, I could hardly tell us apart. That was discomforting. Though I did not like the idea of strangers in my home, I liked less the idea that they might belong better than me.

Wine was served. A string quartet played a merry tune. Queen Mother Althea stood at one end of the hall, the Queen of Hillshire beside her. The two women were of a height, and side by side they reminded me of the Hounds of Sundown, the wolves that must be trounced to reach the River of Reversal. I gave them a wide berth as I strolled the room's perimeter, attempting to steady my nerves. My ears were flooded with heartbeats; my eyes could not settle on any one thing. People observed me cagily, whispering in my wake.

I knew the moment he arrived by the subtle change in my own pulse. Seconds later, the entry doors swung wide, and the crowd gave a cheer. I turned to see Elias entering the great hall in his wheelchair, looking more the king than ever, and she at his side.

Her beauty cut me like a razor. From my window, I had only been able to discern the princess's general appearance, but now every detail came clearly into focus, that shining face, those perfect brows. Her hair was done in an elaborate weave; her cheeks glowed with health. I should have expected Princess Mora's beauty, and perhaps I had, yet the sight of it plain before me dug into a wound I had not even known I harbored. It was said Princess Mora's mother was chosen not only for her loveliness, but for the traits that would pair best with Hillshire's king. The princess's parents made a complementary match, and their daughter was the carefully crafted result. Apparently, this kind of matchmaking was common in Hillshire. The courtiers of Isla praised its brilliance, but all I could see was the ridiculousness. The Queen of Hillshire had been bred like a bitch, and the princess was the prize of the litter.

We sat for dinner. The entire Alder family was in attendance, minus Hobore, whose seat remained empty. I took my place halfway down the king's table, in the spot reserved for the royal physician. From this distant position, I could see Elias and his betrothed at the table's head but could not hear what was said. I tried not to watch too openly, but it was impossible to stop stealing glances. Elias murmured something into Princess Mora's ear. She giggled. He looked pleased. She smiled brightly. The whole scene was perfect, was it not? How convenient, that he had chosen to discover manners for her. Althea, it seemed, was happy with how the evening was progressing. She could be seen bestowing a rare smile on the couple. I stabbed at my broccoli.

I knew Elias had taken his *eithier* before the meal, which meant its effects would soon be setting in. Despite all my petty seething, I could not help but observe Elias' color, the angle of his spine, his hands and wrists. Had his pains begun to vanish? Were his muscles softening, unwinding, preparing to stand? And what of his mind, which he said became looser under the *eithier's* influence? I had a terrible vision of the toast arriving before Elias was ready, of him struggling to push out of his chair in front of all these people, or struggling to speak with the eloquence required from a king. I gripped my dinner knife. He was not ready. He needed more time. I would go to him, I thought, I would intervene…but at that moment, forks began to chime on glasses.

Elias stood as easily as if he did it every day.

There was a roar of fanfare. Princess Mora beamed. Elias gave a toast, which was unrehearsed yet sounded meaningful and sincere. He praised his mother for hosting the dinner, the gatherers for their attendance, the princess and her family for making the arduous journey across spring-wet roads. He did not so much as glance in my direction.

There was dancing. Elias declined to join—this was beyond his ability—but Princess Mora took heartily to the floor and was passed from one lord to the next. Her dress billowed around her. Her hands looked fragile and dainty and perfect. I clenched my own hands, feeling their scars. I wondered if Elias would allow the princess to touch him. He must, if she was to be his wife. But would it be difficult? Would he flinch away, as he flinched from me? I had a hard time imagining Elias submitting to anyone like that, but what did I know? Maybe he would welcome the princess's affections. Maybe Elias was not averse to physical touch when it came in the form of a glowing nymph.

"Find me a glass of wine," said a voice behind me.

I turned to see Hobore speaking to a servant at the edge of the room. It was a sign of my preoccupation that I had not heard him approach; though it was difficult for me to pick out individual heartbeats in a crowd of this size, his was one I always knew to listen for.

I looked closer. Hobore's boots were mud-splattered, his hair tousled. He had a riding crop tucked into his belt, as if he had arrived in a hurry and forgot to leave it at the stables. He caught me studying him, which surprised me into saying, "Where have you been?"

The servant reappeared with the requested wine. Hobore snatched up the glass and took a drink…and then kept drinking, until the wine was gone. He gave the glass back, wiped his mouth with the heel of his hand, and told the servant, "Another."

I thought of Hobore looking subdued at the grim-moon. I thought of a long-ago conversation between him and Elias, how Elias accused Hobore of entertaining an affair with a maid from the King's City. "You were meeting your lover," I said, drawing Hobore's attention back. "Is that why you are late?"

Hobore scowled. "It is impertinent to ask such a direct question."

"Did you quarrel with her?"

"No."

"You seem unwell."

"Do not doctor me," he said darkly. "You cannot fix this."

He stalked away just as the servant reappeared with the requested wine. The servant frowned at the glass, then looked at me. "Care for a drink?"

I was tired, suddenly, and oversaturated, and upset with Elias for reasons I did not wish to examine. I needed the quiet of my workshop, or the forest, yet I also did not want to need those things. I looked around the ballroom, at Princess Mora, the happily dancing couples.

You cannot fix this.

"Yes," I told the servant. He handed me Hobore's abandoned wine. I swallowed a gulp.

The quartet struck up a new song. More guests took to the floor. I finished Hobore's drink and found myself another. It occurred to me that I did not mind the taste of wine so much after all. In fact, by the end of my third cup, I decided the bitterness was quite agreeable. I was staring into the dregs when he approached. "Apologies for being so forward."

Gellert's head dipped as he gave a bow. He had traded his work overalls for trousers and shirt; his beard was neatly trimmed. I stared blearily at the top of his head, thinking I must have missed something. I did not know why he was apologizing.

He straightened, offering me his hand. "Would you do me the honor?"

Dancing. Gellert was asking me to dance. My heart thumped. "I… am no good at dancing."

"Neither am I."

I scrambled, trying to remember what Elias had said about first dances and unwed woman and intentions. "You would not wish to dance with me."

A crooked smile. "On the contrary, I wish it very much."

"Are you…" I blinked through the fuzziness. "Are you sure?"

"Why wouldn't I be?"

We stumbled to the dance floor. Gellert took my hand, his other coming to the small of my back. I glanced around the room, anxious and out of sorts. Had Gellert not seen the way I watched Elias, or how I spoke to Hobore, or how Althea was observing me from her spot across the hall? Did he really think I was a suitable dance partner? Surely this was a mistake. He could not really wish…yet when I looked into his face, my fears quieted. His eyes, I thought, were very blue indeed.

We danced. The room spun, all the colors blurring. I was stiff at first, unsure of my feet, but soon my reserves fell away and I was able to move with a bit less effort. There was a thrill in it. I had never danced with a man before, and I was as bad as I said, though Gellert was a liar—he was in fact quite competent, and guided us skillfully.

"Your earrings remind me of something," he said as we turned, brushing past other couples but somehow never colliding. "Have you heard of the famous Dorithian jewels? They are said to contain magical properties. Some, like these—" he touched the dangling stone, his palm brushing my cheek "—can even enhance the wearer's beauty. But of course, you would not need that."

The compliment flooded me with warmth. *You are too kind*, I might have replied, but it struck me as the sort of thing a doe-eyed courtier would say. I might be wearing pretty earrings, but I was not like that. "That is presumptuous of you," I replied instead, "to think I am not wearing a charm of my own."

"Are you?" His brow hiked. "Perhaps that is why you look even more lovely than usual."

"They do not call me a witch for nothing."

He laughed, friendly and open. "A witch indeed, to have me so enchanted."

I *did* turn doe-eyed, then. His compliment was better than the wine. I did not mind when he pulled me close. I did not mind when his leg brushed the inside of my thigh or his hips joined with mine. I would have allowed him to do anything to me. His attention was a balm to my wounds. It helped me forget, for a time, that I was unhappy.

The song came to an end, but Gellert did not drop my hand. "More wine?"

"Please."

He winked, which made me giggle. I remembered the princess giggling over Elias and my smile fell. But Gellert had already marched off.

"Selene."

I spun. Elias was there in his wheelchair on the edge of the dancefloor, his hair smoothed back, the curls coming to rest behind his ears. He wore a doublet and scarlet trousers; his shoes were polished to a shine. The formal attire reminded me of his father's statue. All those hard, perfect lines.

He said, "I think that is enough."

He was scowling. His mouth was a thin slant, his hands tight on his chair's wheels. I blinked. "What do you mean?"

"You're drunk."

Was I? I brought a hand to my neck to feel its warmth. "Nonsense."

"You have had three glasses of wine, and that boy is off to fetch you a fourth."

"Have you been counting?"

"You will drink no more."

Out of the corner of my eye, I saw heads turning. Our dispute was drawing attention. The quartet continued their spirited tune, the clink of glasses and laughter reverberating beneath the high painted ceiling. At the edge of the crowd, Gellert reappeared with our wine. He took one look at the king's face and ducked away.

I had known our dancing was an illusion. It was like holding a moth in your hand; you must keep your fingers loose so as not to crush it, yet the looser you hold, the more likely the moth is to escape. I felt as if I had just opened my hand to find my palm empty.

"Well," I said bitterly, "the king has spoken."

He wheeled closer. "Do not make a scene."

"I am celebrating your engagement."

"You are acting the fool."

My cheeks turned to fire. "I am in good company."

His mouth opened. "What did you say?"

"I said," I gritted, "*I am in good company.*" My voice rasped out of me. In my periphery, I could see Queen Althea marching our way, but I did not care. I was hurt; I was angry. I was losing control. "You call me a fool, but I am not the one watching a servant more closely than my own bride."

Elias went white; the nearby guests gaped. In those few words, it was as if all the rumors about us had become a mirror held to the light, fracturing around the hall a thousand ways.

Cold trickled through me. Queen Althea was nearly upon us, her face set for war. Elias was still staring at me. For a moment, I could only stare back. "I apologize," I finally breathed. "I didn't...I did not mean that."

I fled before anyone could stop me. My heart pounded; my hands were clammy and shaking. What was wrong with me? If I had to snap back—and why, why had I?—was that really the argument I had to choose? I could not have crafted a more damaging rebuke if I tried.

I pushed out of the great hall and marched toward my chambers, wiping my eyes roughly. Before, surrounded by noise and merriment, it had been difficult to notice the effects of the wine, but there in those quiet corridors it was easy to see the truth—I was indeed drunk. My stomach wobbled; my eyes rocked from thing to thing. I plowed forward, my shoulders finding the corners, my knees every sideboard. I had scarcely made it beyond the first corridor when I heard the scrape of wooden wheels against stone.

I took a deep breath, wishing him away. This was not the time for Elias to chase after me, not after what I had just said, but Elias was Elias, and would do exactly as he pleased. He wheeled to my side, but I could not look at him. My mortification lapped upon me like the shore, wave after relentless wave. I stumbled, and swallowed, and kept my gaze determinedly ahead. "If you care for me at all," I choked, "leave. Please. I do not trust myself to speak to you right now."

"And I do not trust you to be alone."

I threw him a bewildered look. "I will not harm myself."

"Not on purpose."

"I am not so drunk as that."

"No? Does that mean you stand by what you said?" When I struggled to answer, he switched his reply. "It is not merely you who might do harm."

My bewilderment grew. "Am I in danger, Elias?"

"No." His wheels hissed under his palms. His expression was fierce. "Not so long as I am here."

We reached my chambers. I might have probed him further, but my mind was like mist, unable to hold any one thought. I pushed through the small entryway and undid my anthem powder traps, leaving the door ajar behind me. I expected Elias to follow, yet he paused in the doorway. When I turned to look at him, his eyes were dark on mine.

It is the wine, I told myself, that is all. I stumbled to my bedroom. After a beat, I heard him follow. I began stripping off my clothes. These stupid earrings. Elias made a noise. "Selene."

"These are my chambers."

"Technically, they are mine."

"If you are uncomfortable, you may wait in the kitchen."

He did. When I reemerged and moved past him toward my workshop, he followed. "What are you doing?"

I did not answer. My hands seemed to know what ingredients I needed and found them easily. Gingerroot and orange blossom. Witherwart and *melises*. A dash of *istilla*, and the mortar and pestle. As I worked up a paste, Elias continued to watch. I scooped the concoction out with my fingers and swallowed it in one mouthful. It was tangy and bitter down my throat. The room snapped back into focus.

Elias' expression changed. "That," he said, "is useful. Did you invent it?"

"Yes."

Now that I was cured of my drunkenness, I almost wished I was not. Without the wine to blunt things, the intricacies of the evening came clear into focus. The princess. That dance. Elias here in my chambers.

His eyes roamed my workshop. This felt intensely personal, as it had not in my bedroom. I watched him examine this place, the way I had arranged my repaired pots, the cauldron fire always burning. I had the sense that something was coming undone, something I worried would hurt, like a bandage unraveled to reveal a fresh injury. Yet at the same time, I wanted to see the wound beneath.

"You keep it tidy," he said. I do not think that was what he wanted to say. They were words meant to stop himself from saying whatever he was truly thinking.

"What did you expect?"

"A mess." He flashed me a look. "I cannot say why. Perhaps I was hoping I might find some flaw in you."

I could not blame the wine this time. I was hot all over. "I have many flaws. You have always been quick to point them out."

"A regrettable habit."

I blushed. "Elias…"

"No." He cut me off. "Do not apologize."

"I insulted you before your guests. I made us both look like fools. Apparently, I have offended the people of Hillshire so deeply you worry for my safety. And what of the princess? She did not travel across the continent to be insulted in such a way." I toyed with my fingers, wondering if this was the moment I should suggest my own punishment, what punishment might be fitting. Yet I could think of nothing that would make me feel worse than I already did. "You should be furious with me."

"Oh, I am."

"You are not acting like it."

"That is because I am more angry with myself."

"Why?"

He did not answer. Instead he returned his gaze to my shelves. "Your father asked my father to have this workshop built for you shortly after you were born. Somehow, he knew you would need it. I came to see it after its construction. I was—what, nine years old? It was empty then, just a room, but I remember wishing to know what you might make of it."

"Yet you never returned." The king had not visited once, not since I was old enough to recall. "You could have. You could have seen this place any time."

He met my eye again. "I am here now."

Our gazes held. His pulse seemed to tug, insistently, at mine.

Where had all the air gone?

I took a step closer without consciously choosing to do so. His heartrate changed again, speeding like it did when he feared someone was about to touch him. I stopped. He saw me stop. Rubbed his face. "Selene."

I let out a shaky breath and said, "A moment ago, you told me you were angry with yourself."

He gave a slow nod.

"If something has upset you, it is my responsibility to know it. I am your physician."

"You," he said, "are more than just my physician."

Once, when I was perhaps eight years old, I caught my reflection in the window. I was working up a new concoction, absorbed in my work, and I noticed myself in the glass. I remember feeling startled by my own expression. I looked wretched. Stricken. I think all imaginative people have experienced this, that desperation that is only born of creativity. I cannot describe the feeling well, except that there are times when a thing is so meaningful it touches you in a hidden place, and makes you feel as if something has not only been gained, but lost as well.

That is how I felt with Elias in my workshop that night, confessing to me, with his princess just a few floors away. As if something had not only been gained, but also lost.

TWENTY-SIX

I kept my distance for the rest of the princess's visit. I feared Elias would wish to introduce us, and I would have to curtsy and compliment and fake a smile, but I shouldn't have worried. Elias seemed as eager to keep us apart as I was to stay away.

I could not, however, avoid trouble forever. On the morning of her scheduled departure, Princess Mora contracted a cold. Though her entourage included several healers from Hillshire, none of these seemed to appease her. She sent for me instead.

"The princess wants me?" I asked the messenger dumbly. We stood in the center of my garden where I had been deadheading rhododendrons. A storm was moving in; the sky was peppered with clouds. When the messenger tried to hand me the princess's summons, I merely stared. "Does she not have her own—?" I stopped when I caught the man's eye. As a royal messenger, he was well trained in the art of discretion, but I could hear his straining pulse. Like the footman sent to collect Elias' *eithier*, this messenger was noting my hesitations, collecting each reluctance to relay to his associates.

I cooled my expression into bored indifference. "I will deliver the remedy shortly."

I arrived to the princess's suite with my bag of simples in hand. The bedchamber smelled of fresh paint, having been redecorated to suit what was known of the lady's tastes. There were cut flowers rather than potted plants, tea rather than *kriva*, boughs of greenery above each door. The windows were stripped of their curtains, and the bed was outfitted with a sheer canopy tied back to reveal a mountain of pillows. Among these lay the princess.

"At last," she said dryly. "You are here."

Princess Mora rested with a damp cloth pressed to her forehead, her dressing gown buttoned modestly to her neck. Her lady's maid sat on a stool beside the bed, wringing out a spare towel. I could hear both their heartbeats, yet as I drew closer, I noticed a third, accompanied by a familiar change in my chest. I looked over to discover Elias standing at the room's opposite corner with a cane in hand, his wheelchair empty at his side. He saw my open shock and gave a small smile. "Miss Freestone."

I blanched. It was all of it: the king there in the princess' private suite, the empty wheelchair, the cane. After the welcome dinner, I had given Elias several vials of *eithier* to be used during the princess's visit however he saw fit. He knew how to take the formula safely, and I had seen him stand before, but...there was something about his effortless composure, compounded with his presence in a place I had not expected, that had me teetering.

"She works alone?" Mora asked, pulling back my attention. "In Hillshire, our healers work in groups to be sure nothing is missed. How can we be certain your physician knows what is needed?"

"Selene is capable," Elias said simply.

"Forgive me for saying so, but she does not look it. And what is wrong with her hands?"

I had begun pulling the prepared draught from my travel kit, but I paused at that.

Elias said, "There is nothing wrong with Selene's hands."

"She has more scars than skin. And I have heard talk—"

"People always talk," Elias interrupted. "It is of no concern to us."

Mora gave a thick sigh. "Well," she told me. "Go on, then."

I extracted the rest of what I needed from my bag, snapping the clasp with a hard *click*. I thought, for a half second, of my vast collection of poisons.

I began my examination, asking the princess about her symptoms and medical history, checking her temperature, listening for her heartbeat. Up close, the princess's beauty was less like a razor and more like a noose, the kind to wrap around your neck and squeeze. She was younger than I had imagined, only a few years older than me, yet she held herself with all of the authority of a woman used to giving orders. Eager to be done, I finished my examination and tucked the draught back into my kit. "You are well."

"Oh," she frowned. "Do not tell me you are one of those who believes yourself able to heal with a touch?"

"No." I could feel Elias' eyes on me. "I am saying there is no need for me to heal you, because you are not sick."

"What do you mean? Of course I am."

A lie. I would have known it anyway—her skin was a healthy color, her nose unstuffed, with no scent of fever, or even any pallor—but the lie was confirmed by the sound of her pulse picking up pace. As if sensing my thoughts, she bristled and asked, "Do you accuse me of dishonesty?"

"I accuse you of nothing. I am here to give you the facts, and the fact is you are in good health. It is happy news. Now your travel plans may remain as they were."

The princess rounded on Elias. "This is absurd. Your physician is clearly undertrained if she cannot spot something so simple as a cold."

Elias was unfazed. "If Miss Freestone says you are well, then you are well."

I had only a moment to register the princess's shock before Elias looked at me and said, "Thank you, Selene. I will escort you out."

Though the *eithier* allowed Elias to stand, walking with any amount of composure was still beyond his ability, so he returned to his wheelchair, balancing his cane across his knees before leading the way out. As soon as the door was shut behind us, I rounded on him. "You knew she was not sick."

Another tight smile. "It is not my place to tell her so."

"You are the King of Isla."

"And she will be queen."

That sucked the fight right out of me. Elias noticed. He opened his mouth, looking apologetic, but I spoke quickly over him. "If the princess wanted to postpone her trip home, she did not have to fake an illness."

"That is not why she did it."

"No?"

"She wanted to meet you."

I shook my head. "She has no reason to want that."

"Yes, she does."

Why? I could feel the question hanging between us. Elias was still watching me. I realized he had anticipated the princess's jealousy, the confrontation. *That* was why he had come. Which meant he was not as oblivious to the rumors as I thought.

I crossed my arms. "You should have warned me."

"I would have," he admitted. "There was not time."

"It does not take long to write a letter."

"Or to read one," Elias quipped. "Do you trust the messengers to keep their eyes to themselves?"

No, I did not. There were techniques to opening and resealing envelopes without trace, though the couriers need not bother with that; Elias and I delivered our letters unsealed.

I shook my head and grumbled, "You should keep a better handle on your staff."

"Oh? And what method do you suggest?"

Once, he might have made an example of someone, as his captain had done with the young soldier. Elias seemed to read my thoughts. His mouth tipped down. "I wish," he said, "to inspire loyalty. Not demand it."

After he departed, I headed to the forest. The air smelled of hyacinth blooms, the grass shifting under my feet. I had walked this path so many times, I could find my way with my eyes closed. The cherry trees, pretty and pink. The birch with their paperwhite limbs. The green spring valley that would brown in summer, the hunting hawks hanging on the wind. I had named each of these things mine, these elements of the world that spoke to me and seemed to call me home, but the truth is none of it was mine, not the trees or valley, not the flowers or forest, and least of all the man who ruled them.

A familiar feeling was lifting within me. It was the same way I felt when I made a mistake brewing potions. My hand would slip, and the burning cauldron would scald me. I would pull back, hissing, wanting to accuse the fire for being too hot, the cauldron for being too big. Yet I knew where the true blame lay.

I thought of my destroyed workshop. Hermapate's limp body, the shifting eyes of passersby. How even though everyone believed the wrong thing of me, they were too close to being right. I had wanted proof that someone cared for me, and now that I had it, I was faced with that old, sickening feeling: that all my life I had been wanting the wrong things.

...

The princess postponed her departure, despite my assessment of good health. She was courteous to the Queen Mother and approved of her handling of the staff, though nonetheless made it clear she would have her own way of running things once she became queen. Mora was kind to the servants and even came bearing gifts for the palace children, little baubles and forest animals carved from wood. She wished to avoid me, I could tell, and Elias never sent for me again while she was around, which was often—she passed most days at his side. I was not present for much of it, though I did happen to see them together once, walking the path near the forest. Elias' face was firm, hers intent. I watched from the safety of the trees, looking for signs of affection, tenderness, anything. Yet they seemed to be in disagreement.

The princess departed late one summer morning. It would have been a relief, if not for the uncomfortable sense that her visit had changed something fundamental between Elias and me. A crack in the foundation. Still, we settled back into our routines as best we could. I was once again the devoted caretaker, and Elias was unfailingly polite. We spoke around each other, please and thank you and oh yes and if you would?

Our words seemed to run together, rising like rainwater in a river. I wondered what would happen when the banks could no longer contain us. I felt any moment we would overflow.

I stayed busy, working to uncover the missing ingredient for my *eithier*, that final element to make its healing permanent. I kept thinking if only I dove deeply enough into the task, the rest could be forgotten. And yet, my old trick of hiding in my experiments no longer seemed to work. I was constantly lifting my head, looking through my workroom window over the soft lawns, the pastures, the fields scattered with bundled straw. It was misery to be so unfocused. The days moved at an agonizing pace.

It was not until autumn rolled into winter that the princess's presence finally faded from our halls. The ladies stopped carrying her in their gossip, the men in their eyes. Elias never spoke of her, and no longer did she seem to stand between us. Yet still, that feeling. It was with me when I woke in the morning, when I ate and bathed and worked and slept. It was with me when Elias found me in my garden one afternoon and said, "The annual winter festival is in a few days' time."

I shaded my eyes against the sun. The wind was high; I had not heard him approach.

He said, "Do you remember the scene from *The River of Reversal* where the maiden reaches the Pass of Dire?"

It was one of the darker parts of the story, the last of the maiden's many trials. "Of course."

"That scene is the theme for this year's festival. There will be a reenactment. Everyone likes to dress up." A pause. "I will be attending."

I rose to my feet, brushing my knees. I knew all this. The festival was a favored tradition in Isla, and the tale of the River was integral to its success. It had not always been so—the festival was historically a time for prayer and reflection, and the retelling of *The River of Reversal* was a celebratory way to end the night—but over the years enthusiasm for the story had eclipsed the rituals, becoming the festival's main purpose. I knew Elias planned to attend this year. It would be his first festival in three winters. People had been anticipating it for weeks. "Did you mean to ask me a question?"

"Come with me."

My hands dropped to my sides. "To the festival?"

"Yes."

I had never been to the wintertime festival. I had imagined it, certainly: the rush of gaudy colors, the roads wet with snow, everyone dressed in their finest reds and blues. But the size of the crowds made me uncertain, and the noise, and the streets of the King's City, a labyrinth for getting lost. There were men in those streets who would take you, my mother once warned. *They will kidnap you, they will do worse.*

But of course, that is something every parent tells their child. I was not a child anymore, was I, afraid of monsters in the shadows? I had just celebrated my eighteenth birthday.

Still, I had other reasons for hesitating. "I am not sure it is wise for us to go together."

He searched my face. "Tell me why."

"You know why." When he gave me an expectant look, I sighed. "I am your servant, Elias."

"You are my friend."

"It is one thing to enjoy each other's company in the relative seclusion of the palace, but this is a public function. It is just—it's not proper. People will talk."

"People will talk no matter what we do."

It was as close as we had ever come to addressing the rumors. "If I accompany you to the festival, it will send the wrong message."

"Or it could show people the truth. That we have nothing to hide."

TWENTY-SEVEN

The morning of the festival, I stood before my mother's mirror, worrying my lip. How many times had I watched Persaphe stand in this very spot, preening? As a little girl, I longed to be like her. Then I had grown and began to resent my mother's easy beauty. And now?

Well, I was no golden sunrise. Doves would never sing for me. But I did not have to be such a clop, either. I could try.

I attempted to braid my hair in a crown. I wove the thick strands between themselves as I often wound roots for incense, tying it with a string in roughly the same way. I examined my handiwork. My head looked like a fuzzy nest, the strands already unwinding. How did other women manage it? Maybe my hair was too unkept for such styles. Too many years of abuse. Or maybe I was just doing it wrong.

Well, brush it then, and leave it be.

I found a comb and began working through the locks. I added a bit of mallow to help with the tangles, a dash of pressed oil to make it shine. Bolstered by the results, I rummaged through my mother's old cosmetics, dabbing a bit of red tint on my lips, kohl around my eyes. The effect was dramatic. I had always thought my eyes were too round, my lips too wide, everything ruddy and swollen as if I had been crying. Yet I no longer looked like I had been crying. I looked like a flower blown open.

A knock sounded at my door. I opened it to discover a package on the stoop wrapped in simple tissue. A note lay on top. *Wear this*, it read, in a hand I knew.

I tore open the tissue to reveal a dress. It was solid blue in color without embroidery or adornment, yet the stitching showed an obvious quality. The fabric seemed to move with the light, now blue, now sapphire, now so dark as to appear almost black. It was more lovely than anything I had ever owned.

I shucked off my tunic and trousers, racing to put it on. Most women would have worn a slip beneath the dress, with stockings and undergarments to keep themselves contained, but I did not own any of those things. I wore the dress like a kiss, right against my skin. The fabric was cotton, but it might have been silk for how it shimmered. I touched where it lay, running my fingers down my front, over the swell of my breasts, my hips. The length of the dress was perfect—its gifter had a precise eye for my proportions—and came with a matching cloak, thick but surprisingly lightweight, with slits in the sides through which my arms could show. Only children were meant to wear cloaks in this free-arm style, and maybe my gifter had thought it appropriate, but that was his mistake. I was no longer a child, and I did not look like one.

I stood before the mirror. I did not go so far as to spin in a circle, but I swung my hips to make the skirts dance around my ankles, then brought a hand to cover my smile. I thought maybe I understood what those courtiers were always on about after all.

...

The day of the festival split open like a fruit. As I walked through the palace halls, I passed dozens of women dressed like me, all of us meant to mimic the heroine from *The River of Reversal*, who wore blue as a symbol of the ocean city she called home—the opposite of fire, which was the demon's element. Some women took their costumes to the extreme, donning headdresses of rolling tulle waves and scarves of upholstered seaweed, their makeup done in swirling silver and white. The men, too, joined the fun, dressing in head-to-toe black with bright red capes, some sporting lipstick and painted white fangs.

I met Elias in the palace's entry courtyard. He was there waiting for me, his guardsmen standing around in a loose circle. Though Elias had not gone so far as to paint his face, he was dressed the part, wearing the red cape and pronged horns of the demon. His hair caught the sun; his eyes were alight with some joke Arch had just delivered. The merriment that infected the rest of the palace seemed to have touched these men as well, and Elias especially; no longer did he look like a poisoned king carrying the weight of the world, but like the careless prince he might have been.

Freesier was the first to greet me. "That looks well, *rahvika*."

Arch added, "You could have warned us you were going to show up looking like *that*."

"Arch," Kurton admonished. "That's no way to speak to a lady."

"Lady!" Arch threw up his hands. "Now she's a lady!"

I made a show of rolling my eyes, though in truth, I enjoyed this line of teasing. I felt as if I had taken a swig of wine, all the warmth flooding through me.

My giddiness drained when I caught the look on Elias' face. He was staring at me, his lips slightly parted, cheeks pink. Was it fever? Overexertion? I closed the remaining few steps between us, pitching my voice not to carry. "Elias? Are you unwell? There is color in your cheeks."

He swallowed. "I am fine."

"Is it the weather? It's cold out here, is it not, for such a bright day? I'll fetch you a thicker coat."

"Selene." He stopped me with a word. "Don't fuss. My coat is thick enough."

Yet I remained watchful as the King's Guard took up their places in front and behind and we made our way to the carriage at the end of the path. I had brought with me a vial of *eithier*, thinking Elias might like the chance to stand at certain junctions, particularly during the main *River* reenactment when the crowds would be at their thickest. On any other night, special accommodations would have been made for the king and his entourage, but this was the winter festival, where men and women shed their identities to play part in a larger story. Elias was to be treated as an equal.

When I offered him the vial, he shot me a look. "What's that for?"

"To help you enjoy yourself."

"Can I not enjoy myself as I am?"

His tone was clipped. I had offended him. "Of course you can. I was merely thinking of the crowds. Everyone will be standing."

"The crowds do not concern me." He turned his eyes ahead. "People will make room."

"For their king," I corrected gently, "but you are not a king tonight, remember?"

"I am always a king."

"Oh?" Again, I tried for lightheartedness. "I thought you were a demon."

"Are you really going to push?"

His words jolted me. "Of course not." I tucked away the vial, floundering. "I didn't mean to."

He wheeled himself into position beside the carriage. The stairs were tricky, but Elias had become better at managing himself and was able to pull his weight out of the wheelchair and into the cabin without help. Arch lifted the wheelchair into the carriage after us and helped secure it to the floor with straps. The door snapped shut, the four King's Guard mounted their horses, a command was given to the driver, and we were off.

I pulled my eyes around the cabin, its low paneled ceiling, the curtains hanging at each window. The wheelchair took up much of the floor space, meaning Elias and I had to sit on the benches opposite each other. They were close enough that our knees could have touched. The *eithier* sat like a brick in my pocket.

"Elias…"

"I hear the firebreathers will be performing again this year," he said, cutting off my apology. "They have been all the talk."

I understood his attempt to move on from my blunder, and guiltily, I was glad of it. "My father always said the firebreathers were a sight to behold."

"Did you not see them last year?"

"I…no."

"Everyone believes they are the act to beat."

"Everyone except you," I guessed.

He was unapologetic. "They are talented, make no mistake, but much of their act is showmanship. It is easy to dazzle with fire. The tightrope walkers, on the other hand. They have no extra flash or flourish. They do not even dress in colors—their uniforms are all black. When they perform, they perform with skill alone. Their talent is pure."

That was like him, I thought, to prefer the more honest entertainment. It was easy to be enraptured by showy tricks, but Elias had no wish to be dazzled. He liked to see things clearly.

"What do you think about the tightrope walkers?" he asked.

I looked out the window toward the palace, shrinking swiftly in the distance. "I wouldn't know."

"Have you not seen them either?" I fidgeted. Elias had that look on his face, the one when he was discovering things I rather wished he would not discover. "Selene." His tone was serious again. "Have you never been to the winter festival?"

I shrugged.

"Everyone goes to the festival." He spoke as if this was some fundamental truth. "I am the King of Isla and I go. How is it possible you've never been?"

I was beginning to wonder that myself. I knew I had been sheltered, and dedicated in my way, but these excuses sounded feeble even to my own ears. If not for my parents' abandonment, would I have remained closed away in my workshop, forever toiling over my medicines?

"Well." Elias sank back in his seat, bouncing a little with the movement of the carriage. "What do you want to see first?"

I touched my blue dress, which was a gift from him. "I want to see it all."

The King's City grew from the distance, rippling like a pond in the bottom of a depression. I had observed the city from the safety of my forest a thousand times, and had even visited with my father on occasion, yet as we drove through the gates into the bustling streets, I knew my memories did this place no justice. Everywhere, merchants and entertainers called to passersby, shaking out their wares for people to see. Servants, acrobats, commoners and holy men milled about, bickering, laughing, standing in wide-eyed fascination as the king's carriage passed. Nearly every storefront was adorned with wreaths or banners, and over the streets hung stained glass lamps in fragmented shades of red and blue.

The carriage traveled as far as it could before the crush of bodies became too thick and we could go no farther. With the help of the King's Guard, we went through the business of extracting Elias' wheelchair and getting him seated. As the crowd closed around us and the guardsmen faded into the background to keep watch, Elias shot me a smile. "Ready?"

I could not answer. My eyes flitted from the firecrackers, to the food vendors, to the live chickens darting between feet. It was difficult to know where to look; my excitement was beginning to feel more like overwhelm. I wanted to reach for Elias' hand, something to anchor me, though this thought quickly gave way to shame. Had I not just been thinking I was a grown woman? I did not need a hand to hold. I blinked up at the sky instead, trying to breathe through my dizziness. Elias' voice was soft at my side. "Grab my chair's handles."

I clenched my fists. "That is not necessary."

"It will prevent us from being separated."

I glanced at him, but my glance became a stare when I realized he was reaching for me. He seemed to realize what he had done and pulled back the hand. Yet his expression remained gentle. "I am only being practical."

We both knew his offer had nothing to do with practicalities, yet I found myself saying, "Alright."

My palm connected with his wheelchair, and I felt instantly better.

Stepping into the festival was like entering a portal to another world. An overdressed merchant haggled the price of a love potion. A flock of sheep trailed obediently after their herder. Children screeched and chased each other, dancing with ribbons on sticks. Some people recognized their king and bowed as he passed, but most did not. I wondered if that was normal—surely Elias could be easily identified—until I saw a woman jerk out of a curtsy. A man hailed a greeting that trailed into a mumble; eyes loitered and turned away. I realized the citizens did recognize their king, but they knew the rules of this day. At the wintertime festival, Elias was to be given no extra deference. He was a character in a story, just like the rest of us.

We wandered on, watching the firebreathers and tightrope walkers, the tumblers and contortionists and magicians. That last especially astounded me, and when the act was over, Elias introduced me to the magician himself. "Elias," the man exclaimed. "You are looking well, old friend."

"Artevos." Elias grinned. "Staying out of trouble, I hope?"

"Never." Artevos' face was set with powder, his sleeves long and trailing. He looked to be Elias' age. When he turned to me, I could hear his heartbeat quicken. "And who is your friend?"

"This is Selene."

Artevos bent a full bow, taking my hand for a kiss. His lips lingered over the back of my fingers. "You have a magician's hands, Miss Selene. Oh, do not be embarrassed. I mean only to compliment. I can tell you have performed many tricks with these hands. A performer such as myself has instincts for these things." My stomach shrank at his words. I tried to extract myself from his hold, but his grip was firm. "Have you ever considered joining a troupe?"

"Artevos," Elias interrupted. "Are you trying to poach my physician?"

"Your physician? Well. She would do wonders in the circus, my friend, that is all I am saying. There is something…enticing about her." His eyes slid to my bare arms, my hair. "The crowds would love her, I am telling you."

"No," I said a bit too sharply, at last reclaiming my hand. "I mean, thank you, but no."

"Very well, very well." Artevos flashed his performer's smile. "I will say no more about it."

After we departed, Elias threw me a look.

"What?"

"I am not sure it was wise introducing you to Artevos."

I huffed.

Elias laughed. "I know. He's a scoundrel. Artevos was born the son of a lord, yet when he came of age, he rejected his inheritance for life in the circus. We used to make trouble, the two of us, when we were children. Put our mothers through hell. My father, though. He never minded our antics. He used to say I should get it out of my system while I was young." I watched Elias, expecting to see his usual shadow descend, but he was smiling. "I do not think my father would have been so lenient if he knew the kind of trouble we were really up to, but it felt good to have him on my side."

"It is what every child wants," I said, looking out over the rooftops where I could see the spires of The Flame atop the Match, that great temple my own father had so admired. "To have their parent's support."

"All the more," Elias agreed, "when your parent is a king."

Evening was coming, the sky shot through with pink. Elias obtained two ales from one of the vendors. It amused me to see the king order ale like a normal person. He handed one to me and saw my hesitation. "It will not be like last time," he said.

I took a sip and was surprised by the drink's sweetness. "It tastes like butterscotch."

His smile was my favorite kind, the one that seemed to shine from within. "So you like it?"

Another sip, to hide my blush. "Yes."

Though the main performance of *The River of Reversal* would not take place until nightfall, a few smaller street troupes could be seen reenacting the best scenes. We stopped to watch one group perform the part where the maiden uses her enchanted robe to hide the demon-prince from a band of soulless horses. The actress was skilled enough, but the real showstopper was her cape, which shifted to blend seamlessly with the colors of the street. It seemed impossible. Like magic. My mind began spinning as it did when I worked my experiments, wondering what sort of chemicals had been infused into the fabric to create such an effect. I turned to Elias, intending to ask his opinion, yet paused at the look on his face. "Elias?"

"Would you do it?" he asked.

"Do what?"

"Step into the River."

Around us, the crowd compressed and parted, skating past like leaves in a breeze. Elias' question lodged in my chest. Would I choose to step into the River and become some former version of myself? And if so, how far back would I wish to go? According to the legend, the longer you stayed in the water, the more years were wiped away. Would I linger long enough to revert to my childhood, back before the poisoning? My infancy? Even if I could, going back would not undo my mark on the world. It would not undo the hurts I had caused Elias—only those that had been caused to me.

"You are asking the wrong question," I said briskly. "The demon did not choose to enter the River. The maiden made that decision for him. The real question is, would you choose it for me?"

"No," he said easily. "I would not choose the River for you."

The simplicity of his reply cracked something within me. I had not thought of my role in Elias' poisoning in a long time, too long, yet suddenly it was as if all my secrets had been given a mouth, which was Elias'. They stood before me, asking questions I could not answer. He said he would not change me, yet would he be so certain if he knew who I had been and what I had done?

I gazed into his face. I knew its lines better than my own: his full mouth, strong jaw, those green-gold eyes. It was the first time I ever considered telling Elias the truth.

"And you?" He swiveled his chair to face me fully. His expression was open, and full of trust. "Would you lead me into the River if given the chance?"

The sensation began in my fingers and worked its way up my arms. I was no longer aware of our separate pulses; it felt as if our hearts beat as one. "No," I said. "I prefer you just as you are."

...

The rest of the evening passed in a blur. Elias touched my ribs to draw my attention, now to that swooping eagle, now to that illusionist's trick, now to the man with the glowing red mask. It was not skin-to-skin contact—my dress and cloak acted as barriers. Yet each time his hand came in, I felt the touch slide through those layers as if sheer silk.

I looked at him freely. I had not realized how often I resisted doing this. Normally, such open looks would have felt too revealing, my eyes drawn to him again and again, yet that night I was already revealed, stripped back by the ale and merriment and the simple fact of Elias' happiness, lying upon him like the sun. There was nothing left for me to hide. Almost nothing.

We moved on. At first we pointed out the best costumes, laughing at the jesters and clowns, but as the evening wore on, we began spending less time watching the merriment and more time watching each other. Elias continued to reach for me, his fingers finding the inside of my wrist, my bare elbow, my hand. He was no longer drawing my attention to anything. There was no longer any fabric between us.

The sun dipped beyond the horizon, and a great clock struck the hour, indicating it was time for the main *River* reenactment, which would take place at an outdoor theater near the city's center. Elias and I gave our horse driver directions and piled back into the carriage. The door clicked closed, abruptly shutting out the noise. The curtains had been drawn shut; a tiny gas lamp provided the only illumination. I was winter-bitten and giddy, my ears numb from cold. I started to ask if Elias knew any of the actors putting on tonight's performance as he had known the magician, but I stopped at the look on his face.

He was staring at me in a way that made it impossible not to notice we were suddenly quite alone.

Both of our hearts were beating loudly, our hair tangled from the wind. The carriage had not yet lurched to motion, and outside the glass there was dulled chatter and music, laughter and applause. Here, though, all was silent.

It was the ale, I would tell myself later. The afterglow of the day. The way I had allowed myself, finally, to join the world, and be free.

I reached across the space to touch his face.

Elias went perfectly still. Slowly, I drew my thumb along his hairline, down his cheek. His skin was rough with stubble; his jaw was a bundle of clenched muscle. My fingers trembled, yet I continued my perusal. His hands were fists at his sides, his breathing strained. I could tell it was taking every ounce of his control to let me do this. He swallowed hard. "Selene."

He was begging me, for what I did not know. His eyes were molten, and I could see in them his torment mixed with desire, the want and loathing there together. My fingers hovered around his jawline, skating back toward his lips. That full, perfect mouth.

I did not know what I was doing. I had the vague thought that I might have lost my mind. I could smell his earthy scent, the soap he used to bathe. The heat of his breath warmed my fingers. "Close your eyes," I said.

I expected him to stop me then. *You do not*, he once said, *have permission to touch me.* Even if he consented to the physical contact, this was all wrong. I was the royal physician. He was my king, and engaged to another.

Except, Elias did not stop me. He did not say *no* or *wait*. He let out a breath that was almost plaintive, then did as I asked and closed his eyes.

His trust was like an offering to gods long extinct. My mind blanked, leaving no room for anything but the wild, foreign ache of desire. I moved automatically, rising from my seat to lean over him, bracing my palms against his thighs. My mouth hovered over his. It was not a kiss exactly, just the brushing of lips, but I could hear his pulse change again. His hand snaked up the back of my neck, sank into my hair. The ache was worse now. I wanted to grab his face and close the distance between us, but I held myself back, afraid I would push him too far, worried I had pushed him too far already.

He closed the distance for me.

His lips came to mine. He was gentle at first, searching. He ran his teeth along my bottom lip, dipped his tongue into my mouth. I made a gasping noise, and his fingers flexed against my hip at its sound. His breath went ragged, his mouth suddenly hungry. He pulled me down to him on the carriage bench, and I worked my palms under his cape, finding the jut of his ribs, the wings of his shoulders. We began moving in a kind of frenzy. I dragged him closer, desperate and needy as he shifted his hips upward, letting me feel him. My stomach pooled with warmth; my thighs began to shake. I had come awake in ways I had never known, and he was everywhere, everywhere.

"Wait," he said.

I stopped. His hair was a mess, his lips swollen. He looked at me and I saw his expression. Like he was in pain.

"Selene." My name again, different this time. He was no longer begging me.

I flushed from the crown of my head all the way to my toes. I felt dizzy, as if I had just woken from a dream to discover I was in freefall. It took me a moment to make my limbs cooperate; I removed myself from his lap. The carriage ceiling was not high enough to stand fully upright, so I had no choice but to return to the bench opposite him. My fingers curled around its lip.

He brought a hand to cover his eyes. "You must understand—"

"I understand," I cut in quickly. My mortification was building upon itself; the implications of what I had just done swelled through me. I tried to laugh but it came out choked. "I do not know what I was thinking. I should not have done that—I should never have—"

"What? No, Selene—"

"I am so sorry," I stammered before pushing open the carriage door and stepping out into the street. It took everything I had not to run.

TWENTY-EIGHT

Elias did not try to chase me down. I think a part of me had been hoping he might, that it would be like a story, the humbled prince rushing after his beloved. They were the kind of fantasies I wished I could quit.

I pressed forward. The air did not smell of Elias anymore, but of fried food and horse and bodies. I was glad for that. It was awful enough to finally acknowledge how I wanted him, to feel exactly the shape of him under my palms without the scent of him lingering, too. Yet perhaps his scent did linger, because as soon as I had the thought my mind conjured it perfectly, his earthy aroma, that sweet, smoky undertone. It did not matter how far I fled, how much distance I set between us. I had Elias memorized, down to the final hair.

I thought, I am such a fool.

I slowed. I was deep in the crowd, surrounded by the swell of activity. It rose, flooding up to my neck, my chin. I started in one direction and was blocked by a band of acrobats. Another, and a zebra pranced into my vision, her lips drawn back, teeth flashing. Clowns with over-smiling faces dipped forward, their laughter eerie and off-key. Before, the festival had been bright as a flame, yet as night continued to fall, the city shed its playfulness like a second skin. Or maybe that was not right. Maybe it was gaining a second skin, like a devil who comes to possess the living. The streets were the same yet different, brimming with newer, darker energy.

A prickling of my earlier trepidation. I could go back. Chase down the king's carriage, slip behind the safety of its paneled walls, and so what if I was humiliated? I could swallow my pride, say the kiss was an accident, say it was the ale, say nothing at all and pretend it had never happened. That's what I was good at, wasn't it? Pretending.

I elbowed stubbornly forward, ignoring people's complaints, slipping and dodging until I came to a space between two large tents. The canvas glowed yellow from the inside. Behind it, I could see the dark shapes of performers stripping out of their costumes. I inhaled the scents of sugar and oil. My last thought before it happened was, see? This is all you need, a place to clear your head.

A shadow moved at the edge of my vision. My only warning.

At once, someone was on me. A hand came around my mouth, a large form pressing against my back. I did not know what was happening. All the stories my mother told me about young girls being taken and maimed, all the stories I told myself—it was as if those memories had turned to crystal. I had a dozen nonsensical thoughts: someone had slipped and was catching me for balance, I myself had slipped and hit my head. But like a cat falling from a height, my mind quickly righted.

I was being attacked.

I struggled, my breath coming in terrified bursts. There were two of them, one on either side, pushing me deeper between the tents. I bit the hand that covered my mouth, tasted sweat and cigar. There was a hiss of pain, a low curse. A fist came across my face. The impact had me seeing stars.

They threw me to the ground. One of them was heavy on me, pinning my arms with his knees. A knife glistened in his hand, and I caught a glimpse of his rugged face in the wan light. He touched the edge of the blade to the sensitive skin under my eye. "Scream, and I'll gouge it out." He was hard against me, fumbling to undo his belt with his free hand. My skirts were up around my waist. His companion was standing behind us—what? On the lookout? Waiting his turn? I decided I did not much care about my vision. I screamed.

He brought the knife across my cheek. I do not know if it was an accident that he missed the eye, or some kind of mercy. The pain did not come at first. My hair was in my face, caught between my lips. The world swayed even as I fought with renewed vigor, kicking, twisting, bucking. He hit me again, hard enough to make me gasp. "Hold still."

I could not believe this was happening. A part of me refused to believe it. There were noises, the shift of fabric, the huff of an exhale. I tried to scream again, but he set his forearm against my neck, choking me to silence.

I thought of how we come into this world. The quiet safety of our mother's womb. How we do no harm and know no harm. I wondered, is there a single moment when it all changes? Or do we ease into our atrocities as you might ease into the ocean, step after step until your head is beneath the waves?

My assailant shifted again, and I heard the vial of *eithier* crack against my thigh, crushed by the weight of him over me. I could feel the glass digging into my skin through my pocket. I could move my arm from the elbows down. Not much. Enough.

I reached, grabbed the broken glass bottle, and jabbed it into his leg.

He made a surprised noise and pulled back, freeing my arm entirely. I brought the shard up in a wide arc and slammed it into his neck.

Blood spurted. It sprayed my face. He choked and reeled back, all his weight lifting away. It was not a killing blow. The shard was too small, the force behind my attack too weak. But the man did not know that. All he knew was he had been stabbed in the neck, and men died from neck wounds. In a tangle of undone trousers and spitting oaths, he and his companion fled.

I took a small gasp of air, rolled to my knees, and vomited.

It was several long seconds before my vision cleared. I looked down at myself. There was a lot of blood. Dripping over my cheek and neck. Across my palm where the glass had cut me as well as him. But not between my legs. I had stopped him, somehow, from delivering that fate.

"Selene?"

I heard the shout from a distance. I closed my eyes, tried to breathe slowly through my nose.

"Selene? Where are you?"

I wanted to laugh. I could feel it bubbling hysterically. I had wished for Elias to chase after me, and so he had. Maybe the Goddess had been listening. Maybe this was how she punished the damned: by twisting everything so tightly it could never be unwound.

I wiped my mouth and did not stand. I could hear the others then, hollers of King's Guard coming to find me. My legs were made of jelly. I was shaking so violently my teeth chattered. Blood plastered my hair to my cheek, but I was afraid to touch it. I had the sense if I touched it, I would never be the same again.

"Selene!" Freesier's voice was suddenly close. "She's here. I found her, she's here!"

The earth seemed to heave. I crouched as if in prayer, pressed my forehead to the cool dirt. I remembered how it felt to be poisoned, to stare into death's great chasm. This was nothing like that. I was awake, and brutally alive.

• • •

Freesier and Arch departed to hunt my attackers, their faces set for murder. The others took me to the House of Healers.

I did not speak. Not when Elias demanded to know what had happened and how and by whom. Not when Kurton gently put himself between us, set a calming hand to Elias' shoulder. We emerged back into the city streets, and I had to ball my hands into my skirts to stop myself from covering my face. I wanted to hide, and I hated myself for wanting that. I hated that I had reason to want it. I hated that I was so full of hate.

The House of Healers was a sanctuary set high on a hill, rising like a creature from a lake. There, women renounced their past lives to dedicate themselves to the craft, living and working under that pitched roof. All were welcome, either to seek aid or to take the healer's oaths, which could be claimed by anyone, no matter their history. The House turned none away.

I do not know what the House's headmistress thought at the sight of King Alder on her doorstep with a bloodied girl in tow. Maybe she, like me, was no longer affected by the carnage and shock of others. The woman's name was Ishmir, and she was all brusque efficiency, ushering us inside, instructing a young acolyte to guide me to a private room. There, I was situated on a slim bed and handed a cup of murky medicine. "To help with the pain," the young healer told me. It was a halftruth. Under the usual scent of the painkiller, I could smell the sharp, bitter stench of *treebore*, which was a sleeping agent.

I did not admit to noticing this. I did not say, I don't want to sleep. The gore was drying on my clothes. I felt slow and lightheaded, nauseous from the feel of so much blood. I downed the serum in a single gulp.

"You might feel a bit woozy," the acolyte explained. "You can lay back and close your eyes, if you like. We are going to have to stitch your face, and your hand. And..." She hesitated, choosing her words. "Are you hurt anywhere else?"

"No." My voice was cotton. The cup hung loose in my fingers. "Only as you see."

She examined me anyway, her fingers warm on my skin. I had to work not to recoil from her touch. After, she left to fetch a bone needle and thread, leaving the door cracked. For a short time, the hall outside was quiet. Then came Elias' voice, floating from somewhere out of sight. "I want to see her."

"Your Majesty," came Ishmir's reply, "with all respect, we do not allow visitors into our healing chambers."

"You will make an exception."

"Your physician is in a state of shock. She needs the calm, sure presence of our healers and not—forgive me—a distraught monarch. Think of what is best for her."

"I am what's best—" His voice caught horribly. "Give her the choice, at least. Ask her...ask if she wants me there."

There was a pause. "How much do you know about the attack?"

I could imagine Elias' scowl. "What do you mean, how much?"

"It was a man who assaulted her," the headmistress said, her tone quiet but firm. "Maybe multiple men. There was a struggle. It appears they had a knife, or some sort of dagger, but the fighting must have gone beyond that. My healer reports that Selene's scrapes are...extensive."

"I did not see any scrapes."

Another pause. "You would not have."

I felt, in that silence, the moment Elias understood.

I had not been able to sense his pulse before. Now it shot through me, straight as an arrow. He let out a string of curses, and there was a rough noise, like the quick turn of wheels on stone. "No," he growled, "for love of the Goddess, *no.*"

"This is a delicate matter," Ishmir replied. "I say this out of respect to you, Your Majesty. Selene was not hurt in the way you are imagining. She fought to escape. Yet she was still attacked, and brutally. Right now, she needs trained hands, and medicine, and the presence of women. We can provide those things, if you would allow us…"

I did not hear the rest. Everything was going hazy and dark. The empty cup of *treebore* was still in my hand. It had turned sticky with my blood.

I closed my eyes and leaned back, willing the medicine to do its work.

She fought to escape.

My skin was crawling as if with ants. I had the strange yet vivid thought that no matter how hard I scrubbed, I would never be clean again. I might have emerged from the incident intact, yet I felt as if the worst had happened anyway.

I did not know then, but it hadn't.

TWENTY-NINE

I woke later that same night in the bed assigned to me by Ishmir, in a room set off the House's main hall. I did not immediately stir upon waking. My sleep had not been sound, but it was complete, and blessedly empty of dreams. I kept my eyes closed in hopes that I might return to that empty place. I wanted unknowing. I wanted the sweet oblivion of the Goddess' sister void.

Sleep, however, was determined to evade me. It slipped away, leaving nothing but an imprint of memories and frazzled pain. My head pounded; my face stung. Slowly, eyes still closed, I brought a fumbling hand to touch the seam along my cheek.

Thirteen stitches. I counted them with my forefinger one by one.

I came more awake. There was a stale, metallic taste in my mouth. Blood, I thought, but no—it was the aftertaste of the *treebore*, the drug administered by that young acolyte to induce sleep. I knew its properties well. Indeed, I could brew it myself. Yet this was an old medicine. Outdated, even.

The knowledge came thickly. *Treebore* had been invented by my grandmother. I considered that detail, which felt suddenly big as the sun. I considered the sutures in my face, which were perfect, each a tight little knot.

The realization fell into me like a rock into a well. I knew these knots. I knew the one who made them.

I sat up quickly enough to make me dizzy, and saw her.

My mother looked exactly as she had on the day she left four years ago. Delicate collarbones, smooth hands, all the pretty fawn-lines of her figure. She sat in a wing-backed chair across the room, her ankles crossed beneath the fabric of her red robes.

I felt as if I had swallowed a blade. "Take them out."

"Have you hit your head? Do not be foolish."

There was a smell on her I could not place, a stringent mix of bitter orange and acidity. I wondered if she was drugged. I wondered if I still was. It would explain the insanity of this moment. "I want no mark of yours on me."

She had stitched my face. I knew the shape of the seam, which she herself had taught me. None other could make it so perfect. And the *treebore*, too—a recipe my mother would favor, despite its antiquity, as it came from our lineage.

My mind struggled, scrambling to fill in the rest. Persaphe was wearing the red robes that marked her as a member of the House of Healers. Could it be that she sought asylum here? Had she been living in the King's City all this time? The House accepted any into their ranks, but they were not secret keepers. News of the royal physician's reappearance at the House should have flown through the gossip circles and reached the palace within the day. Yet I had heard nothing.

"Never mind," I said. "I will tear them out myself."

"You will scar."

I gave a cracked, feverish laugh. Only Persaphe would worry about appearances at a moment like this.

Her expression changed, becoming less itself. "I regret what happened to you."

My laughter cut away. "Which part, Mother? The part where you used my innocence to lure me into your schemes? When you convinced Father I was best left like a lamb at the altar? Or was it later, when I survived and carried your secrets?"

"Daughter, you are angry, as is your right. But there are things you must understand."

"There is nothing you can say to make me understand."

"It is the fate of the Goddess we find ourselves here together."

"You do not believe in fate."

"I have changed. I want to explain."

Cold fury, like claws in my lungs. I remembered once standing at the edge of the forest imagining my parents had not gone far, that they might come back to claim me. I had scolded myself for such fantasies, yet to think all this time Persaphe had been hiding in the King's City, close enough to watch me grow from afar…

"Tell me something, if you want to explain." I fisted the sheets, spitting the words through my teeth. "Are you here to stay, or have you merely returned to finish what you started?"

"I am here to stay," she supplied readily.

"For what possible purpose?"

"I wish to make amends."

The room was dimly lit, soaked through with night. Persaphe's face was tilted so most of her features were shadow. I listened for her heartbeat instead, picking out the familiar thump. I had known her pulse since my very inception, and it hurt to hear it now, the strength and rhythm, the volume, all as I remembered.

Or…almost as I remembered. I focused through my anger. Did something about her pulse seem…different?

"Your father and I went west for a time," Persaphe said, drawing back my attention. "I wished to return to Isla, but Aegeis did not. His sights were set on the Land of Moore, and the Shadow Temple hidden there—the twin structure to The Flame atop the Match. It is one of the great marvels of the world. He always wished to see it." She smoothed a hand over her hair, touched the spot below her ear. "I tried to convince him to return to the King's City with me, but he was intent on finding the temple. I said to Aegeis, *Do you not want to be near your daughter again? Come, you cannot choose a crumbling building over your own offspring. Don't you miss her like I do?* But he did not."

Her words snapped my reserves. "Get out."

"Daughter, please."

I kicked my legs over the edge of the bed and tried to stand, but I was weak from blood loss and the sleeping draught, and my vision spotted. "I have no intention of sitting here, swallowing your lies."

"I have never lied to you."

"You are right. You were quite clear when you left me to die."

"I knew you would not be harmed," Persaphe said. "I made sure of it."

My eyes narrowed. "What?"

"Did you believe I would abandon you without protection? Why do you think no one ever questioned your role in the king's poisoning?"

"Because I was careful," I said. "I was lucky."

"It is because my charms shielded you."

I stared at my mother. No. That could not be true.

Could it?

I thought back to those first days after the poisoning. How Queen Mother Althea had never once interrogated me, how she had overlooked my explanation regarding Persaphe's nonexistent sister, how easily she had swallowed my story about my parents' death. And there had been others. The messenger in the stables. The guards, absent my back door. Even the king seemed to have a blind spot when it came to me. Was it as Persaphe said? Had they all been under some lingering influence of her spells?

"If you had the power to protect me," I said, "you could have protected yourself as well. Yet you fled."

"My charms only extend so far."

"That," I said darkly, "sounds like an excuse."

Where another woman might have fidgeted, Persaphe sat calmly. "It helped that you were a child, naive and unaware. Innocence is an excellent medium for glamour. And, if the charms failed—" She stopped abruptly, as if she had said too much.

"So I *was* a sacrifice." My lip pulled back in disgust. "You say you have changed, but you are exactly the same."

"I have changed," she insisted. "I am here to prove it."

I gave another unsparing laugh. "And how do you plan to do that?"

"I have the king's cure."

She drew an amber bottle from her pocket. I went utterly still.

"I have watched you, Daughter. I know you have been trying to rehabilitate the king by creating a *gaigi*, a potion of undoing, and your efforts are commendable. But you are missing an ingredient, are you not?" She gave the bottle a shake. "You travel the land in hunt of it, and your dedication is worthy, but you can only be expected to come so far."

Still, I did not move.

"This remedy will reverse the *nightlight's* effects entirely," Persaphe continued. "The king's muscles will decontract. He will regain his strength. In time, he will relearn to walk. I call the remedy *evesama*, and I will give it to you. I only ask for one thing in return." Her face was incandescent as she breathed her desires. "I wish to return to my position as royal physician. I wish for things to be again as they were."

"I wonder," I said coldly, "why you wanted them to change in the first place."

I did not think she would rise to that bait, but she surprised me. "The king fancied himself in love with me. He was isolated after his father's death. Lonely. He believed our relationship meant more than it did and wanted us to be together. When I refused, he grew resentful. I feared he would take extreme measures, perhaps exile, perhaps a forced marriage…"

"So you decided to kill him?"

"At the time, it seemed my only option. I was wrong. Killing the king would have been a mistake." The words were startling coming from her. My mother never admitted her flaws. "I have traveled far. I have seen the lands that wait beyond Isla's borders. They are hard and dangerous, full of people who do not live as we live, seas as vast and barren as deserts. I wish not to spend my days in exile. I do not want to repeat the fate of my mother, vanishing into the distance to never return." It was, I thought, the most honest thing Persaphe had ever said to me. "I hope, with your help, to undo what has been done."

"Impossible."

"Is it? You have grown, Selene. You have come into your power in ways I never dreamed. I think between us, anything is possible."

"Everyone believes you are dead."

"We will come up with a likely explanation. It will all seem a misunderstanding."

"So that is it then. You have it all figured out."

She motioned with the vial. "People believe their eyes over all else. We will simply show them what we want them to see."

"Does everyone fall for your charms so easily?"

A bare smile. "Almost everyone."

My blood was pumping stronger. I took a step, and my legs held my weight.

"Here is my counteroffer," I said. "You will not resume your status as royal physician. You will not live in the palace. You will give me the cure, and in exchange I will give you my oath of silence. I will say nothing of your past deeds, and will therefore spare your life. You will leave, and be happy with those barren seas, and I will never see you again."

She was silent a long moment. "And if I decline?"

"I will tell Elias everything."

"If you tell him everything, you will implicate yourself as well."

"My punishment will be less than yours. I think he can spot the snake in her lair."

Another silence. "If you would take the day to consider—"

"No." I cut my hand through the air. "This is my offer. It is more than you deserve. You must make your choice now."

Persaphe did not quail. Even there, sitting on the ruins of her scheme, she was smooth as water. "I agree."

I held out my hand, and she gave me the cure.

THIRTY

What was my first mistake? Speaking to Persaphe at all? Or maybe it was taking the vial from her hand when I knew it was not the king's cure. I knew, because I understood potions nearly as well as I understood my mother. Her entire story was fabricated, down to the last breath. Elias had never been in love with Persaphe—that was an utter falsity. Whatever motive Persaphe had for killing the king, his supposed affections were not the reason. I would have known it even if I had not finally placed that scent on her. Bitter orange. Something acidic.

My mother had taken a dose of *risphini*, that medication meant to reduce blood pressure. It works to block the effect of the adrenaline hormone, thereby causing the heart to beat more slowly. But Persaphe did not have high blood pressure. She took the drug to reduce her heart-rate because if she did not, her pulse would quicken as she began spinning her lies. She knew I would hear it and uncover the deception of her story. Yet my mother had not guessed, could never have guessed, that I would be able to smell the drug on her.

She had underestimated me.

I felt full of power and hate, brimming with it, a bowl in my hands to carry. I caught her in one lie, and it distracted me. It gave me something to hold, so I was focused only on its weight, and did not see the larger lie until it was too late.

. . .

Ishmir was reluctant to let me go. "Look at you. Pale as a sheet. And those stitches, still fresh. You need rest, dear."

"I feel fine."

"It is scarcely dawn. King Alder planned to return for you this morning. Why not wait? You cannot walk all the way back to the palace in your state."

"I will hitch a ride on a supply cart."

Ishmir crossed her arms. "Better to let me arrange one of the House's carriages, if you are so determined. At least that way you will have some shelter from the winds. The carriages are all in use at the moment, but I expect one should be returning soon."

I wondered if Ishmir knew why my mother sought refuge at the House of Healers.

I wondered if Persaphe requested to stitch my cheek, or if it was Ishmir's idea.

I did not wait for the carriage.

. . .

The palace rose out of the distance. The sun touched its pale awnings; morning light caught the windows and turned them silver. I did manage to hitch a ride on a supply wagon, which was handled by a stout woman and her daughter. I reached down, rubbed my finger against the amber vial in my pocket. So rarely did I see the palace from this angle, on the road riding in. It seemed odd to me, how flat the gardens, how wide the lawn. The building was shaped less like a castle and more like a massive house, its flat roof inlayed with tarnished blue copper, the door a bright spot of red.

By the time we reached the palace's front gates, the sky had brightened. I stepped into the entrance hall and waited for the wash of comfort and relief, but instead I felt only a gray exhaustion. I would have slept then, but there was no time. My mother's schemes were in motion, and we were not safe.

I traversed the stairs to the imperial wing. My head was heavy; the stitches throbbed in my cheek. My bandaged hand felt swollen, and by the time I reached the top of the landing, my breath was coming thin and tight. Ishmir was right, I had overtaxed myself, but I could not worry about that then. I felt exposed, a hare on the high desert. Though I had never been trained in combat, I found myself wishing for a weapon.

Elias was not in his chambers. The rooms were empty, the King's Guard elsewhere. I gave a low curse, hoping he had not already departed back for the city. I stopped a passing servant and asked after the king's whereabouts. She hesitated only a moment, her eyes flicking to my inflamed cheek, before giving her answer.

I found Elias in the courtyard. He was speaking to a stablehand as the boy harnessed two black horses to a carriage. The coach was smaller than the one that had borne us yesterday, lower-set, built for speed. There were a few other people about, a gardener trimming winter hedges, a servant hauling firewood, a handmaiden with muddy skirts rushing on some errand. Most of the King's Guard was there as well—only Arch was missing. I wondered if he was still in the city hunting my attacker. The thought was like a hand around my throat, but I pushed it away, setting my mind more firmly on my current task. That was all I thought of. All I could allow myself to think.

As I came closer, my pulse linked with Elias', his heartbeat rising through me. I had always believed our connection worked one way, that I could feel his pulse but he could not feel mine, yet I was still some distance away when he stilled. His eyes swung to mine.

His face was bare in the sunlight, his expression morphing from surprise to something less easily named. I thought of our kiss. I could not help but think of it. How the king who touched no one had touched me. He started my way, and I moved toward him as well, the whole story ready on my lips. My mother had returned, and though I did not know exactly what she planned, Persaphe would never simply crawl back into exile at my order. She had revealed herself, and that put her in a precarious position, one that would make her unpredictable. We were in danger, and we were out of time.

I do not remember noticing Hobore at the edge of my vision. Only now in my memory can I picture him standing there with an oddly feverish look to his face. I can see the host of guards at his back.

Hobore pointed a finger at me. "Stop that woman—she aims to kill the king!"

It is dizzying, how quickly things can change. One moment your life is moving along its track, but suddenly a rift forms, throwing you off course. That was how I felt then. I was not yet afraid. I was too confused to be afraid. It was as if I had reached the end of a staircase, only to stumble when my foot met flat ground. I had missed the signals, missed everything that mattered, and so when two of Hobore's henchmen sprang forward to restrain me, I did not fight. I did not cry my innocence. I simply allowed myself to be contained.

Elias appeared as baffled as I was. He looked from me, to Hobore, to the guards who held me. "What's this about? Release her."

Their hands began to loosen, but another voice came. "No. Keep your hold."

Persaphe emerged like a vision. She swept forward and went to one knee before Elias, her head bowed, face turned to the stone pavers. She had exchanged her House robes for a gown of rippling silver; her hands were open and clean. All eyes fixed on her, drawn like moons to a planet.

There was a long silence before Elias said, "You are supposed to be dead."

"Your Majesty, you must know the truth." Though Persaphe kept her face down, her voice was undiminished, pure in its purpose. "My daughter drove me out. I have wished to return ever since, but it was not safe. I have only now found a way."

My voice ground out of me. "That's not true."

"Selene has always been an outcast. She believed once she claimed her role as royal physician, people would come to respect her, as they respected me. Yet as the years went on, she grew impatient with waiting and asked that I step down. When I refused, she threatened me, and when that did not work, she threatened you, Your Majesty."

"No." At last, I began to struggle against the hands that restrained me. The men tightened their grip. The feeling brought bile to my throat, but I swallowed it down. "She is lying. I didn't—I would not have—"

"Selene said that unless I left Isla and never returned, she would take your life," my mother continued, speaking over me. "I did not believe her, at first. I stayed, thinking I could talk her into sense, for she is my daughter. Yet she made good on her promise, and poisoned you." Persaphe lifted her face. Her voice was soaked with power. It was as if she sucked all the energy from the courtyard to pull around herself, and her audience was enraptured, the man with the garden shears, the servant carrying firewood, the King's Guard. Only Elias seemed unmoved. His face was a hardened mask.

"Once the poison took hold," Persaphe went on, "Selene made it clear she was not finished. She said, *Now you see I do not make empty threats. Leave, or I will kill the king for good.* It was only then that I realized Selene already had her traps in place. If I made any attempt to stop her, she would have let those traps spring. So I did only what I could, and fled with her father. I did it, Your Majesty, to save your life."

By this point, word of Persaphe's reappearance must have been racing through the palace, for people began appearing at the courtyard's edges, leaning over each other to listen. I looked around, feeling drained of blood. I could sense it, how Persaphe's tale rippled outward, touching the hearts of her audience. Their faces were swollen with ardor, their eyes unnaturally focused. Glamour, I had called my mother's power, but this was more than some sleight of hand. It was true magic, stronger and deeper than I had ever known she possessed. Perhaps stronger than she ever *had* possessed. Where had Persaphe found this new strength?

"Elias." I tried to speak to him directly, to make him look at me. If only he would look at me. "Elias, please—" But at a glance from Persaphe, Hobore was at my side, taking hold of my hair and thrusting me to my knees. My vision wavered, bleeding in from the edges. This could not be happening. There was no world in which this could be happening.

"All this time," Persaphe said, "I have stayed away. I was afraid, Your Majesty. Yet after four years, I could stand it no longer. I came to the festival to tell you the truth, but Selene caught wind of my plan and thwarted me. She once said if I ever returned to Isla, she would finish what she started and end your life. I have learned my daughter does not make empty threats, and now, I believe she aims to make good on her promise." Persaphe aimed a command at one of the guards. "Search her pockets."

That was when I understood. It was as if I had fallen into a rushing river. The water closed swiftly over my head. "No," I said. "Wait—"

The amber vial, which Persaphe had given me that morning, was forcibly extracted from my person. The courtyard hung in perfect stillness. The guard unstoppered the cap and sniffed. "It is Lily of the Night."

Oh, my mother had been clever. Lily of the Night was a poison any half-brain could recognize, the one every child is taught to avoid. When she had given me the vial that morning claiming it was the king's cure, I assumed it was nothing, a worthless mix of water and ash. The bottle was opaque; the liquid inside was masked from sight. I had not thought to check for certain.

What a foolish, foolish mistake.

"It is not as it looks," I croaked. Hobore's fingers tightened painfully in my hair, his other hand on my shoulder, digging bruises. Elias had yet to look at me—his gaze remained on Persaphe—but still his face gave away nothing. My voice trembled. "My mother—she gave that poison to me. She is setting me up."

"I am sorry you must learn of it this way, Your Majesty." Persaphe rose from her knee. "Selene wants you dead. If my word is not enough, we have another witness."

A man appeared. He was dressed in simple trousers and coat, his crop of black hair hidden under a fur hat. I did not recognize him... until he spoke. "The girl came to me in the stables shortly after the poisoning four years ago," the messenger said. "I had been given a letter from the Queen Mother to deliver to Persaphe in Esmond, but the girl said the queen needed to alter the message. She took it from me, and—forgive me—I forgot about it after that. The crown has many emissaries, and I assumed another messenger was sent to Esmond with the updated letter. Yet now I understand; the girl did not want me riding to Esmond, because I would have discovered Persaphe was not there. The poisoner would have been caught in her lie."

Elias' voice was dangerously even. "And Hobore? How has he become entangled in this?"

"I have known Hobore his entire life," Persaphe said. "I brought him to the palace when he was only an infant. He is your brother by blood and has always cared for you. He, too, suspected something was not right with Selene. He tried to warn you, but you would not hear him. When I returned to the King's City and became caught in my daughter's latest trap, I went straight to Hobore, knowing I could trust him to help me stop her." Persaphe raised her voice. "If all this is not enough proof of my daughter's wickedness, I suggest you search her workshop."

I knew, then, that it was over. If they searched my workshop for poison, they would find it, bottles upon bottles of it. I would fight, of course. I would explain everything, how I had searched for Elias' cure, the way I must first invent poisons to find their antidotes. Yet I could see it already, the way the crowd pulled toward Persaphe. How they withdrew from me. Who would believe my story over my mother's?

The blackness was worse now, tugging at my sight. My mind spun down all the wrong paths. It made me say the worst thing. "If I poisoned the king, I only did so because *she* commanded it."

The courtyard, which had already been quite still, turned to stone. Elias' mask slipped as he swung toward me, disbelief showing stark on his face. "What?"

I was coming apart. "Elias, please—"

"Are you saying it's true? No. This isn't—Selene." He broke off, and I realized then that Elias had never believed Persaphe's story. He had only been asking questions to reveal answers, and I had just given myself up for nothing. "Selene," he said again. "Are you my poisoner?"

There were so many things I might have said. *I was different then. I was under my mother's command. If I had known you as I do now, I would have never.* But those words felt like silt in a river, too soft to hold their form. And beneath them was a rising certainty that no matter how many paths I might have traveled, it was only ever going to come to this.

I could not lie. He knew the truth already. "Yes."

There were cries of outrage, the slap of a fist into a palm. Elias was still staring at me; he looked unmoored. I realized with a horrible lurch that I could no longer feel his heartbeat in my chest. Only my own.

Hobore's grip still held me in place. People began chanting, *Down with the witch! Down with the witch!* Yet their cries were not so loud that I missed Elias' next words. "Selene." His face was naked with betrayal. "You ruined me."

And then I put you back together, I wanted to say. And then I came to know you, and love you. Does that mean nothing? My mouth opened to form the words, but Hobore touched a blade to my throat, startling me to silence. I felt myself pale; the knife dug in. My skin split, just enough to draw blood.

Elias' eyes flew to Hobore, but then my mother was speaking again, drawing back everyone's attention. "It is a dark day," she said gravely, "when those we trust turn their backs on us. You have now heard it with your own ears—Selene has confessed her crimes. The accusations she states against me are false, of course, and poorly executed. But all is not lost. What my daughter has done can still be undone. I know a path forward, Your Majesty. The River of Reversal."

Elias' head jerked. "The River?"

"It exists," Persaphe said. "I have traveled the Crossing Sea. I have seen the River myself. If you step into its waters, you can undo the terrors my daughter has wrought. You can be as you once were."

"Elias," I tried, even as the knife beneath my jaw dug deeper. "Please, do not listen—"

"Quiet," my mother snapped. "Have you not done enough?" Then, to Elias, "I will take you there."

I was becoming desperate. My mother was like a hawk with a mouse in its claws, winging away. This was a trap—could no one else see it? The River did not exist, it was only a story. But Elias hesitated.

"I understand if you need time to consider," Persaphe soothed. "The journey to the Land of Moore where the River flows will be long and dangerous. It will require a good ship, and resources, and many willing men. It is not a decision to be made lightly. As for my daughter." She turned her blazing eyes on me. "It pains me to say this. Freestone women only ever bear one child, and she was mine, but her heart has rotted. There is only one outcome for a traitor such as her. Hobore—"

"No," said Elias. His eyes were back on Hobore's blade and the thin stream of blood running down my neck. "Not yet."

"She is an assassin," Persaphe remarked. "Do you mean for her to live?"

"No," Elias said again. He was breathing heavily. "No—I." He mastered himself. "Not here. If she is to be executed, we will do it properly."

I made a sound that might have been a sob. Irritation flashed across my mother's face, quickly covered. "Of course," she said. "The people of Isla should have a chance to witness her death. They, too, are victims of her deceit." She motioned to Hobore and the surrounding guards.

The knife was sheathed, and I was hauled to my feet. "Take her to the prisons. She will be hanged at sunrise."

THIRTY-ONE

The palace prison was small, made up of six little cells each fitted with a barred door. Mine was bare, save for a pallet and a narrow window, through which I could see a slip of the sky.

I did not look at the sky. I did not look at the bars, or the walls, or the guards as they locked my door with a metallic *shick*. I buried my swollen face in my hands and looked at nothing but the blackness behind my lids. I wanted to cry, but no tears would come. I had the terrible feeling of someone who steps too far off the cliff and has time to realize their mistake in those bare moments before they hit the ground.

I had poisoned a life, and loved it, and lost it.

All I could think was, if only. If only I had told Elias the truth from the beginning, if only I had resisted my mother's plots in the first place. A part of me clung to these thoughts, desperate for even the temporary relief of their imaginings, but the wiser part of me knew it was too late for *if onlys*. My sentence had been decided, and now I had only hours.

I lowered my hands. The stone was different here than it was throughout the rest of the palace, dark granite instead of marble. Like Elias' face had been, when he learned the truth.

Was there anything I could have done to make him understand?

I could have said, I was wrong.

I could have said, please forgive me.

But I had not said those things, and even if I had, it would have made no difference. I had not thought it possible to sink any lower, but this was proof even the deepest chests have their hidden bottoms: I was sentenced to die, and that night, I believed I deserved it.

...

The door creaked. A wash of new air breezed into the prison. I came to the bars for a better look, though I knew already who it was.

My mother moved stoically down the corridor as if down a wedding aisle. I had known she would come, yet the sight of her was an assault. She stopped a few paces back, and we observed each other. I could hear her heart beating like a perfectly wound clock.

And again, another sound. The slightest difference.

My attention sharpened. At the House of Healers, I believed this difference in her pulse was due to Persaphe's use of *risphini*, that drug meant to slow her heartrate and prevent me from spotting her lies. Only, I could smell no drug on her this time, nor think of any reason why she might need it. My mother had already won. She had no further reason to lie and therefore no reason to mask her pulse. Yet the change—that soft beat, almost like a murmur—was unmistakable.

"Those were your men," I said raggedly. "At the festival. The attack. You sent them for me."

"I was running out of options." Persaphe was easy, assured in her victory. The truth flowed from her like wine from a barrel. "I needed to speak with you alone. I waited ages for such an opportunity, but you did not venture from the palace, not once since my return. Your attendance at the festival was my chance."

"So you sent—you sent men to hurt me?" My skin crawled with suppressed memories. "To *violate* me?"

Persaphe's expression shifted. "I ordered no violation. My men were instructed to deliver you a single knife wound—one small enough to cause no lasting impact, but large enough to warrant a visit to the House of Healers, and to me."

"And the poison?" I asked. "At the king's reemergence feast? You poisoned my plate. Or..." I thought of Hobore's ill-tempered face. The way he said, *You have not touched your food.* "You had Hobore poison it."

Persaphe's mouth creased. "The palace staff was meant to bring you to the city for treatment. I was there waiting at the House, I had everything ready. But the king called a healer to the palace instead. And of course, I could not be the one who went."

"I would have died that night."

"Daughter." Her face, like a lone candle. "You are going to die anyway."

To hear it said so plainly. My skin was stinging, my lungs battling to expand. Had I ever been anything but a pawn in her games? I was a grown woman, yet I felt little more than a child. "I do not understand," I croaked. "What have I done to deserve your hatred?"

"Hatred has nothing to do with it," Persaphe replied gustily. "The king must be dispatched, and it must happen before he bears an heir. I have spent a lifetime working toward this goal and very nearly lost my chance, what with the failed poison and my exile. But now I have been granted another opportunity to finish the task. I will not risk it for anything."

"I am your *daughter*."

"Would you like a kiss goodbye?" Persaphe rejoined. "This whining is beneath you."

I wish I could say my mother was clutched by madness or terror, something to explain her cruelty. Yet Persaphe spoke with the calculation of a woman who knew exactly what she was doing. She had abandoned me as a young girl, left me for dead, and I'd had four years to come to terms with that. Yet it was not until that night in the prison my eyes opened fully to her true nature.

"If you are so determined to eliminate me in pursuit of this goal," I spat, "why not the night of the feast, then? With the poison? You already had me in your grasp."

"Ending you then would not have served my purposes." She brushed away an invisible piece of lint, her nails catching the lamplight. "I measured the Lily of the Night myself. That dose was meant to make you sick, nothing more."

Did she really believe that? The amount of poison I had ingested that night was many times what was needed to kill me. If not for my own tolerance, I would have died, which meant my mother had erred, just as she erred with the king's poison. But then, potions had never been her specialty. I wondered who else had suffered for her incompetence.

With this thought came another. "What of Father?"

"I already told you what became of Aegeis."

"You lied. I want the truth."

"He lives, if that is what you fear," Persaphe replied with some asperity. "As time passed he became…uncertain of my aims. I knew if we continued on together, he would begin to question me, maybe even resist me, so I set him free. But I did not lie to you. He went to find the Shadow Temple in the Land of Moore."

"Did he—?"

"Enough questions. This is not why I have come. I am here to ask something of you."

"Whatever it is, my answer is no."

Persaphe's lips pulled in. "You have become insolent."

"I can hardly imagine why."

"You have not even heard my request."

I gave a strained laugh. "I do not need to hear it. Why would I ever help you?"

"Not me," Persaphe said. "The king." When I gave no reply, she continued. "His Majesty has been somewhat…reluctant to take my council. More than once, he has asked after your conditions here in the prison. I never believed you gifted with charms, but it is obvious your spells are mingling with mine. Drop them, daughter. Release the king from whatever hold you have on him. I believe you will do this, for his sake. It is dangerous for one man to be under the control of two witches."

My fingers fisted my dress. I did not tell my mother I had no power of glamour. I did not allow my feelings to show on my face, the lurch of sorrow and bitterness and confusion. I didn't know what it meant that Elias was asking after my conditions, and I didn't want to know. What did it matter? I would never speak to him again.

I said, "Why not instruct Hobore to intervene on your behalf? He seems willing enough to do your bidding. If I am correct, he has been doing it for some time." I took a step back. "There were rumors Hobore was seeing a maid in the city. He used to sneak away in the night to meet her. But there was no maid, was there, Mother? He was only ever conspiring with you."

"Hobore has been loyal to me," Persaphe acknowledged. "Yet in this, he cannot help."

"What a shame."

"I did not come here to be mocked. Will you drop your spells or not?"

"I will," I lied, feeling there was little to lose, "if you answer one question. Why? Why must Elias die? And do not spin more tales of his love for you. I want the truth."

But Persaphe was already tiring of me. I could see it in the silver of her eyes, half-hidden under heavy lids. "I cannot agree to that bargain."

"Then I suppose you will have to wait until morning for the spells to lift," I said acidly, "when I am hung."

"Not all charms vanish after the witch's death. Particularly not the charms of the bedchamber."

I choked. "The *what?*"

"Oh, do not feign innocence. It does not suit you. Besides, I have heard the rumors. You would be astonished how much gossip travels through the House. But of course, any intimacy between you and the king must have been bolstered by magic, seeing as you must first circumvent my curse—"

"They were only rumors," I snapped. "Elias was never my lover, we never…" My heart misgave me. I looked into Persaphe's glacial face. "What curse?"

Persaphe merely lifted her brows.

The knowledge seemed to come from far away. I thought of Elias' reputation for callousness. How he had resisted taking a wife, how he hated to be touched. There was a reason he was so withdrawn, and feared human contact, and guarded his heart.

My mother was watching me with an air of impatience, waiting for me to put it together. I made myself hold her gaze, even as my mind rebelled. "It was you," I breathed. "You are the reason Elias fears human contact. The reason he resists all closeness..." My heart was throbbing painfully. "You set a curse on him. I thought you wished to end him with poison, but you've been slowly killing him, for *years*."

She rolled her eyes. "Do not be dramatic."

"He's innocent."

"No man is innocent."

"You've bewitched him into fearing the touch of others, tormented him with your tricks—"

"My tricks?" Persaphe laughed then, as if I was being particularly stupid. "You are so like your father. He, too, could never understand my power. Sorcery is not a *trick*."

Sorcery. That word was not one we used, not for healers, not even for witches. And then there was the curse itself. Physicians—even those as powerful as us—did not have the power to lay curses. I peered at my mother and thought, tremulously, *what have you become?* "It is black magic."

"Call it what you will. I will not be sorry. How else was I supposed to ensure His Majesty never produced an heir? I could sabotage his engagement, but kings still have their consorts. No. Easier to curse the boy into fearing human touch. Address the problem at its source."

"He is *the king*."

"He is a man, as I think you well know." Persaphe's tone dropped its levity. "You say he was never your lover, yet I see the way you look at him. I hear how you call him Elias."

Horribly, tears came to my eyes. "That is not the same."

"Oh, Selene. Do you think it's different because you love him? If you have learned anything from me, it should be this: love does not make you worthy. It only makes you weak."

"I am not weak."

"And yet, you are the one behind bars."

I wanted to stop her, to raise my hands to my ears and shut her out, yet this was what Persaphe did—she took what was good and right and turned it ugly. "Is that why you did it, then?" I asked, my breath coming bare and painful between each word. "Did you try to kill Elias because you loved him?"

She made a face. "Have you not been listening? I never loved the king. I did not love his father, either, but…"

I blinked through my tears. The darkness seemed to press around me. "But what?"

My mother tipped her head to the side, but I was no longer looking at Persaphe. I was remembering the story of the hunting accident that had doomed King Adonis Alder. *It was my duty to ready my father's horse*, Elias once told me, *but I arrived late. The task was given to Hobore instead.* During the hunt, the horse's reins had come loose from the bridle. Adonis had tumbled to his death.

"Hobore," I whispered. "The faulty bridle. That was your doing as well. You made Adonis' death look like an accident, but it wasn't, was it? It was murder."

"His death was a pity," was all Persaphe said. "I rather liked Adonis."

"But *why?*" I burst, in a surge of bitter rage. "Why must they die? Why must I? You were the royal physician. It is one of the most prestigious positions in Isla, short of being royalty yourself. You used to lecture me about power, yet all you had was power, and freedom, and the love of the court. You have been sabotaging yourself, killing kings and forcing yourself into exile—for what? Without the Alder family, we are nothing. What do you possibly stand to gain from these schemes?"

But Persaphe was done with me. I could see it in the lines of her body as she moved to leave. "Apologies, Daughter, but some truths I do not even trust to the grave."

...

Persaphe was gone. There was a sentry standing watch outside the prison door but no one within its chamber. I was alone.

I put my head in my hands. My mother's words looped irrepressibly through my mind, yet the more I replayed our conversation, the less sense I could make of it. How long had Persaphe been scheming? How many threads did this story hold? My mother did not merely want to kill Elias—she wanted to end the entire Alder bloodline. And Hobore? How long had he been entangled in Persaphe's plots?

I bent, suddenly, in grief, as if stabbed through with a knife. Should I have seen this coming? I knew my mother, knew her viper mind. Yet this deviousness went beyond anything I could have fathomed. And what of Elias? How could he accept Persaphe back into his confidences so easily? Clearly, he was unaware of the curse. Unaware that she was even strong enough to lay a curse. Such powers were a thing of legend. How had my mother become so strong?

The prison door creaked, startling me from my thoughts. I came abruptly upright. Was it dawn already? Dread gripped me, but the man who appeared was not an attendant to lead me to the gallows. It was Kurton.

He came forward. Kurton was dressed in his guardsman's uniform, his broad shoulders rounded forward, a platter of bread and porridge in his hands. His face was salt-white, and I was struck with a fresh wave of shame. My admission must have hurt the King's Guard nearly as deeply as it hurt Elias.

"Kurton." I gripped the bars. "You must understand…"

"I do not think I will ever understand." He set the food down in front of my cell but did not move to slide it through the slot under the door. "You are not who we thought you were. You fooled us all, for years, and now we must live with the dishonor that the king's poisoner lulled us while we were wide awake."

"Please, Kurton, listen to me. Persaphe—"

"Enough." He grimaced, raising a hand. "Enough of this. I cannot hear any more lies."

"I am not lying." The air seemed to quiver in my throat. "I do not speak to spare myself. It is too late for that, I know it. But Elias is in danger. My mother wants him dead. She has tried to end his life before, and she is not finished. My execution…it is only a distraction."

He lowered his hand. His eyes were as Elias' had been, cold all the way through. "There was always talk. People were suspicious of you. The king's own brother came to us once, insisting we interrogate you. We laughed at him. People may have talked, but I always thought that was just the court. They love their gossip. And you." His face tightened. "When we first met, you were just a harmless little thing. So eager. Your desire to please was apparent in your every breath. I thought, it could never have been you. And now, as if the last four years were not enough, the king will make the long and dangerous journey to the River of Reversal, where he is sure—"

"What?" I cut him off. "Elias has agreed to go?"

"He is readying for the voyage as we speak."

"But the River does not *exist*."

"Persaphe says it does. She says she has seen it."

"How can you believe her?" I threw out my arms. "How, Kurton? My mother vanishes for years, and returns without warning, and suddenly everyone swallows every word she speaks. Does that not seem odd to you? Do you not see how people go numb around her? Her charms stink the air. Even Elias…" My throat closed. "Have you ever known him to defer to anyone?"

Kurton looked uncertain.

"Please," I tried again. "The king's life is in danger."

"The king's life is always in danger. Such is a monarch's lot."

"I mean, imminent danger."

Slowly, Kurton pushed the food tray into my cell. He spoke his next words carefully. "The king ended his engagement to Princess Mora. He did it last night after we left the House of Healers."

I sputtered. "*What?*"

"The men and I have been telling him for years it's time to stop putting his own happiness aside for the sake of duty. There are more important things. We could never get through to him. But last night, seeing you hurt as you were…I think it shook him awake. Finally opened his eyes to what we have been saying. He sent the letter to Hillshire as soon as we returned to the palace."

"Kurton." I was reeling. "I never—how could he—?"

"He loved you. Do you realize that? He loved you as I have never seen him love another. Selene, you have broken his heart."

. . .

Kurton was gone again, the prison fallen to silence. I stared at the cold plate he had left behind. Bread. Porridge. Simple fare. I did not know why Kurton bothered. It was not as if I needed my strength.

I slid down the wall and tipped my head against the stone. My stitched cheek burned, and I was hot and cold at once—a sure sign of fever. Outside the tiny window, the sky was beginning to pale. I could hear the quick footfalls of early morning workers, the trill of a dove. And then, at last: the final swing of the prison door.

The guards were silent yet efficient. They unlocked my cell and stepped swiftly inside, moving to bind my hands behind my back. I did not struggle, though the feel of their grip made me want to snarl. In the back of my mind, I saw it again: the yellow glow of tents, a shadow in my periphery. That taunting voice saying, *Scream, and I will gouge it out.* I blackened with those images, but I was jolted back into my body by the warden's iron words. *May the Goddess give her justice.*

I allowed myself to be led through the palace. Servants and citizens gathered to watch our procession. They clutched each other, their faces cold with righteousness. *Witch*, they said again and again. *She poisoned the king, she admitted it, we heard it from her own lips. Witch.* Someone spat; the mucus splattered my boot. I kept my chin high, even as fear knotted through me. I had imagined, many times, the manner of my death, but never had I imagined this.

I thought we would go directly to the gallows, but instead I was marched to the stateroom. There, an audience had assembled. I caught sight of Persaphe standing near the raised throne, wearing an embroidered gown and looking displeased. On her opposite side, Queen Mother Althea observed me with tight lips, and behind them, the King's Guard stood together, watching my approach. It was difficult, more difficult than I could have anticipated, seeing Arch's expression of wounded betrayal, and Freesier's incomprehension, and Yorvis' quiet disbelief. Kurton, too, was distressed, clenching and unclenching the sword at his belt.

I was deposited on a small section of black tile at the room's head, which served as a kind of marker where citizens stood to face their king. Sunlight streamed in through wide skylights; frescos of dragons and knights watched from vaulted ceilings. With a shrinking heart, I brought my gaze to the king.

He sat on the throne situated under a half-dome window at the far end of the room. His fingers were bare of rings, his expression like sea glass, worn smooth of all its grooves. He looked composed, authoritative, yet I did not miss the bruises under his eyes. He had not slept, either.

"The terms of your sentence have changed," Elias said in his monarch's voice. He was not quite looking at me, but rather staring at some middle distance over my shoulder. "I intend to travel to the River of Reversal. It seems this may be my final chance to undo my paralysis. I am choosing a small entourage to accompany me. Persaphe knows the way and will guide us, yet I am under no delusions. To journey beyond the Crossing Sea would be difficult for a man with two working legs, and I am not that man." He looked at his hands, which rested unmoving on his thighs. "I will need a steady supply of *eithier* to make the physical aspects of the trek easier. I am aware that this potion requires the use of your blood, and your blood only."

I felt myself go stony. Around me, the court held its breath.

"It has been decided you will journey with us," Elias declared, "and prepare the concoction as needed."

At this, people broke into frenzied chatter. I looked at my mother, standing in stiff disapproval. I looked at the King's Guardsmen, their pale, tired features.

"Make no mistake," Elias said, and now he did look at me. His eyes slid, once, from my wounded cheek, to the crusted blood at my neck, to my bandaged hand. Gone was the emotion from yesterday's courtyard. His gaze was frighteningly remote. "I wish there was another way. If I could have you hung this morning, I would do it. But I am practical.

Even if you were to teach another how to brew the *eithier*, there would still be the matter of your blood. And so you will come with us under guard. If you attempt to escape, or to harm anyone in our party, your life will be ended swiftly, *eithier* or no."

The word was on my lips before I could stop it. "Elias—"

The court gasped, and someone cried, *How dare she!* Elias' fists flexed against the throne's arms. "You have no right," he said, "to address me thus."

"Your Majesty," I corrected, and dropped to my knees. I heard Elias' sharp inhale. I had never knelt before him.

"Get up," he said.

I put out my hands, palms up. "I am a servant, at your mercy—"

"I said, *get up*."

"—and as such, I must tell you—"

Hands closed suddenly around my arms, making me yelp. The guards dragged me back. Elias' eyes were burning, his muscles tensing through the fabric of his trousers. If he could have stood then, he would have. "You are not here to state your case," he said coldly, "merely to hear my orders. You have one day to pack. We leave tomorrow at sunbreak."

THIRTY-TWO

I was marched to my chambers by a host of seven guards. It was more than was assigned to most men. I did not know whether to be flattered.

My rooms were a shock, for how ordinary they seemed. Had it only been the prior morning I had stood in this spot preparing to attend the festival? I looked down at myself, the ruined blue dress I still wore. My feet were clad in winter boots, my hands empty and grimed, the injured palm wrapped in cloth. The guards said not a word, depositing me neatly on the threshold before exiting back the way they had come. Shortly after, I could hear the sound of bolts being driven into the doorframe, barring me in.

I had thought I would be hung that morning, yet instead I had been given a day to pack. Beyond that, I did not know what would become of me. Would they bind my hands in chains along the journey, with only enough links for me to brew the *eithier*? Would I be given a horse, or caged in a wagon? I remembered my old fears, the vastness of the world, towering kingdoms and endless seas, the surety that I would crumble among them. I remembered how it felt to look upon my compass and think, not yet.

I went to the window. Outside, the morning sun pressed against the grass. Beneath me, the stone was worn smooth by generations of passing feet. I could see my forest in the distance, hanging still in the early air as it had for every day of my entire life.

I realized, after a too-long minute, what I felt was not fear.

I went to my wardrobe. I traded my dress for a practical set of fleece leggings and shirt, then extracted the compass from the inner pocket of a hanging cloak. I returned to the foyer and pressed my ear to the door. I could hear the heartbeats of at least three guards stationed beyond, and another four out back. As I moved through my rooms, my eyes were drawn to my shelves of simples, rosemary and poppy, hellhound, wild flax, *istilla* in its clear glass. And last of all, ready in its trap: my anthem powder to induce death-like sleep.

I stepped into my workshop. I had never crafted this brew before, yet the recipe lay within me like a whorl in wood. I pulled a copper bowl from the shelf, a knife from the block. My fingers found the necessary jars, dried ash and spider silk and root. I needed an echo, which was the kind of ingredient that gave me pause, as it crossed that firm boundary between medicine and magic. I looked at my hand around the bowl, the knotted scars crisscrossed over ruddy, wrinkled burns. It was the first time, I think, that I did not mind what I saw.

I drew the bowl to my cold hearth, stuck my head into the chute, and gave a short cry. The sound reverberated back, landing in the bowl. A few more turns of the spoon, and the potion was done.

I knew I could not escape my chambers by force. I was injured, and battling a fever, and heartsore from two days of relentless revelations. Even if I somehow found the strength to make it past the bolts, the guards would see my attempt and cut me down in an instant. So I would not force my way. I waited until the sun finished its duty and night slowly walked across the palace. Once darkness had fallen, I gulped my potion down, then listened again for the guards' heartbeats. Six in total. I did not know if that was too many.

Well, I thought, you are about to find out.

My brew was taking hold, scratching at my throat. I inhaled a breath to steel myself, then began chanting in a voice that sounded nothing like my own. Amplified by my concoction, my words were tinged with a strange ethereality, as if coming from everywhere at once. I drew upon some of my favorite old stories for inspiration, cawing phrases that sounded like spells. *Ath haras, ath velor men dor.* It was all nonsense; the chants meant nothing. Yet the court had long believed me a witch with a penchant for nighttime bewitchings, and for once I could use their superstitions to my advantage.

My performance worked. The guards unbolted the locks, rushing in to stop me from casting whatever spells they believed I was summoning. As soon as they pushed through the doors, my traps sprang, blowing sleeping powder into their faces. I had never seen my powder in action—Hermapate had already been comatose by the time I found her at my door—and so I watched in fascination as a ghostly glaze overcame the men. Their hands loosened; their legs failed beneath them. They had no time to process what was happening before their eyes rolled, and they slumped to the floor.

I hauled their bodies into my bedchamber where they would be hidden from view. I stepped through the back door into the night.

· · ·

The forest welcomed me like an embrace. I dove into its depths, my feet light, my breath coming loud and fast. Deeper I went, past the places I used to play as a child, past my favorite thickets and streams. Through the branches, the stars looked like tiny snowdrops, the air cold and clean. I reached an old stone, the final recognizable landmark and the farthest I had ever gone, and stuttered to a halt.

Overhead, the moon provided white light. Before me, I could see where the trees grew thicker, shadows hanging tapestry-like between them. I was about to cross into new territory, past that invisible line I had always drawn between what was safe and what was not. My sense of self-preservation balked at my intention. *Turn back now, have you lost your mind? There are dangers in this forest. Venomous snakes, spiders the size of dogs, and something else, something you cannot even put to words. You must turn back, turn back to safety.* But there was no safety for me, not anymore. And if I did not go now, I never would.

I stepped forward. Tree limbs twisted in huge, thuggish arcs, their bases creased like the skirts of a lady. There were oaks and *redimens*, but also species I did not recognize, purple-rooted monsters that seemed to sing with age and power. It was not raining, but it might as well have been; moisture dripped from the leaves, splattering my hot skin. The mist was thick and wet and swirling.

The moon continued to rise, dragging the night with it, but under the dense canopy it was difficult to track time. I kept my eyes on the earth, squinting through the dim light, careful to avoid the pits and roots. I had feared the beasts of the woods, but I saw no other creatures. They were wiser than me, it seemed, than to venture into the forest deep.

My energy was flagging; the wind struck like ice on my face. I stumbled onward, gritting my teeth, trying to catch my bearings. Had this been any other part of Isla, I would have laid my palm to a trunk for support, or flopped myself down to the earth to rest, but not there. I passed the black, sucking pit of a bog. A scattering of birch trees, pale as bones. The light seemed to change, and when I looked up, the moon had turned blood red.

There was a reason I had come. Yet how could I possibly find what I sought? The forest was vast, and the compass could only help find my way back, not forward. I tried to think of what my father would say, what wisdom he might have imparted, yet it was Ophelia's long-ago words that came to mind instead. *You have an instinct for these things. You can root out power at its source.*

The chill was truly uncomfortable now, harsh enough to turn my fingers blue. The weight of the trees hung heavy overhead. It was like a blanket, I thought. It could suffocate just as well.

I turned my attention inward, closing my eyes and reaching for the forest as I had once reached for Elias' pulse. I could feel something, almost, rooting there inside me, inside the trees. I moved again. The air was so thick it rattled my lungs. Thin strands of light pierced the forest floor, not from moonlight, but from bioluminescent flowers.

I came to a small clearing. My blood was practically humming. *It is here.* Yet when I looked around, I saw only patches of snow and muddy earth and trees. I had the sudden urge to lay among the leaflitter, to close my eyes and fall asleep and wake in the morning, or wake never. If I lost myself in this frigid dark, I would not have to fight the cold, or feel the stitches pulling at my face, or remember the last two days…

No, I thought fiercely. *You have made it this far. You will not give up yet.* Gathering myself, I did what they did in the stories and spoke into the night. "I am Selene, Daughter of the Freestones. I have come to collect what you may offer and am willing to pay your price. Show yourself."

The forest made no answer.

"I said," I repeated, "show yourself."

I stood, exhaling air into air. My brazenness began to ebb. I was no fell witch, nor did I have my mother's power. I could not summon the world's secrets at my say-so.

"No," I said aloud this time, grinding my teeth against these intrusions. My voice cracked; my throat was bare. "I do not want to be like her. I will not be. My power is my own."

The forest waited like a god.

And what, whispered a voice, maybe mine, maybe my father's, *do gods always want?*

I pulled out my knife and set the blade to the meat of my palm. Blood welled; the offering dripping to the earth. A breeze lifted, and when I looked down again, there was a new cluster of *istilla* at my feet.

A feeling came over me, like wind into a sail. Though I recognized my plant for what it was, this was unlike any *istilla* I had ever encountered. The flowers were large—each as wide as my palm—and bore a shimmery outer coating. As I crouched, the stems reached for me like a child its mother.

I cut those flowers with my most gentle, seasoned hand. I cradled them against my chest, as if a flame that could extinguish. "Thank you," I whispered to the forest. "Thank you."

By the time I made it back to the forest's edge, dawn was coming. I walked to the line where trees met open grass and stared across the valley into the King's City. How many times had I stood in exactly this spot, wondering what would happen if I simply fled? I envisioned rushing into those city streets, vanishing into the labyrinth. I could escape for good. I could be free. Yet if I did that, who would stop my mother from committing more devastation? Who would stand between her and Elias? Indeed, between her and the rest of Isla?

I was past running, I thought. I had been past it for a long time.

I emerged from the forest and started back toward the palace. I was on this path, I had made my choices. There was nothing left to do but see them through.

THIRTY-THREE

I sat in a chair by my kitchen window, a small bag of belongings tucked beneath my feet. The day was like the last, gorgeous and clear. Had this been any other room of the palace, I would have seen dustmotes floating in the sun's rays, but my chamber was warded against such imperfections. The air was pure.

It was there Ophelia found me.

"Your door was open," she said by way of greeting. "The king's entourage is gathering in the midyard. Your guards were meant to escort you there. People are beginning to wonder why you do not come." She swept her gaze around. "Where *are* your guards?"

"Asleep." They were still unconscious in my bedroom.

"I see."

There was a silence. I did not know why Ophelia had come. Perhaps she wanted her own chance to rail at me for my lies. Or maybe she wanted to see me for herself, like a freak at a circus. Here is the witch who has been hiding among us. Here is her true face revealed. Yet all

Ophelia said was, "You have found yourself in quite a stitch."

I turned my eyes to the window so as not to show my grief. There was kindness in Ophelia's voice. How could there be kindness? I thought I must be mistaken, I was only hearing what I wished to hear, yet she spoke again, and her tone remained indisputably gentle. "I saw the bolts on the door. They are treating you like a convict."

"Why should they not?" My words grated. "The accusations are true. I poisoned our king."

"But isn't it also true you did so under Persaphe's instruction?"

I looked up swiftly. "Persaphe denies her role in the poisoning. I attempted to make that case. No one believed me."

"*I* believe you. I also believe you regret your actions and have been trying to reverse them ever since."

"I am no less a murderess."

"The king lived."

"Only because my mother was too stupid to get the poison right."

"So it was not even of your invention?" Ophelia drew up a brow. "That only further absolves you."

"How can you say that?" I rose from my seat, confused and somehow angry. "No one else will hear me. Not even the King's Guard. They witnessed my confession and went deaf to everything else. So why not you, too? Why are you defending me?"

"I am your friend," Ophelia said.

"You are a fool," I snapped, "to claim a friend such as me."

My face was blazing. My words were hurt and angry and bitter. I did not know what it meant that Ophelia alone had taken my side over my mother's, and I did not trust it. Yet strangely, Ophelia smiled. "You may remember I am the oldest of many wild brothers, one of whom owes you his good health. You will have to try harder than that to push me away."

Her words sucked out my fury. Wisely, I said nothing.

Ophelia swept another look around my chamber. I watched her gaze catch on the empty anthem powder traps above the doorways, the too-quiet halls. "Your guards are asleep, you said? Well, we should not be surprised. They must have had too much to drink last night in celebration of your mother's return. Isn't that right?"

My mouth worked. No sound came.

"Isn't it?" she pressed.

"Yes," I said, finding my voice. "Exactly right."

"No matter. You do not need an escort. You meet the king willingly. Is that not so?"

I gave a wary nod. "Just so."

"Good. It will make our journey easier."

My eyes widened. "Our—?"

"The king's entourage requires a cook." She shrugged. "I volunteered. Why not? I have always wanted to see the world. Besides, Kurton will be going. I cannot leave him to face the winter road all on his own. He would miss me too much."

"Ophelia…"

"We had better get moving," she interrupted, offering another smile. This one was crooked, simple, the kind of smile that said there would be no more arguing. I was still uncertain, still expecting…what? A trick? Some rug to be pulled out from under my feet? Ophelia was too pure of heart for that. If I was looking for treachery, I would not find it in her.

The thought calmed me a little. I wished I knew how to smile like Ophelia, in a way that showed my feelings. I wished I could find the words to explain what it meant to know somehow, despite everything, I still had a friend.

. . .

Together, Ophelia and I gathered our belongings and trudged to the midyard where the journeyers were congregating. A small entourage, Elias had said, yet the number of people in the king's party could have filled a ballroom. There were soldiers and wagon-tenders, grooms and scribes, shepherds and messengers and a bard to sing away the hours. There were animals, too, hens and packhorses and even a black ox, which would be slaughtered for its meat once we left civilization behind.

I wondered if anyone really believed a single ox would sustain us through the winter wilderness. Weeks, the journey would take, across barren lands and craggy passes and a wide, endless sea, and that was if everything went smoothly. We all knew the tale. Leviathans, enchantresses, three-headed wolves…during the maiden's fabled journey from Isla to the River of Reversal, she had faced these things and more. *A story*, I had once told Elias.

A legend, he replied. *There's a difference.*

Ophelia and I came to stand at a gate running the length of the yard, watching the colorful assembly of bodies and beasts and sledges. Stablemen stood ready with haltered donkeys, and a troop of well-mounted soldiers gathered in formation, armed with crossbows and swords. I listened to their leader call the men to attention, feeling a sort of detachment. It still did not seem quite real. My mother's return. My sentencing and re-sentencing. All the past day's miseries and revelations.

"Where is the king?" I asked Ophelia, yet as soon as I spoke my attention was drawn to an unassuming carriage pulled by two chestnut mares. The walls were made of lacquered wood; the curtains were drawn closed. Out of habit, I reached with my senses, searching for

Elias' heartbeat, but as before, there was nothing.

"Your guard comes for you," said Ophelia, lifting a hand to shade her eyes. "Persaphe wanted to assign you a full brigade, but the king overruled her. He said one man was enough."

"Who is it?"

Ophelia did not answer, but I saw him then, weaving through the crowd. Hobore's chin was tucked into a tartan scarf, his hands shoved deep in his pockets. He wore a knife at his hip, but the belt was too loose on his thin frame and shifted with every step.

"I will return when I can," Ophelia murmured. She kissed my cheek and was gone.

Hobore came to stand before me, eyeing Ophelia's retreating back. "Where are your guards?"

My fists clenched; the scabbed-over cut under my jaw stung. "I thought you were my guard."

"Your other guards. The ones meant to bring you here."

I started to reply—to craft some new lie—but at that moment I spotted my mother standing at the head of the congregation. She was dressed in boots and layers of fine white fur, and she was speaking to one of the king's men, though her attention wandered. I felt it, like a hand on the back of my neck, the moment her gaze touched mine. Persaphe's expression was unbending; mine, I'm sure, was set with violence. We stood there a moment, each making our silent promises.

You will tell no one my secrets, her eyes warned, *or I will make you suffer as you never have, and you will wish we had hung you after all.*

Of the two of us, I thought back, *I will not be the one who hangs.*

"Now," Hobore interrupted, "none of that."

My gaze swung to his. "What?"

"If you keep looking at your mother like you want to slit her throat,

I will be forced to take action." He pulled a flask from an inner coat pocket—booze, I could smell it—and took a swig. "Persaphe chose me to guard you for a reason," he continued. "She knows she can trust me. I have been instructed to punish you for any indiscretion. With force, if necessary."

I watched him recap his flask. He watched me watch him and stiffened. "Try to poison me, and I will make you sorry."

"If I try to poison you, you will be dead."

His palm flashed so quickly I did not even cry out. He caught my injured cheek right over the stitches, the pain enough to whiten my vision. When I could see again, I found myself on my knees, breathing down at my hands. I looked up at Hobore, expecting to see malice and hate, but he did not look hateful. He looked shaken.

"Every indiscretion," he repeated unsteadily. "With force. I am commanded, do you understand? She has commanded me. Now get up."

I did get up. I touched a tender hand to my face; my fingers came away sticky with blood. The stitches had broken with the force of the blow.

· · ·

Our journey began without ceremony. The midyard gates creaked open and the steeds surged forward, followed by the wagons and pack animals and many far-eyed men. We set a course west into the country, retracing the path the maiden had supposedly taken on her journey; we would travel first to the sea, then sail to the Land of Moore, traverse the Pass of Dire and, assuming all went to plan, uncover the River. Travelers had done this before. The Land of Moore was real enough, though it was so remote, it might as well have been fable. As for the Pass, there were stories to suggest its existence as well, legends of fools like us rushing headlong to conquer it. Most never returned.

There were rules, which were clearly laid out for me. I was to keep away from others, to take my meals alone, to collect only the herbs I needed for the king's *eithier*, which was to be brewed every third night. They did not bind me in chains, for I needed my hands to harvest and work, but I was under Hobore's constant guard and had no opportunity to do anything beyond my assigned task. When the *eithier* was ready, it was first given to a poison tester who made such a show of examining every spoonful that I had half a mind to poison him after all, sheerly for spite. I was not permitted to deliver the medicine to Elias myself, and though it was never stated explicitly, it seemed I was not even allowed to look at the king. Whenever he emerged from his carriage, he was somehow always just beyond my line of vision, blocked by the body of a horse, a wagon, a huddle of men. He did not ask to see me. I did not request an audience.

The land changed as we traveled, hilly farmlands giving way to arid plains and wide, red-tinted shrublands. Persaphe led the party atop a pure white filly, guiding us west along a frozen bank. Whenever we passed close enough to a country village, the bulk of our group made camp outside its walls while runners were sent in to demand the lord's hospitality for our king, and to secure more provisions. Hobore remained a constant shadow at my side, but he was quiet, brooding, often staring into his flask. He rode a tan gelding while I was forced to walk. We did not often speak. There was nothing, really, to say.

I slept badly. I had not suffered nightmares in years, but suddenly every time I shut my eyes there was some new horror awaiting me. Sometimes, it was the memory of my assailant from the festival, the stench of his hot breath, the feel of the glass slicing through his skin and mine. Sometimes it was Elias in the carriage, the heat in my blood, how boldly I had moved over him. Worse was when the dreams were not true memories, but some perverted vision of these things. My assailant would push me into the king's coach, rip at my clothes. I would fight as he heaved over me, and Elias would pound on the door from outside shouting, *How could you do it, Selene? How?*

It was no relief to wake, for wakefulness was its own torment. Every dose of *eithier* required a vial of my blood, and I had begun to feel the effects of those cuttings. It did not help that I was still recovering from my attack, the stitches in my cheek torn and healing poorly. It did not help, either, that I was forced to walk while others rode, a feat that became increasingly difficult when we finally left the tamed lands behind and pavement turned to muddy snow. My muscles trembled; my boots sucked with every step. I collapsed at the end of each day, thirsty, exhausted, but there was no rest for me, as I must gather the *eithier's* ingredients, and cut open my flesh, and set it all to brew.

My arms grew inflamed with thin scores. I wrapped the skin in bandages and did what I could to protect against infection, wondering what would happen if I simply refused to go on. But then I would catch a glimpse of my mother, or Elias, or sometimes, sickeningly, the two of them together. I saw the way Persaphe's teeth flashed with her smiling words, and I imagined what lies she was weaving, what myths she steeped in his heart, and how she possibly intended for all this to end. Elias' face gave no clues to his thoughts. He was wooden, impenetrable: a closed door.

The wind rose, driving sleet into us like a plague. The packhorses huffed in agitation; people eyed me with disgust and turned their backs. Ophelia caught my gaze across the distance, but if ever she tried to venture closer, Hobore would snarl her away.

The wound in my cheek finally healed. I pulled the stitches out myself.

...

The snow fell hard and deep, and after came a white frost that made the air slice through my lungs. There were no roads anymore, there had not been for a long while, but the carpenter and his apprentice crafted skis for the wagons to turn them into sledges. With this alteration, progress sped, for the wagons and for me as well, as I was able to step on the flattened snow-paths they left behind.

It was a rare afternoon when Hobore was not acting my shadow, but rather watching my movements from a slight distance. I stood in the food ration line with my bowl and spoon, trying to ignore the insults muttered my way. *Always knew there was something shifty about her. Bet she's had the king under her spell this whole time. Black magic, that's what I heard. Bewitched him. Well, it explains the rumors...* I kept my eyes determinedly on my feet, even as my cheeks burned. The cuts on my arms itched; the bandages had grown ragged and stained. I thought of Hobore's flask and felt an uncharacteristic pang of desire.

I was returning from the food line when I saw it. My bag of belongings was lying open beside my small fire, the contents torn through. My heart plummeted as I dropped my porridge and gathered up the satchel. When my fingers closed first around my compass and then my small pouch of *istilla* from the deep forest, my lungs opened. My most precious items were there, they were safe. Slowly, with forced care, I sorted through the rest of my possessions. The only item missing, it seemed, was my spare set of clothes, a homespun shirt and trousers that were plain but warm. I wondered what anyone would want with them, yet the relief that neither my compass nor *istilla* had been stolen was so great, I hardly cared to investigate.

The answer came anyway, two days later.

It was a wet, foggy morning, the sun shining valiantly through broken clouds. We stopped to water the horses at an icy river. The path down the bank was slick, with an easy gradient that quickly sharpened into a steep drop. Hobore was at my side, grumbling about the mud as he guided his horse to drink, but aside from him, we were alone; the rest of our caravan was around the riverbend out of sight.

As I came upon the river, I slowed my pace. The water cut hard and deep into the bank, and it would be easy to lose my footing. I crouched by the riverside, tapping a puddle of thin ice with my fingers. Hobore peered sideways at me.

He shoved, and I plunged into the river.

The cold was a dagger to my ribs. It sliced the air right out of me. I flailed, disoriented, fighting the urge to inhale as I struggled for the surface. Though the current was not over-strong, the water was freezing, and the sudden drop in temperature caused my limbs to seize. My pulse stuttered; my cloak tangled around my legs. My back hit something—a large rock, maybe—and the impact sent me spinning. I continued to battle, relying on my arms and what little movement I could wring from my legs until finally, finally, I broke the surface with a gasp.

Hobore and his horse were gone. In their place, a group of witnesses from our caravan was coming around the riverbend, drawn by the sounds of my struggle. I hardly saw them. I was befuddled, shuddering, nearly blind with cold. Coughing, I kicked to the river's edge and crawled onto its rocky bank. My hair hung wet around me, my clothes squelching. My fingers were a startling shade of white.

I made myself take a deep breath. I would not panic. I needed a change of clothes, that was first. I would return to my belongings and make the switch quickly, before hypothermia…

That was when I remembered. My only spare set of clothing had been stolen.

A needle of fear worked its way into my heart. I looked up at the people amassing along the bank. Hobore stood among them as if he had been there all along. Persaphe was there as well, sliding to the group's front. "Are you really so foolish," she asked me in a voice meant to carry, "as to attempt to escape through a frozen river?"

Shakily, I rose to my feet. Water sheeted from me, puddling at the rocks under my boots. I had no blanket to dry myself, no fire by which to get warm. No one moved to help.

"I did not—" I winced, dipping my head. Tremors wracked my body, and I was starting to feel sleepy, confused. "I did not try to escape. Hobore pushed me."

"Pushed you? Impossible. Hobore has been here."

"No, he was right beside—"

"You snuck away," Persaphe interrupted, weaving a bit of power into her voice. "You slipped past Hobore and tried to flee, and once again, you have been caught in your lie."

The crowd shuffled. Some of the onlookers were surely relishing in my public shaming, but others appeared uneasy. These were not palace courtiers, entertained by displays of cruelty; they were servants, like my father had been, simple and honest. They did not seem wholly pleased by the situation, but nor would they stand against Persaphe on my behalf. Not when I was a convicted assassin. Not with Persaphe's charms swirling invisible through the air.

I knew it was pointless to insist on my innocence, yet I could not help but say, "You are lying."

My mother arched a brow. "That is ironic, coming from you."

"I need a fire," I tried weakly, "and a change of clothes."

"Prisoners do not generally dictate their wishes."

"I don't—" It was becoming hard to form words. "I don't feel well."

"I would imagine not."

"Please." I was dismayed to hear my voice crack. The clouds closed over the sun. My sodden shirt was stiffening to ice. "This—is dangerous. I need—" Another swallow. "Fire. Clothes."

Persaphe smirked. "When the king hears—"

"The king has heard," said Elias.

My head swung, and for a moment, I was struck dumb by the sight of him. Elias was there at the edge of the crowd, not in his carriage, or his wheelchair, but sitting astride a slim gelding. His legs were strapped to the saddle, his spine supported by a backrest, which appeared to have been crafted specifically for the purpose. I had caught only glimpses of Elias since our departure; I had not realized he'd made such progress toward mobility. It was impossible, despite everything, not to marvel at how he looked.

Persaphe's face was wide. Her eyes jolted once to the king, in a look of pure hostility, before she closed it down, tranquil again, her mouth set in the temperate shape of a woman doing her duty to her sovereign. "Your Majesty…"

"The girl is no use to me dead," Elias said. He did not raise his voice, yet he spoke as if a pillar of the earth. "Someone, bring her dry clothes."

With a flick of his wrist, Elias turned his horse and vanished.

I stood numbly as the onlookers dispersed. Persaphe watched Elias retreat, and I thought if anyone could see the look in her eyes, they would witness the true murderess revealed. But no one saw. Everyone's attention was on the king and then—as Kurton and Ophelia approached me—on us.

"These are Ophelia's," Kurton told me gruffly, holding out a blanket and wool dress. "She says you may borrow them until your own clothes dry. Then she wants them back, and there had better not be any new stains, or holes—"

"What Kurton means," Ophelia interjected, "is that we are happy to help. I already started a fire. You will be needing help out of those clothes, yes? Preferably before they harden any further."

Kurton glanced at Ophelia. His expression was taut, but when his gaze fell to her, he softened. "Best you go quickly."

I took the items with fumbling hands and followed Ophelia to her fire. Each step was agony on my frozen feet, and though I attempted to hold my breath against the pain, the tears came anyway. I sniffled and wiped at my face. Ophelia lent me her arm, and when that was not enough, she looked over her shoulder and said, "Kurton."

He was there, gathering me up as he had once gathered me in the grand hall. The last time Kurton had done this, his heart pounded with worry. Now, he was steady as the moon, grim-faced and dutiful. He carried me to the blanket next to Ophelia's fire, set me down, and retreated without another word.

"Your mother is a problem," Ophelia muttered as she wiped my tears, then peeled off my cloak. I nodded jerkily, too out of sorts to really consider the implications of what had just happened. "Look at you," she sighed. "Frozen half to death."

There was little modesty to be had on the open road, yet I was thankful no one watched as Ophelia stripped me bare, then hurriedly bundled me in her dress and cloak. She piled more wood onto the fire and began rubbing my fingers, trying to work back some of the blood. Slowly, my shivering returned—a good sign—and my limbs became more cooperative. After, Ophelia told me she would find fresh bandages to replace the sodden ones from my *eithier* cuttings. When I attempted to follow, she set a hand on my shoulder to keep me down. "Rest," she ordered, not unkindly.

"I cannot rest for long," I said through chattering teeth. "I will be left behind."

"We are not going to leave you behind." She pushed me down more firmly. "The king has ordered us to make camp here."

"But…" I licked my numb lips, glancing at the sky. "It is only midday."

"Yes."

"Why are we making camp at midday?"

"I should think it is obvious."

I looked at my hands, orange under the fire's glow. I thought of Elias as he had been on his horse, the way he had referred to me as *the girl*, how he had not once looked at me. "The *eithier* is working," I said quietly. "That is how Elias has the strength to ride. The potion is building up in his system, and day by day, he grows stronger. If he delays our journey, it is only to ensure I can continue brewing his remedy."

"That may be part of it," Ophelia agreed.

"That is all of it."

Ophelia said nothing; there was only the breeze through dry grass, and the faint crackling of the fire. Yet I could see the doubt in her face. I wanted to argue further. *This is not a fairytale, Ophelia. There are no hidden meanings to be found between the lines*. My vision swam with exhaustion.

"Persaphe would have had you killed today," Ophelia said at length. "Hobore may have been the one to push you into the river, but do not think I cannot guess whose orders he was acting under. I have tried speaking to Kurton about the threat she poses. He does not seem to hear me." She rubbed a thumb against the back of her hand. "He acts differently when Persaphe is near. Everyone acts differently. It is almost as if they forget themselves, and see only her."

"It is my mother's power," I replied. "She has always had the gift of glamour. It seems to have grown stronger."

"I would not call it a *gift*."

"Ophelia," I said plaintively. "There is something I need to tell you."

I explained everything. King Adonis Alder's death, Hobore and the horse bridle, Persaphe's curse on Elias, her confessions, and of course my own story, the self-inflicted poisonings and the *nightlight*, the festival and the kiss. I spoke until I was breathless, and Ophelia was putting her arms around me once more and saying, "It's okay, Selene, it's going to be okay."

"I tried to tell Kurton as well," I finished in broken tones. "I wanted to explain. But he would not hear me, either."

Ophelia's eyes were dark as she nodded. "Your mother has always held unnatural sway over the court. I remember how people used to adore her—and for what? She was never kind; she never healed them or cared for them, not like you did for my brother. Yet she had them enamored."

"We should not be surprised," I said. "I meant what I told you before. Persaphe may be to blame for the king's condition, but so am I. I poisoned Elias. I lied about it for years. I abused the friendship of the King's Guard and betrayed their trust. Why should they listen now? They have every reason to hate me."

"But," Ophelia said fiercely, "they have reason to forgive you, too."

That evening, Ophelia was given permission to sleep by my side. She pulled her bedroll close to mine and told me stories to distract me, spinning tales of her wayward brothers and all their many adventures.

It worked; for a time I was able to forget the day's hardships, forget that Hobore had attempted to end me outright on my mother's order, or what that boded for the future. Ophelia brushed my hair from my forehead as a sister might, and held my hand and said, *sleep, Selene.* Yet loneliness rose sharp to my throat, and I fought to stay awake, just to feel the warmth of her presence a little longer.

"Why do they not work on you?" I asked.

The fire was down to embers, the stars pinpoints overhead. Ophelia shifted in the dark. "What?"

"My mother's charms. When she speaks, people go mindless, yet you see her clearly. Why?"

Another silence. "I think," Ophelia replied, "it is because of you."

"Me?"

"When you are near, Persaphe's powers are less. That is why she wants to keep the king away from you. Aside from the secrets you possess, it is probably one of the reasons she wants you dead. Haven't you noticed? You say her powers have grown stronger since her return. But what if her powers were always this strong, but your presence interferes? What if your influence has the strength to outweigh hers?"

I pulled back a little, remembering my mother's words from the prison. *I never believed you gifted with charms, but it is obvious your spells are mingling with mine.* I thought of how Elias had overruled Persaphe to bring me on this journey, how he asked after my conditions as a prisoner, ordered someone fetch me clothes after the river incident. Small things, seemingly inconsequential, yet if Ophelia was to be believed, each of these were small, visible chinks in Persaphe's stranglehold.

"Even if what you say is true," I replied heavily, "my mother is still in control. Whatever small magic I possess has gained me little. It is not enough."

"It is not *much*," Ophelia corrected, "but why should that mean it is not enough?"

THIRTY-FOUR

Elias did not speak to me again, but nor did he remain so hidden. As we continued west, I began seeing more of him as he practiced with a walking cane or rode on horseback. It was true, what I had told Ophelia—with the daily use of my *eithier*, Elias was able to regain his mobility in new ways. His movements were awkward at first, half-bent and jerky, though it was not long before the muscles in his legs and back grew strong. In the evenings, I watched him take up his cane and pace among his men, speaking to the grooms and troops, sitting for meals. He ate as the rest of us ate, seeded breads, hard cheeses, foraged *spinitula* grass boiled dark green and salted like the sea, and people gathered around him to tell stories, smiling and sharing. Elias did not look like a king there on the winter road. He looked like a normal man.

The sight twisted me up, leaving me muddled and strangely achy. It was confusing, watching Elias relearn to walk and ride from afar. It was more confusing still that his newfound strength was due to my *eithier*, which I was forced to brew at the cost of my own health. I might have reminded myself this was the punishment for my crimes, and that I had once vowed to see Elias recover no matter the method, but these were no real comforts. Elias' progress was only a ruse. The *eithier* was not a true cure; his strength would fail as soon as I stopped brewing, and he would again be as he was. If there was a way to make the *eithier's* effects permanent, I had never found it. And now it was too late.

There was a week of drifting white snow, followed by a warm wind and a melt. The sun worked its way beneath our cloaks, and we came across a bounty of wild apples, enough even for the horses. It was there beside that orchard that our party stopped to make camp for the night.

Hobore watched me set my cauldron over a small fire as I did every third evening, his head propped against his pack, eyes half-hooded. Already, his cheeks were ruddy with booze, his pulse elevated due to the strain of all his drinking. We had hardly spoken since the river incident; looking at him tended to summon feelings of rage, so I did my best to keep whatever distance I could. That evening, I ignored him entirely as I sorted through my bag. I had nearly used my entire supply of normal *istilla* to craft Elias' *eithier*, which meant in order to continue, I would soon be forced to take portions from my deep-forest collection. I hated to do it—that *istilla* was limited, and valuable—yet what choice did I have? I pulled out a few more ingredients, glancing again at Hobore, who held my gaze and asked, "Why have you not yet tried to poison me?"

"What," I asked flatly, "kind of question is that?"

"I know you have the means," he continued in slightly slurred tones. "You surely have the desire. I helped your mother spring her trap. I pushed you into that frozen river. I have been waiting…" He peered through the small opening in his flask and did not finish the thought, but only said again, "I have been waiting."

The note in his voice. I felt my disbelief rising abreast my anger, like two eagles circling. "You have a knife," I snapped. "If you wish to die, you know where to stick it."

I had only a moment to witness Hobore's unbridled shock before I sprang to my feet and stalked into the orchard. I wanted to spit with incredulity, for Hobore's brazenness, his cowardice. I barreled forward, paying no mind to my direction. It was only after several minutes of angry stomping that my thoughts began to settle. I looked around, noting the sound of a hidden creek, the carpet of wild moss. Hobore had not followed me.

I moved deeper into the orchard, light-footed with this sudden, unexpected freedom. We were in a region called the Urimond, the *Bright Earth*, which was the final stretch of continent before Isla met the sea. The sun touched the horizon, and it honeyed the trees, turning everything soft and yellow. The air smelled of woodsmoke; the ground was littered with bruised apples.

I thought of the fevered look in Hobore's eye right before he pushed me into the river. The way he constantly reeked of alcohol, the empty longing in his face when he spoke of poison. Hobore believed I hated him, and a part of me did, but I also pitied him. He was not violent by nature—the Hobore I had known as a young girl had been mild, if a bit uninspired. Wasn't he as much Persaphe's prisoner as I had been?

Could it really be that he wanted to die?

So caught was I in these thoughts that I did not notice Elias until I was practically upon him. He was standing by the burbling creek, his cane in one hand, a closed book in the other. I jerked back in surprise, my ankle catching an upturned root. Elias turned, his eyes going round as my arms windmilled and I fell, landing on my backside with an earthy *thump*.

Kurton appeared around a gnarled tree, drawn by the disturbance. He halted when he saw me, his sword halfway pulled from its sheath.

For a moment, the three of us froze like that, as if characters in a painting. Kurton—apparently deciding I posed no immediate threat—was the first to move, sliding back to his original watchman's position.

Elias snapped his gaze away as I rose awkwardly to my feet. I wondered how I must look, rushing through the woods without my guard. As if reading my thoughts, Elias asked, "Where is Hobore?"

I tried to reply calmly. "Back at camp."

Elias tucked the book under his arm, still not quite looking at me. "You are supposed to remain under his watch."

"I do not need a guard," I said automatically. "If I wanted to run away, I would have done so already. Do you really think Hobore could stop me?"

"Is that," he asked, "supposed to persuade me?"

"I am here because I wish it," I insisted. And then, more quietly, "I think you know why."

His gaze darted to mine. Under the early evening sun, Elias' eyes were the hard, shifting anger of the first day after his poisoning. Yet there were memories in their depths that had not been there four years ago. I kept looking. To his hands, strong on the neck of his cane. To his clothes, a thick winter coat, practical boots. There was a broken leaf stuck to the back of his leg, as if he'd been sitting on the ground and had not brushed himself off. I noticed, with that same sense of disassociation, that I could hear his heartbeat but could not feel it.

He said, with some roughness, "Your bandages are filthy."

I looked at my arms. It was true, the wrappings from my *eithier* cuttings were frayed and mud-splattered, but that was to be expected. Clean linens were hard to come by in the faraway wilderness.

He asked, "Do you not worry about infection?"

I did worry, but that fear seemed small compared to everything else.

"My blood is untainted," I said in answer. "I would not add it to your *eithier* if I thought otherwise." He looked away again; a muscle twitched in his cheek. My eyes returned to his figure, his hips in line with his shoulders, his spine upright. I felt a tug at my throat that made me say softly, almost breathlessly, "You are walking."

Not once had Elias and I spoken since the start of our journey. He believed me a traitor, a liar, a witch. If he was going to send me away, this would be the moment. Yet his only reply was, "Yes."

"And…how has it been? Are there any side effects? Of the *eithier*, I mean? We never tested what would happen on a long-term dose. I suspect, given enough time, additional changes will reveal themselves. That is common with most medicines, let alone a *gaigi*, and it seems only prudent…" I stopped at the look on his face. "What?"

"You sound the same."

"The same as what?"

"As you have always sounded."

Silence fell, so that we heard the melting ice drops pattering down from branches. Heat rose unbidden to my cheeks. I did not know how to reply.

"I have often thought of making this journey," Elias said after a moment. "I remember once mentioning the River to my mother. This was shortly after my father's death. I asked if she wished to go there, to undo the suffering that had befallen her. Althea told me I needed to spend more time in prayer if I was truly addled by such childish fantasies. It was—well. I thought…" He pulled the book out from under his arm. It was a copy of *The River of Reversal*, battered and dog-eared. The same copy he had once given me.

"I have dreams, sometimes," he continued in a faraway voice. "I am running through a field. I have regained the use of my legs, without the need for chair or cane. Lately, I have been having this dream every night. And then I wake, and remember the truth, and it is as if I have been poisoned all over again."

My heart twisted. Never did Elias talk so openly about his paralysis. I wondered if I was right about the *eithier*. Perhaps honesty was a side effect of a long-term dose. The lack of pain could be tricking him into speaking freely, and to his poisoner, of all people.

"I asked you once if you would step into the River," he said. "You avoided the answer. Now, I understand why."

My hands were cracked with cold. For once they were useless, unmoving at my sides. "Elias." He flinched at my use of his name. "I made a mistake, and I take responsibility for that. But you must believe—you must know I have regretted it ever since."

Remorse came to his face, like blood to a wound. "I can't—I don't know what to say to you. What you did, how you kept it from me…" His fingers tightened on the book. "How did I not see it? How could I have been so blind?"

"My mother—"

"Your mother." He gave a hoarse laugh. "Persaphe is the only one who speaks clearly in all this."

I felt myself shrink. "You cannot truly believe that."

"She understands the importance of the River. She has seen it, has told me the tales…" Though he was still looking in my direction, his eyes became glazed. I was reminded of the way the guards looked after they inhaled my sleeping powder. That blank mindlessness. "The River is my hope."

"The River is a lie," I retorted.

His attention jerked back. "A lie?"

"I understand why you want to believe in it. Elias, you know I do.

Like there is a simple solution, a way to go back in time, and all you have to do is reach it and everything will be made better. But Persaphe is not your safekeeper. Not now and not…" I stumbled. "Not before. She is setting a trap."

"Of course you would say so." The softness between us—if that is indeed what it had been—was gone. "You are so unlike Persaphe. I often wonder how you two are of one blood."

His words seemed to snag something within me. "What?"

"It is as if you come from different worlds."

The thought landed, light as a moth on wood. I was looking at Elias, but it was as if the scene had vanished from my vision. I remembered, suddenly, how Persaphe had pulled an amber vial from her pocket at the House of Healers. The way she said, *But you are missing an ingredient, are you not?* She let the question dangle without delivering an answer, and I had thought all her words were lies. But I *was* missing an ingredient to make the *eithier's* effects permanent. I had been missing it all along.

The ingredient I lacked was Persaphe's blood.

It was as if I had become snow.

Of course.

Nightlight was made with blood. I knew this, because I had recreated the poison using my own. Yet the *nightlight* used to poison the king was not made with *my* blood—it was made with my mother's. That meant the matching *gaigi*—Elias' one true cure—would require the same.

As soon as I had the thought, I met a wave of despair. I brewed the *eithier* every third night, I could practically do it in my sleep, but I was using my blood as an ingredient when I needed my mother's. Yet how could I possibly secure a dose of Persaphe's blood? I could not exactly ask to cut her open. Maybe there was some other way, some use of trickery, a sleeping potion, a tonic to confuse, but I had already been condemned for my duplicity, and even if I stole the blood straight from her veins, Persaphe would still bear the wound. They would know who did it. And then they really would kill me.

Elias was still watching me. I realized how I must look, standing transfixed in my thoughts. I exhaled, trying to arrange myself without really knowing how. "I am my father's daughter," I said in reply to his earlier comment. "As for my mother…she is not who she seems. I know—" I had to brace myself. "I know why you are the way you are. Why you cannot stand the touch of others. Persaphe…she cursed you, Elias."

He gave a harsh laugh. "What?"

"She is the reason you fear human contact."

"How dare—" His nostrils flared. "How *dare* you invent a story about something like that."

"I invent nothing. Please, believe me. This is all part of her plot to end the Alder bloodline, and she holds you in her grip, even now—"

"Enough." Something beyond memory flashed in his eyes; his voice rose the hair on my arms. "I have heard enough."

"But—"

"Will you continue to defy me?" Elias' face was cold. "This conversation is over. Kurton will escort you back."

That night, I lay on my bedroll peering up at the sky. When I was a child I used to close my eyes and point my finger and guess which star it touched. I did not have to look to see if I was right. I knew the constellations by heart.

My father once told me the story of a knight who wished to slay monsters for glory. The knight went to a wizard who granted him the power, but warned he must use his gift within three days, or else the magic would become uncontainable and kill the knight instead. Yet when the knight hunted a dragon in its lair, he found the creature too beautiful to destroy. He returned to the wizard and begged for mercy, for his three days were nearly up, and soon his unreleased power would consume him. When the wizard refused, the knight found a way to divert the spell instead, and he and the dragon both lived out their lives.

I wished Aegeis was there so I could ask, how did the knight overcome the magic that should have killed him?

A different scene rose to my mind. I saw Queen Mother Althea standing at her window, questioning me about the truth serum. Her words slipped under my skin. *Can you do it?*

No, I had said. Impossible.

Yet even then I wondered. I could brew elixirs of every variety, to heal, to kill, to alter or revert. Sometimes, all I needed was to imagine the outcome and the recipe would spring to mind, ready for my waiting hands. Even absent those moments of intuition, I knew how to experiment, how to gather and collect and remember exactly what I tried, in what proportions, at what time of day.

If anyone could create a truth serum, it should be me.

I had tried revealing Persaphe's secrets to Kurton and to Elias, but they were both too deeply entrenched in her charms, and anyway, they mistrusted me now. I could not make them listen. Yet if I had a truth serum, they need not listen to me at all. I could force my mother to reveal her own plots. I could put an end to this madness, obtain Persaphe's blood, and deliver the king's cure in a single stroke.

It was a wild solution. A desperate one. Yet my mind caught the line of it and pulled.

Inventing a truth serum would be no easy feat, even with the resources of a kingdom at my disposal, and I no longer had those resources. I had a winter road, and a handful of tools, and a weakened spirit. More troublingly, I would have to keep my work a secret—the terms of my imprisonment had, after all, been made clear. I was to brew the king's *eithier* and nothing more. Other experiments such as this were not allowed.

I rolled to my knees and pulled the deep-forest *istilla* from its pouch. The petals were slightly crushed from the journey, but they had not shriveled or browned as a normal plant would have. There were three flowers in total, plus a tangle of stalks and leaves. Three attempts. That was all I would have.

But perhaps it was all I would need. Because I knew—had known, perhaps, for a long time, in some quiet, unexamined part of my mind—that I might one day set myself to this task. I ticked off my suspicions like silent counters. How freely Elias had spoken that evening in the orchard. How he had once followed me into my workshop and said, *You are more than just my physician.* Both times, he had confessed more than the moment warranted. Both times, he had been under the influence of the *eithier*.

That potion has a way of meddling with my thoughts, Elias had told me before the grim-moon. *The lack of pain…it is almost too liberating. Like I lose control of my inhibitions.*

I curled my fingers around my deep-forest *istilla*, not quite squeezing. *Eithier* was a potion to take away pain, to free the body and therefore the mind. Was there a way to modify the concoction? To make it stronger, impossible to resist, and refocus its effects from physical to mental? Yet simply crafting a more powerful *eithier* would not be enough. I would need something to bind the potion to the mind, to bisect thoughts from intentions. That was all a lie was, was it not? A mismatch between what you think and what you say.

I breathed a disbelieving laugh. Was I really doing this? I had not forgotten Elias' story of the potion maker from the king's city. He had died in his attempt to create a truth serum. Inventing such a delicate serum—on the road in secret—was a reckless, dangerous idea, as likely to fail as it was to get me killed, but I had no better ideas, scarcely any allies to call upon, and not much time to spare.

I pulled out my small traveling cauldron, fed my fire. An owl hooted in the night; the trees were bare against the sky. The dark heavens crowned my hands as they began, again, to work.

THIRTY-FIVE

Ophelia came to me the following morning, looking green in the face. I was instantly alarmed. "What is it?"

"I was wondering if you—" But at this she could go no further and bent double, emptying the contents of her stomach across the rocks.

I was there at once, holding her hair, setting a cool hand across the back of her neck. I glanced around, half-expecting Hobore to stop me, but he was nowhere in sight. Since our confrontation the prior afternoon, he had remained conspicuously absent. "Have you eaten something wrong?"

"Oh no," Ophelia said with a smile. "It is nothing like that."

Her smile confused me. I was reminded of the beggars in the King's City, stumbling and laughing wildly at nothing. I wondered if Ophelia was addled. Then she touched a hand to her belly, and I understood. "Ophelia."

"I am only a few weeks along."

"And Kurton—?"

"Is thrilled."

I made her sit on a nearby stump and drink tea brewed hastily over my dwindling fire, with a bit of ginger to help settle her stomach. She thanked me, cupping the mug between her palms and looking cheerfully pale. "Kurton has asked me to marry him. Can you believe it? All at once, I am to be a wife and a mother."

"It is wonderful news," I said, and it was. Yet it also worried me. The journey across Isla had not been easy, and we had yet to even reach the sea. The path ahead held nothing but danger, and if Ophelia was pregnant…

"Quit that," she ordered at the look on my face. "I am stronger than you give me credit."

"It is not too late. You could turn back."

"And leave you on your own?"

"I can handle myself."

"Maybe," she sniffed, "but what of Kurton? I swear, that man cannot brew a proper cup of *kriva* to save his life."

"If that is our greatest worry," I said dryly, "then let us give thanks."

She swatted my arm. "Fine, a poor reason. But if I am gone, who will be there to mend his garments or listen to him snore or remind him to look at the stars? He would be lost without me, and I without him. No, Selene, my place is here." She quieted. "Are you happy for me?"

I laid a hand over hers. "I am happy."

"Good, because I was hoping—"

She was seized by another round of retching, but I already knew what she wanted. "I can brew something to ease the morning sickness."

"I wish I did not have to ask," she said faintly. "You have too much to do already."

I waved her off. "It will only take a minute."

Later that day, I watched from a distance as Kurton and Ophelia announced the news to Elias and the King's Guard. The men went up in cheers, congratulating Kurton, teasing him about cold nights spent under warm blankets. I wished to congratulate Kurton myself, but I knew better than to go where I was not wanted. So I kept my distance, and watched, and told myself a day would come when I could again be among them. After the truth serum was brewed. After Persaphe drank it and her lies were revealed and I had her blood and this nightmare was finally over. Then, I told myself, then all will be well again.

I only wished I could believe it.

. . .

We paused on a rise to observe the terrain. There were sparse oaks to the south and a thicket of birches to the north, their limbs bare, the light pouring through. I could see no more roads or faraway towns, nor any evidence of those things, but there in the distance, larger and more omnipresent than I could have fathomed: the sea.

Later, I would wonder why it did not frighten me to step aboard the king's great ship and traverse those waters. The vessel, named *The Starling*, would speed us over the Crossing Sea, away from Isla, away from everything I had ever known. I should have quaked with fear, yet as we came to the shore and stood in the ship's great shadow, I felt nothing but a restrained sort of anticipation. Perhaps I was too focused on surviving the journey ahead to feel afraid. Or perhaps I was no longer the kind of girl who quaked.

At Persaphe's instruction, our caravan divided itself. Though *The Starling* was a hefty three-mast barque, it had only the space for a light crew and cargo. Three-fourths of our party would return home while the final quarter continued onward. I was ordered into a launch with several others, and together we rowed through the surf out to the waiting ship. Climbing the hull ladder was more challenging than it seemed, up fifteen rungs swinging in the wind, but no one offered any help, and I did not expect them to. In fact, once we were aboard and *The Starling* slid into motion, no one paid me much attention at all; everyone's eyes were on the distance.

The Crossing Sea was famed for monstrous winds and high waves, yet that first day, all was calm. I did my best to stay out from underfoot of the crew as I blinked up at the masts, the sails, the impossible network of ropes and riggings and then out, out at the jeweled sky, the flat horizon, the splash and shine of fish in the water. Though the sea was quiet, it was not still. *The Starling* tossed endlessly, and the never ending motion made me queasy, but a quick sip of Ophelia's nausea potion was enough to steady me. While everyone else retreated below deck to sleep off the seasickness, I stayed above to take it all in.

With dusk came a bounty of colors. I watched the sun's rays stream upwards through gilded clouds, and I glanced unthinkingly for someone to share it with. *Look*, I would have said. *Have you ever seen anything like it?* But the deck was empty save the busy ten-man crew, and anyway, who would I have shown? The King's Guard? Elias? Only Ophelia would have appreciated the scene, but she was down in the storeroom preparing the evening meal.

"The Cup of Life, your father called this ocean."

I swung at the sound of Persaphe's voice. She stood behind me, and though her attention was on the clouds, her eyes seemed to dance with a private joke. "He believed the Goddess created the sea to act as a womb for earth's first humans," she continued. "Men and women incubated under the waves, Aegeis believed, until the day they were grown enough to pull themselves to shore." A huff. "He was always such a bumbling fool."

I stood, breathing the smell of brine and sweat, passive with shock. Persaphe had mostly avoided me since the river incident. The anger—it was difficult to keep the anger from curling up my spine, revealing itself in my bared teeth. I wanted, oh, a thousand things. To shove her over the railing. To sink my knife into her flesh. "Have you come for some purpose?" I asked. "Or do you have nothing better to do than taunt me?"

I wanted to see the anger rise in her as it rose in me, but Persaphe only lifted a shoulder and said, "Your compass."

"What?"

"The king mentioned you carry a special compass. He says it was crafted with a second needle to point travelers toward the Evening Star—a necessary tool, if one is to find the River. I am the one who must guide us over the ocean. It will seem odd if I do not have such a device in my possession." She held out her hand. "Give it to me."

"I don't have the compass." My fingers closed around the strap of my satchel. "I left it behind."

Persaphe sighed. "Selene."

"What? It's the truth."

"We both know it is not."

Hobore appeared beside Persaphe. His eyes were a maelstrom of shame, resentment, violence. I remembered my last words to him had been an exposition on suicide, and I found myself regretting it. I took a step back; my calf met the railing. I thought, I will fight. I will throw the compass overboard before I let them so much as glance at its face. Yet I was aware that if this did turn into a brawl, the compass was hidden in my pack alongside my deep-forest *istilla*. If I lost one, I might lose the other.

I could not let that happen.

"Fine." I shoved my hand into my bag. My fingers closed around cool metal. I squeezed, already feeling the loss of that gift. "Here."

Persaphe took the compass and tucked it into her robes. She nodded once, then looked at Hobore. Her expression could have been called—for the barest moment—affectionate. "Hobore."

He took a threatening step forward.

"Wait," I protested, pressing farther against the railing. The wind rattled the ship's riggings. Below, waves sloshed against the hull. "What are you doing?"

"The king came to me," Persaphe said silkily, "asking the most interesting questions about my power. How it works, what sorts of deeds I might do with it. Curses I might lay. Where did he find this sudden curiosity, I wonder?"

My heart thumped in my ears. "I don't know."

"Did you think you could speak to His Majesty behind my back? That you could attempt to thwart me, and I would not find out?"

"I told him nothing," I lied. "If he suspects you, that is your own fault. Leave me be—I already gave you want you wanted."

"This is what I want," Persaphe said, and Hobore's fist came down.

• • •

I do not know if I fought. I was wrought senseless by Hobore's knuckles, the methodic violence, my face torn and bloodied from the blows. After, I was half-dragged, half-carried, and the world was full of noise: mutterings, questions, a cold, ethereal voice controlling the journeyers, hushing their doubts, saying over and over, *She is a witch. You mustn't forget.*

I was deposited in a small room, which looked to be a converted storage closet. There was a hammock, but I had no strength to draw myself to it. Hands—it felt like many hands touched me, though there was only Hobore's voice muttering, "You should have killed me when you had the chance."

I hurled myself at him in a rush of delayed rage, but he caught my wrists with surprising strength. For a moment we hovered face to face, mine curled with pain, his hazy and hateful. "You blame *me* for your misery?" I whispered, with terrible effort. Blood sprayed from my mouth. "Do you really, Hobore?"

"There is no one else."

"There is, and you know it."

Only then did I notice Kurton over Hobore's shoulder, eyes wide with incomprehension. Hobore punished me again, his elbow cracking over my head, but Kurton's voice came close, saying, "No, stop. What are you doing?"

A gray fog slipped across my sight. I did not hear what more Kurton said to Hobore. I did not see where Persaphe had gone. My lip was broken, my head throbbing. They left me where I had fallen in the doorway. I could hear the crew speaking to each other somewhere out of sight, yet my room was located in a deserted corridor, and I saw no one. I thought, I should find my courage, try to rise. I should brew something for my bloodied lip, check to see if any of my teeth are broken. Instead, I closed my eyes and drifted into unconsciousness.

• • •

There was a palm at my forehead. Feather-light, almost not a touch at all. Kurton's voice said, from a slight distance, and without feeling, "I think he would have killed her, had it gone on."

Silence, from the one touching my face. I felt his fingers tremble, then steady. His palm came to rest more solidly on my cheek.

Kurton said, "Ophelia has been trying to warn me…"

"I know," came the voice of the one touching me.

A cough of discomfort. "I heard Hobore tell Selene she should have killed him when she had the chance. It…well. It has made me wonder…"

More silence.

"She really could have poisoned us by now, if she wished it," Kurton continued. "Hobore is half-worthless, and that food tester is little better. Given what we now know of Selene's abilities…she should have at least *tried* to poison us. Or tried to escape."

"Yet she hasn't," said the other. "Why is that?"

The hand was gone, and the men with it.

. . .

I woke sometime after midnight. I was in the hammock of the small closet-room, my belongings tucked beside me, my cloak drawn over my body like a blanket. I blinked, bleary-eyed, and winced at the pain in my head. Did I climb into the hammock on my own? If so, I could not recall it. I could recall nothing, in fact, except for a hand on my cheek, a voice, two men. A dream?

With effort, I lifted my head and looked around. The room was dark enough that I could not tell if the door was open or shut. I squinted, testing my limbs, trying to find my bearings. My tongue darted out to touch my split lip. I tasted wax paste. Someone had tended the cut with ointment.

That was when the shouting began.

I came abruptly upright. A moment later, *The Starling* gave a violent heave, sending loose items rolling. Bewildered, I clung to the hammock's sides to avoid being tossed, listening as crew members burst from the nearby men's chamber and rushed above deck. My nerves were straining; adrenaline rushed through me.

Clumsily, I rolled to my feet. My headache reared in protest, but once I got my legs under me, the pain subsided a bit. I felt my way out of my room and up the hallway. I was moving through the dark on instinct, unable to wring any sense from my thoughts, the night, the panicked hollers gaining urgency above deck. Reality wavered like air around a flame; the ship tilted again, so that my shoulder bumped the wall. What was happening? I remembered the chapters from *The River of Reversal* detailing the maiden's voyage over the Crossing Sea and all the many monsters she faced. Could this be an attack? A leviathan or cyclops or sea-snake with ten heads? A shadowed figure bolted past me, striding with the urgency of someone fleeing.

When I reached the mouth of the passageway, I saw why.

It was not a leviathan to blame for the ship's jolting, or a cyclops, but a storm. The clouds were massive, omnipresent, shaped like a great wall of smoke. The crew was swift at work, lowering the main sails, raising the storm sails, securing everything within reach. Lightning flashed, quick and strangely green. It was not yet raining, but the waves were high enough to slosh the deck, staining the wood black. I hovered there at the doorway, transfixed by the scene as if caught in a story.

That's when I spotted Elias.

He stood at the railing with his back to the sea, gripping the wood for support. Kurton was at his side, motioning toward the cabin, and Elias was nodding, though he eyed the pitching deck uncertainly. I felt myself come alert all at once. "No," I whispered, in the voice of a girl trapped in horror. Had Elias become caught in the storm before he had a chance to seek shelter? Or was there some other reason he had chosen to venture out at such a dangerous time? His cane, I noticed, was nowhere in sight.

A burst of wind knocked me from my feet. I cried out in surprise, hooking my arms into a coil of rope. Kurton grabbed Elias and held him steadfast while bracing against the spray. An untethered crate flew by the pair, disappearing overboard without a sound. The sight caught my breath, bringing a belated fear.

I shoved upright and began moving toward Elias and Kurton. The rain began to pour then, obscuring the deck. My pulse pounded; the broken skin of my face stung with icy drops. I had no real plan in mind beyond helping Kurton usher Elias back below deck, quickly, before the storm grew any worse and moving became impossible.

Elias spotted me over Kurton's shoulder. He wrenched back, wild-eyed, and tried to speak, but the words were lost on the wind.

A second gale struck, and *The Starling* heaved, everything lifting and then smashing back down. I was again thrown to the planking, though this time I could not immediately stand. I grabbed for something to anchor myself as a wave surged under the ship, tilting the deck impossibly sideways. When I raised my head again, Kurton was still at the railing, but Elias had vanished.

The scene slowed in my vision. *The Starling* continued to lean; a dark canvas of water appeared beneath us. Kurton was gripping an iron cleat, hollering madly over the ship's side. The crew had paused their work, everyone latching to masts and poles lest they tumble into the sea.

I do not remember what I clung to. I do not remember choosing to let it go. I only recall the swift, sharp bite of rain as gravity tugged me through the air down toward where Elias had vanished, and the churning black sea rushing up to meet me.

I hit the water with a great *whoosh*. For a moment, everything went so black I thought I had been struck blind. Then I broke the surface, gasping and spitting. My mouth tasted of fresh blood. My heart labored. Overhead, *The Starling* loomed, still rising on its massive wave. If it capsized, I would be crushed underneath.

I forced my eyes away from the ship and down to the water, searching for a hint of pale skin, a blot of rain-darkened hair. Nothing. I imagined Elias somewhere under the waves, struggling to make his legs kick. He had regained much of his mobility these past weeks, but swimming and walking were not the same. They required different motions, separate muscle groups. Elias would not have the strength to tread water, but if I could find him, pull him to the surface while somehow keeping myself afloat, and avoiding the looming ship, and the storm-battered swells…

It was, of course, ridiculous. I had never been very gifted physically, and Elias was nearly twice my size. Even had I been an expert swimmer—and unweakened as I was from travel, and the *eithier* cuttings, and Hobore's beating—jumping in after Elias would do nothing but ensure we both drowned. It would have been better to stay on board with Kurton and toss out a life raft like a sane person, but I did not feel sane. I felt quite possibly mad.

My boots pulled at my feet. My bandages were weights around my arms. I forced my eyes to do another sweep, and when still I saw nothing, I plunged beneath the surface.

The noise cut away. The water was cold and perfectly black. I sensed the sea's enormity, the press of its ancient depths. I swam down, down, pausing for a moment to focus. In the stillness, I thought—almost—I could feel something.

The water was needle-like on my extremities; my head seemed twice its normal size. In my chest, that sensation continued to grow, as if a second heartbeat had taken up residence and was now trying to nudge aside my own...

My thoughts took on a black-and-white clarity. I could feel Elias' pulse again, as I once had. But where? Where? I had never used our connection to find Elias' location before. I was not even sure such a thing was possible. The ocean pressed in as I strained to sense more, fighting the burn in my lungs until I could hold my breath no longer.

I resurfaced, gasping wet air. This time, I was smarter. I kicked off my heavy boots, tore the sodden bandages from my arms. I took sips of air until my lungs were at absolute capacity before diving under again. There was no more time for doubts—I had to believe I could do this, or we really would drown. I listened for Elias' pulse as I had listened for my deep-forest *istilla*—with the entirety of my being. I thought I could sense something through the blackness beneath me, maybe, so I swam blindly in that direction. My lungs burned. My ears ached from the pressure. I kept my hands outstretched, swimming and swimming until finally, my fingers closed around fabric.

I startled at the unexpected contact and nearly jerked away before better sense took hold of me. I tightened my grip around a handful of jacket and started kicking for the surface. It was the longest, most agonizing minute of my life. My muscles flagged; my vision spotted with the need to breathe. Surely, I thought, I will not last another second, not with death beating at my back, and only storm-ravaged waters ahead. Yet I did last, long enough to pull both our heads above the waves.

As soon as we broke the surface, Elias began coughing. I could have wept then, for relief and fear and the strangest sensation of helplessness. Elias' face was ghastly, his hair plastered to his head. When his spluttering subsided and he finally looked to see who had saved him, his face blanked in disbelief.

Cries sounded from the ship overhead, followed by a great splash as Kurton dove in beside us. I wondered if we had all turned to fools, until I saw the rope. Kurton held one end, while the rest of the King's Guard gripped the other from up on the deck. Kurton tried to wrap an arm around Elias, but the king pushed him back. "Her first."

"No," Kurton clipped. It was the first time I had ever heard him disobey a direct order.

Again, Kurton tried to wrap his arm around Elias and again, Elias shoved him off. "I said," Elias ground out, "her first."

"I heard what you said."

"Then do as I command."

"I will not."

The rain continued to pour, the sea tossing water into our faces. When Kurton moved in a third time, Elias raised a fist. It seemed they might actually fight each other.

"This is ridiculous," I cried over the storm. "Elias, please. We will all die if you do not go now."

Elias glanced at me. Kurton used the distraction to yank him into a firm hold. The king may have been well-built, but Kurton was a bear, and there would be no more resisting. Kurton knotted one ankle around the rope and tugged the line, and their tangled bodies were lifted free from the water, hauled up by the men on board. I watched them swiftly shrink into the sky.

The storm was still coming heavy over my head. Rain galloped across the ocean's frothing surface. After a moment, the rope came back down. I could hear Kurton hollering for me to grab its end so they could pull me up next, but I only tipped my head back and squinted at the roiling clouds. The storm was raging, violent, hungry. But it was honest, too. It was nothing but what it showed itself to be.

That feeling of helplessness was worse. It clenched my heart like a fist.

I had always known I was suffering a bit of insanity to believe I had any chance of righting my wrongs. I was on a fated quest, and if I kept at it, it was only because I was too stubborn to see what was clear before me. *Only the madman believes he has no limit*, my father used to say, yet I think it should have been, *Only the madmen and the doomed*. Where was my limit? Was it there, in those waves? Or had it passed already without my noticing?

The rope was slipping out of reach. It was reeled in and re-tossed, slapping the water right in front of me, yet still I did not take it. Remorse was its own sort of wave. I thought of the beauty of the dusk sky. I had looked around for someone to share it with, though I should have known there was no one. I was alone. I think I had been alone for a long time.

A new voice overtook the last. Elias was shouting my name, leaning over the railing as Yorvis and Arch tried to haul him back. I saw the fear in his eyes mimic what I felt when I had watched him go over. But of course he was afraid. Without me, he would lose his ability to walk.

Without me, he would die at the hands of my mother.

I wondered again—how had Elias found himself out in this storm? I remembered passing a lone figure in the ship's corridor. Tall, shrouded in darkness. Had Persaphe somehow tricked Elias out onto the deck, then fled back to safety? Was this another one of her plots? I had not forgotten the way my mother asked for my compass. She needed the device to keep up appearances, which meant she had never actually been to the River. Maybe she only pretended to guide us there in hopes the king might die along the way, as he nearly had tonight. Maybe that was the real reason she ordered Hobore to beat me—so I could not interfere.

The thought brought back some of my blood. It steadied me. I looked up at the ship, at the men shouting from above, and I remembered the first time I ever poisoned myself. Those old questions seemed to come down upon me with the rain.

Can you bear more?

How much more?

It took every ounce of my depleted strength to grab that rope. I did as I had seen Kurton do, knotting my foot in its length as they pulled me up. For a moment, I was suspended in midair. Then my bare feet hit the planks, hard enough to make me stumble.

Elias yanked me upright. He was still saying the words he had been shouting when I was down in the water. "Don't, Selene. *Don't.*" He shook me once, his fingers digging into my arms, then abruptly let go and covered his face with a hand. "Take her below deck," he croaked. "Somewhere safe. And by the Goddess, don't let her out until this storm is cleared."

Kurton marched me unceremoniously back to my small room. He threw me a glance, his boots squelching wetly, skin pebbled with goosebumps. When we reached the door, he waited until I met his eyes.

"I cannot fathom how you found His Majesty under the waves like that," he said. "The way you dove in after him…you would have to be mad to do that for someone you wanted dead." I curled my arms around my midsection and said nothing. He continued. "I have begun to suspect…" Yet rather than finish the thought, Kurton only shook his head and looked unhappy. He departed, leaving a trail of water behind him.

After Kurton was gone, I felt my way back to my hammock. I changed into Ophelia's spare dress, hung my wet clothes to dry, then simply leaned into the wall and cried. It was everything: the fear and the relief and the exhaustion. The pain. And the fact that somewhere in the distance, I could still feel Elias' pulse beating softly, softly, into mine.

THIRTY-SIX

One of *The Starling's* masts had been damaged in the storm, and wood was needed to mend it. We limped to the nearest island where we would stay until the ship was repaired. I was sitting on the deck, pulling on a spare set of boots to replace the ones I had lost to the sea, when the cry came. Land!

I saw it then, a thin slip in the distance. As we drew near and the shore came into better view, I realized I knew this island. It was crescent in shape, dusted with powdery white sand, and there upon the beach were three great rocks stretching like fingers toward the sky. *Mirir*, the island is called. This was where my mother had once famously come to hunt those rare wildfruit seeds, back when Adonis Alder reigned king.

Arch's slim figure appeared in my periphery. "Selene."

I turned back to the boots, tugging the laces. I had not spoken to anyone since last night, and though I could not say exactly what my plunge into the sea had changed, I was aware of how people had begun looking at me. Their faces were still full of mistrust, but it was mistrust of a different kind, aimed more at their own inner thoughts than at me.

Arch said, "The king requests your presence."

I did not stand, but rather continued working the laces. My voice was hoarse; I had been sick much of the night from swallowing seawater. "You went after my attacker in the King's City on the night of the festival."

A pause. "I did."

I met his eye. "Does the man live?"

Arch's expression was unreadable. "No."

"He died by your hand?"

"In part." Arch's gaze strayed to my cheek. I had not seen a mirror since leaving Isla; I did not know how the scar looked. "It took me six hours to find him. By the time I did, he was in a bad way. A wound to the neck. He had, for some reason, not tended it. I found him half-unconscious in an alley and finished the job."

My hands had begun to tremble. I clenched them shut. "Thank you."

"He might have perished without my interference," the guardsman noted. "As I said, his condition was severe."

"I am not interested in what might have been. He died by your sword, and I am grateful."

Arch nodded. "Come," he said. "The king is waiting."

Though modest in size, Elias' private room was more luxurious than any other on the ship. It was low and wide, filled with dozens of small comforts: hot drinking water, dried fish and bronzed bread, a wolfskin rug. Elias stood behind the desk, his hands resting lightly on his cane. He was dressed in silver and black, and though there were tired lines around his eyes, I thought he still managed to look handsome for someone who had spent the last night drowning at sea. It was an observation I would just as soon have avoided, but once it arose, a dozen other repressed thoughts came crowding in behind it—the cut of his figure, the shape of his mouth, his green-gold eyes that had once looked at me with such affection. I glanced away, frustrated and a bit flustered. Nearby, Kurton sat in a chair, whittling a piece of wood. A toy for a child. He saw my expression and raised his brows.

"There has been a change of plans," Elias began formally. His eyes rested on my cheek, my neck. I felt his heart tighten and wondered what he saw. The scar? Or was it the way my face had purpled from Hobore's fists? I felt a wash of misplaced self-consciousness as I remembered another room, another conversation. My body had been bruised from my first attempt at recreating *nightlight*. The king had taken one look at me and said, *hideous*.

"Hobore has been released from his duty," Elias continued. "He is no longer to act as your guard."

I felt my expression shift. "Does this mean I am no longer a prisoner?"

A tight smile. "Not exactly. From now on, Kurton will watch after you."

My hope—small as it had been—faded. Willing or not, I was still a captive, and though Hobore had been a cruel warden, I was not sure Kurton was the better option. Hobore, at least, had been easy to fool.

"I would ask," I began diplomatically, "that you reconsider. I believe I have proven my intentions well enough to release me from guarding."

"Not possible."

"Is it not? I have no aim to hurt you, nor will I run away. You have my word."

"Your word means nothing," Persaphe interjected as she swept through the open door, "and you insult our king with that act of innocence."

I took an involuntary step back. The sea breeze, once easy, dragged in my lungs. "It is no act."

"Really, Selene?" Persaphe left the door ajar; the sun glared harshly at her back. "Do you think a few weeks of good behavior will lull us into complacency?"

"I have no desire to lull anyone."

"No," she replied, "only to poison us in our sleep."

I found myself swiftly and quite thoroughly out of patience. "I can brew toxins that float in the air," I snapped. "That lay upon surfaces and seep into the skin, that reflect into the eyes with merely a glance. If I wanted to poison you, do you think a single guard could stop me?"

Persaphe's face flashed momentarily with glee. "You dare intimidate us?" she asked with false shock. "After all you have already done? Your Majesty, did you hear her? She threatens you plainly—"

"I heard," Elias cut in.

"And will you do nothing?"

"Your tone," Kurton warned mildly.

The glee was gone. Persaphe glanced between Elias and me. When she spoke next, I could feel the glamour she steeped into her voice, how it welled in the air like sap from a tree. "Your Majesty, I must speak openly, for I believe you are being tempted by dark forces. My daughter is a liar and a murderess. She is not to be trusted, nor given any additional freedoms." As Persaphe spoke, I heard Elias' breathing slow. Behind him, Kurton was blinking heavily. "If we release Selene from guarding, she will only wreak more destruction. Keep Hobore as her guard, or better, lock her—"

"No." My voice grated against the silk of my mother's tones. "I have stated my intentions. They are exactly as I say."

"You have already proven we cannot trust—"

"Enough." Elias was grimacing; he rubbed his eyes as if fighting a headache. "Leave us, Persaphe, Kurton. I would speak with Selene alone."

Kurton tucked away his whittling and obeyed at once, but Persaphe was slower. "Are you sure this is wise? To be alone with your poisoner…"

Elias sliced his gaze sideways. "You are becoming far too comfortable in questioning me."

I could see the outrage crowding under Persaphe's skin. Her eyes flickered with a memory of power; her face was not the face of any healer. Yet she made her words like cream. "Apologies, Your Majesty."

She gave an overdone bow and departed, leaving nothing but Elias and me and the rhythmic rocking of the ship. My earlier bravado slipped as the silence stretched between us. I found myself unaccountably nervous.

Elias said, "I have half a mind to do as Persaphe wishes and lock you up."

"What?" My heart rocked in rebellion. "No, I swear. I will not run—"

"I do not fear you running. Nor do I think you plan to harm anyone else."

The phrasing of this statement made it clear what, exactly, he did fear. My voice was small when I said, "I have no intention of hurting myself."

"No?" His eyes betrayed a sudden anger. "How am I supposed to believe you?"

"Why would you not?"

"You didn't grab the rope."

"Of course I did."

"Not at first. Not quickly enough. You looked like you wanted—" He turned abruptly away, his fist tight on his cane. "I know that look,

Selene," he said to the wall. "I know that feeling."

My eyes dropped to the scar at his wrist. I saw a vision of him bleeding over his bedsheets, the smell of it, his furious plea. *I no longer wish to bear witness to my own death.*

Elias rubbed his neck, then turned again to face me. "I have resisted putting you in chains since the beginning of this journey, against the advice of many. I know the connection you have with the land, and I did not—" His cheeks blazed, as if he had admitted too much.

"You did not what?"

"Nothing. You must gather ingredients for my *eithier*. That is all I meant." He cleared his throat. "You may retain your limited freedom if you make me a promise."

"What promise?"

"You must stay within sight of our camp. No far flung wanderings. No sneaking away from Kurton as you seem apt to do with Hobore. There will be dangers on the island, and I will not see you walk willingly to meet them."

Through the window behind Elias, the full moon rose clear in the daytime sky. In my pocket, there was an empty space where the compass had once been.

"Well?" pressed the king. "Do I have your word?"

"I will not wander," I replied. "I promise."

THIRTY-SEVEN

The sand was a pale expanse marked here and there by jagged stones bathed in afternoon light. We spread out, camping close to the water's edge along a narrow stretch of shore. I made my fire behind a cluster of rocks to shield myself from the wind, and though I could not see the forest beyond the outcrop, I could hear the breeze whisper through the trees. I would have thought it pleasant, had I been in a state to appreciate nature's enjoyments.

Or had the howls not come.

They rose long and mournful from the forest. People lifted their heads, exchanged glances. "Build that fire up higher," someone said, and torches were lit along the dunes to ward off lurking shadows.

I turned my attention back to my small traveling cauldron. Though Kurton had been assigned to guard me, he appeared content to do so from a distance. I could see him there across the beach with Ophelia, nudging her out of the way as he took over the task of driving a torch into the sand. He seemed to be gently admonishing her for attempting such physical labor. He worried for her, as all soon-to-be fathers worried.

The winter sun tilted west, vanishing beyond the ocean. Twilight blued the white sand, and the cold returned, though I was warm from my cauldron's fire. Just as my potion began to simmer, the howls came again.

"They are the Hounds of Sundown," said one of our men, attempting to soothe his anxious horse.

"The Hounds are just a legend," rejoined another, as if he had forgotten this entire journey was predicated on legend.

"They say the Hounds come at dusk," said a third, a young supply-tender with a patchy beard. "They are made of shadow and air, yet they strike as an axe through wood. We are trespassers on their land. They do not want us here."

I waited until darkness draped the beach like cloth. The torchlight turned the landscape golden-yellow, and nothing looked quite solid. When my brew had cooled, I spooned it into a waterskin and tied it to my waist. I glanced around to be sure those nearby were occupied, then drew up my hood and moved around the back of the rocky outcrop. I toed by a small tidepool; I pushed through the marram grass. I had just set my eyes on those distant, looming woods when I heard a heartbeat behind me. "You should know better."

Kurton was there, standing in the knee-high grass under the moon's pale light. My reply came automatically. "It is not how it looks."

"No?" Kurton wore a heavy coat and hat, his sword long at his belt. It was difficult to make out his expression; his face was all shadow. "Because it looks to me like you are running—undefended—toward a wood full of wolves."

I touched the skin at my waist. "I am not undefended."

"A water canteen? How is that supposed to help?"

I admitted nothing.

Kurton gave a grunt. "The king was right about you."

"In what way?"

"You really do have a death wish."

I worried my lip, considering. "This is the Island of Mirir. Have you heard of it?" When he made no reply, I continued. "My mother once came here to collect a wildfruit called damselberry."

"I know the story."

"Yes," I said faintly. "Everyone does."

When I first heard of Persaphe's voyage to Mirir and her subsequent failure, I thought there must be a mistake. I remembered digging furiously for notes about her journey, listening to the bards, tearing pages from botany books, scavenging every detail I could think. When I finally uncovered the reason for my mother's defeat, that too seemed a mistake. The plant she sought only put out fruit one night of the month, during the full moon. Persaphe had simply come at the wrong time.

Like most of the king's court, the story had fascinated me as a girl, and not only because Persaphe was the first royal physician to ever leave her post for such a time—six months, so went the story, on a personal venture. It was because Persaphe had failed to find what she sought. In those days, I had not believed my mother capable of failing at anything.

At the time, I had not thought much about the plant itself, yet through my research I had inadvertently learned about damselberry's properties—namely, its unique ability to bind any agent without altering its composition.

"Damselberry only puts out fruit during the full moon," I explained, motioning to the sky where the moon shone round. "If I am to find the plant, it must be tonight."

"And why," Kurton asked, "must you find damselberry?"

I wished I could better see his face. I wanted to tally my options, weigh the benefits of the truth versus a lie. But then, maybe it did not matter what Kurton's face showed. If I wished him to trust me again, I would need to trust him, too. "As an ingredient, damselberry has certain characteristics of connection," I explained, "which I believe could be used to make a truth serum."

I heard his heartbeat change. "You aim to create a truth serum? But why…?" A pause. "Never mind. I can guess. You wish to give it to your mother. You will force her to admit what you professed to me in the prison. But…do you really believe such an account will prove your innocence?"

"If my serum succeeds, it should reveal everything."

The grass rustled in the wind. Somewhere behind me, a nightbird flitted among the brush. Kurton said, "I will come with you."

My mouth popped open. "What?"

"Our king ordered me to watch over you, and so I will."

"It would be safer for you to return to camp."

"That is not an option."

"You could pretend you never saw me."

"His Majesty would have my head."

"I cannot complete this task with you trailing after me. There is too much ground to cover. You will slow me down."

"Then we are at an impasse."

I did not want Kurton joining me on this quest, and not merely because he might impede my progress. I was breaking my promise to Elias not to wander off, that was one thing, but to drag Kurton with me?

"Elias will have both our heads," I muttered.

"There are worse ways to go," Kurton replied in a rare beat of humor.

With that, it seemed decided. We set out together, forging a path across the short field into the woods. I listened with both ears, to the night, to my breathing and Kurton's, our heartbeats, the heartbeats of small hidden animals. The trees were evergreens and kept their leaves, blocking much of the moonlight. I had not brought a lantern—I did not want to draw unwanted attention, especially after hearing the howls—but instead relied upon those skills I had developed in childhood to navigate the uneven forest floor. Kurton kept up surprisingly well for his size, and we continued deeper, picking around mounds of old snow, gray alders, tall elms. I cast around for something to say, but Kurton spoke first. "I wanted to thank you."

I nearly stumbled over my feet. "What for?"

"Ophelia told me about the medicine you give her. She said it is the only thing that stops her morning sickness. You do this, yet you must also brew the king's *eithier*, and apparently a truth serum as well. I do not understand how you go on."

I turned my eyes ahead, feeling strangely exposed. "Ophelia would do the same for me."

"Still."

Unsure of how to reply, yet unwilling to let the conversation end, I said, "Ophelia will make a wonderful mother. I am happy for her. For the both of you. I wanted…to offer my congratulations. If you will accept it."

There was a pause. "Thank you."

I glanced at Kurton, feeling buoyed, yet he was frowning. He caught my look and said, "Many potion makers have attempted to create a truth serum. None have ever succeeded."

"No, they haven't."

"Do you really believe you can do it?"

"I don't know."

"I have questions of my own I would want answered," he mused. "I have noticed—and I hope I do not regret telling you this—but I have noticed I feel differently around your mother. Ophelia has tried pointing this out many times, but it's as if I could not hear her. Not until recently. Something about the storm, I think. Or—something about my conversation with you after the storm." He cleared his throat. "Now I notice this difference all the time, in myself and in others. The king, especially. It is almost as if…well, I have never known His Majesty to submit to anyone, yet with Persaphe…"

My fists tightened. I focused on the mist veiling the trees and tried to speak calmly. "My mother has powers such that most do not. Glamour, some call it. It is dangerous magic."

He seemed to be thinking hard. "If this is true, it is…upsetting." More silence. "But no. How could it be true?"

I might have said more, but at that moment I spotted it—behind Kurton, under a dangling spruce, a tumble of bright red berries was slowly opening from their pods, reaching toward the moonlight. "There," I said breathlessly, rushing forward to scoop their hard skins into my palm.

I was focused on the berries. I did not see the threat until it was too late.

It happened quickly, almost too quickly to understand. There was no warning. No snarl or growl, no rustle of twig or bush or approach of a new heartbeat. Kurton cried, "Selene!" and then he was there, stepping between me and a monstrous shadow. It seemed to come from everywhere at once, materializing into the shape of a wolf. Its shoulders were of a height with Kurton's; its eyes were black pits. It bared its grizzly teeth, which looked as sharp as the steel in Kurton's fist. The monster vanished into smoke and reappeared on our opposite side, giving a snarl as it went for my throat.

I twisted to dodge the attack and stumbled, falling to the earth. My wrist snapped as I reached to break my fall, pain shooting through me. I gave a cry, scrabbling for the pouch tied to my waist as Kurton again sprang between us, raising his weapon with a roar. The shadow-wolf turned its eyes on Kurton and lunged; it did not break stride, not even when Kurton plunged his sword between its vulturous ribs. Black teeth bit into Kurton's side, and the man made an awful noise, dropping his weapon. I shoved to my feet, screaming, "Away!" as I hurled my sack of poison at the creature's nose.

It was a direct hit. The pouch smacked the shadow's wolf-head and burst, spraying gray liquid. The creature gave a howl and began to dissolve, the poison running over its body like smoke, consuming everything it touched. Black ichor poured from the wounds, but soon that too was dissolved. The shadow-monster flailed, its muzzle gone, then the shoulders, the haunches, until at last there was nothing left, but silence.

Kurton lay on the rocks, his limbs bent strangely, blood leaking from his side. I rushed to him, holding my broken wrist to my chest, frantically looking around for some herb, some magic to stop the blood. Yet the healer in me knew it was too late, that such a wound could not be tended by me or anyone, even if I had the use of both my hands and all the medicine in the world. I screamed for help, and for fear, though I did not think anyone would hear.

"*Rahvika*—" Kurton's breathing was labored. I hushed him, saying he needed to rest, to just breathe, but he was persistent. "Tell…tell Elias…" He closed his eyes. "You are not his enemy. The storm. The *eithier*. All you have sacrificed…"

"Shh," I tried to say. "Rest, reserve your strength."

"It was the right thing," he continued. "The princess. Ending his engagement. He did—the right thing. He must see it. And Ophelia…tell her that I…our child…"

I took his hand in mine, sobbing a broken, "Yes?" But he never finished.

THIRTY-EIGHT

They must have heard my scream after all, because help came, silent and ashen between the branches. Arch appeared first, followed closely by Freesier and Yorvis and finally, on horseback at the rear, Elias. He looked pulled from bed, a coat and boots thrown over his sleeping clothes. When he saw Kurton's lifeless body, his face went blank with shock. Freesier asked what happened, and I did my best to answer, but the tears were coming freely, and all my words were water.

Slowly, carefully, they carried Kurton's broken body back to camp. I followed at a distance, sidestepping the trail of blood. The trees leaned in, catching my clothes. Each stride jarred my wrist, turning me hot, then cold, then hot again. By the time the landscape of tents came into view, the sun had risen, pouring yellow over the horizon.

A crowd gathered to watch the grim procession. No one spoke. I wanted Elias to look at me, even to just glance my way, but it was my mother who emerged. Her voice traveled over the beach. "How can this be? How can a brave member of the King's Guard be dead?"

I knew what was coming, it took no great thinker to figure it out. I would be blamed for Kurton's death. The evidence was certainly damning. What reason could I possibly offer for slipping away into the woods at night, and luring Kurton after me? How could my actions be deemed anything but nefarious, after I had promised—*I had promised*—not to wander off? I had no strength to defend myself this time, though I knew I better find it, and find it fast. And yet, how could I do that when Kurton's death was, in so many ways, my fault? Had I not been blindly set on my task, had I not let Kurton accompany me, he would have been spared. We both heard the howling. We knew the woods were not safe. Kurton should have been asleep beside Ophelia, not out guarding the king's poisoner on her mad quest. I realized I was still gripping the damselberry. It had cost a man his life.

Ophelia appeared. It was as if I witnessed Kurton's death all over again, through her eyes. She seemed to age at the sight of his body, her shoulders bending, her face turning waxen. Under the dawn light, Kurton's wounds were cruelly exposed. His torso was cleaved, the skin and clothes such a torn mess it was impossible to tell one from the other. He had not finished his final words, but given the extent of the damage, it was a wonder he had been able to speak at all.

Kurton's body was born back to the ship where there would be supplies to wash and lay him out. For a time my mother's questions were forgotten, and even I was forgotten. I made my way back to my small firepit. My wrist had swollen enormously; the pain was beginning to send spasms through my arm, but I did not medicate myself. This was nothing compared to Ophelia's agony, the King's Guards' agony, and it was my duty to bear it.

Morning ripened, cloudy and tepid. I sat in perfect stillness. If I moved, I would run, scream, throw the damselberry into the fire. Could this be real? Kurton dead, yet my life spared? I trembled, brought my good hand to cover my mouth. Trying to think was like pushing through a tangle of briars. For an endless hour, I could do nothing but breathe, and smell the poison residue on my fingers, until Freesier arrived to fetch me. "Come," he said.

We returned to the ship. My sweat was cold on my body. I could not help row the launch, but Freesier needed no assistance. Climbing the hull ladder was agony on my wrist, but I gritted my teeth and used the crook of my arm, bearing it best I could. Once we were aboard, Freesier guided me to a room where a small group had gathered: the King's Guard, Ophelia, Persaphe, Elias. Kurton's body lay on a table. He had been washed and redressed, the worst of his wounds hidden beneath a black sheet. Elias stood stoically near his head, all earlier signs of grief wiped clean. He looked at me once, then away, as if he could not bear the sight of my face. The pain seemed to tunnel from my wrist to my heart.

"Selene." Ophelia spoke my name. She looked so unlike herself. Her pupils were too large, her fingernails distinctly blue—both clear symptoms of shock. I wanted to hug her, to put my forehead to hers and weep together, but I knew she would never want that now, so I merely wrapped my arm around my midsection and waited. "I wish to know—they say you were with him in the woods."

I nodded.

"I would like to hear how it happened."

"We know how it happened," Persaphe said from her place beside the door. Her voice struck the perfect note between sorrow and vengeance. "Truly, Selene, you have outdone yourself. Tempting a king's man into the woods at night, slaughtering him like a beast—"

"Persaphe." Elias' voice was tightly contained. "You are upsetting

Ophelia."

"*I* am upsetting? I have warned you from the start, Your Majesty. I never wanted to bring Selene on this journey. Her evils are more far-reaching than even I feared, and here is the proof. Tonight, a man died at her hands."

"We do not know how he died." Elias' tone was not strong, but it was clear. "Let Selene tell her story."

My mother's face shuttered; she turned to me without a word. She must have realized, as Ophelia had, that Elias never went against her wishes unless I was in the same room. Her power reached deep, yet it was as Ophelia guessed—something about my presence seemed to interfere.

Rather than feel bolstered by this knowledge, I was only empty. I could hear everyone's hearts beating softly about the room, and while it was usually easy to blot out the noise, each pulse seemed to chip away at my attention: Yorvis, Freesier, Arch, Ophelia, Persaphe…and there, distinctly, the thrum of something else. My mother's heart murmur? A hidden mouse? I might have paid it better mind had I not been so consumed by my own dismay. As it was, I was using every last ounce of willpower to stay upright.

"Go on, Selene," Arch prompted. "Tell us what happened."

I did not attempt to steady my tone. There was no use. "Kurton saw me leaving for the woods to gather ingredients," I started. "He was instructed to guard me and would not be persuaded to stay behind. I tried—I promise, if I had known what would happen…but everything had gone so quiet. I did not think. We walked for a time. I hardly even realized when—it happened so fast." My pulse was rising, as if I faced the monster again. "The creature came from the dark. It was just like the story. A wolf, like the ones from *The River of Reversal*. Half creature, half shadow. It lunged for me. Kurton—he stabbed the creature, but not—not before—"

I sucked in a ragged breath, then looked at Ophelia. "He wanted me to tell you he loves you." Kurton had not been able to give his final words, but I could guess them well enough. "He wanted me to make sure you know how happy you made him. He knows you will raise your child to be kind and strong, like you are. And he asks—he asks when your son or daughter is old enough, that you pass on his story, so they might know they had a father who loved them."

Ophelia nodded, then dropped her face into her hands and began to sob. I moved involuntarily to go to her side, but Freesier appeared between us, pointing me from the room. I looked at his stiff finger and felt my expression crumple, though I exited without a fight. The hallway outside the room was empty, lit dimly with hanging lanterns. The floor was sandy and wet. I blinked at the warping walls and wondered if this was how it felt to die while your heart was still beating.

The door opened and then closed behind me. I turned to see Elias, still tight-faced, still shielded in stony composure. For a long moment, he simply looked at me. Then his eyes caught my swollen wrist, and his carefully crafted mask slipped in anger. "Are you not going to tend that?"

I looked at the injury as if I had forgotten it was there.

"Selene." Elias braced against his cane, bringing a hand to pinch the bridge of his nose. "Do not dishonor Kurton by leaving yourself uncared for."

His words seemed to slow my blood. "Uncared for?"

"He would not want to see you like this."

I did not understand what Elias was saying. What did he mean Kurton would not want to see me like this? Was I not the reason for his death? Had I not broken Elias' promise? I felt as if we were underwater, everything murky and unclear. "It is only a broken wrist," I replied nonsensically, as if that was not the sort of injury that required tending. Then, falling back on my usual answer: "It will not interfere with my ability to brew your *eithier*..."

"You think—?" He slashed his hand down, somehow even angrier. "You think I am concerned about your *abilities*?"

His fury startled me. I shrank back. "Are you not?"

"*No.*" He let out an explosive breath. "Follow me," he growled, then tore off as fast as cane and legs would allow.

We were in full view of the crew as we marched down the corridor, through the galley and up another hall. I could see their faces; if saving Elias from the storm had changed their minds about me, Kurton's death had changed them back. A man died today, their expressions said, because of that witch. Your own guardsman. He was someone's love, with a baby on the way. Now that son or daughter will never know their father. Yet you act as if you care what happens to his killer? Have you not been listening to Persaphe's warnings?

Elias led me to his chamber on the ship. From a chest in the corner, he tore out a satchel and tossed it onto the bed, ripping through it with his free hand. A smattering of items landed on the sheets: a wrap, some of my own pain tonic, another one of my elixirs to reduce inflammation. "I have seen you work with these before," Elias said roughly. "I do not forget the scars on my own wrist. You will need a wrap to keep the injury stable, and medication for the pain." He was speaking in a kind of frenzy. "I would bandage it for you, but I cannot stay, I—"

He quit the room, leaving me there with his things. I was so mystified that for a moment, I did not move.

I crept out to find him in the small antechamber, his arm bent against the wall, his face pressed into his forearm. His fingers clenched his cane so hard the knuckles showed white. His shoulders shook.

My throat constricted. I wanted to drop to my knees. I wanted to bury my face in Elias' shoulder and cry right alongside him. "Elias," I whispered, stepping closer. "Elias, I am so sorry."

I reached out to touch the skin of his arm. He jerked away, the breath tearing out of him. His eyes were as wild as they had been the day I first touched him all those years ago, but this time, I did not withdraw in fright. Perhaps it was my own sorrow. Perhaps it was Kurton's last words, still raw in my mind. *You are not his enemy.*

"Elias," I said again.

He was stripped bare, grieving and furious and bitter. He pushed away from the wall, which brought us suddenly close, toe to toe. I felt his proximity like a blunted wound. "You promised," Elias said thickly, "not to venture off."

My eyes held their tears. "I know."

I waited for him to ask why I had done it. I would tell him everything—the reason I had come willingly on this journey, the reality of his curse and his father's death, my attempts to create a truth serum, the importance of Persaphe's blood, everything I feared about my mother's schemes. I did not know if Elias was ready to listen—he had been deaf to me before—yet I knew I had to try. *Persaphe cursed you into fearing human touch*, I would say, *as a way to manipulate you, and she holds power over you still. If she aims to bring you to the River, it is only so that you can go back in time to when she had better control of you, but I fear she does not truly intend to make it to the River. She aims for you to die along the way, as Kurton died. She wants it to seem like an accident, as your father's death seemed. There is a reason my mother has been killing kings. There is something she is after, and I fear it will have consequences for us all.*

Elias was still watching me. His chest rose and fell. "Kurton told me to forgive you."

My thoughts swiftly changed course. "He did?"

"After the storm. He saw the look on your face right before you dove into the ocean to find me. He said he had never seen such a look…" Elias' eyes skated away. "You saved my life, and maybe that should—I want to ask Kurton, I want to know exactly what he saw, and now I cannot even—" He covered his eyes.

My tears were coming freely. They poured down my bruised face. "I am so sorry for his death," I whispered again. Useless words, but they were all I had. "I cannot tell you how sorry."

He dropped the hand and made an involuntary noise. "I don't know what to do," he said helplessly, casting about. "I don't know what to do."

Neither did I, and he was breaking my heart. All I knew was this man stood before me, hurting, grappling with the death of a friend, and I was there, and could not do nothing. I moved again, reaching to wrap my arms around his neck in a hug. His breath caught; his shoulders went rigid. My heart was struggling like an injured bird, yet I wound my arms tighter still, sliding my unbandaged hand across the nape of his neck, just holding on.

Elias' pulse rioted in my chest. He made a stifled noise. And then he just…melted. Into me. His cane clattered to the floor as he brought both arms around my waist, pulling my body against his, burying his face in the crook of my neck. His lips parted against my skin. My thoughts turned to cotton as I breathed in the smell of him. Anything I might have said drained from my mind; I was senseless with feeling. There was only him. Our shared grief and stolen comfort and this painful, unexpected truce.

I would have held onto that moment forever.

My mother's voice rang from somewhere nearby, calling for a servant to escort Ophelia to the woman's quarters. Elias seemed to come back to himself. He pulled away from me, using the doorway for support and looking disoriented. Even just the sound of Persaphe's voice was enough to bring the wall back up between us. He shut his expression down and turned away, and I had lost him once more.

THIRTY-NINE

Kurton's body was prepared by his comrades. They wrapped his bloated wounds so they would not leak, dressed him in fine clothes, applied cosmetics to bring some color back to his skin. There was a ceremony much like the one Queen Mother Althea and I had conducted for my parents all those years ago, with tapers and kneeling and ritual verses. They set Kurton in a launch, placed a burning candle between each of his stiff fists, and released him out to sea.

It was hard to go on after that. Another two days we spent on the Island of Mirir while the ship was repaired, and then we set sail. Instead of standing at the prow to feel the wind on my face, or leaning over to watch the dolphins splash in our wake, I retreated to my small chamber to conduct my experiments. I refused to leave that tiny block except for the most vital of purposes. I did not wish to hear the whispers chase me down the corridors. I did not want to witness Ophelia go quietly about her work. She did not ask for me again, and I would not disrespect her by inserting my presence. And so I was alone, pouring my hours into testing the first batch of my truth serum. I slept only when I could not fight it, and though my face smarted, and my injured wrist was swollen immobile, I labored through the pain. It mattered so little to me, then.

The weather warmed as we sped across the sea, spring clouds peppering the sky. I saw Elias, sometimes, in the hall on the way to the narrow hold where we collected our meals, or between the great, wind-filled sails. If ever I tried to catch his eye, he made an excuse to look away. It was as if the moment in his antechamber had never happened, and though I should have known to expect his withdrawal, I suffered for it. Time was running short. Persaphe had begun putting my compass to real use, and soon we would reach the Land of Moore where the River was said to flow. Even if I succeeded in brewing a truth serum, I would need Elias to order Persaphe to drink it. But how could I do that when he would not even look at me?

I gazed down at the deep-forest *istilla*, soft and flat in my hands. One flower I had used, one chance gone, and only two left.

It was a cool, dry morning when Ophelia came to find me. I was hunched over the damselberry in my closet-room, carefully crushing its bulbs. My first attempt at creating a truth serum had gone no worse than I could have hoped—it was an iteration on the king's *eithier*, with extra ingredients to draw out the mind-relaxing effects, bind them, and secure their strength. I had tested the serum on myself with mixed results; though I had felt the urge to speak honestly, I could stifle the desire with a bit of willpower. The binding was not strong enough, so I thought, perhaps a bit more damselberry in the next batch? That morning, I was so intent on my chopping I did not notice Ophelia until she cleared her throat.

"We are set to reach land today," she informed me. "A lookout has spotted the Pass of Dire on the horizon."

I blinked as if into the sun. My mind could not comprehend how

Ophelia had come to stand in my doorway, apparently of her own volition. "The Pass of Dire?" I repeated dumbly. It was the final landmark the maiden had supposedly traversed before finding the River. I had not realized we were so close.

"Most of our caravan will continue forward through the Pass," Ophelia went on, "though some are choosing to return to Isla. The king has been encouraging it. He says he does not want any more innocent blood—" She broke off. "I have decided to return as well."

I had long wished for Ophelia to turn back to safety; her choice to do so now was for the best. So why did I feel as if my lungs were cinched with wire? "I will give you a fresh supply of nausea medication to last the journey."

"There is no need," Ophelia replied. "It seems the worst of my sickness has passed." She touched a hand to her still-flat belly as I rose to my feet; it would still be many weeks before she began to show. "The baby has taken mercy on me, I think. But this is not what I came to talk about. I came because I want you to know I do not blame you for what happened."

The wire cinched tighter. "I blame myself."

"Kurton knew the dangers we faced. We both knew. He gave his life to protect you. If he had to die, this is how he would have wanted it. Doing his duty."

"I wish it could be undone," I said wretchedly. "Ophelia, you must know I would give anything…"

"I know."

"It should have been me. I should be the one—"

"Selene." Ophelia caught my flailing hands. "There are no *should haves*. If you live, it is for a purpose. You have challenges yet to face, but you will do what must be done. I know you will. Kurton's death will not be in vain." She waited until I nodded, then released me, moving her palm back to her belly. "I was wondering," she went on in a different voice. "You are a healer. This babe…can you sense anything?"

Our friendship was gone as I had known it, there would be no bringing it back. Yet Ophelia was there, she was speaking to me. Offering forgiveness and asking my opinion. I felt a flicker of rare hope.

"Possibly," I said. "I have never attempted to use my abilities on an unborn child, but…" As soon as I put my mind to it, the fetus' pulse sprang to my awareness. I let out a surprised breath. "Oh." I could hear the infant's heart beating, though it was different from an adult's heartbeat, fainter, almost like…

My gaze rose to Ophelia's. She saw my startled expression. "What is it?"

"Nothing," I stammered.

"You are white as a sheet. Is it the baby? Is something wrong? Tell me at once."

I was frightening her. "No, no, the baby is fine."

"Then why do you look like you have seen a ghost?"

But I did not know how to answer her question. I did not even know what I was thinking.

A low horn interrupted from the deck: a summoning call. Ophelia glanced around my room, at the final two *istilla* flowers, the partly crushed damselberry, the haphazard array of belongings. "You should pack all this up. You will be deboarding soon."

I began gathering my things, favoring my good arm and trying to organize the havoc of my thoughts. As Ophelia watched me bundle my few possessions, I realized I still wore her borrowed clothes. "Your dress…"

"Keep it," she said.

"I will return it to you as soon as we make it home."

The thought lingered between us. *If we make it home.* But Ophelia marshaled a half-smile. It was the first I had seen on her since Kurton's death, and though it held none of her old spirit, my spark of hope became a small flame. "So you will."

. . .

Once again, our party divided itself. *The Starling* dropped anchor in a gentle bay, and those continuing onward into the Land of Moore set off in small cargo launches in groups of four and six, bending their efforts toward the sandy beach. I strapped my pack tightly across my back and watched *The Starling* shrink behind us, raising a hand to bid Ophelia farewell. She nodded from the deck and attempted another smile, though this one was wooden, worried. I turned forward and tried not to feel as if I was losing my last chance at escape.

By the time we dragged our depleted provisions out of the launches onto the beach, the sun had tipped in the sky, marshalling the late afternoon. The Land of Moore was a rocky, unpopulated continent, windy, pockmarked with brambles. I climbed a rise for a better view, and when I set my eyes on the distant Pass of Dire, I had the same thought everyone has. We must turn back.

The Pass was the single path through Moore's ancient, towering mountain range. Once solid, the centermost mountain had cracked in two, from the very bottom all the way to the top, providing a slim crevasse for crossing. I could see the range's high crags and soaring peaks, the foremost mountaintop dusted with snow. The earth at the base of the Pass was charred black, and though it was still daytime, a darkness seemed to spill from its depths, as if suffused in smoky mist. According to legend, the River was hidden somewhere beyond this obstacle.

At the start of our journey there had been well over a hundred in our party, each person with a purpose: horse drivers, supply tenders, a priestess to pray for fair travel. Now, that number had dwindled to a mere fifteen, few enough to know each man by name. We took up our positions and started forward in silence, keeping to the grass, as it was safer for the horses than the crumbling road. According to legend, it would take three days to cross the Pass' divide, and in that time there would be no food or water, for nothing lived within its walls.

Or at least…nothing natural. Because there was *something* there. I could sense it as we plowed onward; an unknown force seemed to reach across the meadow, prickling cold against my skin.

"Wait," I said to no one in particular. I hurried forward, dodging rocks and weeds until I came even with Elias upon his tall gelding. The remaining three members of the King's Guard watched me approach, but their attention seemed fragmented, their eyes straying to the darkness ahead. I spoke again. "Wait."

Elias did not halt, but I could tell he was listening.

"The Pass," I said. "Do you feel it? There is…something there."

"Something there?" Persaphe twisted in her saddle from her position up the line. Her face was finally showing signs of exhaustion, yet this did nothing to diminish her vividness; even fatigued, she was beautiful, drawing all the light to herself. "And what would you have us do based on this intuition? Turn back?"

Yes, actually. That is exactly what I would have us do. "There must be another way. A route to avoid the Pass."

"There is not," Persaphe replied succinctly, though her eyes skittered toward Elias. "The Mountains of Dire are untraversable. This range stretches thousands of leagues in both directions. If we are to reach the

River, the Pass is the only way through. You must trust me. I have done this before."

"But—"

"We are too close to turn back now," Elias interrupted. Then, low enough that only I could hear, "I'm sorry." He nudged his gelding into a trot, ending our conversation. Persaphe lifted her chin in satisfaction.

I fell back, upset and out of sorts. I was surprised when Arch drew his horse alongside me, casually, so as not to attract attention. "What is it?" he asked, keeping his eyes ahead. "What do you sense?"

"There is something...waiting for us."

A pause. "Can you stop it?"

"I do not even know what *it* is."

"There must be a way."

I clenched the strap of my satchel, feeling how light it had grown. During our journey across Isla, there had been ample opportunity to collect new ingredients, but once we boarded *The Starling* such opportunities had dwindled. I had my final two deep-forest *istilla* flowers, some partly crushed damselberry, plus a small collection of items stockpiled to brew Elias' *eithier*. Aside from that, my stores were used up. "I could maybe craft something," I told Arch dubiously, eyeing the barren landscape. "I do not know. I need time to think."

I spent the next league gathering anything I could get my hands on: wintermite, drooping pieris, snow-glory, wild garlic. These were not ingredients of any great power, but I collected them anyway, until my pack was bulging. A breeze kicked up dust; the sunlight seemed oddly muted. Once, twice, I caught Hobore glancing in my direction. When his eyes met mine a third time, I could not help but snap, "What?"

"Over there," he mumbled. "A patch of lentweed."

I stuttered an incredulous breath, even as I followed the line of his gaze. "How do you know about lentweed?" It was a plant of some actual value.

He gave strange laugh. "I have been watching you gather ingredients for weeks. It figures I should have learned a thing or two by now."

I frowned. I knew Hobore watched me, but that meant…had he realized I was collecting plants besides those needed for Elias' *eithier*? Yet if that was true, why had he done nothing to stop me?

Hobore's skinny neck twisted; he dropped his voice even lower. "I have thought about what you said. About the person truly to blame for my…feelings." His words were reluctant, his mouth downturned. His eyes slid toward Persaphe. "I think…well. Elias is my brother, and I—he has never treated me as anything less. Even when the court whispered about me, even when his own mother attempted to lower my status, Elias never gave in. He doesn't care that I am our father's bastard son. To Elias, we are family."

My frown deepened. "What are you saying?"

"I wanted you to know," said Hobore doggedly.

"Know *what*?"

But he would say no more.

By the time we reached the tall, open-air fissure that marked the beginning of the Pass, temperatures had plummeted. I shivered, thinking of bone-graves and madness, and it seemed I was not alone. Men and horses hunched in fear, their eyes darting, breath streaming white in the cold. The sheer rockface stretched two ways, both high overhead and deep into a ravine. To cross the Pass, we would have to travel along a slim ledge on one side, which was so narrow in places two men could not walk abreast. The horses refused to step upon it, no matter how we coaxed, and so an order was given to leave them behind. The men exchanged wary looks as we packed what provisions we could into our small handcarts, did a hasty headcount, and began.

The wind whined inside the crevasse like a whistle; the shadows were long. More than once, I found myself hugging the rocky wall and glancing down into the chasm below, wishing for a more secure foothold. We were not far above sea level, but it felt as if we stood leagues into the sky; one slip of your boot and you would tumble to your death. It was colder in the mountains than it had been out at sea; I began to shiver again. And still, that awful foreboding. The surety that danger—invisible, unknowable, yet awake to our presence—awaited us.

Can you stop it?

I focused on the gray mountain stone. I knew well the story of *The River of Reversal*. I should be able to remember the tale of some monster hidden within the Pass of Dire. Yet the legend told only of the maiden's hard journey through a narrow alpine trail, not of any creature lurking within. I remembered a line. *The darkness will lead many astray.* But that could mean anything.

There was no sound but the shuffle of our feet against dry rock and the tap and clatter of our packs. My hands were stiff with cold; my back felt tied into knots. Elias kept a strong pace with the use of his cane, though I could see the strain in his shoulders. In my periphery, I thought I spotted a flash of movement deep in the ravine, but when I looked, there was nothing there.

The moon rose like a gaping eye. We walked through the twilight until we reached a ledge that was wide enough to fit our group without fear of slipping. Deprived of our packhorses, everyone had opted to leave their sleeping tents behind—everyone, it seemed, except Persaphe. Hobore carried her poles and canvas, and set to erecting them with short, harsh movements.

"If there is a tent," Freesier noted loudly, "it should be offered to the king."

Persaphe eyed the guardsman before turning reluctantly toward Elias. "Of course. If you wish to have my tent, it is yours."

Elias shook his head. "I will sleep as my men sleep, in the open."

Persaphe put up no fight. As soon as the tent was erected, she slipped inside, pausing at the entrance. "Hobore," she said. "You may join me, as a reward for your efforts."

Hobore's wispy hair flipped in the breeze; his face was tight with some unnamed emotion. He glanced at his brother, who was busy untying his bedroll. "I need no reward."

"Come, do not be prideful. There is room for us both. The canvas will protect you from the cold." There was something in Persaphe's face that was not quite fear. "I insist," she continued, steeping a layer of power into her tone. Hobore dropped his shoulders and submitted. "Leave your weapons outside," Persaphe added in a quieter voice as the young man stepped past her. "You will not need them."

I stared at their closed tent. Something—the frayed thread of an understanding—was beginning to stitch itself together in my mind.

There were no trees in the Pass and therefore no firewood, but we had our torches and used them for light and warmth. I sidled up next to one, and though I had my cloak and a cup of hot water, I could not escape the chill. My ears were attuned to every noise, my eyes to every movement. Fear sapped my strength, yet rather than curl up under my cloak and try for sleep, I pulled out my traveling cauldron and what few supplies were left to me: my meager stock of *istilla*, the damselberry and lentweed, a bit of extra *eithier*. Could I use these ingredients to create a ward of protection? That feeling—like something was watching us, waiting for us—was stronger now. Everything seemed coated in silent menace. I fumbled my way about my task, aware of the camp's mistrustful curiosity. Torchlight twisted the shadows; everything looked strangely liquid. I met Elias' eyes across the space.

"What is she doing?" asked a swordsman under his breath.

"Brewing a spell of some sort," replied another. "A defense to protect us."

"Thought she wasn't allowed to brew anything but the king's medicine."

"Doesn't matter much now, does it?"

"Not taking anything she offers," chimed a third. "Not worth the risk of being poisoned, you ask me."

I pulled my cloak more tightly around myself, trying to work up my little cauldron fire. With groping fingers, I tugged one of the deep-forest *istilla* flowers from its small pouch. I thought I might have an idea for a potion, something to shield our camp from view so any who wished us harm might overlook this space entirely. And yet, was it worth using one of my final two *istilla* in the attempt?

Well, do it, or die. I tossed the white petals into my cauldron, ignoring my unease as they sizzled and dissolved. The liquid gained a silver sheen; I smelled sand and salt. I touched a finger to the potion, hissing at the burn. The fluid dripped like water, which was wrong. A proper ward—the kind to shield a living man from sight—must be thicker. My potion needed more heat, and time to reduce. I locked eyes with Arch where he sat near the ledge and shook my head. *Not yet.*

I leaned over my cauldron, intent on working until this task was finished. Yet unaccountably, my limbs began to loosen. Exhaustion washed over me like a spilled cup. I blinked, startled by the sudden onslaught of fatigue.

Something was not right.

Around me, I could see that same uncanny weariness gripping the others, their heads lolling, eyes drooping shut. Beside me, a man sagged in sudden unconsciousness. I went to him in alarm. I did not need to set two fingers to the man's neck to check for a pulse, yet I did it anyway, just to be sure. He was not dead, only asleep.

My alarm grew. Could this be the black curse of the Pass? To draw us into an endless slumber? I returned swiftly to my cauldron—no matter that the ward was not done, it would have to be enough. I spooned up the entirety of its contents, a single ladle's worth, then strode the short distance across the landing toward Elias. Sleep was tugging at my eyes, but I fought it through sheer force of will and fear and rushing adrenaline. Around Elias, the King's Guard was attempting to draw their swords. They, too, were recognizing the Pass' enchantment. They would try to battle it in the only way they knew how.

"Something—" Yorvis' tongue was heavy. "Something is happening."

"Black magic," Arch managed before tipping sideways.

"Fight it," Freesier warned the king. "Your Majesty, fight it if you—" But he fell unconscious before he could finish.

It was more disturbing than the shadow-wolf, for at least the wolf had been visible. This bleak exhaustion—it was nothing but a blanket of darkness, pulling at our minds. Elias caught my eye as I stumbled his way. His pulse was sharp, his lips parting to speak. There was a look in his face, raw and real as he said, "Selene."

"Drink—" I tried to speak around my failing consciousness. "Drink this. It might help…"

"You—" he growled. "You first…" But then he, too, dropped into oblivion.

Terror made my stomach bottom. I had to do something, stop this, reverse it. My nerves twisted. What if this was it? What if this was just *it?* I would force my potion down Elias' throat. I would force it down everyone's.

I had almost reached the king when my legs gave out. I tried to catch myself, but my arms refused to work. My head hit the ground, the ladle flying from my hand. Darkness crawled into my eyes.

And with it came the dreams.

FORTY

I was in a clearing of white frost. Snow was falling hard, sheeting down. My mother stepped through the storm, parting the flakes like a curtain, yet the Persaphe of my dreams was not as I knew her in life. Her face was ashen, her teeth missing, the mouth a gaping black hole. She came for me, scuttling like a crab, and when she set her withered lips upon my skin, I felt the fabric of my soul tear in two.

Agony. I tried to scream, but no sound came. I pulled away, and my skin ripped, flinging blood. Demon-Persaphe continued to suck; with each swallow, I felt more of my soul fragmenting. She lifted her white eyes to mine, and I felt horribly lucid, as if this was not a dream at all. As if she could truly see me.

No. I strained against the prison of my mind. *Wake up.* This was not the way it was supposed to happen. I would die by poison. By fire or sea storm or the rope of a noose. Not like this, not trapped in my own nightmare.

Demon-Persaphe gulped and gulped. My skin began to wither like a raisin. The fear was such as I had never known. I thought of every torment I had ever suffered, the surety that I could face no worse. That old question sounded cloying to my ears. *Can you bear more?*

No, I thought, no. Let me die rather than endure another moment of this.

My vision fragmented, and through the cracks came a memory. I could see—dimly, somewhere in my final recesses—a courtyard under a clear sky. I could hear Elias' voice saying, *I do not value you for your likability, Selene, merely for your mind.* At the time, I had found the comment irksome. He had intended it to be. But now...it nudged at some soft, unexamined part within me.

I remembered a different day, a different room. My own voice as I said, *We are more than our bodies.* I remembered comparing myself to Princess Mora, a lifetime spent comparing myself to my mother. The way I had rejected such comparisons to find the deep-forest *istilla*. I had always viewed my physical form as a tool, an apparatus meant to serve my own ends. My hands, particularly, were troublesome. Sometimes, I appreciated their ability. Other times, they were merely to be tolerated. But my mind—my ability to craft potions and poisons, to encounter a problem and imagine a solution and then just *invent* it...that was who I was.

Had I survived poison, escaped assault, overcome a sea storm only to die in a dream?

Demon-Persaphe continued to suck. Beneath her maw, my body looked like a shrunken husk.

No, I thought. Enough. I am stronger than this.

With that thought, the monster lifted her face and hissed. I brought my bare fist between us. *Begone!* In life, the motion would have done nothing, but this was a nightmare, it was *my* nightmare, and I would command it. Persaphe flew back as if struck. She landed in a snowbank and gave a screech, tearing at the ground in her rage. "You will not have me," I breathed, and woke.

I was lying where I had fallen, uncovered, shivering convulsively. Tears had frozen to my face. It was still night, but the shadows were deeper; all but three of our torches had been extinguished. For a moment, I stared at the thin splinter of sky visible through the cracked mountaintop overhead, wondering vaguely why I was not dead. It was quiet, except for the faint whistle of wind across stone. Gingerly, I put a trembling hand to my skin, remembering the feel of shrunken lips and oozing blood, searching for the wound...

Nothing.

I sat up, inhaling the scent of torch fumes and rock. My pulse was unsettled; my body was chilled and stiff. It was then that I noticed what lay around me, illuminated by the feeble light. Three men from our party had been slain.

I scrambled to my feet. The rest of the camp was still asleep, and they jerked in their dreams, battling their own monsters. One man had a dagger in his unconscious grip. He came partway awake, his face sheet-white. I started to call out, to stop him, but I could see the terror hanging in his sightless vision. Whatever he was dreaming, he was not strong enough to survive it. He thrust the blade into his own belly and slumped over, dead.

I ran to Elias. He was tossing in his sleep, fisting the bedroll. "Elias." I shook him, but he did not stir. "Elias, wake up, wake up." No response. Nearby, the King's Guard were trapped in their own nightmares, thrashing and crying out. Arch pulled his sword into his dreaming hand. I snatched it from his grasp.

I went through the encampment, grabbing weapons out of fists, collecting them all in a pile where they could do no harm. After, I returned to Elias' side to wait out the remaining twilight hours. I would not leave him. I would not even look away until this terror was over.

I feared dawn would never come, yet finally it did, in a river of blue light. When Elias fell still and opened his eyes, I nearly burst into tears. He looked at me and shuddered. Like the slain man, I could see his dream lingering in his harried face. "Selene?"

Then I really did sob. It was the relief, yes, but also the tone of his voice. He had not spoken my name like that—unguarded, full of concern—since the day he learned I was his poisoner.

My face was in my hands, my shoulders shaking. I heard him shift upright. "Selene," Elias said again, grabbing my forearms to pull my palms away from my eyes. The feel of his skin on mine—the shock of it—abruptly stopped my tears.

His voice was thick when he asked, "Are you hurt?"

Was I? I ached everywhere, and I was sweating from the strain of those long night hours. My soaked shirt clung to my skin, my stomach was a ball of coal, my broken wrist smarting from the lack of care I had employed as I gathered the camp's weapons. But I was alive, and my mind was still my own. "I am not hurt."

Reluctantly, Elias released my arms and swept a bleak look across the camp. I was not the only one in tears. All around, men wept openly—for themselves, and their dreams, and the sight of their dead comrades.

"I gathered the weapons," I told Elias, wiping my wet face with the back of my sleeve. "But I was too—I was too late to save…"

"You did what you could," he told me quietly. "It is over."

"No, it isn't." Yorvis spoke from his nearby bedroll. "We will endure two more nights of this, if legend is to be believed."

Elias said nothing.

"Your Majesty." It was Arch this time, coming forward to take a knee. His face was written with worry; his hands were not quite steady. "Beasts and men, those we can slay, but these night terrors…I have never faced anything like them. If we continue onward, I fear we cannot uphold our oaths to protect you. It would be the greatest failure of our lives."

Elias stared. "What are you saying?"

"I do not ask this lightly," Arch continued. "I know what the River of Reversal means to you. But what good will its waters do if we die before we reach them? Abandon this quest. Let us turn back now, while we still can."

Elias looked stunned. "Abandon it? Now?"

"It is the only way."

Emotion scoured Elias' expression. "I would not hold you here. None of you. If you wish to turn back—"

"Who wishes to turn back?"

We all spun at the sound of Persaphe's voice. She was emerging from her tent, Hobore hobbling slowly behind. I expected her to look brighter than the rest of us, for surely my mother had met her kin there in the night, yet she appeared pale. "Do you really mean to stop now, when we are so close?" she asked the King's Guard. "What will people think when their sovereign returns to Isla a failure?"

Arch colored. "Better to fail and live than to die."

"That is not what the bards say."

"This is not a song."

"No. It is a dull reality, full of cowards."

Arch's hand went to his belt, though his sword no longer hung there—it was in the pile along with everyone else's weapons. He clenched the hand to a fist. "We are not cowards. Only men who know their limit."

"And have you reached that limit so soon?" Persaphe drew her lip back; the sight of her disapproval caused several men to flinch and bend away. "A few nightmares and you are ready to give up?"

Arch, though gray under her accusations, held steadfast. "Did you know of this? You said you have come this way before. That you have seen the River with your own eyes. And yet, you've made no mention of nightmares with the power to kill."

"It was not a nightmare that ended these men's lives. The blades, as you see, were wielded by each man's own hand."

Arch went red with anger. Yorvis and Freesier appeared unsettled. Even Hobore frowned. It was the first time I had seen them look at my mother with anything but blank obedience.

"Arch." Elias pushed himself to his feet. It was a slow business, marked by stiff pauses, but at last he stood upright, without the help of any cane or hold. I blinked rapidly. I was not even sure Elias realized what he had done. "If you wish to turn back now, there is no shame in it. No shame for any of you." He raised his voice. "Many of you have families waiting at home. Wives and children. I will not be the reason you do not make it back to them. I give you the same option I gave those on *The Starling*—if you wish to retreat, you may do so now, with honor."

"Yet you will not return with us," Arch said flatly.

Elias looked down at himself, and I realized he did recognize what he'd done—recognized it, and felt it was not enough. He could stand on his own, could walk with the use of a cane. My *either* had brought him that far. But this was not the recovery he desired.

"Years," Elias said softly. "Years, I have endured this condition. I have done my best to bear it as my father would have, with bravery and patience, but I just—you cannot imagine the daily frustration, the indignity. The *relentlessness*. I want to walk again. I want—" He closed his eyes, and I closed mine, too. His words were like a thousand tiny daggers. I felt where each of them pierced my skin. "The River is my chance to undo what has been done. To reverse these last four years as if they had never happened. If those waters exist, I must find them. I am too close to turn back now. I understand if you cannot continue with me."

Arch was shaking his head as he passed the king his cane. "Your battles are ours, Your Majesty."

"We will not turn back," Freesier agreed.

"I stand with you," Hobore added softly, though it was unlike him to speak at such a moment. He glanced at Persaphe, then at me, and I noticed his eyes looked uncolored by alcohol. "Whatever may come."

To this, the rest of our party gave a low cheer, the *hear hears* ringing between dark stone. Elias looked from man to man, offering a solemn nod. "If we move swiftly, perhaps we can make it out of the Pass in one more night rather than two, with no more loss of life."

Persaphe took her place at the head of the group. Though her face was stoic, I did not miss the twitch of her mouth when she said, "Then it is best we get moving."

There was another long day, another hard walk. I drank from my canteen and chewed dried jerky to keep up my strength, but my stomach hurt, and my heart was knotted with worry. We drove ourselves hard, yet too soon the sun was sinking again. No one wanted to stop to make camp, but it would not be safe to wander the Pass after dark, blind to all the cracks and footholds. Mist hung in the ravine. Already, that feeling was returning, the uncanny blanket of exhaustion. *Close your eyes,* the coming darkness seemed to whisper, *just for a moment. Close your eyes.* My head grew heavy; my thoughts were thick. When I looked at my hands, they did not quite seem my own.

Elias ordered everyone to turn in their weapons. The steel, the rope, the spare box of nails for mending handcarts. No one was to carry anything that could possibly do harm. And yet, even muddy-headed as I was, I could see the futility. The Pass's crevasse yawned beside us like a gaping mouth. All anyone had to do was take a running leap.

As I stared into that deep ravine, I noticed a section of rock midway down that looked like a carved doorway. When I blinked, the image was gone.

Elias came to my side. As with the prior night, we had made camp on a wider section of the path. It was enough to give us a bit of space, but still too slim for my liking. "We have lost too many men already," Elias told me in a lowered voice. His tone was as it had been, tinged with true feeling. "That potion you attempted last night, the ward. Can you make another?"

I was aware of my mother watching us, and of the listening men, even as they pretended great interest in their separate tasks. "I never finished the ward," I replied hoarsely, "nor did I have a chance to test it. I am not even sure it would work."

"Will you try?"

I could. Yet to do so would mean using the very last of my deep-forest *istilla*. If I did that, I would have nothing to create my truth serum. Yet if I did not, would we even survive the night? I bit my lip and said, "I...yes. I suppose I must."

Elias ordered his men to chop up a wooden handcart so I could have fire. I gathered the splintered chunks, doing my best to make my limbs obey. The skin around my broken wrist was painfully tight. I piled the wood and accepted the flint Elias offered, lighting the tinder, blowing gently on the flames. Elias walked away, then returned, his cane in one hand and his bedroll in the other.

I shot him an incredulous look. "What are you doing?"

"Keep working as long as you can fight the darkness. I will guard you."

I squeaked. "You?" When he began laying out his bedroll without giving an answer, I pressed, "Why not assign someone else?"

He held my gaze. "I do not want anyone else."

The moment expanded. I thought, do not dare to hope, you would be a fool to hope, and yet...the way he was looking at me. That emotion, running through the depths of him. But...of course he would look at me that way. I was his only chance of protection against the night terrors. That explained things. Yet my heart was erratic.

I started to brew. I thought, I will not sleep until it is done, though I knew it did not work like that. The Pass of Dire was drenched in dark magic, and sleep would soon pull me under, whether I wished it or not. Persaphe started toward us—to question my intentions, I am sure—but Hobore was suddenly there, a hand on her arm. She pulled up short; she seemed astonished by his interference. They began to speak in rough whispers.

I toiled and toiled, yet too soon, the sky purpled and darkened to black. Nearby, the first man dropped suddenly to sleep. Then the next. The feeling came over me shortly after, that waterfall of exhaustion. I still had not finished the ward.

"I'm sorry," I told Elias. "I need more time."

He was looking at me with open concern, and for a moment, I allowed myself to imagine his worry was for me alone, and not my abilities as a potion maker. I had been so strong for so long, but my will was beginning to fracture. Fingers of darkness curled around me. I longed to find somewhere I could be safe. I longed to sleep as I had slept as a child, without fear or dread.

I remembered my dream from the prior night. Persaphe's sucking maw. The toll it had taken, the way the pain lingered even after I had woken.

"I am afraid," I whispered as my eyes drooped closed.

Elias' voice came close at my ear, though I had not heard him move. "You are strong enough to fight the nightmares. You have already proven that. You woke when the rest of us could not, and in doing so, you helped save lives."

"I cannot do it again," I murmured. "Not alone."

"You are not alone," he said.

FORTY-ONE

That night, I did not dream of monsters. I dreamed of my father.

He looked different than he had when I last saw him, his manner gentle, his eyes serene. He stood in a winter forest, snow falling softly all around, and though he was wearing only a simple shirt and trousers, he did not look cold.

"You have come to ask for forgiveness," I told Aegeis. "You want me to forgive you, as I want Elias to forgive me."

"It would make for a good tale," my father agreed.

"But neither of us deserves it."

"Do you know the story of the Goddess and the winged man?"

I shook my head.

"Once," said my father, "there was a mapmaker with a heart for adventure. He dreamed of sailing to the four corners of the world and mapping all he discovered. He found himself the best crew, the most revered captain. He even had the backing of the king."

"Which king?"

"Shh," Aegeis said. "For many years, the mapmaker explored without limit. He made a name for himself, charting new lands, traveling to the world's farthest reaches. But he became overconfident. He allowed his pride to blind him. And so he did not listen to his ship's captain when the man warned of a coming storm.

"The boat wrecked. All the crew perished, save the mapmaker. He found himself stranded on a barren island. For six nights, he waited for a vessel to pass so he might call for help, but the island was remote, and no one appeared. Despairing, the mapmaker spoke to the Goddess, begging her aid."

"And she came?" I asked, then pressed my lips together at his look.

"She did," he agreed, "on silver moonlight. She gifted him a pair of wings—white like a swan's, shooting straight from his back—so he could fly home. He returned to his country full of hope, yet his people did not see his wings as a gift. To them, they were a disfigurement. A curse. The mapmaker was shunned, and lost his status among his people.

"He called once again to the Goddess and begged she remove his wings. The Goddess was offended. *I give you a gift*, she said, *and this is how you show your gratitude?* At his look of devastation, however, she relented. *I will not take the wings away myself, but you may travel to the River of Reversal, to be as you once were.*"

"Am I the mapmaker in this story?" I asked. "Or the Goddess?"

My father ignored me. "Using the Goddess' directions and a special compass, the mapmaker flew to the River. He stepped into the water. His wings vanished, and he rejoiced. But while he was admiring his reflection in the water's surface, the River continued to work its magic, drawing the mapmaker farther back in time, back to an age before he had charted a single new land. When he finally stumbled from the water, he could not remember any of his accomplishments. And so was revealed the true magnitude of the River. To be as he once was—no one.

"The mapmaker returned home to his family. He was confused by his time away, and uncertain of his welcome, yet his children simply ran into his arms and admonished him for being gone so long. He gripped them to his chest and wept for joy and relief. He spent the next years at home raising his children, and tending his land, and doting on his wife, who was pleased her husband had finally given up his far-flung quests to be with his family. Together, they went on to live a life of quiet reflection."

I waited for the rest, but my father seemed finished. "That is a terrible story."

"Is it?" He tipped his chin. "Did not the mapmaker get exactly what he asked for?"

"No." I crossed my arms. "He would never have asked for help if he knew what would follow. The Goddess tricked him."

"That is the Goddess' nature."

"It is a cruel nature."

My father did not deny it.

I said, "I suppose the moral is that if we are stupid enough to fall prey to the deceptions of others, then it is our duty to bear the consequences. Well, there is no need to impart that wisdom, Father. I have learned it well enough."

My father's eyes were so clear, I was suddenly not sure this was a dream at all. "Or," he said, "what if the moral is that sometimes, everything we desire already stands before us, if only we are wise enough to see it?"

FORTY-TWO

I woke with the morning sun full in my face. For a moment, I did not move, caught in the tangles of my dream. It had been so unlike the first—not a nightmare at all. My heart felt light; my breath was full and real. I had not finished the ward, so how had I escaped the Pass' torment? Had the others been spared as well? Yet when I pushed to my elbows and looked around, I saw it was not so.

Men thrashed in their sleep, their eyes open and sightless, fingers bloody from clawing the dry rock. Veins bulged in their necks and temples, pulsing thickly with the strain of their terror. I counted three bedrolls empty. The men had thrown themselves from the cliff.

Elias was there beside me. In the night, he had moved closer; only an arm's length away. When I set a hand to his shoulder, he came awake gasping. His breath caught at the sight of me. After a blink, he asked grimly, "How many?"

There was no way to soften the truth. "Three."

He sat up to take in the scene but seemed to forget himself, his eyes returning to my face, searching for signs of damage. I was reminded, vividly, of him once doing this at the palace, hunting for new marks from my experiments. His throat worked. "You are unhurt?"

I did not know why I blushed. I nodded. "And you?"

"The same."

I stood and went through the camp, shaking each person one by one. We were under the light of day this time, and they stirred easily at my touch. When I returned to Elias' side, he was frowning. I bit the inside of my cheek. "What did you dream?"

He threw me a look. "You first."

"I...dreamed of my father. He came to me with a story."

Elias studied me. "It was not a nightmare?"

"I do not know what it was," I admitted. "But no. Not a nightmare."

"Then you are lucky."

Around us, men were getting dazedly to their feet. Yorvis had his head buried in his hands. Arch set a comforting palm to the man's shoulder.

I rose to my knees and peered into my cauldron. The fire was dead, the half-finished potion congealed. I touched the cold iron with a tremulous hand; the last of my *istilla* was buried in this concoction. "Well?" I prompted Elias. "What about you?"

I did not think he would answer. His eyes were distant, his fingers moving tightly as he began packing up. He spoke to the bedroll. "I dreamed of you."

It was foolish, foolish, the way my heart squeezed at that. I busied myself with the firewood to hide my emotion.

After a moment, Elias glanced at my cauldron. "Is it salvageable?"

I sighed, tipping the jug toward the light. "I am not sure. I would need to get the fire restarted first. Then I might see if I can recover these ingredients."

"Is there any way for you do that while we are on the move?"

I pursed my lips. "No."

"I didn't think so." He looked away again. "How much time do you need?"

I was already shaking my head. "Elias, no. We should press onward. We still have another night to endure, and if we delay…"

"Another night in this place means more lives lost. If you managed to finish your ward before then, it would protect us from the dreams. Men would be spared."

"*If* I am able to finish it," I emphasized.

"You will."

"You cannot be sure of that."

"I am."

My skin felt thin, as though it would tear with a touch. "You would trust me with this?"

He did not answer. Instead, he merely said, "Work on the ward. See how much progress you can make this morning. In the meantime, I will inform the others of our delay."

The men, as expected, were dismayed. When Elias explained we would not be breaking camp that morning, they stared at him as if contemplating an intervention. *You want us to spend yet even more time in this place? Have you gone mad? I thought we were not to trust your poisoner.* Persaphe, unsurprisingly, was the loudest opposer among them. *My daughter is not brewing a ward of protection. It is poison, it is a trick. We must not take anything she gives.*

The debate continued, but I shut it out. Lives were in my hands, whether they believed it or not.

I restarted the fire, worked the congealed liquid until it began to bubble. My potion had cooled in the night, but I added more crushed damselberry, a bit of rock-dust from the Pass itself. I breathed new life into the brew, and soon it began to shimmer once more.

After Elias had wrangled his men into unhappy obedience, he returned to sit on a nearby rock in order that he might observe me. His eyes were green, cautious, hopeful. "Tell me how it works."

"At first, I thought perhaps I could invent something to keep us hidden from the Pass' magic," I replied, stirring the potion in even motions. "Yet what good will hiding do, if the danger lies within us? The Pass is tricking our minds into believing we are under attack. The terror is so great, it is driving us to end our own lives as a means of escape. The solution is to force each of us to see…" I trailed off.

Elias peered at me. "To see what?"

"To see things clearly," I said faintly.

"Selene?" He was concerned. "What is it?"

But I was looking at my hands. I was looking at the ward, half-made.

What if sometimes, said my father's voice, *everything we desire already stands before us, if only we are wise enough to see it?*

Once ingested, this ward would prevent our minds from lying to themselves. That's how we would remember our dreams were only dreams. But this would come with an unintended consequence.

I looked at Elias. Sunlight wove through his hair, and his shadowed face seemed suddenly brand new. "This potion will protect us from our own minds," I said, forcing my dry mouth to work. "But there will be side effects."

"What kind of side effects?"

"It will make you see only what is real." I swallowed. "Only the truth."

I saw the moment Elias understood. "A truth serum."

My fingertips had gone numb. My tongue moved on its own. "Yes."

The answer, as so many answers, seemed obvious now that I had it.

To create a truth serum, I did not need to stop a person from lying to others. I merely needed to make it so you could not lie to yourself.

I remember little of the following hours. I saw only my hands before me, my charred cauldron, my knife smeared with the residue of my ingredients. The day moved onward; clouds boiled up in that sheer slip of sky. Elias alternated between hovering and giving me space, talking with the men and waiting in anxious silence. I kept at my task, ignoring the strain in my shoulders and eyes. All day I worked, frothing, distilling, drawing out the weak power of the overwrought *istilla*, all the while quivering with hope. It will work, I told myself. It must work.

When the ravine was blue-hollowed and the sun falling, I held the finished serum in my hand. There was not much to go around—just a single vial's worth. I tried to move calmly. There were less than ten people left in our party. We would all drink a small dose, including my mother. She would ingest the serum, either on her own or by order of the king. I would ask her questions. She would be forced to reveal answers.

"It is finished," I said.

The group descended at once. The men seemed to have forgotten their earlier trepidation—they had already faced two nights of terrors, and here loomed a third. Poisoner or no, my ward was their best hope of survival.

Persaphe approached first among the group, looking haughty and indignant. Yet beneath her cold exterior, I thought I sensed true interest. My mother would never openly defer to my power, but not even she was immune to the nightmares. Surely she wished to face them no more than the rest of us. I wondered what she had dreamed.

"What is it?" she asked as she accepted the vial and unstoppered the cork. The liquid inside was emerald green.

"It is a ward of protection," I said, trying to breathe normally. "It will prevent the night terrors."

Elias had come to my side. My blood drummed; I did not know where to look. "Just a small drink will be enough," I told Persaphe, though I wanted to make her down every last drop. As soon as she drank my truth serum, I would begin my questioning, and she would admit everything—the curse she had laid upon Elias, her desire for his death, the true purpose of this quest. Her role in the king's poisoning would be revealed, and Elias would see I was not the lone villain he believed. They would all see.

Persaphe sniffed the bottle. I felt the tick of every agonizing second. I could scarcely stand it. She lifted the serum to her lips.

Before the liquid met her tongue, Persaphe turned and flung the vial from the cliff.

I watched it sail through the air. My mind seemed to skip. The bottle caught the light as it twirled once, sloshing out its contents. It disappeared into the black depths of the ravine.

"*No.*" I lunged, as if to hurl myself down after the vial, but Elias' arm came around my waist to stop me. All my blood was draining. "What have you done?" I choked out at my mother. "How could you do that?"

"You are a *prisoner,*" Persaphe seethed. "You are responsible for the king's poisoning. Has everyone forgotten that? Do you think I would trust any serum you create?"

"That draught was going to save us," I cried. "It was going to save *me*—" The horror was morphing in my lungs. After all this time, all I had sacrificed, my one hope had just been destroyed. I was out of deep-forest *istilla* and had no way to summon more. The wind was higher now; the men's faces were coated in shock. I felt Elias' arm around me like a band. His breath fanned my hair, his heart thumping violently against my back. I could hear the rest of their heartbeats, too, including—when I sought it—that soft addition. The one that had been there ever since my mother's return. I closed my eyes and fought a wave of blackness.

"Come," Persaphe told the others, with a note that said she had noticed how their faces were hardened with anger. "Let us not have—"

"I know everything," I interrupted with my eyes still closed. I was not sure if I was speaking to Persaphe, or Elias, or no one. It did not matter. My path to absolution was gone, burnt to cinders, and it did not matter. "I know what you have done, Mother, and I know why." Elias released me, and I stepped away. I needed to stand on my own for this.

Persaphe eyed me. Hobore watched with a grim kind of wariness.

I said to my mother, "You are pregnant."

Silence. Persaphe blinked once, then gave a sharp laugh. "Excuse me?"

"At the House of Healers, I noticed something different about your pulse. I thought it was due to your use of the heartrate drug *risphini*. You know I can hear heartbeats, which means you knew I would be able to hear your pulse quicken when you lied about Elias' cure. You took the drug to reduce your heartrate. That seemed to explain the change."

"What kind of nonsense—?"

"Later," I barreled on, "in the prison, I switched my theory. I thought maybe you had a heart murmur. Wouldn't that justify the change? It was not until I heard the pulse of Ophelia's unborn child that I realized the truth. I would not have recognized it before then—I had never listened for such a sound. But now it is clear; the noise I have been hearing is not due to a drug, or a heart murmur. It is the pulse of an infant."

Persaphe did not even hesitate. "Well done, daughter. How clever you must feel, to have it all figured out. There is only one problem—you seem to have forgotten the rules of our lineage. Freestone women can bear only one child."

"Can they?" I challenged. "It's true, our ancestors have seemed to only birth a single daughter, but patterns do not equal rules. That is something every potion maker must learn—sometimes coincidences arise in nature, sometimes false correlations. What if the same is true for our lineage? What if Freestones have only ever *seemed* to bear a single daughter, but really, we can birth sons as well? Or," I continued darkly, taking another step, "what if the tales of our lineage were a lie, perpetrated by you?"

"What are you asking?" Persaphe snapped.

"How many times *have* you been pregnant, Mother? Was I really your firstborn child? Or have there been others?"

Persaphe glanced around. Yorvis, Freesier, Arch, Elias—everyone was watching our exchange in utter silence. The orange-colored sunset had diminished to a faint hue in the west, and the wind was oddly calm. Persaphe replied, in a voice soaked in power, "You are my only child."

"I don't think so," I replied in a voice of my own—the only kind that seemed able to dismantle hers. "We all know the story of your journey to the Island of Mirir. Over the course of six months, you ventured there in hunt of a wildfruit called damselberry. I have always wondered how you failed to find that fruit. Half a year is a long time. Having been to Mirir myself, I can say with certainty you could have accomplished that journey much faster…unless your aim was never truly to find damselberry. What if instead your disappearance was meant to conceal a pregnancy?"

"Do you hear yourself?" Persaphe asked. "You are speaking like a madwoman."

"You would have been young at the time," I continued, "not yet married. Conceiving out of wedlock would have brought shame upon our family, but I suspect that is not the only reason for your deception. Shortly after this journey, you returned to Isla and a woman approached you in the King's City with a child in her hands."

I saw the men of our party remembering the story. This tale, too, was well known among our people. A mysterious woman had shoved the baby into Persaphe's hands and said, *Please, you must take him, this is a son of the king.*

"You brought that child to the palace," I said. "You begged Queen Althea to allow him a place in our halls. You even named him, and had a hand in his raising. But why, Mother? Why go through the trouble with this baby? Why insist that King Adonis Alder's bastard live among the court?"

Everyone's eyes went to Hobore.

"It's true," I told Elias, spinning to face him squarely, "that Hobore is your half-brother. Your father Adonis sired you both. But what we have never known is the identity of Hobore's mother. Persaphe is his mother."

At this, there was a general intake of breath. Elias looked unwell; Hobore met his brother's eye in open regret. My own thoughts were rushing through me like a broken dam, and the world seemed to sway, but with terrible effort, I continued.

"Persaphe killed your father," I told Elias, and it broke me, a little, the way his face split with pain. "The hunting accident was a setup. Your father's death was contrived. Then Persaphe tried to kill you. She did it, because once you were disposed, Hobore would be next in line for the throne. He would take his place as king. It would make Persaphe Queen Mother."

I had questioned my mother's sanity for wishing Elias dead. She was the royal physician, afforded every comfort, every luxury. Without the

Alder bloodline, I had believed Persaphe would fall from glory, but I was wrong. There was still a final rung for her to climb. I could picture it, how she would gleam in her newfound power. How easily she could control Hobore from the shadows, much in the same way she controlled him now. Persaphe had always feared imprisonment; watching her own mother kidnapped by a band of enemy horseman had born in her a deep fear of powerlessness. The memory had poisoned her mind. And what better way to combat powerlessness than to claim a position of royalty? This had always been Persaphe's plan: she would rid the world of the king so that Hobore could take his place, and make her queen.

Persaphe was still standing where she had been on the cliffside. She did not look afraid; the emotion in her eyes was much closer to rage.

Elias looked at his brother. His expression was not unlike it had been when he discovered I was his poisoner. "Brother. Is this—could this be true?"

"Hobore," Persaphe warned, "say nothing."

"Tell him, Hobore," I urged. My words seemed to scrape against my mother's, like two halves of a split bone. I felt how they strangled her authority. "You love Elias. He has always treated you as family, no matter your lineage. You told me so yourself. This is his life. He deserves to know."

Hobore cast about like a cornered animal, then dropped suddenly to his knees. "What Selene says is true," he cried. "I am sorry, Brother. Persaphe has aimed for your death since the start of this journey. I'm sorry, I'm sorry."

The King's Guard needed no further confession. They swung toward Persaphe and drew their weapons, prompting the rest of the men to quickly follow suit. A half-dozen swords gleamed in the fading light, but Persaphe only sneered. "Hobore lies," she said. "They both lie. My only aim is to bring the king to the River. *Drop your weapons*."

I could almost see it, the way her command flowed over the men, only to part like water around a rock. The swords did not drop; the group moved closer.

"I said," Persaphe repeated, with more conviction, "drop your weapons."

"They will not," I answered. "You have been revealed; you cannot bewitch them any longer."

"What would you know of it?" she spat. "You, with barely a scrap of power to your name?"

"More than just a scrap," I said evenly.

My mother took a menacing step toward me. "I should have killed you when I had the chance."

With that admission, the final threads of her spell broke. I felt them snap in the air, as if Persaphe's power was a plank that cleaved beneath her feet. The King's Guard rushed forward, but I yelled, "No, she must live. The baby—her blood. Persaphe's blood is the key. With it, I can create a *gaigi*. I can undo—"

Persaphe lunged for me. I had only time to register the murder in her face before Elias was there, Elias without his cane, Elias with strong hands and a growling mouth, stepping between us. He seemed to tower over me, and I thought, had he always been so tall? He shoved me behind him, and Persaphe nearly reached for him instead, but the King's Guard gripped her from behind and halted her progress.

"Touch her," Elias told Persaphe, "and I'll kill you."

The King's Guard hauled Persaphe back as she screeched, "*Unhand me.*" Her voice held no enchantment; she looked more human than I had ever seen. "You fools," she snarled, twisting and bucking like a wildcat. With one surprising heave, she tore free from their grip. Our eyes met for a single moment, and I knew, with a sickening jolt, what she intended. *My mother is not one to be commanded by another.* Persaphe wrenched backward, spun, and hurled herself from the cliff.

I screamed and reached out. For a moment, she seemed suspended in midair. Then she plummeted.

FORTY-THREE

The sky was nearly faded of color, the cliffside ragged with shadows. For an endless minute, no one moved; the only sounds were the groaning of the wind against the rockface and my own broken breathing. We stared at the chasm, frozen with shock, as if expecting Persaphe's long-fingered hand to appear over the ledge to pull herself up to safety.

And then—it *did*.

I made a noise like a dying thing and stumbled backward. Elias' palms came up to steady me, and I clutched at him blindly, my eyes on the figure coming over the cliffside. Dark cloak, dark hair, hands worn from years of labor. But this was not Persaphe.

It was my father.

Another mangled cry from my throat. I thought, I must have gone mad. This was madness.

Aegeis was not alone; four men emerged from the ravine after him. They all wore matching black cloaks, and their heads were shaved on the sides in the manner of priests. Still, I did not understand. My voice came out gasping. "How are you here?"

Aegeis met my eye and said, "This is the Shadow Temple."

"You—I don't—this is *what?*"

"The Shadow Temple," he repeated with unnerving calm. "Home of the Shadow Priests."

It was the place of worship Aegeis often used to speak about, the twin temple to The Flame atop the Match. I remembered my father taking me to see The Flame in the King's City long ago, the open yearning in his face when he spoke of those who'd built it. *I did not lie to you,* Persaphe had said to me in the prison. *He went to find the Shadow Temple in the Land of Moore.* It had always been Aegeis' dream.

It seemed, really, as if this was all a dream.

Aegeis moved forward. I thought he meant to embrace me, and I recoiled. Aegeis caught the motion, and something shifted in his eyes, but in the end he only turned toward the king. The King's Guard hefted their weapons, though my father was unarmed. He knelt. "Your Majesty."

"You," said Elias.

"I have much explaining to do," Aegeis said with a nod, "and much apologizing as well. But night is coming, and your men are exhausted. We must retreat to the safety of our halls before the curse of the Pass descends. My brothers and I can offer you shelter and rest. We have food and hot bathing water. Beds."

At the mention of these comforts, the others in our party stirred from their shock. Elias looked at me, a question in his face. *Can we trust him?*

I did not know the answer to that, but night was indeed coming. If we did not find shelter soon, the night terrors would return, and more men would die. I would have to put my disbelief aside, and my grief, for now. "It seems we have little choice."

Elias gave Aegeis a nod. "Very well."

"There is a hidden passage," Aegeis noted. "We can make it there before dark if we move swiftly. My brothers will lead the way."

The other four Shadow Priests began silently guiding our men down the path. I did not immediately join them, and neither did Aegeis. When Elias noticed our delay, he paused, but I merely shook my head. "Go on," I said shakily. "I will follow soon."

Elias did not go on. He planted his feet and crossed his arms, stubborn and resolute and…and it was so strange to see him like this. Standing, walking without a cane, without any assistance. The King's Guard, too, planted their feet, turning their mistrustful eyes on my father. Aegeis, for his part, seemed not to notice. He had moved a few paces back and was watching me apprehensively. I hoped I did not faint. I felt as if it was taking all my effort to stay upright.

"I need to know something," I told my father, "and it cannot wait."

He nodded, yet now that I had his full attention, I found it difficult to form words.

"Mother…" I started, and faltered.

At last, Aegeis' face showed something other than calm. His eyes darted away. "I have many things for which to apologize. Your mother's death will be the first."

"It…will?" I blinked. "Did she tell you what she planned? Did you know we would pass this way? Have you been…waiting for us?"

"For you," he corrected softly.

My exhaustion was suddenly unutterable; the world was backwards, my mother was dead, and nothing was as it seemed. I no more knew the man standing before me as I knew the Goddess, yet Aegeis' frank look had me speaking again. "You once told me not all of us are magic."

"Magic comes in many forms."

"Last night, I dreamed—"

"I know what you dreamed," he said gently.

I swayed slightly on my feet.

"Your question," Aegeis prompted.

"Yes." I braced myself. "It was important for me to obtain some of Persaphe's blood. This is…difficult to ask. But she fell from the cliff. I do not go so far as to believe she could have survived, but…her body. Is there any way to retrieve it?"

Aegeis shook his head. "This ravine has no bottom. Persaphe has passed through the Shadow Void. She is gone." He must have seen my dismay, because he looked suddenly pitying. "There will be more time for talk later, but we really must not delay."

Aegeis led us down the dusty mountain path. He paused before a blank sheet of rock, and when he set his palm to its surface, a door materialized. I scarcely reacted; it seemed my capacity for shock had run dry. Beyond the door was a well-lit staircase, which wound down into a reception hall built straight into the rock. There, the rest of our men were gathered, speaking in hushed tones as they surveyed their surroundings. I felt Elias' presence at my back; he and the King's Guard were not straying far. Hobore caught sight of us and worried his lip.

"You will be safe here in the Shadow Temple," Aegeis told me. "You and your companions may stay as long as you require."

I managed a nod.

"And…" He pulled something from his pocket. "I believe this is yours."

As it turned out, I did still have some capacity for shock. "My truth serum? But how, I thought you said—?"

"The vial did not fall into the Shadow Void. It became trapped on a ledge just over the cliff. Perhaps the Goddess intervened, or the Temple did. Such is the way of this place." He eyed the glass bottle. "A truth serum, you say? Are you sure? Potion makers have been attempting to create such serums since the beginning of time. They have all failed."

I took the bottle from his offered hand. I was aware of Elias' eyes on me when I said, "I have not failed."

...

The Shadow Temple was a place of darkness and light. Cut deep into the earth, the rooms bore no windows, save for faraway skylights in the worship halls and common areas. Some of the Temple's chambers were little more than dugouts, while others were arching, cavernous, engraved with carvings of beasts and men. The Shadow Priests were soft-spoken, gathering like leaves in the breeze of our wake. They were curious, but respectful, and perhaps even a bit shy.

Aegeis had promised food and hot baths, and when one of our men asked suspiciously, "Why help us? The Shadow Priests owe our king no loyalty. And that man—the leader—was the husband of the golden witch. Is this meant to be another trick?"

My father merely said, "It is penance," and walked away.

We were shown to the bathhouse, which was a spacious room built over a natural hot spring, which bubbled merrily from its center. Our men began undressing as soon as they stepped inside, leaving me to stutter and excuse myself. An acolyte approached me in the antechamber, looking chagrined. "Apologies, miss," he said. "We are not used to hosting women."

I stifled my discomfort. "No apology needed."

"Brother Freestone instructed us to prepare a heated tub in a separate room for your use. You may bathe there in private. I will show you—"

"Where?" demanded Elias.

The acolyte and I both startled. Elias stood—still clothed, no cane—in the doorway of the bathing chamber. I wondered dimly if he was doing this on purpose, using his newfound mobility to confound me at choice moments.

The acolyte pressed his palms together and bowed. "We have set aside a room down the hall for the purpose."

"I will come."

I made a noise in the back of my throat. Elias' eyes flashed to mine. The tips of his ears turned slightly pink as he clarified, "To guard the door. Outside."

"I can assure you," said the acolyte, "she will be perfectly safe—"

"I do not care for your assurances."

"Your Majesty." This was Arch, poking his head around the bathhouse door. Of us all, he alone looked in good spirits. "You bathe. I will guard Miss Freestone."

"I don't—"

"It's what I'm trained for," Arch insisted with a smile, "and you stink."

Elias snorted. "So do you."

"All the more reason to relegate me." Arch stepped around the door, giving Elias a friendly nudge. They did not seem, in this moment, like guardsman and master. The formalities had been dropped—a sure aftereffect of our unusual situation—and now spoke only as friends. "Go on."

Elias glanced my way one last time, but nodded.

And so I bathed in a private chamber with Arch, not Elias, standing watch outside the door. I tried to be thorough, though my hands kept drifting to stillness. I stared at the cooling water and thought, *My mother is dead. My father is a Shadow Priest. The truth serum survived, but Elias' gaigi is lost forever. And me?*

After I had dressed in the clean robes laid out for me, tended my broken wrist, and emerged from my makeshift bathing room, Arch gave me another smile. "We've missed the dinner hour, but the priests have set out some food. Our men have torn through most of it—greedy good-for-nothings—but they saved you a plate. His Majesty made sure of it." Arch still had that amused look on his face. I did not know what he found so funny. This day had been a disaster. "The Shadow Temple," he pondered as we walked, tipping his head back to peer at the carved ceiling. "I never would have believed it."

We entered a modest hall of stone, which had mostly cleared out by the time Arch and I arrived. There was a fire in the hearth, and a long table draped in cloth. Elias sat in a wooden chair near the mantle, speaking with Yorvis and Freesier. When he saw me, he stood. I stopped in the doorway. The room fell suddenly quiet.

"Here." Arch guided a prepared plate into my hands, and then—when I made no move to sit—led me to a chair. I followed him wordlessly, as though I had lost the ability to function without help. Elias was still watching me, but he did not come closer, and I felt…lost. So lost, and confused, and exhausted. There were still problems to work through, things that needed resolving, but when I tried to think on them, my thoughts turned to mist.

I set my plate on the table and rubbed my face, sinking into the winged-back chair. My father had mentioned something about clean beds, but I did not have the strength to ask after them. My eyes drifted back to Elias, who had resumed conversation with his men. I wanted to ask, *What now?* and *How does it feel to walk again?* and *Do you still hate me?* The nearby fire warmed my cold hands. My fatigue was of a natural sort, untouched by magic. I remember thinking, *I should not fall asleep here.* But I did.

. . .

When I woke, my plate of food was still on the table, the fire still burning in the hearth. The room, however, was empty, save for Elias.

He was standing with his back to me, facing the fire. My chair creaked as I stirred, and he turned. "There is a bed for you," he said. "You need not sleep in a chair."

"I didn't mean to." I pushed myself upright. "The others—?"

"Have more sense than us. They've retired to their chambers."

I nodded, dragging a hand through my hair. My neck was sore from dozing upright, but the rest had done me good. My head seemed clearer, and I no longer felt as if I would be sick, from terror or shock.

"Your father surprised me," Elias said. "I would never have imagined the fate of a Shadow Priest for one such as him."

"We are in agreement," I grumbled. "I believe him an entirely different person than the one I once knew."

"He probably thinks the same of you." I felt Elias' attention like sun on stone. "Come here."

The hair stood up on my arms. I did not move.

Though his eyes were full of dark meaning, he kept his voice light. "Afraid?"

"No." I stood from my seat and came closer, and then at his arched brow, closer still. We were within arm's reach of each other. I was tense, uncertain. I had no defense, nor—truthfully—the desire to muster one. *Whatever may come*, I thought.

"Do you have the truth serum?" he asked.

I pulled it from my pocket. Much of the concoction had spilled from the vial when it went over the cliffside, but there was still a finger's width left, shining emerald in the firelight.

His hand came over mine, clasping the bottle in my fist. He did not seem to reject the contact; his heartbeat went on steadily. I wondered, with a surge of blinding hope, if Persaphe's curse had lifted with her death. Did this mean Elias could touch again without fear? Had he been released from her spell?

My pulse sped, and I thought perhaps he could feel it rising through my skin when he said, "You will take it."

I inhaled. "What?"

"You will take the truth serum, and you will answer my questions." Up close, Elias' eyes looked lit from within. Gold and green, longing and loss. I could see it all there, all the emotion he usually kept hidden. "If this is poison, and it is a trick, you will die."

"Do you really believe it could be poison?"

"I am ready to believe anything."

"Well," I said in a scolding tone, "it is not."

He did not smile. "We will see."

· · ·

The thing about a truth serum is that so long as you are in its power, you cannot lie, not even to yourself. The sensation is not a comfortable one. It is as if your thoughts become clear fluid, stripped of every imperfection. In their place stands only what is real, what is uncompromised and objective.

There is danger in this unveiling. Not everyone can handle the reality of their own minds. It is only human to avoid what hurts, to wrap ourselves in fantasy and falsities. If the curtain is lifted, it can break us.

But I did not think of these concerns then. I thought only of Elias as he looked before the fire, his tawny hair gilded from behind, skin smooth against the press of his clothes. Handsome. Achingly so. He always had been, to me. I unstoppered the cap and swallowed half the contents. It burned cold down my throat, as if it had been sitting on ice. I brought a hand to wipe my lips and was surprised to find it trembling. I had not yet tested the truth serum on myself and did not know what a full dose would do to my mind, what sorts of secrets I might spill, or what they would change along the way.

Before I knew what was happening, Elias plucked the vial from my fingers and downed the rest of the serum. I heard the sharpness in my voice. "What are you doing?"

"How else will I know if the serum is real?"

"You could have called for someone. One of your King's Guard. They would have tested it for you."

"I thought you did not believe in testing your potions on others."

I flushed. "I have changed."

He threw me a look. "Undoubtably."

"What if it *was* poison?"

"Then we do not have much time."

A wild laugh threatened to burst from me. Already, I could feel the truth serum working in my belly. "Are you not worried what you will say?"

"I am worried," he replied easily, then blinked. An honest answer. I watched his expression dawn. "Oh."

"Oh," I repeated dryly. "You should have just left the serum to me. You will see soon enough I cannot lie."

"No need." He waved his hand, then stopped to look at it, frowning. "This feels strange."

"Yes," I said, and was startled to find myself smiling. "No more hiding behind your masks."

"Nor yours." He cut me another look. "I have only one question."

My smile fell. Nerves swarmed my stomach. "Yes?"

"Do you regret it?"

The silence was loud in my ears. Firelight dripped gold against the walls. It was a simple question, four words, yet it seemed to encompass my entire life. Entire worlds. Did I regret poisoning him? "I do not."

He drew back, his expression openly wounded.

"I regret hurting you," I hurried to explain. "I regret the pain I caused, the frustration and suffering. I wish I had told you the truth sooner—I wish I had said so many things. And this is selfish, it's selfish…" My throat tightened. "But if I had not poisoned you, I would never have changed. You would not have, either. We would have remained exactly as we were, me absorbed in my work, and you closed off to your subjects, believing everyone preferred your father over you. Without the poisoning, I would never have known you as I do. I would not have…"

"Yes?"

The serum was begging me to speak, yet I was suddenly overcome. I clamped down on the words, though I knew it was futile. I would not be able to fight the power of this potion for long. I should know. I was the one who made it.

"Selene." Elias' breath was slightly jagged, his eyes darting between each of mine. He took a step closer, so that I had to tip my head to look at him. For a moment, we only stood there, breathing each other. My lips parted, and the thought dropped through me like a rock into a pond: I wanted him to touch me. I burned for it. This thought was chased quickly by another: I had no right to want that.

Yet, the truth. He had asked me a question. I must give an answer.

I gulped and said, "If not for the poison, I would never have known what it was to love you."

His expression changed, blanking in astonishment. He made a stifled sound and dropped suddenly to his knees. I was alarmed—my first thought was the *eithier* had failed, and his ability to stand had somehow been cut out of him. Then I realized he was crying.

"Elias? No, no."

I sank down to my own knees, reaching for his face, but he grabbed my wrist and held it there between us. "I have been so blind."

My own tears began to rise. "Not in everything."

"In the things that mattered." He lifted his head. "Do you mean that? Could you…but how could you ever…?"

"I love you," I said again. "I always have. It's the truth."

He looked like he was flailing. He had clearly not expected my admission. He did not know what to do with it. "You betrayed me," he started hoarsely. "You did, and I was so angry. I'm angry still. Your mother returned and fed me stories of your treacheries, and it was all too easy to listen. I wanted to believe the worst in you—that you were nothing but a murderess, that you had once poisoned me and aimed to try again, and everything that happened between us—the stories, hours spent in each other's company, by the Goddess, that *kiss*—" His voice broke "—was all just a plot to lull me." He loosened his hold on my wrist, stroking the skin with his thumb. "I was so hurt. I was confused. It was simpler, so much simpler to hate you than to think I might not hate you at all, I might care for you and want to forgive you. But I was wrong. I was wrong." He gave a weak laugh. "What is happening? You are supposed to be confessing to me right now. This truth serum has me in tatters. Or you do. You make me all tangled up."

"You are not the only one who was wrong," I choked. "Elias, I poisoned you. That is a truth that cannot be undone. But I hope—I have wanted—"

He kissed me. It was happening before I understood, his palms cradling my jaw, his lips coming down on mine. The world tilted, then righted itself as I gripped his shirt and kissed him back. He pulled me roughly closer, fingers sinking into my hair. The kiss was a wild, depraved sort of thing, and my mind went blank of everything, except for him. We were both still on our knees; his heart beat into mine. There was no fear in him, no resistance. He was the mold and I was hot wax, pliant and ready to surrender.

The kiss changed, gentled. His fingers spanned my face, smoothing invisible lines. His breath sighed out of him as his lips moved softly over mine, and I thought, *I am pushing him too far*, before I remembered I was not the one who started this kiss.

Elias kissed me like he did it every day, and yet not like that at all, because this was a kiss to move worlds.

When we finally broke apart, Elias pressed his forehead to mine. I was dizzy with feeling; golden light moved through my veins. I tried to settle my racing pulse long enough to say, "There is still so much to explain. Things we must discuss. I want—"

"Later," he murmured, and kissed me again.

The shadows curled around us. I smelled woodsmoke and cliff-dust and him. We glowed under the light we created between ourselves, and the heat of it kept the night at bay.

FORTY-FOUR

The following morning, the Shadow Priests conducted a ceremony in honor of those who had died in the Pass, including Persaphe's unborn baby. We gathered in one of the Temple's many antechambers and lit prayer candles, hundreds of them all around the room. The Priests sang a hymn I did not know, but the tune was simple and looping, and it was easy enough to catch on. Elias and I stood side by side, him in silence and me joining the chorus. I once said I did not want a brother or sister, yet I had been young then, and ignorant in so many ways. I did not know who the baby's father was—Aegeis, or someone else—but that did not matter, either. This was a life lost, and I mourned it.

And yet…even as I had the thought, my eyes sought Hobore standing among our men. He was the king's half-brother, by their father. But he was my half-brother, too, by our mother. I did not know what to do with that revelation.

It felt, sometimes, like I was waiting to wake up.

Hobore caught me looking and went rigid under my scrutiny. He seemed smaller lately, his eyes rimmed in red. The King's Guard had questioned Hobore last night and revoked his weapons, but his fate was still to be decided. His presence here—and indeed, his freedom in the face of his crimes—was conspicuous, and I was conflicted. Hobore had tried to kill me. He aided in a conspiracy to murder the king, and the king's father. Yet he had done these things under Persaphe's iron command, just as I once had. And in the end, Hobore had stood against her.

When the ceremony was complete and the men began to file out, Hobore surprised me by approaching. "This belongs to you," he said, offering my compass.

I cradled the object between my palms. The gift of a gift—one I thought I had lost forever. When I lifted my gaze to thank Hobore, he was already gone.

"What would you have me do with him?" Elias asked darkly, watching his brother's retreating figure. At my look, Elias continued. "He was an accomplice to your mother. He tried to have us both killed. And," Elias darkened further, "he is responsible for the death of our father."

"Persaphe is responsible," I replied. "Hobore was not in command of himself. He was compelled to do her bidding through glamour. He was, in many ways, merely her tool."

Elias scrutinized me. "Still."

I thought of a soldier pinned to cobblestones, punished for the sake of punishment. I thought of my father, and myself as I had been, and said, "Give him another chance."

. . .

The letter arrived on a silver platter, delivered by a young acolyte who looked not a day over thirteen. The boy approached after the grieving ceremony and bowed to Elias, but held the letter out to me. I plucked it off the platter and broke the wax seal. The note inside was written in swirling cursive on simple parchment. An invitation. Elias took it from my hand, studying the flowery print.

"It's addressed to me only," I noted.

Elias heard my unhappiness. "Do you want me to come?"

"That is my point. You are not invited."

"I'm invited everywhere."

"Let me guess," I said archly. "Because you are a king?"

He shrugged. "As a matter of fact, yes."

I snatched back the letter in mock exasperation, though his teasing helped soothe some of my anxiety. "Being a king is not always the answer."

"You would be surprised."

I tried to shoo him with the letter, but he caught my hand, cradling it in his. I was aware of curious eyes on us. I cared, but not enough to pull away.

"I have noticed," I said abruptly, nodding toward our twined fingers, "that this does not seem to bother you so much."

"Hmm."

"Persaphe's curse," I pressed. "Do you think…?"

"I was not aware of being under any curse." He linked our fingers more fully. "Only of feeling different than others, and not understanding why."

"And now?"

"Now…I am not sure the sensation is gone."

I was unpleasantly surprised. "It isn't?"

"I still feel…hesitant, over physical contact. Or—perhaps it is that I remember how it felt to be trapped, and the memory *feels* like entrapment. Does that make sense?" He offered a small smile. "With you, though, it's easier."

I twisted my mouth. "I was once told I have some power of interference."

That made him grin. "Undoubtably." His thumb began making small circles along the back of my hand. The sensation was turning my legs to butter. I felt shy, new to this open affection, though there was a sweetness there, too. Though the truth serum had worn off, we still remembered the things we had said.

"So," he prevailed, "your invitation. Am I coming?"

I sighed. "No. This is something I must do alone."

I met my father in the library at his requested time. Wine was served by priests who knew Isla's customs, alongside warm bread and cheese. All of it—the invitation, the servants, the wine—seemed absurdly formal. This was not the king's palace. I was no special guest. Yet I understood why Aegeis was falling back on old conventions. It was easier for us to interact under the constraints of courtly formalities.

"The strides you have made with His Majesty's recovery are extraordinary," Aegeis said conversationally from his cushioned leather seat, offering me a tin of chocolates. "I was told about your so-called *eithier*. Is it true you invented it yourself? A potion to cure all ailments?"

"The results are not permanent," I said, accepting the proffered sweets. "The *eithier* only lasts as long as it is in the bloodstream, and anyway, it only works on members of the Alder family—our twined blood is key." Aegeis' eyes fell to my bandaged arms. I drew them back, tucking my elbows in as I sorted through the tin. "Elias has been taking a daily dose of *eithier* since the start of our journey. That is how he can walk. Without it, his progress would revert, and he would return to his wheelchair."

"Regrettable, but not entirely unforeseen. True *gaigis* are rare."

I glanced up, surprised he knew the word. Even for someone married into the Freestone family, our terms of healing could be tricky.

"Does His Majesty still seek a permanent cure?"

"I think Elias would do anything to walk again." I turned a small chocolate heart between my fingers and added, "I would do anything."

"You feel guilty."

"Wouldn't you?" I asked. "Don't you feel guilty for things you did, or didn't do?"

"Are we still talking about His Majesty?"

"We are talking about *everything*," I burst, breaking the chocolate heart in half. I clamped my mouth shut. I had not realized how deeply the last days' events—indeed, the last four years' events—had burrowed inside me, or how they waited now, ready to lash out at the most minor provocations. "The king's paralysis was my doing," I said in cooler tones. "Under Persaphe's order, yes, but by my hand. Of course I feel guilty."

Aegeis did not immediately refute this. He sat back in his seat, and I took the moment to study him. Brown hair—partially shaved now—brown eyes. Small in stature, a quiet face. He inhaled deeply through his nose. "You are angry, as is your right. More than that, you have questions. That is the reason I wanted to meet—to give you answers."

I was glad I had not drunk much of the wine. For this, I wanted a clear head. "You are right, Father, I do have questions. Just one, actually, and a borrowed one at that." I braced myself. "Do you regret it?"

Aegeis did not react as I had when Elias posed this query to me. There was no balking, no thickly swallowed emotion. But then, Aegeis was not under the influence of a truth serum.

"What you should know," my father began, "is that I was aware of Persaphe's aims for many years. I knew she seduced King Adonis Alder in order to bear his heir. When she brought Hobore to the palace, I knew the boy was her son. Later, when she began plotting to kill both Adonis and Elias, I understood her goal was to ascend to power and become Queen Mother."

"Yet you did nothing."

"Actually," he corrected lightly, "I did quite a bit. As much as was within my power to stall her. Why else do you think it took her eight years to make it this far? I was there, planting delays veiled as suggestions, sowing doubt in her ability to remain uncaught. I would say I am ashamed for not thwarting her entirely, but the truth is that Persaphe had me trapped under a spell of my own, just as she had the king trapped, and Hobore, and even you, once. I could not raise a hand against her directly, only through circumvention. Still." He gave a tired sigh. "I do not evade responsibility for my role. Like you, I feel accountable, whether or not I had any real power to choose otherwise."

"You have not answered my question."

"My answer is yes," he said, with sudden intensity. "I regret abandoning you, and everything that has happened since. I will not ask for forgiveness." He looked away; his eyes turned to the floor. "For all that has happened these past years, I do not deserve as much. I ask for your mercy."

Words failed me. If I had any anger left, it was gone now. I tried to see my father in this man, who had somehow found his way to the Shadow Temple, and wore the robes of a priest, and knew things without having been told. There was a part of me that ached to throw myself into his arms as I would have when I was little, to let him comfort and protect, but I was a grown woman now, and we were lost in a mountain at the edge of the world. Things were not as they had been. Nothing ever would be again. "I need time," I said.

"You will have it."

I returned to the chocolate, seeking a better piece. "You say you regret everything," I said casually, so that he knew I was not trying to provoke him. "But what about the Shadow Temple? It was always your dream to find it."

"I only intended to meet the Shadow Priests," he admitted, "not join their ranks. And in fact, even that did not go entirely according to plan. My original goal was to find the River of Reversal."

I surprised us both with a cutting laugh. "You? Find the River?"

"I was in a dark place. I had just left my daughter for dead, my wife was plotting the downfall of our monarchy, and I was helpless to do much about any of it. I wanted a way to go back."

"But the River does not exist. I thought you of anyone would be wise enough to know that."

Aegeis merely looked at me, in that same, too-clear way he had looked at me in my dream.

"Father?"

"I have committed many wrongs," he said slowly, "which cannot be undone. I understand, more than you know, how it feels to encounter the consequences of your actions. To see the harm you have caused another, and wish to take it back. You told me you would do anything to see your king walk again."

My hands felt suddenly cold. Yet I could only say, "Yes."

Aegeis nodded. "You will be needing some horses."

・・・

Elias and I departed the following morning. We followed my father's directions, which circumvented the Pass and its nightmare curse, leading us instead through a series of caverns into an open plain. We rode on borrowed horses, listening to the dry grass hiss under their hooves. The earth-rock smell of the foothills gained a newer, greener note; the sun was wide as a saucer, streaming brilliantly in a clear sky.

The first night, we bedded down in a grassy hillock. Elias—it is difficult to describe the mixed joy I felt at seeing him so fiercely hopeful, while at the same time understanding the need to relinquish my own hopes. His words from the Pass seemed to come back upon the breeze. *The River is my only chance to undo what has been done. To reverse these last four years as if they had never been.*

I had not managed to create his *gaigi*, and Persaphe's fall into the Shadow Void ensured I never would. Yet even if I had succeeded, the *nightlight's* cure would not undo Elias' suffering entirely. It would not erase my involvement. And yes, after drinking the truth serum, and hearing the things Elias said...my heart had swelled with hope. Foolish, stupid hope. I knew Elias. Stubborn. Determined. Once set on a course, he could not be turned away. He had always dreamed of finding the River, and really, he had more reasons than most to want it. Maybe we would discover those fabled waters after all. Maybe he would step into them, and the River's magic would draw him back in time, erasing the last four years...and all his memories of me.

"Bread," he announced, unaware of my silent turmoil. He looked around our small camp with the air of someone who wanted to be useful. "What if I warm some bread?"

He burned the bread, yet was adamant about eating bite after brittle bite. I clutched my stomach in laughter. "What's funny?" he demanded around a mouthful of char. "It is delicious. Try it. Come here, I insist."

He chased me, waving the bread like a hatchet. I screeched and dodged, giddy with exhilaration, scarcely able to breathe. When I fell to the grassy earth and he tumbled down beside me, I listened to the sound of his laughter and thought, *If he chooses to step into the River and forget me, so be it. I have him for now. It is more than I deserve.*

Elias quieted. The sky was a riot of color; the sun had just dropped beneath the mountains. He propped himself up on one elbow, resting his cheek in his hand as he looked at me. Crickets began to sing.

"It is like a symphony," I sighed, the laughter still upon me.

"Then dance with me," was his reply.

He rolled to his feet. Not perfectly, not gracefully, but with the newfound enthusiasm of a man who had rediscovered an old ability. We were a bit of a sorry sight—my face, bruised and scarred, my broken wrist, my cut arms, and him, with—well, I had no real complaints. His smile was almost bashful, cheeks flushing when he admitted, "I've wanted to do this with you for a long time."

My own cheeks flushed in response—pleasure and pain, pleasure and pain. I rested my head on his chest, and he threaded our hands together, and there under the golden light, we swayed. My breath—why could I not breathe? Tears threatened. I kept my face turned so he would not see.

"I have been wondering," Elias began, rocking us. "You said you can hear pulses. Is this...some sort of ability of yours?"

"I can hear the heartbeats of others," I said, "though I have long kept this a secret. When I was younger, I did not want..."

"Others to judge you more harshly than they already did," Elias guessed.

I nodded.

"My heartbeat, too?" he asked. "Can you hear it now?"

"With yours, it is different. Not only can I hear your pulse, but I can feel it in my chest. Almost as if your heart is sitting beside my own."

He went still. "How long have you had this ability?"

"I do not know, exactly." I pulled back slightly to look at him. "The first time I noticed was many years ago, in your chamber. The day I touched a cloth to your forehead and you ordered me out."

He was staring at me. "I can—" His mouth worked. "I can feel yours, too."

I gaped at him. "What?"

"I never understood it. I'm not...well versed in matters of magic. For years, I ignored the feeling. Denied it. I thought—that is, I believed it was all in my head." His words came haltingly. "It was only, well, that day at the House of Healers, when you were hurt, I think maybe I realized its nature then. But after, when your mother returned, the sensation seemed to vanish. I thought...I should have understood, but I didn't..."

I tried for a smile. "It's alright."

But Elias was not looking at me as if it was alright. He was looking at me as if everything had changed.

When he kissed me, he was gentle, yet there was something new lurking under this kiss, something urgent. His skin was warm under my hands; I was shivering all over. It was quite rapidly too much: hunger and heat and a rising tide of need. We were soon tugging at each other, the kiss turning mindless. He pulled away, resting his forehead on mine. "I want—"

"I know."

"Do you—?"

"Yes."

We found the bedroll. I thought I knew what it would be like, but I knew nothing. The weight of him over me, the raw scrape of his scruff at my cheek. The way his breath became tattered, his expression so full of plaintive want that my heart seemed to double in size, even as I feared the breaking to come.

I thought it again: *I have him for now.*

It may be all I will ever have. It is more than I deserve.

I gripped his shirt and tugged, my hips lifting. Elias seemed to be battling his own desire; he wanted to be soft, harness his greed. But I did not care for softness. I wanted everything: his fingers digging into the crease of my thighs, teeth marks in my skin, his tongue and his urgency. My frustration must have been apparent, because he bowed his head and laughed into my neck. "You really will be the death of me."

I nipped his ear, and he groaned.

Our clothes came away. The world condensed. There was nothing left but shadows and heat, strong arms on either side, his desire heavy at my belly. Elias dipped to kiss my throat and I dug my fingers into his hair, arching. I wanted more. I was dizzy with need. When he finally moved inside me, I could hear the noise I made. I do not know where that sound came from, but he sank deeper, and I made it again. I gasped and dragged him closer. I was wine in a cup I was begging him to drink.

There were no thoughts anymore, only sensation. He moved again, and for a moment I saw those old fears cross his face. His eyes became distant, staring into the past. I cupped his jaw. "Elias, I'm here." He blinked, and seemed to see me. For a moment, we merely looked at each other, breathing, shaking. I whispered, "Stay with me."

He curled his fingers into mine. "I am with you."

FORTY-FIVE

We rise at dawn. I study Elias as he dresses, the tousle of his hair, his capable hands. He meets my eye and I blush, remembering where those hands have been. But there is a newness between us now. It is the kind of feeling that cannot be scrubbed away.

Two more days of travel, I tell Elias, consulting the map, yet it is only hours after we set off again that we hear a great thunder of water, smell the cool-mist spray. The landscape is rolling, mellow, sunny. Dragonflies hang upon the wind, their bodies like armored jewels. We dismount our horses and follow our senses, crossing through a line of trees.

The River of Reversal stands before us. My mind blanks in the face of its power. It is larger than I imagined, and perfectly clear. Nothing grows around it, for any plant that touches its water is reverted to seed. When we walk to its edge and lay our eyes upon its surface, we do not see ourselves reflected back.

I continue to stare. The aura of the River's force is so deep as to numb me—stronger than my forest, stronger than the storm of the

Crossing Sea. I think, I could step into these waters and be free of my scars. I could forget my mother's betrayal, the pain of my youth, all my suffering. And Elias. He will enter this river and go back in time to an age where he is strong again, agile, happy.

The thought brings back some of my blood. I take a step away. I want to grab Elias, shake him, beg. Who would we be without our scars? Who would we become without our pasts?

I don't say these things. I have meddled enough. We are here now, and it is his choice.

Elias is a stone at my side. I am afraid to look at him. I fear I will see the longing in his face, the eagerness and the excitement. I know how many years he has dreamed of finding the River, what it means that we have reached this place. He will step into this water, and I will be forced to watch the years strip back, and with them, all his knowledge of me.

The silence expands. Elias does not move. I cannot bear it any longer—I look at him. And yet, it is not excitement I see in him, or eagerness, but peace.

"I find," he says, "that I am in no hurry to become again who I was."

The sun is a blaze of yellow. Overhead, gulls dip and weave. "Elias... are you... but this is what you wanted."

He holds my eye. "There are things, I think, that I want more."

Together, we turn away from the water. The roar of the River fades behind us. As we find our way back to our waiting horses, Elias takes my hand in his.

We return to the Shadow Temple. As soon as our party is rested and recovered, we bid farewell to the Shadow Priests, thanking them for their hospitality. There is nothing more holding us here; it is time now to return home. As the men load up a set of gifted pack mules and enough provisions to last us the journey home, I pull my father aside and ask,

"Will you return to the Kingdom of Isla with us?"

He gives me a hesitant smile. "There are a few repairs that need to be done to the Shadow Tower. An expansion, too, for a new worship hall. I have drawn up the plans and presented them to the high priests. I am hopeful my proposal will be accepted soon, and we can begin construction." He pauses. "But, if you wish for me to return, I will."

It has always been Aegeis' dream to build a temple. He would have done so already, if not for my mother's interference. That is something she stole from him; I will not steal it, too. "No," I say. "Visit us, I hope, but you have found your place here."

His expression softens. He glances at Elias. "You have found your place, too."

I hug him. He does not hesitate to hug me back.

Spring is in full bloom by the time we traverse the Crossing Sea and return to Isla. There, we share our story: the storm, the Pass, the truth serum. My reunion with my father. Persaphe's death, and Kurton's, and that innocent unborn child. Yet when anyone asks about the River, Elias and I shake our heads. *We never found it*, we say. *It was only a myth.*

Ophelia is there. She is heavy with child, and there are lines around her eyes, but her mother Daphne is with her, as well as her many brothers. I am thankful she is not alone. She pulls me into a hug, and I think, I am not alone, either.

As the weeks wear on, the *eithier* leaves Elias' system. His strength fails; his muscles grow weak. He returns to his wheelchair, and when I attempt to leave a vial of *eithier* on his nightstand, he clasps his hand over mine. *Didn't you once say*, he asks, *that you prefer me as I am?*

His touch lingers. My skin heats under his gaze. I slide into his bed and pull him over me. *I did say that*, I reply, *and I meant it.*

The years slip by. Elias and I bear a daughter together, that single girl that is so common among the Freestone line. Palladine, she is called. I like to think she is more her father's daughter than she is mine. She is a brave child who grows into a brave woman, sharp-witted and fearless. When she is very little, I ask Elias what is to become of her. She is heir to the throne with the blood of a healer. Never before has such a person existed. What is her destiny?

He smiles, soft as a whisper, and says, "Whatever she wants it to be."

I still think of the River. I look at my hands, their burn marks and scars. I look at the wrinkles around my eyes, my sagging skin, the age that is taking hold of me and him. Time will claim us. We could undo it if we wished, we know the way. Sometimes, when I lie beside Elias at night, the fear resurfaces in a great surge. I grip him to me and wonder what ever possessed me not to throw him into that water when I had the chance. I could undo his age, make him live forever, and so what if he forgets? I used to list the things I had sacrificed for him, how I poisoned myself, bled myself empty, abandoned my home, forsook my mother. It was a long way of saying what I could have put simply: I would do anything.

He wipes my tears and says, shh, Selene. It will be alright. I regret nothing, do you hear me? Not one thing.

The bards sing songs about Elias. I hear them sometimes as I walk through the city. They are not songs about overcoming hardship, or defeating it, but rather settling into it with grace. Allowing yourself to soften, so when the world tests you, as it always will, you bend but do not break.

Have you ever tried to hold onto a moment? Over the course of my life, there were many times I wished I could; the good moments and the bad, for they are all a part of me. But you cannot hold onto moments, only memories, and these I forever will.

Acknowledgements

Writing a novel is a lot like throwing yourself off a cliff and hoping there's water down there and not a pit of spikes. I am so grateful to everyone who's continued to believe in me on this journey. And for those who come with buckets of water to fill the ravine, just in case.

To Monster, first and forever, who can look me in the eye and say *You've got this*, and make me believe it.

To James and Catherine, who read these words before anyone, and helped make them better; you gave me courage in the story when I needed it most. To Skyler and the rest of the Ebook Launch Editing team for all your copyediting skills. To Nathaniel, deeply, for your proofreading ninja powers. I'll never understand how you do it. To Andi and Tabby, for your willingness to jump into another story as beta and sensitivity readers; I'm grateful to you both. To Rosie, for your endless endurance as a friend and cheerleader. To Dad, to whom this story is dedicated, for getting it. To my street team, who've championed the book with cover reveals, early reviews, blog posts, and overall enthusiasm. You all are the best.

And of course, to my readers. I like to say that I write books for myself, but I publish them for you. You've made this possible, and for that, thank you. I'm more grateful than I can say.

More By This Author

A Reader's Most Anticipated Fantasy and instant bestseller from debut author S.G. Prince, *The Elvish Trilogy* is perfect for those who enjoy gritty action, flawed heroes, slow-burn romance and surprising twists.

Elvish (The Elvish Trilogy, Book I)
Elder (The Elvish Trilogy, Book II)
Ember (The Elvish Trilogy, Book III)

Follow S.G. Prince

To stay updated on events and future releases from S.G. Prince, subscribe to her newsletter at sgprince.com/subscribe.

Website: sgprince.com
Instagram: @sgprince.books
Twitter: @sgprince_author

Printed in Great Britain
by Amazon